JACK: K9 Warrior

KEVIN L. BRETT

Stafford, Virginia

ISBN-10: 0981935060
ISBN-13: 978-0-9819350-6-5

V:1.15

For more information, please contact the author at
KevinBrettStudios@yahoo.com

Jack's Facebook page is:
Jack: The Christmas Collie

Dedication

This book is dedicated to dog rescues everywhere and to those caring souls who answer the call to help discarded, abused and lost Collies and Shelties so they may have the chance to find their forever homes. Every Collie deserves to be surrounded by a loving family and to become the hero of their story.

"All good stories deserve to be embellished."
Gandalf the Grey. *"The Hobbit"*

JACK K9 WARRIOR

Soon after the world was first created, during a bitter cold winter, First Dog gave birth to her pups. She was unable to find food for them and they began to starve. First Dog approached the warmth of the fire of First Man and First Woman. She asked the humans to share their fire and their food with her pups so they would not perish. To the humans she said. "You will raise my children with love and kindness and call them Dog. In return, they will be your guardians. They will alert you to danger, keep you warm, guard your camp, and even lay down their life to protect you and your children. They and their offspring will be loyal companions to you and all your generations until the end of time.

Lakota Sioux Legend – The Pact of the Fire

-1-

Reservations

The young teens straggled along the chain link fence. The tall barrier protected a rusty, metal warehouse, as if such a structure really required protection from anything. It was the crappy part of town. Just about every part of the reservation was crappy. They didn't care. It was their kingdom. They were the princes of this territory.

They continued tracking, trailing behind their target, closing the gap slowly, taunting their prey by their mere presence as they prepared to fire their initial shots. The message had to be made clear about who belonged and who didn't.

"Hey half-breed! Yeah, we're talking to you! Ya loser!"

"This reservation is for full-blood Lakota."

"Yeah, tell your mother she should have married a real Lakota, not some white dude."

The boy they targeted continued walking; ambling along, tuning out his tormentors. His dog emitted a throaty, almost imperceptible growl. "Com' on Sierra. It's ok." He continued on his course and the tormentors continued theirs.

"Hey Dixon, tell your mother that since she married a white man, she's not really a Lakota *either*! She's a traitor."

"You don't know how to talk to people do you? Just dogs."

"Freak."

The boy continued walking, but looked down at Sierra briefly as their eyes met. After a short glance, Sierra stopped and turned. She took several steps toward the boys. They halted their advance as she growled and snarled fiercely, emitting several warning barks. She stood her ground, silencing the royalty temporarily.

Dakota turned and faced the jerks as Sierra continued projecting her displeasure.

"Call her off jerk."

"Yeah! Get your dog out of here."

Dakota grinned as the devious idea took shape in his mind.

"I'm sorry guys. My bad. I think what she wants is for you to take your pants off and leave them. Then I'm sure she'll leave you alone."

"Not likely, freak!"

Dakota and Sierra's eyes met again. He nodded to her and that was all.

She growled more fiercely and snapped at the boys who became increasingly tense, drawing closer together. She stepped forward and backed them up against the fence.

"Dixon. Make her leave us alone!"

"Guys, I'm sorry. I really think she wants your pants. She's really into rank-smelling blue jeans like yours. What can I say? It's just a thing with her. Maybe if you'd wash them occasionally she wouldn't care."

Sierra growled and barked more as the boys began to remove their pants, leaving them in a pile in front of her. They stood backed up against the fence, in only their shirts and underwear, holding their shoes in their hands.

"Better get running guys. She wants to enjoy those jeans."

The boys hesitated, but were too intimidated by the vicious presentation Sierra provided. They began trotting away from the scene.

"This isn't the end of this Dixon! You'll pay! You're one dead half-breed."

Sierra stood and growled even more viciously as the boys ran off.

Dakota turned and continued walking. He snapped his fingers and she turned toward him, trotting to catch up. The boys continued to hurl insults as they ran.

"We'll get you Dixon!"

"Why don't you learn to fight like a man!"

"Don't ever think you're one of us!"

"You don't belong here! You never will!"

On his 13th birthday, Dakota's grandfather, Running Deer, took him camping for the weekend. Mountains and wilderness surrounded the reservation and the two enjoyed hiking and fishing whenever they had the chance. Since Dakota's father was not part of the picture, the esteemed Running Deer was the one Dakota most looked up to and admired. From his grandfather he had learned many of the old ways, the history, and traditions. One evening, after a day of venturing about, the two sat enjoying the warmth and atmosphere of their campfire.

"Dakota, you know that every Lakota has a spirit-destiny."

"Yes."

"It is understood by our people to be the reason for which we were put on this earth. Sometimes we must discover it on our own, but sometimes our elders are able to catch a glimpse of what it might be and they share that destiny with us. In this way your destiny may just discover you."

"What are you saying grandfather?"

"I have had several visions about you over the past few years."

"Visions. … Like what?"

"I believe they tell of your spirit destiny."

Dakota listened intently as the firelight flickered across their faces. He noticed how the warm glow danced over the gold lettering and pins on his grandfather's red Marine Corps Veteran cap. The atmosphere was imbued with a sense of mystery, even anticipation. The distant howl of a lonely wolf periodically punctuated the crackling of the fire.

"I believe with your gift, you will do great things and be of service to our people and all people."

"My gift?"

"It is a gift that only appears once in a great many generations, the gift of being a dog whisperer."

"Oh that. …Feels more like a curse sometimes than a gift," he muttered.

"You are wrong. Since ancient times, our people have shared a kindred spirit, first with the wolf, then with their dog descendants. Not many have had the way as you do."

"I'm not sure what the big deal is."

"Dakota, a dog whisperer is an honored destiny among our people and a source of great pride."

"But grandfather, I am *already* good at training dogs. Am I not a dog whisperer now?"

"Dakota, a dog *trainer* can teach commands to dogs, but a dog *whisperer* learns to listen and hear the very spirit of his canine partner."

"Dogs don't speak."

"They do, but you must learn to hear them and sense their spirit so the two of you can learn to function as one. It will take time, but when you learn to calm your soul and quiet your spirit, you will be able to begin to hear your partner. That is the beginning of a great power. But that power must be used carefully. With it you can do great things."

"Is this like mind reading? I'm just sayin', cause it sounds a lot like mind reading to me."

"Dakota, I'm being serious."

"Serious mind reading, I get it Grandfather."

Running Deer grinned and shook his head.

"Sorry Grandfather. You know I like messing with you." Dakota re-positioned himself on the log so he appeared to be more serious and focused on what his grandfather was saying. "Ok, serious Indian stuff. Got it. Take two, camera rolling, and cue Indian Chief," as he pointed at his grandfather like a movie director.

"Dakota, I must warn you. A time will come when your canine brother will tell you something that is the most important thing he will ever share with you. When that moment comes, you must recognize it and be in tune with him, trusting him completely."

"I understand. I think. Maybe when I am a dog whisperer I can then become a great warrior like you Grandfather. The others will accept me as if I was a full Lakota. You will see. I will make you proud."

"Dakota, I am already proud."

"But you were a Marine. You helped win the war and beat the Japanese."

Running Deer smiled. "Warriors fight many different types of battles Dakota. Not all of them are on the battlefield."

"Yeah, but the cool stuff happens on the battlefield. You know, like the hand-to-hand combat, the helicopter gunships. Man that would be cool to fly one of those. Is this the part where you give me my own light saber?"

"Dakota."

"Sorrrryy!"

"Some of the most difficult battles are within ourselves, and some may be with those closest to us."

"I hear *that*," shaking his head in acknowledgement, as he looked at the fire.

"But the mark of the greatest warrior is knowing that not all battles must be fought."

"How lame is that? What's the point?"

"Know when to use your skill and your gift. Not every attack requires a response."

"Well that sucks."

"You have a great power to control animals, but that power is most effective when you build a bond of trust with your partner. Without trust, your gift may not work when you need it the most. Learn to control the power you have for the greatest result and the good of others."

"I'll try Grandfather."

"Someday, this will make more sense, but for now, just try to remember what I have told you tonight."

Dakota felt his eyes well up before the words that followed.

"I just want to fit in somewhere. ... I'm *so* tired of the crap I get. ...It's like Sierra is my only real friend. I'm not the only half-breed on the reservation, but they give me so much garbage about it....Someday I'll prove myself to everyone and then they'll treat me like the adults treat you Grandfather."

Running Deer grinned. He understood Dakota's struggle. He leaned in toward his grandson. Dakota stopped his fidgeting, sensing his grandfather had more. Even the distant wolf paused his lonesome howls seemingly in anticipation of Running Deer's words. He lowered his tone and spaced his few words carefully for emphasis.

"Dakota … You are more of a Lakota than many full-bloods. … You were born to do this. … Even though a wolf has his pack, … he may still be lonely. …Being part of a pack does not cure the wolf's longing."

"Longing for what?"

Running Deer inhaled slowly, then exhaled as if clearing a path for his words.

"Sometimes the wolf is longing to know his purpose."

Dakota waited long enough for the words settle.

"But how will I know when I have achieved my spirit destiny?"

"Every dog whisperer has a different journey. When the time is right, yours will be revealed to you. Only then will it become clear what will be required to complete your quest. Listen to your canine brother. He will not fail you. But he will not share with you if you misuse the power you have. Teach him to trust you, then in your moment of need, if you listen to what your canine companion tells you, then you will prove yourself worthy of your spirt destiny."

Dakota pondered the words for a brief moment.

"I just have one question Grandfather."

"What is it Dakota?"

"If I become a Marine, will I get a cool hat like yours?"

Running Deer sighed and grinned the patient grin of a grandfather.

KEVIN BRETT

-2-

Sands of Takhar

Fourteen Years Later

Master Sergeant, Eddie Robinson landed hard, face down in the sand. The senior Marine lay battered, sweat-drenched, and stunned from the impact. The Afghan sun beat down on him relentlessly as he took a deep breath to replace the wind that had just been knocked out of him. He choked and coughed on the dust and sand, then drew a second slow breath before he opened his eyes.

A few seconds later, he wasn't really ready, but he got up anyway. He slowly dragged his arms to his sides and pushed himself up. He struggled to muster enough saliva to spit out a mouthful of sand. His teeth were gritty, his dark brown skin scraped raw from the many slams he had taken from his partner. Dixon kept pulling new techniques out of his bag of martial arts tricks. Most of them involved the tall Native American sending Eddie's compact, five-foot five self, airborne.

Sand coated Eddie's head and stuck to the sweat. Sand stuck to his soaked t-shirt and found its way inside his boots and other inconvenient places. Grains of the stuff were everywhere, rubbing, itching, chaffing, and grinding. It did just about as much damage to people as it did to equipment and vehicles. Sand was a constant foe that had to be battled and guarded against almost with more vigilance than battling the Taliban and the barbarians of Al Qaeda.

Eddie pulled himself up into a squatting position and turned toward Dakota who towered over him like Goliath. Dakota had streams of sweat running down his head and face, but wasn't covered in sand like Eddie; probably because Eddie was the one being thrown around like a rag doll. Dixon's short black hair glistened in the brutal sun as he stood grinning at his platoon sergeant, twelve years his senior.

Robinson groaned. "Are we done yet Lieutenant? We've been at it nearly two hours."

"Seriously?" replied Dixon. "What's wrong 'Top'? Too much for the old man? Come on, you know you love it."

'Top', was the nickname often used to refer to Master Sergeants since they are typically the top enlisted member of a unit. Dixon was the Kung Fu guy, the 'Karate Kid', as Robinson saw it. He had a brown belt in the Marine Corps Martial Arts Program (MCMAP) and loved working out, slamming, flipping, and sweeping down his fellow Marines. It was both gritty and graceful at the same time; maybe that's why they called it an 'art'.

"Sir, you're gonna break every bone in my body. Then I won't be able to do a very good job of protecting your sorry butt when we're on patrol. Besides isn't there some Marine Corps Order against brown belts beating up on lower-ranking green belts?"

"You're right. I forget that you senior citizens are a little more 'delicate' than the rest of us! I'll give you a reprieve. Besides, I don't want your wife getting all pissed off at me for messing up your pretty little face, but don't worry, no one will ever mistake you for Denzel Washington. You ain't that pretty!"

"Keep it up Sir. That's okay. I just want to be in one piece so I'm able to shoot some hoops with my son when we get back, … and I don't mean from a wheelchair!" he said, grinning. Dixon reached out and helped Robinson up.

"Oh … Dude! … I'm sorry, I forgot to bring some cheese!"

"Cheese? … What?"

"You know … some cheese to go with that whine of yours! Come on, get ready. One more time."

"That's what you said two hours ago. Can't we just hit the Taliban with close air support? It's less painful for us than using all your Kung Fu crap."

"This time you throw me."

Robinson was secretly convinced that the Native American in Dixon enjoyed exacting just a little revenge on non-Native Americans in the form of grueling martial arts training sessions, but Robinson still respected the kid. When he wasn't running on endlessly with about anything and everything that entered his mind, or pulling some pisser of a prank on the very person least likely to appreciate the genius behind it, he was downright tolerable. He was a good egg and he had heart, and that's what mattered to Eddie. He saw potential in the kid.

Robinson snatched his 9mm pistol from his thigh holster and trained it on Dixon. "Sir, I don't want to have to do this, but-"

Suddenly Dixon's German Shepherd, who had been calmly watching her master practice, jumped up with a fierce growl and leapt toward Eddie's pistol. She took it down with the full force of her seventy-five pounds of pure muscle. When Eddie attempted to stand up, Dakota nodded subtly toward Zoe.

Zoe growled fiercely toward Eddie and circled him closely so that he dare not attempt to stand up or move.

Eddie shook his head and slammed his fist down on the sand. "I'm seriously having to rethink this whole friend thing. Now, would you tell your dog to give me back my damned weapon?"

Dakota looked at Zoe and then swung his head toward Eddie. She walked calmly to him and dropped his pistol beside him. It thumped in the soft, dusty sand. Eddie looked down at the dusty firearm for a moment, taking in his defeat. He picked up the weapon and brushed off the sand, then stood up slowly, feeling the punishment of the past two hours. Once again, he whipped his pistol into a single-hand grip and pointed it at Dakota. Zoe growled. DX stared at Eddie. Neither man moved. In an instant, DX executed a gun disarming technique. It resembled someone extending his hands forward and clapping once. With one sudden 'clap' of his hands against the barrel of the 9mm pistol and the inside of Eddie's wrist, he broke his partner's grip on the weapon. He rotated it in the palm of his hand as Eddie's grip dissolved, transferring it smoothly to his own hands. In roughly a quarter of a second, DX was pointing the pistol back at Eddie, gripping it firmly with both hands as he slid back one step away from him.

"Didn't your mother teach you to hold your weapon with both hands Eddie? Common man, you make this too easy for me."

"Seriously, I'm good Lieutenant. You and your dog have embarrassed me enough. We need to get started prepping and reviewing the intel reports from Bravo sector for tomorrow."

"I hear ya. You're right. Let's go. ... Damn. What are you, my wife?"

Dakota reached down and picked up their hydration packs, handing one to Eddie. They sucked down some water from the drinking tubes and Eddie swished and spit out a mouthful, trying to rinse out any remaining grains of sand.

"No Lieutenant, but you might give that some consideration. It's actually a pretty awesome thing. 'Specially when you start having little ones. They're a blast and they're more fun as they get older. Phase one though, ya gotta get a girl. That's a must. We'll work on that."

"Naw, not me Eddie. I like the idea. Sounds good. Maybe someday, but I'm not so sure I'm 'Dad' material. Besides, being around women, I just get all stupid and end up blowing it. I don't think anyone could tolerate me except you and you're just not my type."

"Thanks for clearing that up."

"What you're saying sounds pretty scary."

"You kiddin' me Lieutenant! You lead forty-eight men into a combat zone every day and you're afraid of going home to a skirt and some rug rats?"

"You got it 'Top'. The Corps provides training for what *we* do. There's *no* training for what you're talking about."

"I hear ya Sir. ...It's not that hard. You just show up every day, give your best, show 'em all that you love 'em and just be there for 'em, kinda like you do with these kids. They all think the world of you Lieutenant. That's all I do with my kids and they think I'm some kinda flippin' super hero; piece of freaking cake Sir. You do that and they'll wanna put a cape on you, or at least a pair of tights."

"Yeah Eddie. ... *me* in tights. Now there's a visual."

"Lieutenant, the way I see it, the sooner you get married, the less time you have to beat me up."

"Don't worry. I always have time for you."

The two walked back toward their barracks. Dakota whistled for Zoe, who jumped up from her spot in the shade and trotted alongside.

She was Dakota's girl, a beautiful German Shepherd. Other than Eddie, she was pretty much his best friend in this desolate, terrorist-infested part of the world. Dakota had a special connection with her that prompted Eddie to dub him 'Dog Whisperer'; a connection resonated to his core.

With Zoe, it was more than just demonstrating tricks. Most of what she could do went against the book, but the 'book' didn't concern Dakota. His company commander knew about Dixon's K9 training expertise prior to entering the Marine Corps. He allowed him to include her in the platoon as an experiment. Dakota was excited that she had begun to show real potential.

Eddie broke the silence. "So, have you heard back from the K9 School yet?"

"Nope. Gettin' a little antsy about it. I hate waiting."

"So if you get accepted, you're just going to dump us all and go play dog tricks with Zoe is that it?"

"You got it 'Top'. Whatever it takes to piss you off."

"Not funny. ... The guys will miss her. Oh, and you too Sir. She kind of gives a little feeling of being back home ya know?"

"Yea."

"Kinda helps them decompress when they're out playing catch with her. But that's ok, you go ahead and do your own thing."

DX turned and watched Eddie as he rambled on. A grin slowly formed on his face as Eddie continued.

"Don't let that bother you one bit. I'll just have to break in a new platoon leader, that's all. Maybe the next one won't have this thing about beatin' up on little guys like me. Know what I'm sayin'?"

"Still with the whining thing huh 'Top'?"

Eddie shook his head.

"Ya know Eddie, this whole K9 training thing of mine is going to help me prove something big, and if I'm right, it could just change everything about the role of K9s in the military. They're capable of much more than we know."

"Roger that Sir. It's cool the stuff you've taught her and it definitely helps having her on patrol with us. All the stuff she does, like those sneak attacks and - I mean, she's doing stuff that usually takes a team of different K9s. You got her doin' it all."

"That's the idea."

"I just don't get how you get her to do all that stuff and, ...I mean, you don't even really give her any commands. She just seems to know what you want. How does she know?"

"It's just a thing Eddie."

Eddie shook his head in disbelief. "I don't know. It's cool, but it's creepy too. It's like, my wife does that to me sometimes. Just freaking reads my mind. That's what Zoe does to you isn't?"

"Well. You know, women's intuition. I'm sure that's part of it."

"Must be."

'You know, it's gonna to be an uphill climb to get the leadership of the training school to buy off on some of my concepts. I can't exactly go walking in the door and tell 'em they're all wet and I have it all figured out."

"Roger that. ... So maybe that's why you should stay with us."

"Nice try."

Dixon admired Eddie. He was experienced, knowledgeable, and loyal to his Marine 'kids'. As far as humans go, Dakota felt that he and Eddie made a good team. Chemistry was important, even if he outranked Robinson. There was a good balance between the two.

DX continued. "This is why I became a Marine; at least partly. My grandfather was a Marine; a code talker during World War II."

"You never mentioned that before."

"I told him I would use my gift and become a great warrior one day and make him proud."

"Oh, I get it. Big bad warrior likes beating up on little guys," snarked Eddie.

DX grinned.

"You sure have something when it comes to dogs. I don't totally get it."

"I was bullied a lot as a kid. Since I wasn't a full Lakota, the other boys on the reservation just wouldn't let up, so I spent more time with dogs than with the kids my age. I just didn't fit in."

"Sure. I get it Rudolf. The other reindeer wouldn't let you join in any reindeer games. Poor Dakota. That's it. Now I know why you're so big on pulling pranks. You're just trying to get back at those jerks who bullied you back home. ... Yep. I nailed that one. Just call me Doctor Eddie. Weekdays at four, after Oprah. Uh huh!"

DX shook his head. "The sun is definitely getting to you brother."

"Brother! Do we *look* related? Cause I'm not seeing the family resemblance."

DX's grin couldn't catch a break. "Do you *ever* shut up?"

As they walked near the company headquarters barracks, DX opened the door. He knelt down and whispered in Zoe's ear. She took off inside the temporary building and DX let the door swing shut behind her.

"Sir, do you *enjoy* being punished? You know the CO is going to take a chunk out of your backside, maybe the whole thing."

"Ah, common Eddie. You know he loves it."

"What is it this time?"

DX looked at his watch. "Wait for it. In three, two, one. Cue pissed Company Commander."

Right on cue, Zoe rushed out of another swinging door along the far end of the building. In her mouth flapped a pair of olive drab men's briefs. A second later, the CO, with only a towel wrapped around his waist, ran after her cursing. Suddenly he stopped when he spotted DX laughing.

The CO screamed and shook an angry finger at DX. "No more Dixon! You hear me! No more! This ends now!" Then he ran off toward Zoe.

"Aye Sir!"

Dakota sat at a laptop in the ops tent checking his email. The last one was from the admissions clerk with the Marine Corps Special Operations Command Canine Tactical School (CTS).

He screamed out in what sounded like a Native American war cry. "Yiewwww Heeyaaa! I'm in! Got it! Got it! Got it!"

Several Marines seated at workstations looked toward him casually, curious as to what he was screaming about this time. He had applied every session for two years. Each time, he was turned down, but this email informed him that a seat had been reserved for the spring training session.

Dakota craved the tactics, techniques, and procedures for training canines. He was ready to devour every bit of training. With Zoe, he was determined to demonstrate that it was possible to develop a new breed of canine warrior. His whole life had been building to this point. During his martial arts studies, he had discovered a book that espoused the importance of the well-rounded warrior with a wide range of skills and capabilities. He believed that, given time and a lot of work, it might be possible to do the same with canines. He was obsessed with proving that K9s could play a wider role and that they should not be limited to a small set of skills as they were currently. It didn't matter if that role was in military operations or civilian activities.

Rushing out of the ops center with a copy of the letter in his hand, he bolted across the base and found Eddie.

"Eddie! Check it out," as he thrust the letter in front of him. "I made it!"

"The school?"

"Yeah, look!"

"Congrats Sir. That's awesome."

Dakota began a high-speed babble. "Eddie it's all coming together! This is so stinking awesome! When I was young boy on the reservation, my grandfather shared a vision with me. He saw the spirit that I share with dogs. He could see how I communicate with them! It's what I've been training for my whole life!"

"Congratulations young Skywalker."

Inside the UOC, Robinson sat beside the S2 (Intel) officer. They reviewed patrol reports and drone surveillance. Robinson would need to brief this intel about enemy encounters and threats in the sector to Dixon and the platoon in the morning as part of the pre-mission brief.

Dixon was at the motor pool inspecting the vehicles with the motor transport chief. The routine over the past three weeks was to take a patrol of several Mine-Resistant Ambush Protected (MRAP) vehicles out to a series of mountain ridges where they would dismount, leave a squad of thirteen Marines to protect the vehicles and secure the area. Robinson, Dixon, Zoe and the other two squads would head overland to the higher third ridge to gain a vantage point over the valley on the other side. From there the unit would stay on post to observe, coordinate with the Brits, and call in air support for different operations taking place within their range.

The MRAPs were huge, bulky, and awkward, but they worked. Some versions stood twice as high as the better known Hummers, towering over the ground. These monsters had saved many lives and literally only a handful of troops had been killed in them. The introduction of these vehicles forced the enemy to change tactics and focus on IEDs that aimed at taking out personnel on foot patrol rather than those who were well protected inside their MRAPs. Maybe that was some type of progress. It was just a constant game of cat and mouse with the Taliban.

Dixon sat beside the driver in the lead vehicle with Robinson, Zoe, and several other Marines. The young Marines chewed gum with an anxious intensity that was a combination of nervousness and boredom. The ride was slow. The convoy averaged twenty-five miles per hour over roads the combat engineers had graded so that they were level and solid. Too many MRAPs had fallen prey to soft roads in Afghanistan or weak bridges, causing them to roll over in ditches as portions of the roads collapsed under the 14-ton weight of these beasts.

Overhead, drones, or more properly, Unmanned Arial Systems (UAS) kept a nearly constant eye on the region, feeding sensor data up to the satellites, then down to the dishes outside the UOC so that the boys inside at the S2 (intel) post could monitor for hostiles and provide intel based on Dakota's priority intelligence requests. As the system tagged the data and the S2 team confirmed and analyzed it, they fed unit data to the vehicles in the convoys to keep the crew apprised of enemy targets. It was the new age of net-centric warfare, like online, multi-player video games.

While all the electrons swirled around in space and down at ground level, the Marines inside the MRAPs kept a sharp eye out, but still found time for plenty of idle chatter.

"So Lieutenant, when you get out of the Corps are you going to partner with me in my pizza shop like we talked about? I think we should call it 'Tops' Pizza," said Robinson.

"Get out of the Corps? I'm just getting started old man. I don't know 'Top'. Are you forgetting that I just got accepted to the canine school yesterday," replied Dixon.

"Hey that's awesome Sir," grinning at the other Marines. "I'm sure you'll make an excellent dog, Lieutenant. I have complete confidence in you," joked Robinson.

"Okay, Robinson. You can joke about it, but the tactical K9 stuff is my thing. It's personal. Besides, tell me, do I really want to be a business partner with a guy who thinks that MREs can be used as pizza toppings?"

"Sir, the guys in the chow hall thought that shit was awesome. They gobbled it up in a heartbeat. What's wrong with Beef Stroganoff pizza or scrambled eggs and cheese on pizza? You have to think outside the box. Could be the next big craze."

"Robinson, I'm not sure that pizza like that *belongs* in a box! That's just plain wrong and secondly, they're Marines! ... What do they know about quality food? They live on Ramen Noodles!"

"They were hungry."

"Exactly, they'd been on patrol for 48 hours. You took advantage of their heightened state of hunger, made pizza with that garbage, and then tried to convince them that somehow Dominos had just delivered! I'm sure there has to be a Marine Corps Order against that."

The other Marines inside the MRAP chuckled at the mock conflict between the Master Sergeant and the Lieutenant.

"Sir, they were willing taste testers taking part in a great experiment," replied Robinson in mock defense of his actions.

"Yeah, we'll go with that," said Dixon, shaking his head with a grin.

"Besides Sir, you know the drill, make do with what you have – improvise," continued Robinson.

"Why don't you improvise some coordinates and make sure we don't drive past the Brits and leave them hanging all alone out there. We're approaching the first ridge."

"Aye Sir."

About twenty minutes later, the massive vehicles slowed. Their brakes squealed as they came to a stop. Dixon gave the order to re-position the vehicles in a protective configuration so that the force protection squad would be better able to monitor and protect the vehicles. Gunners stayed in the vehicles while other Marines set up a protective perimeter. They were approximately forty-five miles out from the base in an area often referred to as "Hell's Back Yard."

Dixon, Robinson, Zoe, and the Marines in 1st and 2nd squad dismounted from the vehicles and headed toward the base of the first ridge. The vehicles could take them no farther. They would be on foot until they reached their initial coordinates. Staff Sergeant White took the point, followed by Robinson, Dixon and the two squads. Zoe tagged alongside Dixon. The unit formed two staggered columns about eight feet apart, but that distance fluctuated as they passed between boulders and narrow gaps in the hills leading to their destination on higher ridges in the distance.

As the unit neared the base of the first ridge, Dixon turned to Robinson and imitated characters from Lord of the Rings. "Take us to Mordoor Froto. My precious."

Robinson, turned slowly toward Dixon in disbelief. "You realize you're nuts, right Lieutenant?"

"Probably", said Dixon with a grin.

"And we're following you into combat. … I'm the one who's nuts. Sir, were you kicked in the head a lot when you were learning all that Kung Fu crap? Just askin'."

"I don't remember," joked Dixon.

Clearly, the sand, the heat, the months on end could drive you batty or cause you to develop weird quirks from boredom, stress, isolation, monotony, whatever it was. In Dixon's case, his personality was to relieve stress with humor, sarcasm, or just act a little batty.

Robinson looked at him. "Sir, you need a woman, or something. Problem is I don't know any as crazy as you."

Dixon's eye met Robinson's for a few fleeting seconds. "You know I'm just screwin' with ya right? I'm fine, just havin' a little fun with ya 'Top'. Relax."

"You're *fine*? Mixing metaphors and all that!"

"I'm not mixing metaphors. I'm mixing movies – duh." In his John Wayne voice. "Come on pardner, we're burnin' daylight," pointing ahead excitedly. "Look! The Emerald City."

Robinson, looked down, shook his head, and started to grin a little at the unreality of the conversation and Dixon's off the charts zaniness. Then he muttered under his breath. "Shit. You gotta be kiddin' me."

Dixon motioned with his right arm for Robinson to go ahead of him and lead the way.

Robinson responded. "Oh, no. You go ahead. I'm good. Besides, I don't want you and your dog behind me doing any of that Kung Fu Ninja shit when I'm not lookin'."

Dakota went ahead of Robinson, following just behind Staff Sergeant White. Zoe, well, she just tuned out the banter and began to sniff.

A few minutes on the trail and the radio operator for the squad came forward to Dixon. "Sir, the UOC reports that there is no overhead UAS coverage of our sector. The drone squadron comm relays were not working this morning, so the drones were grounded. ... We're on our own Sir."

Dakota was silent for a moment, then commented to the Corporal. "Nice of them to let us know. ...Thanks Corporal."

"Aye Sir."

Robinson spoke into his comm to the platoon. "Alright boys, look alive. We don't have eyes in the sky so you need to watch the rocks. We've been blind all morning and just found out. Stay focused. We don't know what kind of creepy crawlies might be out there."

The platoon continued on their route. The hills became steeper and the pace of the troops slowed. Zoe looked at Dakota and whimpered.

"What girl?"

She gave him a look. He had never seen this expression in her eyes. She was anxious. He sensed it.

"Ok girl. Scout!"

He sent her ahead to scout out the trail since there was no drone coverage to provide that capability for them. Dixon estimated they had about a twenty-minute trek to get to the top of the third ridge where they would have a commanding view of the region and provide the unit more security being able to see the lower terrain. The men continued scanning in silence.

Zoe moved out of sight a ways ahead. She growled and barked angrily twice, then yelped out with a sudden shriek of pain, then nothing. Suddenly Robinson took in a terrifying sight. Toward the front of the platoon, a Taliban fighter shouldering an RPG launcher stepped out into the clear and fired. The lethal projectile raced toward the lead element. Dakota spotted the perpetrator a split second after Robinson.

The hostile stood higher up the ridge about fifty yards ahead of them. Immediately Robinson yelled out into his comm. "RPG! Hit the deck!" A split second later, the projectile struck a rock formation near the middle of the platoon's pair of columns, exploding and blasting the rock like shrapnel, creating a deafening explosion. A second RPG fired from a position to the south of the column and rocketed forward. It too struck a large rock formation near Dakota, Robinson, White and the lead members. Zoe had met her end when she passed by the lead component of the Taliban ambush, just before the first RPG had launched. The shriek she made was her last.

Several lethal shards of rock shrapnel pulverized Robinson, inflicting grave injuries before he even hit the ground. A firestorm of lead erupted from several concealed hostiles and ricocheted around the men making either pings when it hit rock. Rounds seemed to spray in every direction and those rounds that hit the ground, made odd little thumps as they burrowed into the sand. It was like being trapped in a spider web of crisscrossing bullets. Dakota raced toward Robinson, yelling into his comm. "Corpsman!"

Robinson was hit bad. Dakota pretty much knew it as soon as he saw him. "Corpsman, get over here!" The Navy Corpsman attached to the platoon provided their medical support. These field medics had many capabilities if they could get to the injured party quickly enough. The Corpsman's job was to stabilize the injured and prep them for evacuation to a field surgical care facility.

Staff Sergeant Bob White went down too; struck in the head as a large section of a rock formation collapsed on him. Several AK-47 rounds found their way through gaps in his body armor.

The other Marines put up a wall of fire in carefully structured patterns in all directions where the Taliban were positioned around them. The Marines knew what to do. It was second nature. Unfortunately it was a perfect ambush in a semi canyon-like land formation and without the eyes in the sky, which they had not been notified about, pretty much everything was against them; really, it was a perfect shit storm.

Dakota arrived at Robinson before the Corpsman. Heavy enemy fire from several directions pinned the Corpsman down. Dakota knelt down and tried to lean over Robinson to cover him. "Hang on Robinson, 'Doc' is on his way. We're gettin' you outa here 'Top'. Just stay with me."

Robinson struggled to breathe. He became weak from the loss of blood and started to shiver as his body temperature began dropping.

"Lieutenant -"

"Save your energy 'Top'."

"Sorry Lieutenant – Don't think I'm gonna-"

"Shut up Eddie. You stay with me dammit!!! Doc's almost here."

Robinson coughed as he began to speak "Sir. Do the family thing. You'll make an awesome dad. You care about your family half as much as you care about these kids out here, you'll get those tights."

"Shut up. Just hang in there Eddie. Doc's comin' Don't you leave me!"

Eddie struggled with each word, because of his injuries and because of the emotions he was feeling about his final moments. "Sir. ...I need you to tell my wife and kids how much I love 'em. ...Maybe you could shoot some hoops with my boy. He'd like that. ....and try not to let my wife know you're nuts."

Dakota quietly accepted the reality of what was happening. 'Doc' wasn't going to make it to them, and even if he did, Robinson was going fast.

"Eddie, ya gotta teach me how to make that crappy pizza like you do man. I need you to teach me that."

"Sir, it's not that hard. Just smear whatever you got on a big-ass piece of round bread and cook it for a while; presto, one crappy pizza. ...You'll get the hang of it."

The gunfire quickly subsided as the fire teams took out the enemy fighters and quelled the storm of lead. Dakota's voice became quiet; almost a whisper. "Eddie. Come on man."

Eddie's eyes slowly closed. He could no longer hear Dakota.

"Eddie, please."

Dakota looked at his friend for a moment. He felt a hot wave of grief wash over him as his friend slipped away. Dakota's eyes welled up and his vision became blurry. A tear rolled over the bottom edge of his right eye, creating a small stream as it mixed with the sand on his face. He hugged Eddie close and whispered. "Great Creator, please accept my brother into your magnificent presence. May he live in peace with you and his ancestors."

The AK-47 fire now seemed to come from only one position; down from the ten or twelve positions that seemed to radiate bullets when the attack first began. Dakota snapped back to the reality of the ambush and squat-ran, trying to stay low as he headed over to his Sergeant. He gave a few brief orders and then headed off toward one of the fire teams.

Suddenly a hand-thrown explosive hit a large rock formation near him. The shock knocked Dakota to the ground. Rock exploded and fell on and around him, pinning his legs and his right arm. He felt light-headed. His ears rang from the concussion of the blast. Everything seemed to spin and become hazy as he lay there. The pain in his legs and arm didn't feel like pain, it was just hot and numb at the same time. He lay on his back, pinned down by an avalanche of rock. His eyes flickered a few times and he had to work hard to keep them from closing. He tried to lift his head to look around, but he couldn't keep it up. His head fell back to the ground and rested against the inside of his helmet. All the noise around him began to fade as though someone turned down the volume, just before he passed out.

KEVIN BRETT

-3-

Dogs Just Help Kids Grow Up Right

Sixteen Months Earlier

The three Barnes children camped out in the family room watching the most recent Lassie movie for the zillionth time. A family embarks on a cross-country road trip and finds a stray Collie. The son and daughter plead with the parents to let them adopt the dog. They beg them to take the beautiful Collie with them to their new home in the country.

"Please Dad," pleaded the daughter. "We need a dog. Besides, dogs just help kids grow up right."

Keith and Linda Barnes got the hint, all five hundred of them. They needed a dog too. Why? Because, dogs just help kids grow up right.

The Barnes were very much the typical suburban family. They lived in a pleasant neighborhood in North Stafford, Virginia. They attended church, played soccer, participated in Scouts, and engaged in all the other activities that seemed to define life in suburbia.

Allie, Sandra, and Wes were all bright, caring, sweet kids who would thoroughly enjoy and love their new chum. It wasn't just about them though, Keith really wanted a dog again, a Collie to be precise. He longed to relive the joy and magic of owning Collies in his childhood. He and Linda wanted to share that with their children, just one of the simple joys of parenthood.

The kids were already in bed and Keith and Linda prepared to do the same. Linda turned back the bed sheets. "I've always loved Golden Retrievers. I'm not too crazy about really small dogs. They make me think of some type of rodent. They're cute and everything, but ya have to be able to hug 'em around the neck."

"So a larger dog."

"Not a drooler though." Linda had a real issue with saliva and to Keith it was only fair that he got to push her buttons occasionally; one of the perks of being married.

"Hey! I know. A big guy like Beethoven! You know, huge and drooling a lot! That would be awesome! We could slip on big gobs of drool that he leaves on the kitchen floor and have our clothes stick to the drool that he leaves on the couch. It'll be great."

Linda instantly felt a twinge of queasiness in the pit of her stomach as the muscles in her throat constricted. "Ok! Stop. I'm going to lose it if you don't stop! You're not funny Keith." She tried to change the subject. "It would also be good if it were a guard dog to protect the family."

"Of course, I agree. He could drool all over the bad guys and they'd be slipping in it everywhere while we call the cops."

"Okay. I'm done with this conversation." She left the bedroom and went into the bathroom. Keith chuckled. "It's all good fun until someone hurls," she warned.

"You know I grew up with Collies."

"I know."

"My first one was Macintosh. He was a beauty; dark red like the apple. He was a wild one though. He would run loose to nearby farms and chase the sheep. One night he came back and some farmer had shot his hind side with birdshot or something."

"I know and you've read every Collie book and watched every Lassie movie. I get it."

"I'm just saying. I've had a Collie in my family since I was five. Piney Branch Lindsay Lad was another Collie we had. Piney Branch was the dog breeder, and Lindsay Lad was his Scottish name."

"Keith, I get it."

"It is almost required, or at least should be, for any Collie to have a Scottish name. It's tradition you know- or should be."

"Pushing. Pushing."

"I want the kids to enjoy the companionship of a gentle and lovable Collie and see them all grow up together."

Linda stopped, folded her arms, cocked her hip to one side, and gave Keith a quizzical look, followed by a wifely look. "And what am I, chopped liver?"

"I'm just sayin' ... It's an awesome dream. ... It's ok. You can talk about other types of dogs if it helps you feel like you're part of the process, but it's going to be a Collie."

She continued her stance and her look.

"I'm being completely reasonable here."

Her look didn't change.

The cold light of a winter morning invaded the kitchen as Linda sat at the small round wooden table. She stared out through the French doors at the waterfall in the back yard. Colorful leaves still speckled the hillside providing the last evidence of fall. The branches of everything but the evergreens were stripped bare since the trees had completed their autumn color spectacle. The aroma of freshly brewed coffee wafted through the air as Keith poured Linda her first steaming cup.

To Keith it was a waste. Coffee didn't wake her up like it did him. She enjoyed the taste and the ritual; usually only a few sips at that. Keith never ceased to be perplexed at how he could make it through two or even three cups of coffee while she struggled to complete one.

As he poured, he opened with the topic du jour. "So it looks like my plan is working. The dream is becoming a reality."

"Yes. So I hear, and apparently the Collie is the perfect dog, and it would make the perfect Christmas gift, and our kids will turn out better by having a Collie, and ... Did I leave anything out?" She grinned. "You know our life is about to change. It's almost like having a baby. Now I'll have five kids to take care of."

"Five? ... Wait. What? ... You're not funny."

"That's going to be such an awesome gift for the kids. I can't wait to see their reactions when they first see the little guy."

"I know what you're saying, but I'm still worried about all that hair. You know I'm going to be the one to vacuum up the hair and give the little growing fur ball lots of brushings to keep the house from becoming hairy."

"It's all for the cause. ... I'll make sure to walk him and take care of him when the kids don't. And, I'll help groom him as often as needed to keep the hair under control."

"Wow. Which kid did you borrow that line from?"

Keith grinned.

Linda stared at him; her head cocked to one side, not believing she was having this conversation with her husband. Her sarcastic baby-talk kicked in. "Ok Keith. You can have your widdul doggie as wong as you pwomise to be a good boy."

He tried to tune out her mocking of him.

They didn't want a show dog, just a healthy, well-bred Collie. Linda settled herself in front of the computer and searched Collie breeders in Virginia. After much surfing of the web, Linda was comfortable that she had finally narrowed it down to two breeders in Central Virginia. She called one to see if they had any pups for sale. Sunrise Acres was run by a husband and wife team and had some sable and white Collies from a recent litter and were expecting another mixed litter soon. They hoped to get a puppy from a litter that would be ready closer to Christmas.

After her call, she suggested to Keith. "I think the timing of the second litter would be perfect. The breeder said that the Collies were carefully bred. She seemed pretty knowledgeable and none of them had any medical issues in their history. The breeder said they had inherited three Collies with perfect health and no medical issues in their bloodline. They were guaranteed to be free of all major medical issues including hip dysplasia."

"I've heard of that before, hip displaysia is so serious that many dogs often have to be put down. Fortunately, the condition is very rare in Collies.

Linda was giddy with a sense of anticipation about the idea of owning a dog again.

"It will be fun having a new fury bundle scampering around the house."

The line from the Lassie movie echoed in her ears. ... It was true; dogs just help kids grow up right.

Linda emailed Carol with a few follow-up questions. She wanted everything to be perfect.

"I'm worried. What if something ends up being wrong with the dog after we bring him home? What if he has some ailment or condition that no one had noticed? I would just hate to see something happen. What if he didn't end up being the ideal pet and couldn't play with the kids, or worse. What if something *really* bad developed and he had to be put to sleep? It's just making me sick!"

"It'll be ok babe. Quit *worrying* so much. Focus on the exciting side. We're getting a Collie! It seems to me that you've discovered a really good breeder. She knows the breed, and she's gone to great lengths to make sure they are really good dogs."

"I feel like an expectant parent."

Linda wanted a storybook beginning, middle and ending.

"It isn't that I can't deal with imperfection, or problems, I just don't want the children to have any negative experiences the first time with a new pet."

The butterflies in her stomach had to work themselves out.

-4-

The Perfect Christmas Gift

Linda was up on email early the next morning hoping for any word; some comfort for her worries, just something from Carol that would let her know that everything would be fine. Carol came through. Her email assured Linda, that after many puppy litters; they had never had problems with any of their Collies.

Carol explained how the dogs were checked out by vets and specialists to ensure the highest quality dog; the perfect Collie; the perfect Christmas gift.

"Shew! That email arrived just in the nick of time - what a relief! I guess everything will be ok after all."

"I told you," teased Keith. "Carol said it would be. You can trust her. She and I go way back. Glad that's over. Now, tell ya what would brighten me up – a little breakfast!" Silence; followed by a wifely look. "Okay, so maybe I'll fix it myself."

A wave of relief washed over Linda. "My goodness. All this about a dog!" She looked at Keith as though she couldn't believe how worked up she had gotten.

The phone rang in Carol's kitchen just after nine-thirty in the morning.

"Hello Carol. It's Linda Barnes. How are you?"

"I'm fine. What can I do for you?"

"I was calling to check on the puppies. When can we come by to see them?"

"They're doing great. All beautiful and healthy, and they've all been checked by the vet. None of them have any problems at all."

"Wonderful!"

"They will be ready to take home on December 20."

"Oh perfect! Just in time for Christmas. We'll pick him up that morning after we take the kids to school."

"That will be a wonderful surprise waiting for them when they get home."

Before this perfect plan could happen, they needed a dog. Keith and Linda first had to make a visit to the Acres to check out the litter and decide which Collie would join the Barnes family.

As Linda drove south on Interstate 95, Keith checked the map, looking for the turnoff for Interstate 64 West, which would take them southwest toward Sunrise Acres. They turned off the exit from 64 West to Route 522 South, which passed directly through Johnson's Corner. Keith checked the map, for the thirty-eighth time. The countryside was beautiful, with an even mixture of small farms and forests; one quaint scene of red barns and cows behind white ranch fences after another. The sprawling metropolis that was Johnson's Corner sported a total of three stoplights running the length of the town. They turned left onto Sully Road, on the outskirts at the intersection with the Johnson's Corner Fire Department. A little ways ahead was the entrance to Sunrise Acres.

As their Ford Expedition cruised down the oak-lined road, they spotted the sign for Sunrise Acres Farm and pulled onto the main driveway. They headed down the two-hundred yard road toward the main house. White wood fencing lined the sides of the drive. As they drove along the road, several Collies ran beside them, keeping a close eye on the unknown visitors.

Linda spotted a pair of blue merles and several sable and white Collies. Seeing them, Keith had flashbacks of that visit to Piney Branch Kennels when he was a boy when he and his parents went to pick up Lad.

"I just think there is some special kind of magic at a Collie kennel that must come only directly from the sunlight."

"You think?"

"Yea, I think it has some kind of reaction when it comes into contact with their coats. It's the only thing that explains all the amazing qualities these guys have. No other breed has that special magic. I'm sure of it."

Linda grinned as she felt the excitement building. What a grand sight. At least six mature Collies were scattered about the property and three younger ones that appeared to be about six to eight months old. They sprawled beneath very large Oak trees, enjoying the cool morning breeze.

Linda commented. "With their thick roughs and lounging around in the shade like that, it makes me think of pride of lions somewhere in the African Savannah."

She pulled over to a small parking area on the front side of the white farmhouse. Exiting the vehicle, they took in the scene as the Collies approached the couple cautiously; checking them out. The leader of the pack fired out two loud announcing barks toward the main house to signal Carol that visitors had arrived. Keith and Linda were under close watch by three very capable Collies. The Barnes merely thought the Collies were being friendly, but being the good shepherds that they are, these wolf-descendants were actually keeping the Barnes safely in check, watching their every move. Although Keith and Linda might not have felt it, they were surrounded. The Collies escorted them as they walked toward the house.

Carol walked out on the front porch. "Hello Mrs. Barnes! Come on up. Don't mind the security detail. They're just greeting you."

The farmhouse had a small, front living room to the left of the front door and a cozy library office to the right.

"Please excuse me a moment while I get one of the girls to bring out the pups."

A moment or two later, Carol and two assistants walked out with a Collie pup in each arm. There were six furry, lovable pups, two blue merles, and four tri-colors. Keith and Linda were in awe at the tiny fur balls.

One of the blue merles was significantly larger than any of the other Collies. It was a female, with a thick, beautiful, blue-grey coat. The other blue merle was about the same size as the four tri-colors. Although they both found the blue merles beautiful, Keith and Linda gravitated toward the tri-colors. Their stunning jet-black coats, brilliant white ruffs, rich sable face markings, and sable edging around their legs was striking.

Carol and her helpers placed the puppies down on the slick wood floor. Keith and Linda immediately sat down on the floor to be with the pups. Linda petted one of them and watching how it played with her. Keith was busy with two tri-colors of his own. Linda made one of them run in circles chasing after her finger. Her Collie was alert, but when she held him, he acted very nervous and hyper and did not seem to enjoy being held. She played with him a little and then moved to one of the others. Keith found one of the tri-colors, who seemed to be very alert and playful. When Keith tried the same thing with his finger as Linda, this little tri-color made a soft purring sound.

"Look Linda. He's showing his stuff!" Keith laughed.

"That's not a purr. That's a growl!"

Keith reached out to pet the little fellow. He ran his hand along the Collie's back and felt his tiny, bony frame below the thick fur. He played keep-away with his finger and felt the Collie's body vibrate as he made another fierce "growl". When he held him in his lap, the tiny Collie rolled on his back comfortably and showed his tummy. He continued to try to nibble on Keith's finger with his tiny needle-like baby teeth.

Keith gently rubbed this little guy's tummy. The Collie seemed happy to continue playing with Keith's finger as he lay on his back. Keith had a good feeling about this pup. He continued to play and roughhouse, slipping on the wood floor. He scrambled around, slipped sideways, and crashed in a tiny thump of fur. Immediately he wrenched his little body from being on his side, and pulled his legs underneath him in a sudden flip. Instantly he was upright. He stood up again ready for another daredevil run at that circling finger. Linda was amazed watching this little furry wonder. The pup was quite happy, lying in Linda's lap, comfortably chilling out, or burying his sharp little teeth in her finger.

"Keith, I think this is the one."

"Yep. I agree. He seems really alert and playful, but he's able to be calm as well."

They decided he was the Barnes new Collie. Soon, the Barnes children, Keith and Linda would all have a new chum.

On the ride back, Keith began exploring possible names.

"He's a Collie, so there has to be a Scottish name in there somewhere. My previous Collies had Scottish names – Laddie and Macintosh. Can't get much more Scottish than that. So we have to find him a Scottish name."

"Okay. I think we've established the fact that it has to be a Scottish name. So, how do we know, which names are Scottish?"

"My dear wife, have you not heard of this wondrous thing called the internet?"

"Smart alec. I don't suppose you have a Scottish internet to look at?"

"I might."

"I don't just want to pick a name. I want it to be a name that fits the personality of the dog."

"I know. We'll find something that's just right."

But what was the personality of this little fur ball? The pure black color of his fur made Keith think of a pirate. His personality was comical and sneaky, but very lovable.

"Linda, what about Captain Jack. After the character in that pirate movie the kids love?"

"The kids? I don't know. I have to think about it some."

"Oh, c'mon, let's have a fun name. He's black, like a pirate, and playful and rascally. You know the kids would love that. With his personality, and the fact that he was mostly black and mischievous, the name seemed like a perfect fit. Besides, he even has the movie character's eyes!"

"Is Jack a Scottish name?"

"Yes. It is a name with a Scottish origin. According to these web sites, Jack means – mischievous and fun loving. That fits."

"That would be a lot of fun." It was settled, Captain Jack would be coming home to Stafford in a few weeks.

The pickup day arrived. It was December 20, and the children would be at school when their special Christmas package arrived home. Keith and Linda had already made their first trip to the nearby pet store for all the necessary dog accessories and so they would be ready for Jack. Then they headed back to Sunrise Acres.

Jack was soft, fluffy, even more adorable, and larger than before. He was alert and looked right at Linda as Mark handed him to her. Keith gleamed like a proud father as he looked on at their new family member. Jack's paws were snow white. He had a white ruff, a white tipped tail, sable muzzle, two little sable-colored patches above the eyes and sable on the front edges of his rear legs. He was beautiful.

"Carol. Thank you so much for all your help," said Linda.

"Oh, no problem, it was my pleasure. We just love when these little guys get settled into a good home, and from what you have told me about your past experiences with Collies, I think he will have a wonderful home and family."

"We're so are excited to get him home and surprise the kids," said Linda, turning to Keith. After Carol implanted the microchip in Jack's neck and the paperwork and transaction was completed it was time.

"I guess we'd better get going so we can be home before they are."

They all walked outside toward the Barnes's vehicle. Keith had put the little padded dog bed in the back seat. Keith would sit in the back with Jack while Linda drove. They buckled in and turned the vehicle around to head down the driveway toward Johnson's Corner and the route home.

Nearly two hours later, Linda pulled the Expedition into their driveway. Once they were in the house, she went upstairs to find a box of ribbons and bows that she kept for gifts. She settled on a red Christmas bow. She also purchased a gift tag with the bow. Keith saw the bow and smiled, knowing that she planned to put it on Jack.

It was 2:45 PM, and the Barnes's children normally arrived home from the bus stop at about 3:30 PM. "Here, let's put this bow on him. The kids will be home shortly."

Once Linda attached the bow, she arranged it so that it lay just right. On the gift tag, she wrote "To: Sandra, Allie, and Wes, From: Mom and Dad"

Finally, at 3:22 PM, Keith, Linda, and Jack heard the sound of the school bus pulling up to the bus stop about one hundred yards from the house. Keith heard the familiar screech of the brakes as the bus came to a stop. Linda decided to sit outside on the front steps to wait for the children, while Keith stayed inside, seated on the kitchen floor with Jack in his lap.

Several long moments passed as Keith sat with Jack. The tiny Collie was still, calm and soft in his hands. Finally, the door opened as little Sandra walked in. Her bright freckled face lit up as her mouth opened wide, followed by her older sister Allie, with the same expression and finally Wes, with a huge smile on his face and eyebrows rose so high on his forehead they practically touched his hairline.

"Oh my gosh!" gasped Allie. "It's a puppy!"

"Oh wow!" exclaimed Wes.

Sandra's expression shifted from an open gape to a sweet, excited smile. "Mama, Daddy, who's is it?" Sandra asked.

"Who's do you think it is?" asked Linda.

"Ours?" wondered Sandra.

"Yes it is sweetheart," replied Linda. "Merry Christmas guys," announced Linda to the three kids.

"He's ours?!!!" inquired Allie, still in disbelief.

"Yes," replied Linda.

"Oh my gosh! I can't believe he's ours!" exclaimed Allie.

"He's so cute and fluffy," said Wes.

"What's his name?" asked Sandra.

"Look at his name tag," said Keith.

"Captain Jack," read Wes.

The Barnes kids were blown away. They each took turns holding and playing with Jack, and the whole time, Linda was, yes, taking pictures for the scrapbook. Jack had instantly entered the hearts of the Barnes children. He was home and nothing would ever be the same.

The first night was rough for Jack and for Linda and Keith. Jack cried, whimpered, and pawed at the metal fencing of his sleeping area in the kitchen. Keith and Linda listened from upstairs in their bedroom and felt pity for the poor puppy.

"He must be lonely," worried Linda.

"He'll fall asleep in a little bit."

Eventually, everyone made it through that first night okay, but it was a pitiful routine for the first several days, until Jack became accustomed to his new sleeping area.

As he grew older, Jack's personality began to develop and manifest itself in different ways. He was like many Collies, a troublemaker. In fact, *'trouble with a tail'* is what Allie began to call him. He was curious about everything and that wasn't always a good thing! As Linda prepared dinner in the kitchen, Jack scampered around on the slick floor around her feet. She couldn't walk anywhere without having a tiny Collie circling around somewhere. Eventually, Keith divided the kitchen so Jack was in one-half near the kitchen table and Linda could work safely in the other half, making dinner without being tripped up by Jack.

Jack's fur grew thicker and less fuzzy; almost the way a baby chick starts out with fluffy fuzz and begins to lose it as it grows. His coat had several interesting features. Normally a Collie has a ruff, the thick, white band of fur around his neck and chest; like a lion. This fur provides natural protection, like armor, making it almost impossible for a Collie to be bitten on the neck by a wolf or other attacker. Normally, the white ruff wraps completely around the neck and connects to the large white "bib" of fur on the Collie's chest. Yeah, not so much with Jack though. He was somewhat of a loser in that area.

"Notice how the white fur on his chest doesn't wrap all the way around?" commented Linda.

"Well, that is a very unusual marking."

"Does it make any difference?"

"Not at all. In fact, we'll call it his lucky break,"

She smiled.

The Barnes had inherited a comfortable-sized log home from an uncle of Linda's in Colorado. It was part blessing and part curse; more curse. It required significant repairs and fixes, so they decided to take a late fall, early winter trip to work on it.

"You know I love this cabin Linda, but it's pretty close to bankrupting us. We've tapped just about everything we have trying to get it up to code."

"I know. I keep feeling like we're almost there though. How much more could it need ya know?"

"I just want to see how much we can get done ourselves so we don't have to pay local contractors for everything. The Bank of Barnes is empty and I'm about ready to throw in the towel and sell it as is."

"I know. I know."

At the cabin, Jack was out of his little Collie mind with excitement. While Keith and Linda worked, Jack enjoyed playing with Wes and the girls in their own winter wonderland. One had to wonder if maybe way back inside his Collie consciousness, something in his DNA told him that he was back in his ancestral Scotland. He was perfectly at home in the cold, wintry weather; as snow fell all around him; he raced up and down his very own backyard Scottish highlands.

Soon, Jack's first winter with his new family was behind him. These winter adventures would be displaced in his young Collie brain with new experiences as winter gave way to spring.

KEVIN BRETT

The snow thawed and disappeared into the ground and the days became warmer and longer, but still cool and blustery at times as though winter was not yet ready to leave town. Jack was almost six months old and resembled a small, lanky black wolf instead of a black and white ball of fuzz. His legs were like stilts and his tail was unquestionably longer than it needed to be.

Keith and Linda watched Jack in the backyard one morning. "Linda, look how fast this guy is changing. It's crazy. He's growing so fast."

"Yeah and he's really curious about everything *and* mischievous!" He had been training his amazing nose and building a library of different scents inside his Collie brain.

"You know most dogs just take in new scents and features in their environment, but with Collies and their herding instinct and protective ways, they actually map out their surroundings in their mind. They're much more aware of what is around them and constantly on guard for threats."

"I guess that makes sense when they have to manage large numbers of livestock on their own."

"I know he's still a puppy, but I'm tellin' ya, he can sure act in ways that might make you question all that intelligence, and all those smarts make him really skilled at creating problems."

"Problem solving; problem creating – it's really a fine line."

Jack's herding instincts became more apparent to Keith and Linda. At times, he treated the family like part of his pack and chilled out when they were all in one spot doing something like eating dinner, but at other times, he treated them as if they were his flock of sheep. He herded them around where he wanted or scolded them with very upset sounding barks if they got out of line by doing such things as leaving the dinner table or just playing and joking around with each other.

Maybe it was the black and white colors. Possibly Jack thought that he was a referee for the family.

-5-

A Thanksgiving Lesson

Linda looked at Jack with concern. "Have you noticed Jack's right rear leg? It seems to drag behind the other one sometimes. Every once in a while, it almost looks like he has a slight limp on his right side. Why do you think that is?"

"I don't' know. I don't really see him doing any limping. I think he's probably just having difficulty with the slick floor."

She folded her arms, shifting her weight to one side and frowned as she watched Jack. "I don't think so. I've been watching him for a while now, and he seems to do it even when he's on the carpet. I think he has some kind of kink in his hip, or it might be binding or catching in some way."

Keith watched as Jack walked around, looking for anything strange in his walk.

For the next several weeks, they kept a close watch. Possibly, he was experiencing some form of canine growing pains. After several weeks, they became convinced that they needed to have Jack checked.

The vet examined Jack closely and observed his gait, but when the x-rays came back, she confirmed that Jack had hip dysplasia.

"I don't understand?" said Keith. "He was guaranteed *not* to have hip dysplasia."

"Here is the main view," said the doctor as she put the X-ray sheet on the viewing board and flipped on the light panel. If you look at this area here, showing his right hip, it is just being ground away by the top of his femur, and his left hip has already begun to do the same. The bone of his hip socket is all jagged and that's causing a lot of pain."

Linda frowned. "That's awful."

"I understand what the breeder told you, but even if there has never been hip dysplasia in Jack's bloodline, it could still always appear randomly. I'm afraid this is a very serious case. It's just a shame to see this in a dog at such a young age."

"What options do we have?" asked Linda.

"Well, until just a few years ago, most owners would put the dog down to save the animal from the terrible pain, but in recent years, surgery has become possible in some cases. There are two possible procedures. Either of them have the potential of eliminating the pain and giving Jack almost complete use of his hip. Unfortunately, the procedures are not a sure thing and they are very expensive."

"You said they have the potential," inquired Keith.

"Yes. There have been many successes with these procedures, but there have also been failures and unfortunately, if it does not go well, then Jack might have to be put down anyway. If it does go well, we won't know for several months afterward exactly how strong his hip will be. In other words, if it works, he may still have limited mobility, but at least he would not be in pain."

"I see," said Keith.

Linda stared down at the floor. When she looked up again, a tear rolled down her left cheek. She wiped it away and sniffed.

The vet continued. "It is likely that Jack will need the same procedure in a year or two for his left hip and there are the same risks with that as well. ... I'm sorry to be the bearer of bad news, but this is just an awful condition to have to deal with. He is a very stoic dog though. He shows very little sign that anything is wrong."

Linda's eyes welled up with more tears at the thought of Jack in terrible pain and not even really showing it. In her mind, Linda leapfrogged right over any discussion about whether to have the surgery.

"We just need to know which surgical facility to use for the procedure."

The vet continued. "I'm sorry I've just delivered a nightmare scenario for Jack and your family." There were no guarantees of how things might work out; many unknowns, lots of money that they didn't have.

As Keith drove them home, Linda was the first to break the long silence. "I don't even see an option. We don't just buy a new puppy, then turn around and tell the kids we have to put him to sleep. We've only had him a few months Keith!"

"So you think he should have the surgery?"

"And you would consider putting him down? He's not even one year old yet!"

"The doc did say it was a really expensive procedure and it might not even work … and then he might need to go through the whole thing again. You know we're tapped out of money and have had to go into a lot of debt to work out the repairs on the cabin. Everything's just hitting at once. I'm just looking at the money side of it and that's the problem. There isn't any. We're talking about a really big gamble that anything will even work and that's times two hips."

Tears ran down her face. Linda's voice broke up as she tried to speak. "If it were one of the kids, or *me*! – Would you just say, 'Sorry! Don't have the money honey?'"

"Of course not!"

"Ok! Well. Jack is part of the family. You wanted a new family member. If he can be saved and he won't be in pain anymore, then I say we do it. If he was a really old dog and only had a short time left, that might be different, but that's not the case. There are payment plans and options. I'm sure."

"Okay. Okay. I get it. I'm sorry. You're right. We'll figure something out."

"We'll handle it. It'll be okay, but we're not putting that sweet dog to sleep and just take the easy way out. Too many people just think everything in life is going to be perfect and when it doesn't turn out that way they just want to drop everything and run away from the problem. Sure, we were hoping he'd be the perfect Christmas gift and everything would be wonderful, but there will always be unexpected problems. That's just life. It's how you handle them that really matters."

"I know. I know. You're right."

"I can't believe the irony. Here we spent so much time searching for an outstanding breeder who even guaranteed that the dogs were free of hip dysplasia."

That evening they looked again at the x-ray.

Keith shook his head. "Wow. You don't have to be a doctor to see that his right hip socket is all chewed up and jagged. What a mess."

They called the children into the family room for a family meeting. Linda sat down in the large double-sized chair and Allie climbed up into her lap. The others came in and took seats.

"Hey kids, Dad, and I have some news we want to share with you."

Allie was the first to become excited about imagining the surprise. "What is it? Are we going to Disney World or Busch Gardens?"

Sandra chimed in with her best four-year old sarcasm in a low tone. "It's probably something lame, like we have to clean up our rooms."

Wes snapped at her. "Stop it Sandra. You're such a loser."

Linda looked at Keith with a look of mild frustration. "That went well," she sighed. Linda started over. "Guys, we want to talk to you about Jack."

"What about him? Did he poop in the living room?" giggled Wes. "You should make the girls clean it up! They could be poopie cleaners! Loser, poopie cleaners."

"Shut up Wes, you chicken-head!" snapped Allie in response.

"Guys, stop it! We have some really serious news about Jack, now behave – nicely that is, and listen."

A worried frown replaced the smile on Allie's face. "Is he ok?"

"Yes, he's going to be ok honey," assured Linda. "Come here," she motioned to Sandra who suddenly became concerned as she reacted to Linda's tone.

Sandra climbed up in her lap and snuggled close to her with Allie. Linda wrapped her arms around them in preparation for her third attempt to get past the brother-sister bickering.

"Jack has something wrong with his hip. It's causing him to limp and walk funny. But the important thing is that his hip is causing him to be in a lot of pain. Even though he runs around a lot, his hip is actually hurting him. Because he's still a puppy, he doesn't know enough to stop running."

The heaviness of the situation hung in the air as everyone focused in on Linda's words. Tears welled up in her eyes again and her voice became weak as she tried to explain.

"Daddy and I took Jack to the vet today while you were at school. They took some x-rays of his back legs and hips. One of his back legs is causing him a lot of pain."

Allie's eyes began to glisten with tears and her voice weakened as she asked. "Is Jack going to die?"

"No sweetie," replied Keith. "But he's going to have to go to the dog hospital and have an operation to fix his hip."

"Can the doctors fix him?" asked Wes in a hopeful tone.

"Yes," answered Linda.

"We're going to take him to a really good animal hospital that we've found. They fix hip problems like this all the time, and they're going to make Jack all better."

"That's right," added Linda. "So there's nothing to worry about." She said, trying to perk up her tone of voice to a more hopeful level. We just wanted you guys to know what was going on with the big guy. I also want you guys to be thankful and appreciate how fortunate we arc that we're able to take care of Jack so that he will be healthy and with us for a long time."

"We'll take good care of him mom," assured Wes.

"Jack is very lucky to have us as his family because we *are* going to take good care of him. So, like we're always trying to teach you guys, we have to give of ourselves and help those who are in need right?"

Linda wiped her eyes. The tears were suspended in front of her eyeballs, blurring her vision. She began to feel joy and relief after making it through the difficult conversation. She smiled through her tears and thought to herself how she cherished everything about her children.

"So, guys, think about this. It is almost Thanksgiving and Jack's operation is actually going to be the day before Thanksgiving. We talked with the doctors, and we will be picking Jack up from the hospital and taking him home on Thanksgiving Day," explained Linda. "Pretty cool Thanksgiving huh? Jack is going to get a second chance. It will be a sort of new beginning for him."

"Yeah," replied Allie. "So Jack will have a really good Thanksgiving with our family, because we all love him so much, right?"

"You bet sweetie," answered Keith.

Wes reflected on the conversation. "Well, …that surprise sucked."

As planned, Jack had his surgery on Wednesday morning; Thanksgiving Eve. Thanksgiving Day, Keith went to the hospital to pick up Jack. A member of the nursing staff brought Keith to a private consultation room where he waited for Jack.

A few moments later, the nurse walked Jack into the room. Jack immediately pulled his ears back, happy to see Keith. He tried his best to get in a few wags of his tail, but he was still wiped out from the ordeal. Jack had been shaved to the skin on his left rear side. There was a long incision, about six inches, where they had worked on him. When the nurse walked him into the room, she held Jack's belly up with a wide cloth sling to minimize the weight on his hips. She went over the therapy procedures and explained Jack's medication. Jack would require physical therapy for the next several weeks until he had fully recovered. He would also require a lot of help, attention, and care.

"The operation was a complete success," she explained. "He did wonderfully and has been a great patient. The good news is that Jack is not in any pain from the grinding hip. He will feel some soreness and tenderness from the surgery, but we have pain medication for that along with his antibiotic. He will probably always have a little bit of weakness and wobble in that joint, but other than that, once he's recovered, he will become stronger and more flexible with exercise."

When Keith finally pulled into the Barnes's driveway, the whole gang was there waiting to see their beloved Collie patient.

"Happy Thanksgiving guys!" proclaimed Keith as he stepped out of the van.

Sandra grinned from ear to ear and bounced in place, wondering what Jack would look like and what this surgery thing was really about. "Happy Thanksgiving Daddy!"

"I have a big, furry Thanksgiving gift for you guys. Remember we can't pet him on the hips because he's really sore. Only pet him on the head or the neck, ok?"

All three Barnes children ran to the driver side door of the van as Keith carefully lifted Jack and carried him into the house. He helped Jack over to a large padded ottoman in the family room. There he let Jack lie down and rest.

"Oh, Jack," exclaimed Allie trying to comfort him. "You poor baby, it'll be okay." Allie put her nose up to Jack's and rubbed noses with him as she stroked his neck and back. "I don't like the look of those stitches on his hip mom," she frowned.

"I know sweetie, but the doctors did a great job on him, and he's going to heal just fine," assured Linda.

Every day, Jack's legs became stronger and more stable. Keith and Linda took turns lying Jack on his side so they could move his right, rear leg through some range of motion exercises that the doctor had recommended. Often Allie or Sandra would kneel down at Jack's head, caress him, and talk to him calmly, while Keith or Linda gave him the therapy. For the first few weeks, Jack was nervous about the therapy, but as his mobility increased, it became easier for him, and he gradually grew accustomed to the twice-daily routine.

Jack still limped, but he took it slowly; concentrating on each step as he gradually worked his way up and down the sidewalk on his daily walks. Neighbors on the street watched as Jack struggled. They observed the effort he put in to walk at a normal pace, following his progress each week. Almost every day, one or more of the kids walked along with Jack, talked to him, and petted him as he worked his legs. Soon, Jack was able to run around in the backyard. He ran up and down the hill almost as if the handicap had never existed.

The family took to heart that while even the best plans like trying to find a perfect pet might not work out, Jack's imperfect handicap was a blessing in disguise and actually made him the perfect pet for the Barnes. The situation gave them the opportunity to be grateful that he could be helped and that they could help him. The kids learned to be thankful for the gift of Jack. Jack healed and strengthened rapidly in the months following his surgery and it looked as if Keith and Linda's vision of having a great canine companion to help the kids "grow up right" was already working.

KEVIN BRETT

-6-

A Healing Paw

Dixon leaned back against his pillow and adjusted the sheets and blanket. The midmorning light coming through the hospital room window filled the space with warm, bright light; flipping on the overhead would just ruin the effect. That touch of the outdoors actually boosted his mood. He picked up the newspaper from the tray beside his bed and held up the length of the paper for a quick scan of anything that might capture his interest or distract his mind and transport him out of this place; just some brief diversion.

Twelve insanely long weeks - he had been stuck there all summer. Each day, the same routine, fruit juice before breakfast; usually grapefruit, with a specimen cup, not your typical breakfast menu. The morning pee in the cup was always fun. The best part was the evil nurse with the hideous glasses. Dakota was certain she had stolen them from Cat Woman back in the early 60s. It was her awesome duty to collect his pee and take it to the lab for analysis. So, for her, serving her country meant collecting pee? Weird. The whole gig here was lame, and who wore glasses like that anymore? Didn't those go out of style back in the 50s about twenty-minutes after they were introduced? She was like a character from an Hitchcock movie, but he was pretty sure she wasn't acting. Sadly, that whole ritual and visit was one of the few highlights of his day.

Being cooped up like some lab rat, giving samples of this and extracts of that was the worst. He was an active, outdoors guy. He thrived on being busy, getting things done, just experiencing as much life as he could. That was the old Dakota Dixon. Only twenty-seven, he felt seventy-seven; beaten, sore and tired, like a spent racehorse that should have been retired or turned into glue already. The surgical recovery period was approaching its end. Four major surgeries were required to repair the damage. Soon he would be transferred to a rehabilitation center, with a long, difficult journey ahead. Two of his close buddies were gone; two outstanding young men, full of life, gone in an instant. They never had a chance.

Because of his injuries, he could not escort their caskets home. Being unable to carry out that duty brought an anguish he had never experienced. It was his obligation, his honor to go and express to their loved ones how much these Marines had meant to him and how they had served honorably beside him. He wanted; he needed to sit with their families and help them to know that their husbands and fathers would always live in his and others' memory as brothers. Not being able to be there for them doubled the sense of loss and guilt that he felt and carried with him every day. He vowed that when he was able, he would make that journey. It was his duty.

The initial physical therapy accomplished what it was supposed to; getting his broken and beaten body parts working and moving again. After multiple surgeries on his legs and right arm, the pain was still epic. His joints were swollen. The doc called it effusion, but whatever, and any normal level of mobility was months away. Meanwhile, it was incredibly difficult to bend a knee, ankle, hip, or elbow. An image of Tin Woodsman in The Wizard of Oz came to his mind. He thought, if someone would just oil his joints, maybe he would be able to move again.

Once the doctors and physical therapists decided that they could do no more, he would be evaluated and released. That's when they would determine if he could return to active duty. That wasn't an issue in his mind however. He had plans. He had new orders. In Afghanistan, he had suffered crushing injuries to his legs and right arm, nearly losing all three. Each limb now had enough screws, pins, and plates to build a toaster oven. At least he could walk again, somewhat, but only with the help of a walker. His right arm was partially useful, for now. Time would be the judge and he simply had to wait for the verdict, but he was grateful, if not impatient, for every bit of progress. He brought all of his energy and will to each therapy session, seeking his old self, his old strength and agility. It was out there somewhere.

He assumed that giving it everything he had would bring his old self back, but a small part of him had trouble believing it. He needed progress soon. It was September, and fortunately, the school did not start until June. That was time enough. It had to be.

Each time he applied to Marine Corps Canine Tactical School he was not among the small group of selectees; those who would become operators in the K-9 special forces. Finally, he had made it, if he could only recover quickly enough to get there.

Dixon considered himself one of the lucky ones. Even so, with all the repairs and metalwork, his condition reminded him of Iron Man, but without the cool suit. He did wear a suit however. It was an invisible suit made of the interwoven threads of guilt, responsibility, and anguish. He *was* responsible … period. It was his job to ensure everyone returned safely to the forward operating base, and they didn't. He was also guilty because he had survived and they didn't. It was a common emotional response for warriors in situations where they have lost close buddies. They called it survivor's guilt, how convenient, but it wasn't rational. He had done nothing wrong, they had simply been attacked, but he was the leader. Maybe they should have pulled back when they lost their overhead drone coverage. Maybe they could have avoided the ambush. He was in charge, and that part of him demanded answers. He tormented himself with events of that day constantly, but the only conclusion he came to was that he failed and that haunted him.

He was already shaven for the day and his otherwise thick black hair was cut to regulation. He scanned over the newspaper when Nurse Bittleman came in with the dreaded juice and the plastic specimen cup. Same crap every day. She grinned stupidly at him and he returned a half-smile and half-stupid grin or frown or something. He wasn't sure, maybe her look had something to do with her liver or maybe it was just the fact that she realized that she had a stupid-sounding last name. It sounded like 'bitter', which she seemed to be. Either way, they had developed this unspoken language; a new form of communication made up of stupid grins. It was an odd ritual. After several months of being there at Bethesda Naval Medical Center, the only interaction he had with this particular member of the nursing staff was this bizarre ritual of peeing in a cup and exchanging stupid grins. To Dakota it was just freaky and wacked out, but he played along. After all, what does one say at a moment like that – thank you for letting me pee in that stupid little cup … have a terrific day? She left and Dixon continued looking at the newspaper. He stared blankly at the page for a moment as he recalled the World War II song. "Praise the Lord and Pass the Ammunition." He wondered if her take on that one was. "Praise the Lord and Pass the Pee." He shook his head and then began to scan the paper.

In the local section, he noticed an article about a young Boy Scout who had been rescued by a Collie during a hiking trip on the Appalachian Trail. Dakota laid the paper on his lap for a moment, staring blankly out into space. He saw nothing in front of him in his room, but in his mind were visions of his times hiking as a scout. His memories brought back the bonds that he shared with his closest buddies as they trekked across the wilderness in North Dakota.

His brain suddenly swapped out that memory with a similar one that brought back the feeling he had with the Marines in his patrol and right before the attack. The memory of the patrol ended with a brief vision of his platoon hiking along a mountain trail with Zoe. He hit the pause button in his mind and stopped it there. He knew what was next. Dixon picked up the paper again and read the rest of the article about the scouts.

A little more than an hour had passed when he realized that Bittleman would probably be making her rounds to collect his pee. Then it hit him in a flash. He knew what needed to happen. He was so caught up with the newspaper that he forgot to drink the grapefruit juice. He reached for the juice bottle, opened it and poured it into the specimen cup. What wouldn't fit into the cup, he drank, quickly putting the lid back on both containers and setting them on the bedside tray. He busied himself with the paper and the sports section.

Bittleman approached his room with her lab cart, probably thinking about how she could improve upon her stupid grin. She wheeled the cart into the room and over to the side of the bed. She looked at Dixon. He pretended to be too busy reading didn't bother to make eye contact. She picked up the cup, and formed a frown as she raised it in front of her face for a closer look. Surprised, she said the first words Dixon had heard her speak in nearly three months. "Hmmm... We're a bit cloudy today."

Dixon lowered the paper, looking both surprised to see her and surprised at the appearance of the liquid in the cup. He paused before he reached out, took the cup from her. "Well ...Let's run it through again."

He unscrewed the lid on the specimen cup and drank the grapefruit juice quickly, gulping heavily for effect. With a sense of accomplishment, he placed the empty cup on the bedside tray, smacking his lips slightly and taking in a much needed breath of air. "Ahhhhh. .... Guess I'll see you in a couple of hours."

Bittleman was appalled, but at the moment he put the cup down, her brain finished processing what he had just done to her. Smiling stupidly back at her scowl he asked. "Oh, could you be a dear and check on my breakfast while you're out? And don't forget to include juice."

Bittleman clenched her jaw muscles in disgust, said nothing more, and turned her lab cart around and quickly exited Dixon's room.

It was nearly lunchtime when Dr. Neustatter came in for a word with Dixon. Neustatter was a Brit; part of an exchange program that the Navy had going with the United Kingdom.

"Hey doc. What's shakin'?"

"Hello Lieutenant. How are the legs?"

"Still connected I guess. What's the word on getting out of here?"

"Well, that's what I came to see you about. You are scheduled to be transferred to the Stafford rehabilitation center next Tuesday," he said looking down at his clipboard.

"Ok ..."

"They will continue your long term therapy so that you can really get those stiff joints moving again and improve your muscular strength in your legs and arm."

"Shew. Good to know. I've been giving it everything I have. You know, trying to do extra strengthening exercises all the time and work the joints. Gotta get in shape for that Canine Tactical School."

Dr. Neustatter exhaled, stared down at his clipboard for a moment, then he raised his head slowly until his eyes met Dixon's. He paused for a second. Dixon noticed how the doc's facial expression became serious.

"Dakota. ...I'm sorry. ... But, there isn't going to be any Canine Tactical School."

"Uhh... What are you talking about? As soon as I'm recovered I'll be good to go. I'm already all Rogered-up for my next duty station. Got it covered."

"Dakota, you're being given a medical discharge from the Marine Corps. You won't be returning to duty. The Medical Evaluation Board has already reviewed your case. You'll still do all your therapy and follow up with the VA, but you can't return to active duty, or reserve status."

The two men stared at each other. "Doc. I *have* to get to that school. I mean, I don't have my dog anymore, the freaking Taliban sent her back to the Creator, but I have to get to that school to prove what I can do. It's a Native American thing you wouldn't understand.

"Try me."

"Doc, that's my big chance. Dog training is in my blood. It's something my people call spirit-destiny. It isn't what I *do*. It's what I *am*. I've been training my whole life for this. I have to have this chance Doc."

"Dakota-"

"Doc, dogs respond to me. I have a connection to them. It's like we are of the same spirit. I need to prove to myself that I can make this new training approach work. I have to get back in the game."

"I'm trying here Dakota ..."

"Doc, any other trainer would just be teaching movements and commands. I know this all sounds crazy, but I can talk to certain dogs and we understand each other. We can communicate on a level that others can't, but I can teach other trainers how to teach most of these skills to their K9s. Ya gotta fix this Doc. Don't let them do this. I'll recover. I'll get in shape and-."

"Dakota ... It isn't my choice. In your condition, with what's happened to you, you're lucky to be alive. Be thankful for that. After injuries like yours, the body just isn't the same. Your injuries won't permit you to perform at the required level to return to duty. ... I'm sorry. I sense how much this means to you."

Silence replaced Dixon's plea. He felt somewhat embarrassed for putting himself out there like that, but the Doc was a good guy. He knew he could talk to him. Dakota sensed that Neustatter empathized with him, but it was the technicality of the matter; the medical parameters of the situation that were against the young Native American. A quiet acknowledgement of reality spoke to him, telling him this was not the way. Dakota's spirit knew that his connection to his K9 brothers was not over. As he said, it was part of him, but he realized his Marine Corps chapter had just ended. The few words uttered by the doctor brought his career to an abrupt end. Dixon looked down at the newspaper and fidgeted with it. "Wonder if they have a jobs section in here."

"You'll be set up with a career monitor to help you with your transition to civilian life. Don't worry about that."

"Oh, no sweat doc. No worries. I'm good. You know ... Ooooh Rahhh, Semper Fi."

Dr. Neustatter looked at Dixon quietly, deciding that there really was nothing more he could say. Then he turned and started walking away. He stopped and turned back around facing Dixon again.

"Dixon. I really am sorry. I know you were looking forward to that school."

Dixon's voice resonated an unmistakable tone of total disappointment mixed with sarcasm. "No doc. I wasn't looking forward to that school. Training dogs is my life. It's what I do best; relating to dogs; people, not so much."

Neustatter paused. "There are always possibilities."

"Sure doc. … thanks. Thanks for all you've done. … I mean it."

"I'll be by later to check on you."

"Roger that."

"Dixon …"

"Sir?"

"What is this affinity you Yanks have with saying OoohRahhh all the time? What on earth does that mean?"

"Doc, it's not us Yanks. It's the Marines that say it; and it's Turkish. It means, 'Yeah baby! We beat those Brits. We're It.' You know, the Revolution – 1776. … Nothing personal of course doc."

Neustatter shook his head as he walked out muttering to himself. "Yanks."

"You're welcome," grinning to himself.

Tuesday morning Dixon was in the head folding his bath towel. He hung it neatly on the towel bar beside the shower. He worked his way out to the room using a walker and stuffed the last of his personal effects into the duffel bag lying open on his bed. A moment later, Dr. Neustatter walked through the door.

"Good morning Lieutenant."

"Sir, how are you?"

"Oh, just another fabulous day in Her Majesty's Navy."

"What can I do for you skipper?"

"I just wanted to come by to see you off."

"Appreciate that Sir."

"Dixon. … keep in touch. Seriously, email me. I want to know how you are doing, if I can help. I'll be heading back to England in a few months, but keep in touch. Let me know how your therapy is going and what your plans are after you're out of the Marines."

"Sure thing Doc. Who knows, maybe I'll just stop by your side of the pond next summer and we'll have a Fourth of July cookout to celebrate old times."

The doc looked at Dakota confused. "I don't understand."

"A cookout … where we burn meat on the grill, drink a few pints … you know…."

"I understand the cookout bit, but why the Fourth of July?"

"Oh, well. It's a date that we Yanks like to celebrate with cookouts and fireworks," Dixon waited for Neustatter to acknowledge, but the doc just looked blankly at him, completely at a loss.

"Common Doc …. You know … Two-hundred years ago when we kicked your guys' butts? The Revolution?"

Neustatter finally got it, rolling his eyes in disbelief.

"Ohhhh Please! You Yanks certainly know how to hold a grudge."

"Doc, no. No, not a grudge, it's called pride. I don't know about you boys, but on our side of the pond, the Fourth of July is a pretty big deal."

Neustatter shook his head. "I would imagine so. Anyway, please keep in contact with me. But if you're planning any more revolutions, keep me out of it."

"Sure thing doc. … and we can do the cookout any time. Doesn't have to be the Fourth of July," grinning.

"Oh. Well … that just changes everything."

The two shook hands and Neustatter left. Nurse Bittleman came in pushing a wheel chair a moment after the doc left. Bittleman donned her stupid grin one last time. "Time to go Lieutenant."

"Check," as he zipped his duffle bag and limped over to the wheel chair.

He lowered himself into the chair and laid the bag across his lap. Bittleman turned the chair around and wheeled him out of the room. The two headed down the hall to the elevators. They emerged from the elevators on the level for patient discharge. She stopped at the admin desk and retrieved a manila folder with some papers for him to sign. Once signed, she wheeled him out to the curbside where a car waited for him. He forced himself up slowly. Taking a step toward the car; he turned back to Bittleman. He had a sudden flash of the movie Casablanca.

Putting on his best Humphrey Bogart. "I'm sorry things didn't work out between us. Of all the gin joints, in all the towns, in all the world, you walk into mine…. It just wasn't meant to be."

Recognizing that Dixon was mocking her one last time, Bittleman clenched her jaw muscles tight, but remained speechless, waiting for Dixon to finish acting stupid, if he was acting at all.

"Shweethart, we'll always have Bethesda," he saluted quickly.

Bittleman clenched her jaw tighter. Dixon threw his bag into the backseat and climbed in after it. She closed the door for him, turned and walked back around behind the wheelchair as Dixon rolled down the passenger window in the back seat.

"Nurse."

She turned and looked toward him. He tossed an empty specimen cup out the window to her. Continuing as Bogart. "Here's lookin' at you kid."

Reflexively, she caught the cup just as the car drove off. Another stupid grin appeared as she looked at the cup in her hands. In the back seat, Dixon smiled and chuckled to himself.

The joking was a shield, one of those useful human coping mechanisms. It protected Dixon from everything inside or it took his mind off it temporarily. Heck, it felt better to laugh anyway. They say laughter is the best medicine right? Dixon needed that medicine. The death of his two friends and the guilt he felt in simply being alive when they weren't sent him into episodes of depression. As if that wasn't enough, receiving a discharge and unable to attend the training school where he hoped to become an instructor was like having all hope of a dream taken away. It felt like a perfect storm. All the pieces came together and crushed his spirit, his hope, and his optimism. He didn't feel like that adventurous, take-on-the-world, go-getter. But the Marine in him kept reminding him; adapt and overcome. That's what Marines do. They run *to* the fight, not away from it.

As he sat in his wheel chair in the community lounge room at the rehab center, he didn't feel like that old Dixon or rather the young Dixon. Instead of feeling as if his whole life was ahead of him, he kept having this sinking feeling that maybe his best days were behind him. Some invisible adversary had just chucked a grenade in the middle of his life.

His future or his horizon just felt like one massive storm cloud heading right for him. Several months ago, he had a purpose, direction, plans, goals, dreams. It was all set; now nothing. Where the heck was he? More stinking therapy? More grueling work to get his young body not to feel so old and beaten? What was the point?

Looking around at other service members in the patient lounge, he could see that they were in worse shape. Dixon briefly wondered what was going through their minds. Most of them lacked one or more limbs. He did still consider himself lucky in that regard. At least he had all of his limbs even if they were half-metal. Then he stopped questioning everything. He didn't really care right now. He had to figure out a way to figure this thing out. What would today be about? What was tomorrow and the rest of the week and next week going to be about? He needed a plan, but for what? He had no focus. He needed goals. It all just sucked – big-time.

It was gorgeous, a mostly blue sky, shirtsleeve temperature, slight breeze and low humidity; perfect for an afternoon run. Linda had Jack on a short leash as she jogged down the road leading to her church. She planned to run down to where the street came to a "T", hang a left and follow that street two-hundred yards to the entrance of the church parking lot. Once on the church campus she would make a loop around the perimeter for extra mileage. Jack trotted along beside her, happily taking in all the scents carried by the air.

"Good boy! Jack ... doing good big guy!"

Jack panted lightly from the jaunt, ears folded back. He could feel the breeze rustle past them as he and Linda pushed on. The two continued along the approach to the church parking lot. Jack occasionally lifted his nose a little just to see if he could scoop up any interesting scents along the way. It was probably like a dog version of the game that kids used to play on long road trips, before iPods and in-car movies; you know where you would look out the window and see how many license plates you could count from different states or countries.

As the pair rounded the corner, they headed toward the left parkway that wrapped around the church campus. Melissa walked down the sidewalk past the playground pushing a young man in a wheel chair.

Linda didn't recognize the man, but she smiled and waved toward Melissa as she approached the pair.

Melissa called out. "Hi Linda!"

Linda slowed down and walked her last few steps with Jack.

"Hi! How are ya?"

"Linda, this is my brother Trevor. He's back from Afghanistan."

"Nice to meet you Ma'am," reaching out his hand to Linda.

"You too Trevor. ... This is Jack. Captain Jack ... You know ... the pirate."

"He's beautiful."

"Thank you."

"Is it ok if I pet him?"

"Certainly. ... He only eats small children," she teased.

Trevor smiled as he leaned forward to rub Jack's neck and ears.

"He's a beauty."

He just quietly enjoyed Jack and kept smiling as he scratched Jack behind the ears. Jack panted gently, really getting into the ear thing. Jack thoroughly enjoyed having a friendly stranger with a knowledge of the right parts of the ear to rub, scratch and massage. Jack could feel himself going into a temporary trance as Trevor worked an area behind Jack's left ear.

"So what are you and Trevor doing out here?"

"Oh I just took Trevor around the church to see the place. He's never been here before. We visited with a couple of the pastors. He just got back from the hospital in Germany last week."

"Is that where you were injured?"

"No. Ma'am. It happened in Afghanistan."

"Oh, I mean, yes, not Germany, Afghanistan. I'm sorry. ... Trevor, thank you for your service and all you do."

"You're welcome Ma'am," as he continued petting Jack.

Melissa noticed how Trevor was so involved with Jack. "You two seem to be hitting it off pretty well."

Trevor didn't even look up. "Jack doesn't seem to mind ..." Trevor just smiled as he played with Jack.

"Well Lady. It was great running into you guys. I'd better be heading back with this crazy Collie."

"Ok Linda. Good seeing you too."

"Trevor it was great meeting you."

"Likewise Ma'am."

"It's Linda ..."

"Yes Ma'am. .... Ma'am it was really fun meeting Jack. Do you think there might be a possibility of meeting up with him again?"

"Well sure Trevor. That would be great."

"Actually, I was wondering if maybe it would be possible to bring him by the rehab center some time when Melissa comes to visit. You know, sort of like those groups that bring dogs around to visit with patients and kids."

The request caught Linda by surprise. "Uhh ... well ... sure."

"It's not for me. ... Ma'am there are a lot of guys there who have some real emotional issues. They act all upbeat and gung-ho a lot of the time, but when they're alone they start to drift. Get really down and it's hard to find a lot to be positive about. I think if they could hang out with this guy some and see this beautiful dog that it would really have a positive effect on them. It would keep them from slipping too far down. Especially if you came by once in a while."

"Well ..." started Linda.

The impact of what was happening suddenly hit her. This young man had lost a leg, but wasn't worried about himself, he was concerned about other troops and how they were doing. They had sacrificed so much and all he asked was for her to take Jack to spend a little time with these men; letting them know that someone cared and allowing them to share a little of Jack's time.

Trevor interrupted her. "I know it's a lot to ask."

"No. ...No, Trevor it's not. I'll talk with Melissa and we'll make it happen."

A huge smile spread across his face. Linda saw how just a short visit with Jack had such a positive effect on Trevor and immediately pictured a room full of other troops and the potential positive effect it could have on them. She decided that that vision in her mind; that one humble request from an injured service member had to become a reality.

"That would be wonderful Ma'am."

"Under one condition Trevor."

"What's that Ma'am?"

"Stop calling me Ma'am. ... The name's Linda."

"Yes Miss Linda. Anything you say Ma'am."

Linda grinned and shook her head.

Keith sat at the kitchen table looking at the back yard through the French doors. He thought about how the foliage of the miniature Japanese Maples around the waterfall and pond would soon begin turning a beautiful golden hue for the fall. He ran his thumb up and down along the outside curve of the handle on his coffee mug as he stared out the window. He looked down briefly at the pool of black liquid inside his mug before looking across the table at Linda.

"So you want to use Jack as a therapy dog for these guys at the rehab center."

"Yes. I think it could do them some real good."

"But Jack isn't even trained or certified for that kind of thing."

"Neither were the first service dogs. They learned as they went. Besides, there's a real shortage of this kind of thing."

"I've never considered Jack anything other than the family pet and guardian. So how often are you planning to do this?"

"I don't know Keith ... and what do you mean me?"

"Well ...I have a pretty full plate."

"This is both of us ... and Jack."

Silence hung in the air for a moment.

Linda tried getting inside Keith's head. "You don't seem too thrilled about this idea."

"First of all, it wasn't my idea. I just think about all that Jack has been through ... and us. We brought him into our family so that we could have a family dog, plain and simple, no strings attached."

Linda watched Keith, waiting for him to finish.

"I just want to have a normal life, just Jack and the family. Doing our thing."

A few silent seconds ticked by.

"What about those troops? They're sitting there in that stupid rehab center feeding off each other's misery. What if this crazy pirate of a Collie would go trotting in there with his infectious Collie smile and brighten their day; bring them some enjoyment more than watching a football game on TV; something that really touches their hearts and their souls. What if Jack could do that? ... He touches our hearts and brightens our days. Don't those men deserve a little of that?"

"Exactly. He's ours. That's why we bought him, but he had this hip problem and we still don't know if the other hip will need surgery and he wasn't a year old when all that happened and then he had all the therapy and recovery so we haven't had any really normal time with him practically since we got him. It's all been about his medical problems. ... The hiking trip with the scouts was some of the first normal stuff we've done. You know ... having a Collie for the family to enjoy."

"You're sounding a little selfish Keith."

"What? ...Just wanting have some normal family time with our kids and our dog and not have to start sharing him with half of Stafford."

"Quit going to the extreme. It doesn't have to be an either or situation. It's possible to do both. We will enjoy him, but that doesn't mean we can't let others enjoy him too. Think outside the box a little."

Silence filled the space between them. This time Linda stared out into the backyard as Keith continued rubbing his thumb aimlessly along the edge of the handle on his mug. She turned her head back in his direction.

"Keith, I understand what you're getting at. I love the idea."

"Yeah, I can tell. ... It would be ideal. It probably doesn't seem like it right now, but having Jack is a blessing to this family in many ways; but not necessarily in the way you might have planned. Why can't he be a blessing to others? If we had a sick relative nearby we would be going to visit them and taking up time ... and maybe even taking Jack with us to cheer them up possibly. How is visiting some troops any different from that; especially when they've sacrificed so much?"

Keith took a moment to process her words. Man ... another case of Linda being right. How did she keep doing that? "I see what you're saying. I'm sure we can do it. It just isn't the way I pictured things."

"I know, but that's okay."

"Not sure where this is all leading, but let's just go ahead. Call who you need to and let's get this thing going."

Dixon didn't have a plan yet. He had nothing to latch on to in his mind. He had been struggling to let go of the idea of the CTS school; that wasn't going to happen. It was like he had never been accepted to it in the first place. He was trying to move on. There was nothing, just a vacuum. He felt like he was flipping to a new chapter in a book, but there was nothing on the pages and he didn't know what to put there. He didn't know who the new Dakota Dixon was.

The topic of the future was closed for now. He shifted back to the present. He found the remote control and flipped on the TV in his room, surfed briefly, then flipped it off. Nothing appealed to him; couldn't really focus worth anything. He didn't even have Nurse Bittleman to mess with. Was he missing her? No, that couldn't be it, he thought. He was just missing the routine. No more cups to pee in. At least that routine was familiar to him. It was something he could count on. Ok that was just disturbing on many levels, he thought.

Today was only the second day. The rest of the week couldn't be like this. Something had to change; what and when was another issue. Dixon did something counter to his character, instead of seeing how much he could accomplish in one day, he decided not to expect too much from any day, just focus on the therapy; make that the adventure; see where that took him. He was trying too hard.

As for the present, his stomach told him it was time for chow. He cleaned up his act; shaved, showered and dressed. Then he pulled his walker in front of him and held on to the handles for balance as he maneuvered downstairs to the cafeteria for breakfast. Partway down the hall, he paused. The stiffness in his knees and ankles took its toll. He looked down at the walker, took a deep breath and exhaled, trying to push out thoughts that wanted to come in again. He just tried to focus on moving. Food sounded good. Food was a good goal.

Linda, Keith, and Jack stopped to pick up Melissa on the way to the rehab center. The plan was to meet up with her brother Trevor and have him help them become acquainted with some of the troops and introduce them to Jack. Keith and Linda both felt some nervous anticipation. How hard could it be? Let Jack goof-around with some of the patients right?

The Barnes Expedition pulled into the parking lot. Keith opened the rear hatch and reached inside for Jack, who looked at him with anticipation. With Jack's hip issue and the height of the vehicle, jumping down onto the pavement wasn't the best idea for now. Keith picked up the seventy-pound Collie and placed him on the ground. As they walked toward the building, Melissa explained that she had already spoken with the facility manager and she was expecting them. They were going to check in with her and then go track down Trevor.

Dora stood behind the receptionist counter organizing some folders. She looked toward the door when the door chime rang. to see three people and a happy Collie gently swishing his tail back and forth. Melissa she recognized from previous visits.

Her hospitable Jamaican greeting made Keith and Linda feel as though a close relative was greeting them. Her island accent was rich and smooth as it resonated from her soul outward.

"Hello Ms. Cantor. How are you my dear on dis beautiful day?"

"I'm well Dora. How are you?" replied Melissa.

"I kont complain. Wooden dooo any good now wood it?" she laughed. "I see you have brought your friends en dare dog. He's soh pritee."

Jack sat down waiting happily for the humans to finish their conversation.

"Thank you," responded Linda.

Dora queried. "I take it you've brought him to see dee payshunz?"

"Yes. Hi, I'm Linda. This is my husband Keith and this is Captain Jack – our pirate."

Dora let out a deep laugh. Clearly, the surprise of naming a large black dog after a pirate caught her in a funny place. Somewhere in her psyche, the oddity of connecting the two was unexpectedly humorous to her. Her resonate laugh exited her mouth and raced across her face turning into a wide smile as she arched her head back with the laugh. She chuckled so suddenly that when she tilted her head back it almost appeared as though she did it to take in more oxygen to feed her laugh.

"He looks like a pirate. Black, wid dat bit of white on him is true pirate colors!"

"That's for sure," chimed in Keith.

"I kon see in trew his eyes into his soul that he is sweet, but troublesome too … am I right?"

Melissa laughed as Linda answered. "Yes, very troublesome. Sometimes we call him trouble with a tail."

Dora echoed Linda's comment, starting another round of laughing. "Trouble wid a tayul. (laughing) Dat is truly funny girl. (laughing more) … Oh my. … You make me laugh. … Now den. I suppose we should find your brudder Miss Melissa."

"That would be great."

Dora came around the end of the counter and petted Jack briefly before leading the group down a short hallway that opened up into a large community lounge area.

The scene quietly startled Keith. It was so different from anything he had ever witnessed. There were couches, easy chairs, various tables and coffee tables, racks of books and magazines, a couple of large-screen TVs on either side of the room. It looked like any typical hospital lounge area, but what Keith clued in on was not the appearance of the room, but the occupants. Scattered throughout the room were about a dozen service members. Some in wheel chairs playing cards at a table, others with walkers or crutches. Probably half of them were missing an arm a leg or both legs or some combination. They were all occupied; engaged with something, but the sudden impression that formed in Keith's consciousness was that many of them simply had the appearance of incomplete people. So many of them were missing limbs, yet otherwise looked like a normal bunch of guys, hanging out. A new thought quickly replaced that instantaneous impression. What was going through their minds?

Were things as normal as their activities appeared or did they have a completely different set of thoughts, worries, regrets? He quickly realized that he had no idea what they felt; how they were dealing with their situations; what kind of moods they might be in. It could be anything.

He took a reset breath and mentally braced himself. He just wanted it to go well. He wanted them to know that he was sorry for their loss, but he didn't want to bring too much attention to it and have some negative effect on their spirits; that would defeat the purpose of coming. Keith decided it would be best to skip that topic unless they brought it up and focus on visiting with them. Let them enjoy Jack; let the conversation go wherever.

Melissa spotted Trevor in his wheel chair at a round table playing cards with a couple of other patients. Dora led the group in that direction.

"Here we are Miss Cantor. Trevor, you have some friends to see you. Dey have brought a surprise. Dis is a pirate dog named Captain Jack."

"Hello Dora," replied Trevor.

He put down his hand of cards as Linda approached. "Thanks for coming Ma'am."

"You're welcome Trevor. Still workin' on that Linda thing aren't we?" she laughed.

"Yes … Miss .. uh, Linda. Some habits die hard."

Linda smiled.

Dora prepared to exit. "I will leave you folks to enjoy. Let me know if dare is any ting you need."

"Thank you Dora," replied Melissa.

"All righty now," ended Dora as she turned and headed back down the hall.

Trevor took over introductions. "Guys, you've met my sister Melissa. These are her friends Keith and …. Linda."

The men each nodded or replied with some greeting or acknowledgement as they paused their game.

"I asked them if they would bring their dog Jack. I met him last week and he was just cool; thought some of the guys here might get a kick too."

Keith walked around the table where the other two men sat so they could better see Jack. Smiles came across their faces immediately as they reached out and pet him and rubbed him behind the ears.

Jack was in heaven; people who understood his language; rubbing and scratching his ears. The Collie smile appeared on Jack's face as he tilted his head to one side to increase the pressure on the backside of his ear. The men pushed their wheel chairs back from the table and moved them around slightly to better reach Jack. They were immediately drawn to him. There was silence; a smiling Collie, two smiling men and Linda, Melissa, Keith and Trevor all looked on, smiling at all the smiling taking place!

The visiting party pulled some table chairs around or took a seat on a nearby couch while the men enjoyed running their hands through Jack's thick fur, petting and talking to him. Jack, well, he did his duty and sat happily soaking up all the attention.

No one had to *do* anything; it just happened … as Trevor had hoped. Jack worked his magic and he didn't even know it. The group eventually made some small talk. The men asked about Jack and the visitors asked if the men had owned dogs before. The group exchanged fond memories and dog stories that served as sidebars to break the ice. The focus of the moment was Jack and, of course and Jack was cool with that.

The men enjoyed Jack completely. He stood up and walked around casually within his circle of visitors. When one of the men wasn't petting and roughing up his fur, they leaned back in their wheel chairs and watched enjoyably as one of the others did.

Having a dog in the visiting lounge was definitely a new and welcome experience for them. Everything else they seemed engaged in was really just passing time between therapy sessions. Visiting with Jack was an escape. Linda saw it in their eyes. While the men looked at Jack and played with him, she could tell that somehow they had really gone somewhere else; a good place, even if it was just for a little while. The physical and emotional effects of having gone to that better place would linger after Jack had gone and they could summon them back if desired. A calm peace enveloped Linda like a soft warm blanket. She quietly experienced her side of the moment as she watched the men experience their side of the same moment. Jack, well, he was good with all of it.

Keith, Linda, and Jack approached the entrance of the rehab center. It was their third visit since Trevor had requested they come by. Jack became a familiar fixture around the patients' lounge. Keith and Linda had met and come to know several of the troops. Some had completed their therapy and moved on. For their military careers, it was the end of the line. A few might end up in the Wounded Warrior Regiment (WWR that helps Marines and Sailors determine their suitability for returning to duty or assisting their transition to civilian life and new careers. Dixon had already had a visit from a representative from the WWR headquarters just up the street at Marine Corps Base, Quantico. He knew he would not be returning to duty. For him and many of the rest, being at the rehab facility was an ending and a beginning; uncertain and fretful beginning. Each faced a different and very personal struggle to adapt to their physical limitations from having lost limbs and other injuries along with the challenge of reintegrating into civilian life in a meaningful way.

"Oh, here come dee pirate Captain," exclaimed Dora with a broad smile as she looked up and saw Jack, Linda and Keith walk through the door toward her desk. "Good day Miss Linda and Mista Keith. How are you on dis glorious day now?"

"Doin' great Dora."

"Go on bach. Dee boyz are waitun for you"

"Thank you," nodded Keith, as the trio headed down the familiar hallway to the patients' lounge.

"Take care Dora. We'll stop by and see you on the way out."

"Ok child. We'll see you. ... Now be gone wit you," as she smiled and waved them off in the direction of the lounge.

Dixon sat reading a magazine when he noticed Keith walking in with Jack. Jack caught Dixon's focus and he continued to watch as Keith walked Jack over to a couch where a few men watched TV. They greeted Jack and chatted briefly with Keith and Linda. Dixon continued to watch Jack. As he stared blankly at Jack, an image formed in his mind. His imagination had him running and playing in a grassy park with his German Shepherd, Zoe. The image disappeared when he blinked his eyes and refocused on Jack.

While Dixon experienced his brief vision, Keith noticed Dixon and he and Linda walked Jack over toward him.

"Hi. ...I'm Keith and this is Captain Jack."

"Hello, he's beautiful. ... A Collie right?" asked Dixon.

"Yes. He's a tri-color. Instead of the typical sable and white ones that you usually see."

"Sorry. ... I'm Dakota. Dakota Dixon."

"Nice to meet you," replied Linda.

"Do you know Trevor Morrison? He's a patient here."

"No. 'fraid not."

Linda explained. "I met him a couple of weeks ago and he asked if we'd bring this crazy puppy by to hang out and visit."

"That's a great idea. Gets kind of mundane around here. Nice to have something different going on. ... So how old is he?"

"Almost two, pretty much full-grown now," explained Keith.

Dakota ran his right hand along Jack's side with long smooth strokes before starting to rub the backs of his ears. Jack groaned, panting gently, then let out a big yawn as he sat down in front of Dakota.

Keith smiled. "Obviously you've found the secret to creating Collie happiness," ending with a slight chuckle.

"It's so funny how you can almost hypnotize a dog by working that sensitive area behind their ears and the back of their head. It makes the nerves tingle down their spine and puts them in a highly relaxed state. It's as good for them as it is for us humans."

Linda commented. "You seem to know a lot about dogs."

"Yes Ma'am, I'm a trainer; or was. Won't be doing any of that now that I'm being discharged."

"You trained military dogs?"

"Yes, Ma'am. I had a German Shepherd. Zoe. She was my girl. I was admitted to the Canine Tactical School. Was hoping to change over to training and special ops work with dogs."

"Wow. That sounds amazing."

"Can't do that now though. The injuries and all that. The docs say I won't get totally back to normal to be able to work in that type of unit. So, I'm out of here in a few months."

"I'm sorry. I don't know what to say," replied Linda.

"Oh, it's all good. I have plans. Once I'm cut loose from here I'll kick those plans into high gear. … Always have a Plan 'B'."

Dixon continued playing with and petting Jack and making small talk with the Barnes. After visiting a while, the Barnes were ready to stop by and check in on some of the other troops. Dixon roughed up Jack's fur a little with some rapid side-to-side rubbing on the back of his neck.

"Great to meet ya Jack! Ya big hairy beast! You folks take care," as he reached out to shake hands first with Keith, then with Linda.

"You too Lieutenant," replied Linda.

"Oh, please Ma'am; just Dakota. You can lose the Lieutenant bit. Won't be keeping that part much longer."

"Got it … Dakota," replied Linda.

"Thanks a lot for bringing Jack. It feels awesome to spend some time with a beautiful big guy like him."

"We're glad you enjoyed him," added Keith.

"He's awesome. I'd love to take him on a run. Unfortunately, he'd leave me in the dust."

Linda laughed. "Oh, believe me, you're not the only one. I run with him sometimes and he's ready to pull me like a sled dog! I should put on roller skates and make it easier on both of us!"

"Take it easy Dakota," said Keith.

"You too Sir. Thanks again. …. Say, when do you all think you'll be coming back. I'd love to see this big pirate again."

"Uh. I don't know, probably this weekend," answered Linda.

"Could you please have Dora ring my room if I don't happen to be here in the lounge?"

"Absolutely. We'll see you then."

The week went by uneventfully. Keith put Jack in the back of the Expedition while Linda waited in the front seat. They headed off again to the rehab center. Dixon was expecting them.

When they arrived, Linda asked Dora to check to see if Dixon was in his room. She rang his phone and notified him that Jack and company were on their way to the lounge. Keith, Jack and Linda stood in the entrance for just a few seconds when Dixon came rounding the corner slowly with his walker. It was obvious that movement with his legs was still a challenge and he appeared to rest much of his body weight on his left arm as he leaned on the walker for support. Nonetheless, he smiled the instant he saw Jack. Jack's tail swished from side to side in wide sweeps. It was apparent that he recognized a friend in Dixon and the feeling was mutual.

Dixon reached down over the front of his walker and started petting Jack. "Hey Jack! How ya doin' buddy! Hi Linda. Hey Keith. How are you guys?"

"Good," replied Linda.

"Hey Dakota, you're moving a little better," noted Keith.

"Well. I don't know, but I've been working on it. The stiffness in the joints is ridiculous. I'd be all ready to go and just get my strength back if it weren't for the joints holding me back. … Did you happen to bring any oil? Maybe if I drank a quart or two it would help," he laughed. "Say, it's a beautiful day out. Would you all mind if we walked and talked outside? Something I'd like to try."

"Sure," replied Keith.

Dixon took a couple of steps over to a rack of canes, picked one out of the holder, and pushed his walker over against the wall. He took the cane in his left hand and shifted his weight on that side.

"Wow," explained Linda. "Look at you."

"Told you I've been working on it," replied Dixon.

"Nice," said Keith.

"By the way, my friends just call me 'DX'."

"Got it DX. Roger Dodger. Alpha Charlie," joked Linda.

Dixon turned to Keith jokingly under his breath, but loud enough for Linda to hear. "Is she always this nerdy?"

"Always."

"Ok boys. Y'all think you're so *it*."

"'Yeah. What else could it be?" joked Keith.

"Seriously," added Dakota, siding with Keith.

The group headed down a short hallway toward an exit that led them to the outside garden area. Jack sauntered casually along; ears perked, checking out the surroundings. Once outside, Dakota walked away from Jack a few yards. Keith let him off the leash and Dakota called him. Jack came running happily and wagged his tail as Dakota stroked his back. Dakota told Jack to sit and stay. Jack sat for a second, then got up and followed Dakota as he walked toward Keith and Linda. Dakota looked at Jack with a serious stare. Jack eyes met Dakota's and then he sat as he had before, but without a word from Dakota. Then Dakota walked away and called Jack to come. Jack had accepted Dakota. They had come to know each other and Jack responded well to Dakota. When the visit was over, the group returned to the lounge to spend a little time with some of the other troops.

-7-

Dog Whisperer

The training and interaction with Jack increased over the next few weeks, becoming a regular event. With each visit, Dakota became more mobile, using the cane less and less and moving, squatting and slowly trotting around the grassy areas with Jack chasing him and jumping at him. Dakota had Jack chasing down Frisbees or tennis balls. On one visit, Keith and Linda watched as Dakota chased Jack and squatted down with relative ease to pet him. To Linda it was obvious that Dixon was improving significantly. She was convinced that regular visits from Jack gave Dakota a reason to continue pushing hard with his conditioning and therapy. Dixon and Jack jogged back to where Keith and Linda sat on a bench. She was surprised to see Dixon moving quickly and with ease.

"Wow. You're picking up your pace more every week Dakota."

"Well, I've been trying to get back into some of my martial arts drills and stretches. Some of the low stances can really help get your muscle tone and loosen up the old joints. So far I haven't noticed any metal rattling around inside, so it must be working."

"So you're into martial arts?" asked Linda.

"Well, yes. All Marines are required to train in the Marine Corps Martial Arts Program – MCMAP."

"That's interesting. Keith is into martial arts too. He used to be an instructor."

Keith intervened. "What Linda is doing a poor job of explaining is that *we* used to be instructors. We had our own martial arts school that we started with several other instructors up in Alexandria."

"Really?"

"Yes," responded Keith. "We met when we were white-belts at another dojo."

Linda interjected. "Yes, but we waited. We didn't start dating until we were green-belts. ... I had to make sure his kicks were good enough. Ya know ... Jess sayin'"

"So you're both black belts? ... Instructors? That's pretty cool! Married black belts. ...Fight much?"

"He knows I can beat him," laughed Linda.

"Helps keep the kids in line," added Keith.

Linda smiled. "Yea, we just drop kick 'em to the moon if they get out of line.

The three laughed.

Keith asked. "So what belt level are you in the MCMAP?"

"I'm a brown belt. Nearly ready to test for 1st degree black belt, but that isn't going to happen either. Just freakin' stinks ya know. I had plans and dreams and I knew where I was going and why. Now, nothing." Dixon looked down at the ground. Suddenly his mood changed and his shoulders sank. He felt like someone had pulled a drain plug on his enthusiasm and dropped quickly into a depressed state. His voice became lower and he spoke under his breath.

"Damn. Everything changed."

The Marine who only moments ago seemed so uplifted and exhilarated, suddenly appeared visibly transformed as he relaxed his stance. He leaned more on the cane and allowed his posture to give in subconsciously to the collection of strains and aches in his muscles and joints that he had happily been ignoring until now. Linda responded to the shift.

"DX, I'm sorry. I didn't mean to bring up a sore subject."

"No. You didn't. It's all good. I just have to keep reminding myself that the future I *had* isn't the future I *have*. Adapt and overcome. That's what Marines do."

"I understand."

Keith tried to change the focus a little. "DX, you're really looking a heck of a lot better than when we first met you. If you keep up this pace, by spring or early summer you'll probably be at least eighty-percent back to normal or more."

"I hope so."

A spark of an idea flashed in Keith's head. It was clear from the look on his face. He was excited about what had suddenly hit him. "Hey! I have an idea."

"What's that?" asked Dixon casually.

"How 'bout if you train Jack and I train *you*?"

Linda cocked her head to the side almost the way Jack would. "Train for what?"

"I train Dixon in martial arts. I could use a training partner. I'm familiar with a lot of the techniques in the MCMAP already, it's a lot of the same stuff you and I have studied and taught forever Linda. Then at the same time, Dixon, trains Jack. I mean after we workout. Seriously, Jack is sweet and lovable, but he doesn't exactly have the best manners, and he isn't the most obedient Collie on the planet."

Linda and Dixon both tried to visualize his idea.

"What do you think?" finished Keith.

Dakota tried to make sure he had the picture straight. "You would train me in martial arts?"

"Yeah. You know. Close quarters combat, gun and knife disarming techniques, survival drills, the works; fun stuff. It will help you get back in shape and it will help me too. We can take turns beating each other up. It'll be fun, in a twisted kind of way."

"For real?"

"Dude. ...Linda and I have trained tons of Marines, Army Rangers, local police, and feds. We even trained the JAG of the Marine Corps. We've done this for years. Don't believe me, check out some of my books on the internet."

"Whoa, you write books too?"

"Yes. So it's settled. We'll start next week at our place. I use my garage as a dojo, so we can start in there and then train Jack at the nearby park afterward. Be at our place at zero-nine hundred or I'll sue for breach of contract," smiled Keith.

"So wait. ... What's one of the books you've written? Name one."

"Uh, well, the first one I published was called, *The Way of the Martial Artist: Achieving Success in Martial Arts and in Life!* It's kind of a motivational and informational book. It covers -"

"You're kidding right?" interrupted Dixon.

"No. It does."

"No. I mean. I've read that book. I chose it for one of the required book studies in the MCMAP. ... You wrote that? That's you?"

"Yeah."

"Cool ...And that was you in there with him in some of the pictures right Linda?"

"Yes."

Dixon's mood changed rapidly and Keith and Linda could see him coming back out of the dark place he had briefly slipped into earlier.

"Dudes, I feel like I'm at a Ninja Turtle convention or something. This is *awesome*," turning to Keith. "So does this mean I have to call you Obi Wan or something?"

Keith pointed at DX and looked at Linda. "Funny guy."

"So which one of you is the better fighter?"

"Oh. That would be me," interjected Linda.

Keith shook his head and looked at Dixon.

Keith complained to DX. "Ya know, it's bad enough that she's a Cowboys fan. Then she starts talking smack about martial arts. ... Whenever we watch a martial arts flick or some action movie with a good fight scene, she starts analyzing the techniques and picking it apart, talking about how impractical some of the moves are and why that move wouldn't work or what they should have done differently."

Dixon laughed. "Seriously?"

"Yeah, I just wanna watch the movie and she's acting like she's judging at a karate tournament."

They chuckled. Linda felt compelled to respond. "Hey, if they're gonna put it in a movie, they need to make it practical or not do it at all. I'm jess sayin'."

Linda confirmed the plans. "So next Saturday, we'll pick you up at nine o'clock. You come to our place; pound on each other for a while and then we can go watch and see if you can teach Jack some manners."

"Sounds like a plan," agreed Dixon. "And, actually, once we get Jack through some basic obedience training there are a few techniques I'd like to try on him; sort of special tactics if that's okay."

"Sure," said Linda.

"Almost like canine martial arts. We'll all be getting some fight training in," smiled Dixon.

Linda smiled. "Sounds good."

The weather was cool. Keith and Linda both loved the fall. The air was crisp and invigorating and the typical Washington area summer humidity had left. The holidays were approaching and the foliage prepared for its magnificent annual display of fall colors. Keith went to the physical therapy center to pick up Dakota. The Barnes children were excited about meeting Dakota. Sandra and Allie played soccer in the back yard with Jack. He loved being "monkey-in-the-middle" and chasing the soccer ball as they attempted to kick it back and forth to keep it from him as he barked constantly.

Shortly after nine-thirty Keith's Expedition cruised down the street toward the Barnes's home. Wesley was in his room playing a video game and the girls were in the kitchen helping Linda bake sugar cookies. Jack stood guard at the top of the hill in the back yard, observing his domain. He sat upright and dignified; as dignified as a misfit pirate of a Collie can be as he scanned the area, occasionally sounding out a few barks to see what other canine pals were out there willing to speak back. It was ritual.

Keith and Dixon climbed out of the Expedition. Dixon was able to open the door and climb out without the aid of a cane. He was fully mobile, but still working out stiffness and soreness as he focused on building muscle and joint strength. That would just take time; time that Dixon was impatient to burn through. They walked in the front door and immediately caught the aroma of fresh baked cookies.

"Well," said Keith. "Maybe we just skip the workout and chow down on some nice warm cookies."

"I'm game," agreed Dakota.

Linda quickly wiped her hands with a dishtowel and walked toward Keith and Dakota. She hugged Dakota. "Hey stranger. You look good! You're walking and everything," she observed with a smile.

Keith stood by awkwardly; looked comically from side to side, then back at Linda and Dakota before injecting a little snarky sarcasm.

"I'm good too. Thanks for asking. … And don't worry, I already know I look good."

Linda smiled and moved toward Keith with a hug and some sarcasm of her own. "There. Do we feel better now?"

Keith stood there arms down to his side as if he was in a bear hug, waiting for her to finish. He pursed his lips indignantly. How lame, he thought. Linda unwrapped herself from hugging Keith. Then she snapped the dish towel toward Keith' rear.

"The cookies are for *after* the workout. Think of them as recovery cookies. … DX these are my girls, Allie and Sandra."

"Nice to meet you girls! Your cookies smell amazing!"

Sandra took on a very curious tone. "Why did mommy call you DX? Sounds like a video game?"

Sandra sat on a stool at the counter. Dakota leaned forward and crouched slightly to Sandra's level. He made a silly scary face with a mock Indian accent. "No, little princess. I am an Indian! DX is my short name. My real name is Dakota Dixon, but my friends call me DX," staring Sandra in the eyes with a funny intense, wide-eyed look.

"You're an Indian?" inquired Allie.

Dakota maintained his funny, serious bug-eyed look as he remained in position only turning his head to make eye contact with Allie across the counter.

"Do you live in a tipi?" asked Sandra.

"No, but I have slept in one many times. My grandfather taught me how to make one and set it up."

"Coooool!" squealed Allie. "Like on Survivor."

"Yeah …. Something like that. But I've never been voted out of the Tipi."

Sandra was still curious.

"Where's your Mohawk?"

"Well, you know Sandra, the Marines aren't too crazy about Mohawks, so we're not allowed to have one."

"It might scare off the bad guys," she suggested.

"You know. I think you're right Miss Sandra. Maybe I'll give that suggestion to my big boss and see what he thinks."

"Is he an Indian?"

"No, not that I know of."

"Are there any other Indian Marines?"

"There are a few."

Linda called off the investigation. "Ok girls; let's get that next batch of cookies going. Dad and Dakota have some things to do."

Dakota grinned at the girls as he stood back up. "Nice to meet you girls. I can't wait to try some of those cookies."

Sandra had one more question. "Are you going to train Jack? Dad said you were going to teach him not to be such a pirate all the time. He always takes our things."

"Yes I am sweetie. Is that ok with you?"

"Sure! Sounds good. The way he acts right now is unmackceptable. That's what mom says."

"Well, I'm pretty good with dogs, so I'll see what I can do. If he's a real pirate, that might be difficult. Maybe we can give him some manners. … Deal."

"Deal DX!" exclaimed Sandra.

"Cool!" as they high-fived.

Keith and Linda grinned as they watched the girls interact with their new friend.

"We actually have a son too, but I believe at the moment he's glued to a video game upstairs in his room. I'll see if I can introduce you to him later."

"Sounds good," replied Dakota.

Keith and DX were already wearing sweats for working out. "We're going to head out to the garage and get started babe."

"Okay, you boys have fun. Don't hurt yourselves."

"The garage is not really a garage, it's half workshop and half dojo," explained Keith.

They entered the garage. Dakota explained to Keith what type of training he had been doing to improve his flexibility and strength.

"One problem I've been having that feels weird is my balance. With all the problems in my knee joints and ankles and hip, it's actually tricky to maintain good balance. A lot of it is just stiffness and weakness of the joints and some of it's where a lot of the muscles in my legs are not equally balanced and strengthened yet, so that throws me off easily. It won't matter what techniques I know if I can't stay upright."

Keith listened and began visualizing a series of warm-up drills that would help improve balance.

"Well, ya know, if you remember in my book, I explained that balance is actually not something you're born with. It's a skill. It can actually be improved upon by practicing the right drills. Let's go through some things that can help get you there."

Keith proceeded to go through a number of different balance and conditioning drills with Dakota, explaining how he should practice these twice or three times per day.

"I think within three or four weeks you're going to see a major improvements. So, I'll write those down and a few others you should be familiar with. Do those a couple or three times per day and mix them up for variety. ...Sounds like a prescription."

"Whatever you say doc."

Keith and Dakota got past the warm-ups and conditioning into some actual common attacks and defenses. They continued exchanging and varying up the techniques, each gradually becoming in-tune with how the other was moving and responding. As the workout progressed, the intensity increased. They continued, focusing on common chokes, grabs, and pin-downs. Keith showed DX how to formulate the basic components of a response to an assailant and how to vary and adapt his response to the attack. Dakota's fluid movement impressed Keith, not only considering his injuries and physical condition, but even accounting for his relatively short time in martial arts.

"How long did you say you studied martial arts in the Corps?"

"Well, since I was here at Quantico for Officer Candidate training. That was about three and a half years ago."

"You have a very natural ability. All you need is to make your skill set more robust and versatile, work in the strategy and spirit aspects and you have the makings of a very good martial artist."

"Thank you. I remember those were some of the chapters in your book. I also liked the last chapter, '*Success for Life*' I could probably use some work in that area."

"We all can. We're always growing, hopefully. You'll get there. One level at a time. It's the best journey you'll ever take. What do you say we go check on those cookies and then see what you can do with that crazy Collie?"

"Roger that. Let's do it."

They headed back inside to the kitchen. The cookies sat on some metal cooling racks on the counter, but their aroma filled the house. The girls watched TV and Linda sat in front of the computer in the family room.

"Hey guys. How'd it go?" asked Linda.

"Your husband beat me up mercilessly," said Dakota.

Keith balked. "Yeah, beating up injured warriors. That's my thing."

Dakota grinned as he reached for a cookie. Linda got up and walked over into the kitchen on the other side of the counter. The girls heard the conversation and became interested in Dakota's story. They came into the kitchen and sat at the table, leaning forward, and propped themselves up with their hands. They were ready to learn more about their new friend.

"Milk?"

Dakota's eyes lit up. "You're never too old for a glass of milk with cookies."

"Okay. ... Keith?" she asked.

"Yes please. I need my milk and cookies."

Keith changed the subject. "So what got you interested in the Marines?"

"My grandfather. I practically grew up with him. He taught me the old ways; hunting, trapping, survival, scouting, spiritual rituals."

"I don't understand. How did learning the ways of your people make you want to become a Marine?"

"He represented his people honorably as a Lakota and a member of the Lakota Council. He was also a friend to your people. During World War II, he was a Marine, a code talker. He used the Lakota language to communicate with other Lakotas to send secret messages about battle plans for the U.S. forces. Since the Japanese had no one who could understand his language, they could not decipher the messages and figure out what was happening. It was the perfect code."

"Oh... I've heard of the code talkers. They just dedicated a new Code Talkers Hall over at Quantico recently and had some of them there for the ceremony."

"My grandfather served his people honorably, but he also believed that he served America, because this was once his people's land and it was his home, so he volunteered for the Marines. Since this is my home. I wanted to play a part in keeping it strong and free."

Linda leaned forward with her forearms on the kitchen counter as she listened quietly to Dakota's story.

"That's a wonderful story. It makes me think of every time I hear the cannons practicing over at Quantico … it makes the house shake and I just tell people, that's the sound of freedom."

"We Lakota have always been proud warriors."

Sandra had a question that taxed her brain. "So you're an Indian *and* a Marine?"

"Yes little one."

She was quiet and had to think about that one. Meanwhile Dakota finished his last cookie.

"So, we need to get that crazy pirate Collie over to the park and get him some training," said Dakota.

Jack, who lay flaked out in the family room, lifted his head lazily and looked at the gathering in the kitchen. He kept lying on his side, but watched the group for a moment as he continued holding his head up. Once he knew that everything was good, he dropped his head back down on the raised edge of his large dog bed.

Keith called Jack. "Jack! Come on! Let's go."

Jack popped up and walked with a lazy swagger from his bed near the fireplace over to the kitchen. Once he was around the group, he stopped and panted gently with a smile. Dakota reached down and roughed up Jack's fur as Keith went to get the leash.

Keith, Jack, and Dakota took the Expedition to the park down the street. They stood at the edge of a soccer field, where not long ago, Jack chased and successfully herded a bull that had escaped from a local farm just in time for animal control officers to take over for him. Dakota turned toward Keith to explain his plan. "I want to focus for about ten minutes on some basic obedience just to establish a baseline. After that I have a few tactical techniques I'd like to work on with him."

Keith handed the leash to DX who walked with Jack, further out into the field away from Keith. Keith took a seat on the corner of a picnic table bench under a small pavilion at the edge of the field. He watched Dakota work with Jack. Dixon worked through the basics, 'sit', 'stay', 'come', and 'down'. He went over these rapidly with Jack who responded eagerly. As Jack accomplished the tasks, Dakota rewarded him with training treats, returning several times to earlier commands just to keep reinforcing Jack's memory of them.

With the obedience training completed for the day, it was time to try some of Dakota's tactical concepts. Dakota and Jack walked over to Keith.

"He did really well on the obedience training. We just have to keep working on that to program it into him."

"Great," replied Keith.

"I can tell he's smart because he knows the commands. It's just a matter of whether he's in the mood to obey them or not, but that's fixable."

"Okay."

"So here's what I have in mind. Back in World War II, the military began utilizing war dogs. They even used some in World War I. When the military takes a dog, they train them for a specific position. Those positions are typically: scout dog, messenger dog, ambulance dog, mine dog, and sentry dog. In recent years, groups have begun training personal protection dogs with specific skills. These dogs are trained to attack intruders and assailants and to take their guns, knives, or clubs. They literally are personal bodyguards and very effective. Jack and Collies in general are naturally very protective, so training them to do this is pretty easy."

Keith listened with interest as Dakota continued. "Each of these military positions requires specialized training and what you have at the end is a dog that is very good at one type of assignment. My theory is that if you find dogs of exceptional intelligence, such as Collies, that a single dog could be trained to perform in all these areas, or at least in several of them."

"That sounds intriguing."

"Remember in your book where you talk about the idea of a martial artist needing to be very versatile; always learning new skills; having a large library of skills and tactics to be able to handle a wide variety of situations."

"Sure."

"That's what I'm talking about, except with dogs; warrior dogs. The idea really came to me from reading your book. I wanted to try that with the dogs to see if it could be done. That's the reason I wanted to attend that canine school in the Marine Corps. It was to eventually propose the idea of a whole team of highly versatile dogs. It would be like a canine version of a SEAL team, or a Ninja."

"That's an awesome concept. I didn't know that much about canine tactical training and all the different uses of the dogs."

Dakota's eyes lit up, as he was clearly passionate about training highly skilled dogs. "See, the sentry dogs are trained to make a lot of noise when they are guarding an area like a home or a military base or outpost. The scout dogs are trained to seek out enemy troops or intruders silently, then come back and give signals to their master whether there are intruders and where they are located. The ambulance dog goes and finds an injured person and goes back to his master and leads the rescue team to the injured person. Then there's the mine dog that sniffs out explosives or drugs and can also detect trip-wires and booby traps of different types. In more recent years other skills like man-trailing and man-tracking have been added as well."

"That's a pretty broad set of skill you're describing."

"But imagine if you had a dog that could do many or all of those tasks. As far as I know, no one has ever tried to train a tactical dog that could do everything, but if one existed, he would be the ultimate tactical dog; way beyond anything that exists now."

"Sounds like you're trying to create some type of super hero almost."

"Yeah, I suppose so."

"Does he get to wear a cape?"

Dixon laughed. "So, you understand the idea though right?"

"Oh absolutely, really cool stuff. You're basically experimenting with Jack to make him into a canine martial artist."

"Pretty much."

"Well show me some stuff."

"Alright."

Dixon began the second half of Jack's training session by teaching him some of the techniques for guard dog; warning of intruders. When Dakota finished the session, they headed back to the Barnes's home. Keith and DX explained to Linda about DX's training concept and how the first session went.

"Jack has some typical Collie instincts; protective, aggressive when necessary, like a wolf! He's ridiculously alert and smart. He learns really quickly Keith. I see a lot of dogs who just kind of don't think much about what's going on around them, but Jack is really in tune with his environment. He is what we call in Lakota oyuskeya (oh-yue-shkay-yah), meaning 'alert'."

Linda listened as the three sat at the kitchen table. "So what's the next step?"

"Well if you two are ok with continuing, I'd like to keep working with him on the basic obedience training because that's a foundation for everything. It's kind of like his white-belt training, but then each time we train, I'd like to keep going over the tactical techniques with him."

"Sounds cool," said Linda.

"You guys can even help in some cases. I would like to teach him at least a handful of techniques in each of the different roles in which dogs are typically trained."

Linda was intrigued. Her face perked up and her eyes grew larger. "I'd like to do some of that; and see how it all works."

"Awesome," replied Dakota. "It'll take a few weeks to see how well Jack is able to integrate the wide variety of techniques, but by then we should know for certain whether he will be capable of becoming good at many different types of tasks in different roles."

"This is exciting," she said.

"See, normally most canine training schools are a few weeks at most and the dogs come out with specialized training, but it's just in one area. What I was telling Keith is that Jack will be learning a broad set of techniques that would take much longer than the usual few-week courses, but if he is able to learn all these different tasks that usually require separate dogs, then that would prove my theory."

"I like it," responded Linda enthusiastically.

"Thanks you guys," said Dakota in a partly sheepish way. "You don't know how much this means to me and how much I appreciate everything you all have done."

"We're glad to help," added Linda.

"I mean, sharing Jack with me and taking him to the rehab center to spend time with the other troops is just huge."

"Well, ..." Keith started.

"Just know that, while you might not think about it that much, it has a big effect, and it's helped me tremendously. I'm not sure what the future holds once I am discharged, but for now, working with Jack and you guys makes me feel like someone threw a life line out into the water before I was about to go under. It's just awesome, so thank you."

Dixon looked down for a second after speaking. Keith and Linda were silent and as looked at him. The impact of Trevor's request hit home. It was hard to describe, certainly a good feeling, grateful. They were able to bless Dakota by sharing Jack and the same for the other troops as well.

Linda broke the brief silence. "Say, it's approaching dinner time. Dakota you are staying for dinner."

"Linda …" he started.

"That wasn't a question. That was a statement, besides you know I can kick your butt if I have to."

Keith turned to Dakota. "See what I mean. She doesn't look it, but she does have some moves."

Dakota nodded. "Yeah, well, even we Lakota know that when we are in the village and the hunt or the battle is completed, the women are in charge of the Tipi."

"Then it's settled. You will dine in our Tipi this evening."

"Yes Ma'am."

Linda smiled, proud of her small victory.

Jack sat on the floor at the edge of the dining room as the family finished dinner.

"Linda that was the best Buffalo meat I've had in a long time."

Wes looked down at his plate and frowned. Before he could say anything Allie, responded. "That was *Buffalo* meat?!"

"Yes," responded Dakota. "Your Dad and Jack and I tracked a herd of them this morning and shot one of them for dinner."

Sandra was curious. "Did you use your bow and arrow?"

"No ...," laughing. "I was just kidding. It's not Buffalo meat, but it was really good Linda. Thank you."

Wes didn't let it go quit so quickly. "You know Sandra, I think it *was* from a Buffalo ... It was..."

"Enough Wes!" said Linda, giving him a motherly stare. Wes giggled to himself.

"You're very welcome. Glad you all liked it. Anyone interested in some German Chocolate cake? It's Keith's favorite."

"Sounds good to me," replied Dakota.

After dinner, everyone hung out in the family room. Keith, Linda, and Dakota had one conversation going, while the girls and Wes watched TV quietly, and Jack lay in the center of the room. He was in the center of his pack, content, looking around at everyone, panting lightly and smiling.

"Are we going to do more training tomorrow?" asked Linda.

"Well ..." started Dixon.

"I would hope so. It's going to take a while, no point doing it once a week. You need to get in a lot of sessions to teach Jack everything you're trying to teach him," said Linda.

Dakota didn't want to push too hard to have access to Jack and the blessing of Keith and Linda to continue training him, but he was encouraged to hear how supportive Linda was of the idea.

"If you're ok with it, that would be great. I'd love to."

"Okay, so Keith and I can pick you up after church tomorrow."

"Awesome," said Dakota.

"Girls, I believe it's time for little ones to hit the hay," suggested Linda.

"Let us finish this episode. It's almost over," said Allie.

"Of course my dearest, I wouldn't want to interfere with your television viewing priorities. ... Come on girls. Time for bed."

"Oh Mom," said Allie.

Dakota laughed. "Before they go up, I have a little something for the kids. If it's ok?" asked Dakota.

"Well ... Sure," said Linda.

"Let me get it. It's in my training bag."

Sandra whispered. "What do you think it is?"

Wes had the answer of course. "Probably a hatchet so he can scalp you're ugly hair, butt-turd."

"Stop Wes!" shouted Sandra.

"Wes!" added Linda. "*Really?*"

Dakota came back with his training bag. He sat down, unzipped it and pulled out a white plastic bag. He took something out of it for each of the children.

"Kids, this is just little something I thought you might like."

"What is it?" asked Sandra.

"Oh! I know," started Allie. "It's a ….."

Wes jumped in again. "It's a dream catcher stupid."

"Wes," scolded Linda.

"Well ... she is," returned Wes.

Linda shook her head to herself, and then turned her attention back to Dakota to explain the gift.

"Wes is right. ... Not that you're stupid Sandra, (*laughing*), but that it's a dream catcher. My people created these."

"What's it for?" wondered Sandra.

"Well, there is a legend behind the dream catcher."

Sandra turned hers around curiously, to see if something was behind it. There wasn't.

Dakota explained. "The legend goes something like this...

>   Long ago when the world was young, an old Lakota spiritual leader was on a high mountain and had a vision. In his vision, Iktomi, the great trickster and teacher of wisdom, appeared in the form of a spider. Iktomi spoke to him in a sacred language that only the spiritual leaders of the Lakota could understand.
>
>   As he spoke, Iktomi, the spider, took the elder's willow hoop, which had feathers, horsehair, beads and offerings on it and began to spin a web.
>
>   He spoke to the elder about the cycles of life...and how we begin our lives as infants and we move on to childhood, and then to adulthood. Finally, we go to old age where we must be taken care of as infants, completing the cycle.
>
>   'But,' Iktomi said as he continued to spin his web, 'in each time of life there are many forces -- some good and some bad. If you listen to the good forces, they will steer you in the right direction. But if you listen to the bad forces, they will hurt you and steer you in the wrong direction.'
>
>   He continued, 'There are many forces and different directions that can help or interfere with the harmony of nature, and also with the Great Spirit and all of his wonderful teachings.'
>
>   All the while, the spider spoke, he continued to weave his web starting from the outside and working towards the center.
>
>   When Iktomi finished speaking, he gave the Lakota elder

the web and said....'See, the web is a perfect circle but there is a hole in the center of the circle.'

He said, 'Use the web to help yourself and your people to reach your goals and make use of your people's ideas, dreams and visions.

'If you believe in the Great Spirit, the web will catch your good ideas -- and the bad ones will go through the hole.'

The Lakota elder passed on his vision to his people and now the Sioux Indians use the dream catcher as the web of their life.

It is hung above their beds or in their home to sift their dreams and visions.

The good in their dreams is captured in the web of life and carried with them...but the evil in their dreams escapes through the hole in the center of the web and is no longer a part of them.

We believe that the dream catcher holds the destiny of our future....

And that my friends, is the legend of the dream catcher."

"Wow! … That's cool," declared Sandra.

Linda prompted the kids. "What do you say kids?"

Replying in unison. "Thank you Mr. Dixon."

"You're welcome guys. If you hang those near your bed I bet they might start working tonight."

"Ok kids, time for bed; everyone upstairs," ordered Linda.

"Good night guys," said Dixon.

"Good night," replied the trio of Barnes kids as they headed upstairs.

After the kids were in bed, Keith Linda and Dakota chilled out in the family room, enjoying the silence for a moment before Keith commented.

"That was a neat story DX. Thanks for getting those dream catchers for the kids."

"No problem. You guys have done so much for me; I just wanted to make a little gesture."

Linda returned the topic back to Jack's training. "So DX, you have this theory about training dogs and you were hoping to use it in the Marine Corps. So if you can prove this theory works now, what will you do with it?"

"That's where I'm stuck. I don't exactly know. I'm just grateful to you two for giving me the chance to find out if it might work."

Keith tried to encourage DX. "Well you said that the Lakota believe that the dream catcher holds the destiny of your people and that it catches good dreams. Maybe you need to get your dream catcher and see what good ideas it has captured that you could pull out of it. Maybe you can change your destiny."

"I suppose. That will definitely take some thought."

Linda chimed in. "I would think that if you're really serious about dog training that is a good thing for you to consider pursuing. You know … follow that dream. Corny, I know, but…."

"No," interrupted DX. "That's not corny at all. I'm just not quite sure where to go with it yet. I'll have to sleep on it."

Dakota continued training Jack several times per week. Keith and Linda helped where they could. As the weeks passed and fall surrendered to winter, Jack became more capable of new tasks and commands, increasing his versatility. It was really something for Keith and Linda to stand by the edge of the field at the park and see their friend, the dog whisperer, work his magic with Jack. Jack learned how to disarm someone with a firearm, attack an intruder, scout out an enemy in the woods, and other tactical techniques. It appeared that Dakota's theory was paying off.

During one training session, DX tried to make Jack go through a smoke screen that he had created with a smoke bomb, but Jack refused. It was all part of teaching Jack to function in simulated battle conditions. Initially he approached the smoke, but then backed away. DX tried to coax him and call him to come through the wall of smoke, but Jack after an initial approach, he would, again, back away.

The kids were already in bed as Keith and Linda sat at the kitchen table one night. Keith had returned from dropping DX off at the rehab center. He only had a couple more months left before his discharge. Then he would have to find a place of his own. Keith noticed that Linda had a blank stare.

"Are you here?"

"Yes. I was just thinking about DX and Jack and what he might do when he's discharged. Seems like he could start a dog training business or get hired by a group that does that type of work. He must have connections in the Marine Corps or something."

"Actually, I could ask Jim Boone. You remember Jim, he's with the FBI. I've heard him talk about working with dogs. I don't know if he does, but maybe he knows someone."

"He needs to start getting some leads about what to do when he's out," commented Linda.

"I'll call Jim tomorrow and see what he says."

"Okay. Maybe this was the purpose that Jack was intended to serve."

"What do you mean?"

"Well… We wanted a family dog. That's it."

"Oh. Yeah, … then we end up using him as a therapy dog, now he's being trained as a tactical canine warrior, Ninja thing."

"Right. So what happened to the simple idea of the family pet? It's not exactly turning out the way you envisioned."

"Well. The training is good for Jack. He's much more obedient, but still majorly mischievous. It's not like this is going to go on forever; maybe another few weeks of training or so. Then things should start returning back to normal."

"I mean, you and DX can still work out and do self-defense. That's cool."

"Sure, but at some point DX will most likely get his own dog once he finishes testing his theory with Jack.

"That's true."

"Besides, at least for now, having Jack to train is helping DX recover more than just physically. You can see how he lights up when he works with Jack or talks about him."

"I know. I was skeptical when you first suggested going to the rehab center, but it's worked out really well."

The day was chilly with a slight breeze. The cool crisp air of fall had definitely left town and been replaced by the much colder air of its sibling season of winter. Keith stood at the edge of the field, watching DX work with Jack on the latest round of tactical techniques. He and DX had already spent a little over an hour working out in the garage on self-defense; then it was time for Jack to do a little canine marital arts.

DX had set up a perimeter with stakes pounded into the ground and connected with string to form a makeshift fenced in area. Jack stood inside the twenty by thirty foot zone. DX called Keith over to him so that Keith could pose as an intruder trying to approach the perimeter. Whenever Keith approached, Jack barked wildly at him to warn of his approach.

After the session, Keith, Dixon, and Jack walked back to the Barnes home.

"DX, when you went into the Corps, you learned a new way of being. You became a Marine."

"Certainly. I can safely say that I'm not the same person I was when I went in."

"So it was a kind of transformation right?"

"Most definitely."

"So that transformation prepared you for the life you had ahead of you in the Marine Corps right."

"Where are you going with this Keith?"

"You see my point. If you know what you're heading for and you put in the effort and make the change or the transformation, then you are prepared for what is ahead."

DX knew there was a point, he could see that there was a point, and Keith tried to get DX on the same page with him.

"Your career in the Marine Corps, unfortunately, is over."

"Hey thanks for cheering me up."

"Sorry. I didn't mean it like that."

"No. It's okay. I understand. Just jerking your chain."

"What I'm trying to say is that looking ahead; you're going to have to change your thinking some and consider some new ideas."

"Well, yes, I realize that. I'm just a little short on ideas at the moment."

"Well. I had one."

"Yeah?"

"I have a friend. He's an FBI agent, here in Stafford. He works at the academy at Quantico. I contacted him to see if he knew anything about a need for a dog trainer or handler. If that's ok with you?"

"Uh .. Sure. I guess. ... Thanks."

"I haven't heard back yet, but I'll let you know what he says. Even if he doesn't know of anything, I would bet there are some tactical canine training schools in Northern Virginia or elsewhere that would be interested in your ideas or at least take you on as a trainer or instructor trainer or something."

"I hadn't really thought of that. Thanks Keith. That could be a possibility I could look into."

"Don't thank me, it was Linda's idea."

"That's really cool."

"Maybe a way to get some interest from some organizations would be to put a YouTube video together showing what Jack can do? Kind of a video resume."

"That's a cool idea. Heck, we could just about shoot that now with what Jack has learned so far."

"That's true."

"Wow. This is really cool Keith! See, now you're getting me all excited about this."

"Nothing wrong with that!"

Dixon was silent and looked at Jack. He leaned over and roughed up his fur with both hands.

"And DX, there's something else."

"What?"

"Linda wants to talk with you when we get back to the house."

"Is she threatening to kick my butt again?"

"No, not quite."

Keith, Linda, and DX gathered around the kitchen table. It had become somewhat of a ritual, chatting over a cup of tea or coffee. Linda started this particular conversation. "DX. ... Keith and I want you to join us and the kids, *and* Jack, in Colorado for Christmas. We have a log home there that my Uncle left us and there's plenty of room."

DX was silent as he looked down at his coffee cup. He appreciated the gesture and it sounded wonderful as he had grown very fond of the Barnes family, and of course, Jack, but he didn't know how to handle or feel about the offer. He straddled the fence between simply giving in and going along with what he knew would be very enjoyable and pulling back from committing. He didn't have a solid reason for saying no; just that he felt awkward saying yes. He was torn as he paused.

"... DX?" asked Linda.

"...I'm sorry. ... That's a great offer. I really appreciate it, but I have a couple of Marine buddies I was planning to visit down at Camp Lejeune. I was going to take the AMTRAK down there and see them for a week or so. That would give you all and Jack a break."

"A break from what?" asked Linda.

"From dealing with me."

Keith started to respond. "Dude ..." Linda motioned to Keith by shaking her head slightly when DX wasn't looking at her. She took over.

"DX. We aren't *dealing* with you. You're our friend. We'd love for you to spend Christmas with us; just hang out. No pressure, we like to keep it simple, have fun, and enjoy a change of scenery. So, we'd really like you to come with us. Now do you actually have plans already made with your buddies?"

The Marine in him kicked back in.

"Yes Ma'am."

"Okay. Well, we just wanted you to know that we'd be thrilled if you could join us."

"That's really outstanding of you all to ask me, but I already have those plans. Train ticket is already paid for."

"Okay. If something changes, the offer is still there."

"Thank you very much guys."

Keith and Linda prepared for bed. She walked out of the master bathroom into the bedroom as Keith lay in bed reading.

"Do you believe him?" she asked.

"About what?"

"Going to visit friends."

"I don't know. Either way he isn't going to join us. So it doesn't really matter."

"I know. I just thought it would be good for him to join us."

"Well, he does have his own life ya know."

"I suppose. I had just hoped that he would say yes."

Keith headed over to a friend's café. It was a charming neighborhood spot about two miles from the Barnes's home. Josh owned the *"Before 'N After Café."* He attended the same church as Keith and Linda. In fact, Linda was part of a women's bible study group that met each Tuesday morning at the café.

As Keith walked in the door, Josh stood behind the counter. He spotted Keith and raised an arm in acknowledgement. Keith waved back and took two steps in the direction of the counter when he noticed DX. He was sitting at one of the small two-person bistro tables near the window eating a sandwich and looking over a newspaper on the table in front of him. Keith shifted direction and headed over to DX's table, sitting down at the empty seat. DX had not even noticed Keith until he sat down. His head was down as he held his sandwich with both hands. He didn't move his head, but raised his eyes to see who had just sat down at his table.

Keith spoke first. "So … How's that train trip working out for ya?"

Dixon had a mouthful of sandwich. "Uhh.…"

"Do you need some money for the train?"

Trying to swallow enough of the sandwich so he could speak reasonably clearly. "No. I'm good."

"Can I refresh your coffee?"

Dakota swallowed. "No thank you."

"I'm waiting."

"… for what?"

"For you to finish your lunch. … And then you're coming with me."

"Where?"

"To Colorado for Christmas."

"Seriously, thank you, but-"

"Just eat. Besides I could use some help doing some work on the cabin before I go broke paying contractors. I'm sure Jack could use some more training, or at least you could show me some more about how to handle him."

"Keith, really ..."

"Don't talk with your mouth full. You'll set a bad example around the kids."

Dixon lowered his eyes and grinned, shaking his head as he tried to finish chewing the large bite he had taken before Keith joined him.

Keith continued. "I knew that story about going to see some buddies was fake. What kind of crap is that? You make up some lame story that you're going to Camp Lejeune. Seriously?"

"Sorry Keith. I didn't mean to-"

"How's that whole Semper Fi thing working out for ya? 'No' is a perfectly good answer, but don't give us some line of bull. Now we want you coming with us. We like having you around and you know there's a crazy Collie and three kids who have grown pretty fond of you, so eat your chow so we can get going. I'll take you by the rehab center so you can get packed."

Dixon chewed.

"I'll text Linda and let her know you're coming."

"I suppose she'll want to kick my butt or something."

"Probably. ...You don't want that Texan pissed at you. That's all I know."

Keith looked down at Jack as the two walked along the sidewalk. A slow and steady current of thoughts started filling his mind. Things had evolved since Jack came into their life. The reality was that Keith's original, simple plan of having a Collie as he did throughout his childhood was not working out as planned. First the hip problem, then the whole deal with using Jack at the rehab center as a therapy dog, then meeting up with Dakota and sharing Jack with him for tactical canine training. None of it was part of the plan. The way things were working out was about as far from simple and perfect as Keith or Linda could have imagined. He could have predicted none of the events that had occurred, and yet, somehow, they all seemed to flow into each other in a sort of unpredictable way that actually kind of made sense when he looked back on them. They all connected logically.

They enjoyed their friendship with Dakota. The children really liked him. Keith had trouble letting go of the idealistic vision in his mind. Part of him just wanted Jack, healthy, no complications, no other involvements, no tactical stuff going on, no therapy dog, just Jack and the family. Another part of him realized Jack had been through a lot, yet so had DX and things were working out well. Keith had this nagging sense that the vision would have to go. He would simply have to learn to roll with how things *were* instead of how he *wished* they were. As he accepted his new reality, he realized he was doing the same thing he had been trying to get across to Dakota and his circumstances.

His vision faded and this new reality began to take its place. He was adapting and becoming comfortable with it. He really enjoyed having Dakota as a friend. Maybe it wasn't that big of a deal. They had Jack. That was the general idea anyway. Keith was kind of proud that Jack had become a servant of the community. Keith was learning to see this idea of a simple Christmas gift as something bigger than he had imagined. Keith realized that Jack had changed him and the Barnes family in ways that he had never expected, good ways.

"Come on Jack! Let's run!"

-8-

This Old Cabin

The Barnes loved Christmas in the Colorado Rockies. This trip was both holiday and work as Keith hoped to fix more of the problems with the cabin. The list of issues seemed to keep growing and was draining their finances, forming an expanding mountain of debt, but Keith was thankful that Dakota was along to lend a hand.

After driving two-thirds of the way across country, the Barnes's Expedition, with Jack in the back, finally pulled into the small, valley town of Simpson's Creek, population six-thousand and one. Simpson's Creek was a former gold mining town dating back to the 1840's and the days of some early Colorado outlaws. It was rich with history and small-town mountain charm.

As he pointed the vehicle down the main street in town, Keith announced. "I need to make a quick stop in town before we head out to the cabin. I need to check Hank on some blueprints for the cabin." He drove up to Hank's office and pulled into a parking spot out front.

"I'll just be a minute or two. Why don't you guys take Jack and stretch your legs."

Sandra was thrilled. "Okay, Dad! Goodie!"

Keith headed into Hank's office for a quick status update. A few minutes later, he emerged from the two-story brick building with a cardboard tube containing the updated blueprints based on some modifications and adjustments he and Keith had discussed.

As Keith climbed back into the Expedition, the rest of the crew migrated back and piled into their seats. Linda walked back toward the vehicle from the sidewalk just as Hank came outside and waived to everyone.

Seeing Jack, Hank sauntered up to him and squatted down to pet the friendly Collie. Jack's ears folded back and he smiled in his customary way as Hank stroked his head and petted him. "Wow, this guy has really grown and turned into a real beauty."

"Yes he has," replied Linda. "Although he's had some rough patches, but he's doing great now, thanks to the kids helping out with his therapy and our friend here," motioning toward Dakota.

Keith introduced Hank. "Dakota this is Hank. He's working on the cabin. Hank, this is Dakota Dixon a friend of ours and Jack's. He's been training Jack."

Hank extended a hand. "Nice to meet you Dakota. Welcome to Simpson's Creek."

"Thanks. You as well Sir."

Hank waived to the group as he stepped back up on the curb. "Well it's great seeing all of you again. Hello, kids. I'll come out to the house tomorrow and check on the progress."

"Great. We'll have some hot cider waiting for you," replied Linda.

The family drove away down Simpson Street. Peering out the windows for a glimpse, everyone marveled at the beautiful small-town decorations strung across the street and the strands of garland wrapped around every lamppost, topped with a wreaths. The shops were each decorated in their own unique ways as well. To Linda the main street was a Currier and Ives post card, except for the lack of snow. People strolled along the sidewalks with their packages and bags from the local stores. The sound of Christmas music floated in the air, adding a merry soundtrack to the scene.

As the Barnes drove toward the outskirts of town, a few medium-sized snowflakes began drifting aimlessly down from the wintry-grey sky. The flakes were widely separated; not a major event to be sure, but even so, each flake fell, silently seeking its landing zone. The postcard was complete.

Jack looked out the window, intently observing everything. He had been out here once last year before his surgery. This time he would be able to play and romp in the snow since he was completely healed and much stronger.

The family soon arrived at their log home. Linda was first inside and sought out the thermostat to start up the furnace. "Wes, let's get a fire built in the fire place."

"Okay mom."

Keith let Jack out the back of the Expedition as the girls started carrying their bags into the cabin. Jack sniffed around the property, investigating all the new smells. He scoured the ground in the area around the front door. His only concern was detecting the presence of any recent four-legged visitors. You know, Fido pee'd here a week ago; that kind of thing.

The family finished settling in. In the kitchen, Linda and the girls were making hot chili and cornbread for dinner. In the living room, the fire crackled as Wes nursed it to strength. Keith looked over the current work that the contractor had done on the cabin. The sun began to set and the final glow of light in the sky slipped quietly away into the darkness. DX and the family gathered for a warming winter meal in the dining room.

"Wes would you call Jack inside please?" Keith requested.

"Sure Dad."

Jack came bounding inside the house with his smile and a slight pant. He had been enjoying himself, romping around the property. The place had been out of his Collie brain for a year, but some scents like that of some of the cedar in the cabin were familiar and his canine brain reconciled them with those of nearly a year ago.

As they cleared the dinner table, Linda asked Keith. "Are you thinking about doing some riding around on the ATV's tomorrow?"

"Yes. Wes, would you like to go ride around a little tomorrow? It would give you a chance to practice some more."

"Awesome! Yeah, Dad, I can't wait!"

"Okay. After breakfast we'll fire those beasts up and see where they take us." Keith turned to Dakota. "DX, you game?"

"Sure."

"Great. Sounds like a plan. Ok, kids, help me clear the table and cleanup."

The central feature of the cabin was a cozy and inviting two-story great room with a large stone fireplace. The walls were, of course, log and the portion of the upstairs that was visible was an open hallway with irregular shaped log railings. The scent from the fire wafted throughout the cabin as Keith and Linda each quietly enjoyed a book by the fire. The kids enjoyed themselves in the game room off to the side of the kitchen. DX was engrossed in something on his laptop as he sat on one of the stools by the kitchen counter.

Linda closed her book and stretched her arms out slowly. "I think I'll turn in."

"Okay, be right there as soon as I shut everything down and lock up."

She called toward the game room. "Guys, time for bed. Let's head upstairs."

DX continued working quietly. Linda patted him on the back as she walked by. "I'm really glad you're with us Dakota. ... I've put some linens and blankets in the guest bedroom for you."

"Thanks Linda, ... for everything."

"Good night," she said with a smile.

Everyone made their way upstairs in turn and within a few minutes, the whole family, except Jack and DX, was upstairs preparing for bed. Jack took up a strategic position at the base of the stairs. From there, he could look across into the great room and up the stairway while still hearing his adult masters upstairs as they occasionally tossed and turned in their beds.

A few minutes later, DX shut down his computer and turned in. He petted Jack and roughed up his fur gently. "Good night Jack buddy."

The family awoke to a beautiful, sunny, winter day in the valley. Linda cooked bacon on the open grill in the kitchen's center island. Soon everyone came downstairs, drawn by the combined scents of fresh coffee and bacon wafting upstairs. Jack paced around the kitchen area, sniffing at the ground. He had to consider the possibility that some morsel of food might have found its way to a lower altitude than the counter top or the table; if so, he would find it.

After breakfast, Keith, DX, and Wes headed out to the garage and opened it up to connect the ATV trailer to the back of the Expedition. Since they were not going very fast, Keith decided it would be good exercise for Jack to tag along. They took the ATVs further out into the valley to some open areas with wide passageways between the fir trees and other evergreens that dotted the landscape.

The mountains were jagged and beautiful. In an odd sort of way, Keith thought they felt like a backdrop of very tall, old friends watching over the group as they played on their ATVs.

When the group reached a pleasant meadow area at the base of some of the mountains, they stopped and parked.

"Dad how about you and DX show me some of what you guys have been working on? You know. The cool stuff!"

"Seriously?" questioned Keith.

"Yeah Dad, common. I wanna see DX beat your butt."

"Oh! Thanks Wes. I'm loving the sound of that already."

DX grinned. "Wes. What if we practice on you instead buddy?"

"Oh no! I'm not falling for that trick."

Keith demonstrated a few flips, throws and takedowns, and put on a bit of a show for Wes. Like any boy, he gobbled it up, especially when DX would turn the tables, sweep Keith, and take him down.

Several minutes later, the mini-workout ended and the two walked toward Wes and sat down on their ATVs. Both men breathed in the cold mountain air rapidly as they recovered from their exertion.

"So Keith, I've been thinking about some of the things I remember reading in your book; strategy and stuff like that. In the military, when it's a combat situation, your only objective is to defeat the enemy, but when it's a self-defense situation, how do you figure out what action or outcome to accomplish in a split second in the heat of the moment? What's your decision-process like?"

"Before the battle you have to know where you stand and what you would do. Get your priorities straight, that kind of thing. It's something I like to call the line of conviction. It's your tipping point. If someone goes too far or the situation reaches a certain point, you've already decided that's when you act and what action you would take."

"Ok, I think I see what you're saying," nodded DX.

"It's kind of a double edged sword, though. You also have a line of conviction about how *far* you will go. There are some actions or paths you simply won't take. It's not as black and white as combat on a battlefield. In the civilian world you have legal limitations depending upon the threat."

Dakota nodded as he thought through what Keith said.

"Not every threat requires a response. You have to make that call."

"Wow, that sounds familiar."

"Really?"

"Sounds like something my Grandfather taught me."

"Sounds like a wise man."

"He was."

"So you think these situations through and set your limits. When the time comes and you find yourself in one of these situations, the decisions have already been made. You know what to do. In a battle or a self-defense situation, you don't always have time to rationalize."

"Right. More reflex or reaction than conscious action."

"For the most part. You simply come to the realization that some line has been crossed that you have already thought about and you respond with an appropriate level of force. That's really what it's about – like law enforcement. You match your response to the level of the threat. So, I guess the answer to your question is, you have to assess the level of threat very quickly so that you know how to respond without going too far."

"Ok."

"The key is that you have to trust yourself and the decisions you have already made and trained for. You're already convicted in what you will do. Being in a real situation mainly comes down to recognizing when the time is necessary to do what you know must be done. ... That's my two cents anyway."

"Copy that."

The sky began to weave a very wintry blanket over the valley. The boys enjoyed several hours of exploring before the first light snowflakes began to fall. These new flakes quickly replaced those from yesterday, which had already nearly evaporated into the thin, Colorado air.

Later in the day, Hank stopped by to meet with Keith to review the progress on the repair work. DX joined them so that he could see where he might be able to pitch in and help. Keith and Hank came into the main house and visited with Linda for a short time as she delivered the promised hot cider. The rest of the day passed uneventfully and evening arrived at its usual time.

Allie and Sandra enjoyed playing outside with Jack just before dinner, but the sun had nearly disappeared behind the mountain peaks and it was time to head inside for the night. Jack, Sandra and Allie all tracked leaves and debris from the yard into the entrance where they hung their coats. At the end of the evening, Jack was once again at his post at the base of the stairs.

The few snowflakes that had fallen that afternoon and the day before were barely enough to qualify as even a light dusting. Several inches of snow fell earlier in December, but a few scattered patches of white stuff were the only remnants of that event. The new dusting looked as if it attempted to connect the clumps of older snow and blend them into a thin white blanket, but the result was not enough to pass for a blanketing of snow; not yet.

DX sat near the fireplace reading a book as Keith came in with a cup of coffee and sat on the couch near him.

"What are you reading?"

DX held up the book for Keith to see the cover. It was Keith's book. "The Way of the Martial Artist"; the one that had originally inspired the ideas DX had taught dogs to become more versatile and more well-rounded in their tactical skills.

"Thought you'd already read that?"

"Yes, but, like you say in here, 'review it often'."

Keith grinned.

"I'm reading the part about pursuing your passion."

"That's what it really all comes down to."

"Mine was getting the whole K9 training worked out. Breaking out of the old system of dogs trained for just one type of task. They are so much smarter than you can imagine, but we don't give them the time to show it."

Keith sat down with his coffee and listened as DX continued.

"They can tell us so much Keith. It's amazing."

"You certainly seem to have a way with Jack. It's like you two have your own wifi communications thing going on. I don't know how you do it."

DX looked down, searching for a way to tell Keith without revealing too much. "There are ways, very old ways. Most people don't take the time to learn or practice them, so the messages from Spirits are not always heard."

"Ok…." said Keith, as he raised an eyebrow partly out of fascination and partly with skepticism.

DX shook his head as if he had already said too much.

Later that day, a low-pressure front moved in and with it a frigid breeze that channeled its way directly through Thompson's Gap. Thompson's Gap provided a direct path from the northwest through the mountains. Through this pass, a steady stream of cold Canadian air began to blow. Linda saw on the local news channel that the weather forecast called for temperatures to drop into the teens overnight, and a storm front was expected to move in behind the low-pressure system, bringing significant accumulations of snow.

The next morning was Christmas Eve. The Barnes family woke up to more than two feet of new fallen snow, and large flakes were still coming down in a dense snowfall.

Sandra was slightly concerned and curious. "Daddy is Santa Clause going to be able to get through the snow?"

Linda answered her. "Now Sandra, you know that Santa always finds his way, especially since he has Rudolph's nose to light the way."

Christmas Eve afternoon, the snow finally ended. Linda called out to the kids. "Hey gang, time to get dressed and ready for Christmas Eve service."

The family was about ready to depart for town. Linda walked up to the breakfast bar and rested her palms on the counter top as she spoke to Dakota as he put a glass into the dishwasher. "DX. Would you like to join us at church this evening? They have a lovely candlelight service."

"I would like that a lot."

"Good. Oh, and thanks for helping Keith with the snow plow out in the driveway. That would have taken days to shovel by hand."

"Yeah, in earlier times, we would have just stayed in our Tipis and watched ESPN until it melted."

They both laughed.

The next morning, the family awoke and made their way to the family room. Santa had found his way through the blizzard. An array of beautiful packages was nestled under the tree, but one was slightly damaged. It had been torn partly open. Jack had already been busy.

"I guess Jack found the present with Christmas dog treats," laughed Keith. "Hey. Collies have to have a little Christmas too!"

Sandra looked at Keith somewhat confused. "Can Jack read the label? How did he know that present was for him Daddy?"

"I think his nose did the reading for him," responded Linda

"Oh yeah," she said as she realized the logic in what Linda said.

Jack barked as Keith knelt down to help him finish opening the package. Once Keith opened it completely, he handed Jack one of the treats. He gratefully gobbled it up.

"Merry Christmas everyone," exclaimed Linda.

Jack barked happily two times with his trademark smile and ears pinned back.

"Merry Christmas to you too Jack!" said Keith.

Jack barked two more times, getting in the last word-bark.

Thursday: January 3

Christmas in Colorado was memorable. With Dakota's help, Keith made good progress on some of the issues with the cabin. It was their last day in Colorado. The kids were theoretically in their rooms packing. Theoretically because Keith and Linda knew that a minimum of five requests were often required for kids to begin to even think about what Linda had asked them to do. Jack paced around the kitchen and dining room. There was always the possibility that something waited for him on the floor, or just maybe someone had left something on the table that he could snatch when no one was looking.

Keith and Dakota were outside in the driveway with the first group of bags. They were busy strapping them to the roof rack of the Expedition.

"DX?"

"Yeah?"

"I heard back from my agent friend at the FBI academy. I sent him the link to the demo video of you and Jack."

"Yeah?"

"He was very impressed. He'd like to meet you when we get back."

"Really? ... That's cool. I think... Any idea what he wants to talk about?"

"No, but he is interested."

"Right ... Wow. Thanks Keith. I don't know what to say."

"You'll like him. He's real laid back and easy going. He's a country boy from Georgia. He said he wanted to set something up for the week after next."

"This is great Keith. Not sure what it's about, but it's something. …I'm excited. So he wants to know more about Jack's training?"

"That's what he said. You never know what possibilities there are until you just start looking and asking."

KEVIN BRETT

-9-

The Unit

Monday: January 7

Dakota and Keith returned to working out a few times per week and training Jack, running him through a variety of tactical scenarios including obstacle courses. He set up several of these on trails in the woods behind the middle school.

After training with Jack in the fields or on the trails, Dakota stretched and worked to keep loosening his joints.

"How the body doing DX?"

"My joints are moving well and becoming stronger every day."

"Excellent."

"Even so, I'm still not at the level I was before."

"I hear ya."

"I was in rock solid shape – my unit was high-speed, low drag. Our motto was 'Lightning from the Sky, Thunder from the Sea'."

"That's intimidating."

"That's the idea. I'm moving with a lot more confidence and speed, but there is still a level of resistance in my knees and ankles when I run or jump. It's just like there's this subconscious wall or barrier, and I know it's there waiting to hold me back."

"Training will get you past that."

"I know. In the back of my mind, there's still that feeling of being trapped in my own body like the Tin Woodsman right before his joints got oiled up."

"Understood. ... Suppose we head back to the Emerald City and see what the Good Which of the South is up to?"

"Sure. ... Jack! Come!"

Linda heard the front door open. She stepped forward and leaned into the passageway from the kitchen to see who it was. "How did it go?"

"Good. Real good, Jack is amazing. He really inspires me. He's so eager. His surgery seems to have been a success. He's becoming quite strong and fast. Guess we're both recovering together. Kind of cool to have him as a partner."

"That's so awesome DX. I'm glad he's helping you. We sure appreciate what you've done for him."

"Linda. I need to let you and Keith know something."

"That almost sounds ominous. What is it."

"No, not at all. This whole meeting thing next week at the academy is great. I can't thank Keith enough, but before I go, there's something I need to do."

"What?" asked Keith.

"Well. I'm scheduled to be discharged in two weeks. I don't know what will happen with this meeting or interview or whatever it is at the academy, but this is a time when I feel that I must go back to tradition."

Linda looked interested, like she was trying, but it just wasn't clear where he was going. "I'm hearing ya DX, but what are you getting at?"

"My people have a tradition called Hembleciya. It means, 'crying for a dream'. Many know it as a vision quest. It is something that is often done when one reaches a turning point in life where we need to find ourselves and our intended life direction. "

"Okay ..."

"You might think of it like in martial arts where you meditate before or after a workout to clear your mind and focus on what you are about to do."

"Sure. I see what you mean. So how does your Hemb…"

"ham-blay-che-ya"

"How does it work? I mean. What do you do?"

"I must spend a few days alone … in the mountains, mediating, listening to nagi tanka – the Great Spirit. During this time, I cry out for a dream. … a dream of the future. It is how we see where we must go and know what we must do. Once the dream reveals itself, then we chase after that dream with the guidance and insight we received during the vision quest."

"That's really amazing. I love that. When will you begin?"

"Tonight. I will be heading out for about three days."

"Do you need one of us to give you a ride somewhere?" she asked.

"No. Thank you though. I have it covered. Thanks, but a buddy of mine should be here shortly to pick me up?"

Dakota read the map as his buddy Melvin, a fellow Marine, drove the Jeep west on Rt. 17 toward Warrenton, Virginia. DX had a small backpack with a few basic survival items and a small amount of food and water. They drove toward the Blue Ridge Mountains where Dakota would begin his vision quest.

A few hours later, they approached the entrance to the state park. Dakota grabbed his pack, said goodbye to Melvin and took off for the hills. Melvin backed up, turned the vehicle around, and glanced at his rear view mirror. He saw that Dakota had his pack on and a hiking stick then he drove off, heading east again. He knew Dakota possessed not only the survival and land navigation skills from years in the Corps, but even without that, Dakota carried with him the ancient ways of his people. It was still daylight as the half-Lakota set out to catch a glimpse into his soul and his destiny.

Saturday: January 12, 9:36 AM

Keith tried to balance the wireless phone on his shoulder while pressing it against his cheek as he spoke with Dakota. At the same time, he was mixing a batch of pancake batter. It was Saturday morning and he was finishing making the last few pancakes. He already had bacon and scrambled eggs with shredded cheese ready to go. It was a Bob Evans, down on the farm kind of morning.

"DX. You're missin' it buddy. We've got pancakes, eggs, toast with apple butter, bacon, OJ, coffee – the works. … You know, your basic white-man breakfast feast. You should come on over and get fat with us."

"You have a strange approach toward persuasion."

"Lemme guess, you're drinking pine cone tea with grass and dirt mixed in or some crap like that. You're probably trying to cleanse your colon or whatever – right?"

On the other end of the phone, Dakota read the morning paper as he savored the taste and the aroma of a cup of gourmet coffee at the *Before 'N After Cafe*. Beside his cup was a plate with the remnants of one of the café's specialty pastries with a few crumbs scattered around for effect; total white man food.

Dakota waited for Keith to finish expelling his sarcasm before responding with a little of his own. "You know Keith, for a white man …. You're just not funny dude? Your faster kicks don't mean you're also quick-witted. And for your info pal, my colon is just fine. But you're right, I'm sitting here at the cafe drinking pine cone tea with two teaspoons of dirt mixed in … Yeah, we'll go with that. And when I'm finished, I plan to eat the paper napkin for a little extra fiber. Now what do you want?"

"I want to know if you're planning on coming over here any time soon. We have your appointment at the academy in just over an hour."

"Well. I suppose if you guys can finish stuffing your faces sometime this morning I could mosey on over there. Melvin let me borrow his Jeep, so I can be there in five minutes."

"Do you have Jack's training gear and equipment?"

"Yes. It's in his training bag in the Jeep, all ready to go, and yes, I brushed my teeth this morning. Anything else Kimosabe?"

"Okay Tonto. We'll see you shortly. Finish drinking your dirt and get over here. If you want some real food, I'm sure we'll have plenty left. I think I made about six hundred pancakes."

"No thanks. They make my thighs look fat. … Later."

Keith grinned as he pressed the "end" button on the phone and continued flipping pancakes.

Saturday: January 12, 9:52 AM

Keith was planted in the passenger seat as Dakota drove the Jeep east on Garrisonville Road. They turned left on Onville Road next to the CVS Pharmacy and headed toward the Onville Gate for Quantico Marine Corps Base. The base was home to the Marines, but it also housed the FBI Academy within the Marine Corps Base in a separately gated campus. They traveled northwest until they reached the Onville gate. Once through the gate, Onville Road ended and the road name changed to MCB-2. They followed MCB-2 to MCB-3. Once they reached the intersection of MCB-3, Dakota turned right on MCB-4. From there it was a short drive along Lunga Reservoir where Keith often took the scouts camping. They approached the FBI gate at J. Edgar Hoover Road. Dakota slowed and gently coasted up to the gate where he waited for one of the FBI Police Officers.

"Can I help you gentlemen?"

Dakota lowered his sunglasses. "Yes Sir. We're here to see Special Agent Boone. He's expecting us."

"I'll need your names and IDs please."

"Sure thing."

Dakota and Keith both produced government IDs which Dakota handed to the officer.

"Wait here."

The officer went back to the guardhouse to verify the ID's and to look up in the visitor control system the names of Special Agent Boone's expected visitors. After verifying their IDs and matching them to the visitor log, the officer returned to the waiting vehicle.

"Your IDs check out, but according to the visitor control log there is supposed to be a third member in your party – a Captain Jack Barnes. Is he or she with you?"

Dakota responded. "Yes Sir. He's in the back."

"There's a dog back there," replied the officer.

"Roger that. He is Captain Jack – check the name tag."

"Okay. Check. You're good to go. So, you're a Lieutenant and he's a Captain?" inquired the officer.

Dakota grinned. "Yeah, he got promoted before I did."

"I hear you Sir. …Wait for the gait to lift and then you may proceed. Welcome to FBI Quantico."

"Thanks. Have a good one."

The gate rose and Dakota pulled ahead and proceeded down J. Edgar Hoover Road toward the office where Agent Boone waited.

Once they arrived, Dakota got Jack out of the back of the Jeep and put him down on the pavement. The three approached the building. They checked in at the front desk where they received visitor badges. The receptionist called Agent Boone to come meet his visitors. Jack sat and panted happily, as they waited. A few moments later, Jim came through one of the security turnstiles to greet them. He had a slight drawl as he spoke with a soft Georgia accent.

"Hey Keith. How are ya?"

"Good Jim. Thanks for having us. … Jim, this is Lieutenant Dakota Dixon. You already know Jack."

Jim reached out his hand toward Dakota who quickly shifted Jack's leash from his right hand to his left so he could shake hands.

"Nice to meet you Sir."

"Follow me and we'll walk back to my office."

Keith went through the turnstile as Jim opened a gate to allow Dakota to walk through with Jack. They headed down the hallway and around a corner to Jim's office.

"I have to say guys, that video you sent me gave me a bit of a chill."

"In what way Sir?"

"Please. Name's Jim. Least that's what my wife calls me most of the time," the three laughed before Jim continued.

"What I mean is Lieutenant, I've never seen a single dog trained to perform such a wide range of skills as what you've been able to teach Jack. That video was just amazing."

"Thank you Sir. Uh, Jim."

"Lieutenant …"

"Please … Dakota. I won't be a Lieutenant much longer."

"Dakota, as far as I know, tactical dogs are not taught such a wide variety of skills. They're usually just taught a single job and they do it very well. What you've done is … well, I hate to put it like this, but you've created a 'Jack' of all trades. … But a master of them too. It's really incredible to watch."

"Thank you Sir – Jim."

"It's almost like he can do anything."

"Well. That's pretty much the theory I had."

"What possessed you to take on such a task?"

"Well. I know how smart certain breeds are, and like you said. They're trained to do one job very well, but I thought, why couldn't I find a smart dog that could learn even more. You know, push the limits."

Jim nodded. "Right."

"Just because they normally only have one or maybe two jobs doesn't mean that, given time, a single dog couldn't learn many jobs, and then if you had that, you'd have a really versatile partner."

"I agree. I've just never seen it done before."

"Keith's book actually gave me the idea, the whole concept of the well-rounded and versatile martial artist with a broad range of skills."

"Ah yes, Keith and I have talked about that before. It certainly makes a lot of sense. I'm sorry guys. Please, have a seat. I just got started so quickly wanting to talk about the amazing work you've done that I lost my manners. Can I get you all some water or coffee or a soda or anything?"

Keith answered. "Oh, no Jim. I think we're good. Thanks."

Jack lay down between them and Jim continued as Keith and Dakota sat down. "So let me explain why I wanted to meet with you and Jack."

Dakota listened eagerly. "Sure."

"First, I wanted to see Jack go through some of his stuff in person," Jim smiled. "… or, in dog. Then I wanted to explain some new things that are going on around here at the academy and how I think we might have a use for you and Jack."

"Okay," responded Dakota.

Dakota and Keith both looked at each other curiously at Jim's phrasing, 'you and Jack'. Both ran the implication through their minds at the same time and their immediate reaction was slightly discomforting, but neither spoke. They listened as Jim continued.

"So what do ya say we head over to Hogan's Alley. Dakota you may be familiar with it. It's where we have a mock town that we use for training exercises and practice for new agents. It's a lot of fun."

Keith stood up as Jim did. "Sounds good. Let's go see what Jack's got up his sleeve."

"Great. I've got another agent I'd like you guys to meet. He's a tactical dog trainer and handler also."

"Let's do it," said Dakota.

Saturday: January 12, 10:12 AM

The trio of Keith, Dakota, and Jack followed in the Jeep as Jim led the way in a government car to the mock town Hogan's Alley. They parked their vehicles and Jim walk toward his visitors.

"So here we are. This town was named after an 1800 era cartoon about a bad neighborhood with a lot of crime. The FBI decided that was an appropriate since there are drug dealers on every street corner, fights breaking out in bars, and the local bank is robbed like clockwork several times per week, and that's not even counting all the potential terrorists lurking in the bushes."

"Sounds lovely," grinned Keith.

"Of course, the perpetrators in the town are actually role-players there to give us and other law enforcement agencies the chance to hone our skills in a realistic setting." Jim held up his index finger. "I'll be right back."

He walked a few yards away to a small group of people on the sidewalk outside of a brick townhouse. They listened to one man who was giving them some pointers and tips about handling a certain type of situation. Jim waited a moment for the man to finish, and then the speaker turned to Jim and greeted him. "Hi Mike. I've brought the folks I told you about and the dog. They're waiting over there in the parking lot."

"Great, let's check it out."

The two headed toward Keith, Dakota, and Jack. Jack sat politely, panting slightly, observing the two men as they approached. Jim introduced everyone. "Guys, this is Special Agent Mike Pearson. He's a tactical dog trainer with the Bureau."

"Mike, this is Lieutenant Dakota Dixon and Keith Barnes, and this guy here is Captain Jack."

Keith and Dakota nodded and everyone shook hands.

Jim led the conversation. "So, Mike, I asked them to come over here today because Keith sent me a link with a video of Jack doing some really great tactical drills and exercises.

"Ok."

"Dakota is scheduled to be discharged from the Corps shortly and I was thinking that his training skills and Jack's special abilities might be a good fit for some of the things we discussed last week."

Again, Keith and Dakota looked at each other with a slight cringe when Jim mentioned the idea of Jack being a good fit. Jim probably meant well, but his comment about Jack came across a bit presumptuous.

Mike picked up from Jim's lead. "Okay, well, I don't know what you all have in mind. Why don't we head over into that grassy area near the edge of town and Dakota, I guess you can take it from there and show us what Jack can do."

"Yes Sir." Dakota looked at Jack and their eyes met. Immediately Jack stood up and Dakota walk forward with Jack at his side as the group walked to the field. Keith had Jack's training bag, with props and other accessories. As they walked, Mike inquired about Dakota's training. "So, Jim tells me that you've been teaching Jack a lot of different tactical concepts."

"Yes Sir. I've had this theory that if you had a smart dog breed like a Collie, you could teach the dog a wide variety of techniques that are normally taught to separate dogs with separate roles and duties. Kind of like an ultimate tactical dog or K9 warrior."

Mike was polite, but clearly, skeptical. "Hmm. Interesting. Never seen that done before. Dogs just normally can't handle all the different training modes and behavior adjustments required to play multiple tactical roles. That's why we have several dogs so that each has his own specialty, just like with human specialists. Keeps things simpler and doesn't take as long to train them."

"I understand."

"Also makes it easier to replace one if he gets injured or becomes too old, the dogs that is."

"I understand. My thinking was that if we put the dog through a lengthier training program, you could build on his skills from there. Then only one handler would be required with one or maybe two of these dogs instead of multiple handlers for multiple dogs. It would make for simpler logistics. One dog could do more."

"Sounds good in theory, but …"

Jim interrupted. "Mike, let's just give him a look. If there's anything to it, this could change the way we train. An open mind is a beautiful thing."

The group stood at the far edge of the field as Dakota removed a few items from Jack's training bag. Jack proceeded to spend the next twenty minutes going through his paces and performing a variety of stunts, tactics, maneuvers, guard tactics, attack maneuvers, weapons disarms, and search and rescue techniques. The drill clearly demonstrated that Jack possessed many more skills than the average tactical K9. He moved with ease through the material Dakota had taught him. When he finished, he and Jack came over to the edge of the field where Keith and the agents stood.

"That's just a sample of what I've been working on with him, but I think you get the idea."

Mike's skepticism still lingered. "Nice moves, but I would worry about a dog being overwhelmed in a real situation and freezing up. It's just too much responsibility for one dog and one trainer to have to maintain the level of training and proficiency required to perform in a reliable manner. We have really high standards and expectations for all of our dogs. They have to perform their jobs with almost 100 percent efficiency and reliability."

Dakota tried to address Mikes' concern. "Obviously I've never taken Jack out in a real situation, but I've been working with him for months and I can vouch that he is quite reliable."

"Like I said, the standards are high and the more you pile on, the harder it is to meet them."

"My only point was to prove that it could be done and that a single dog *could* take on multiple roles. Jack is obviously capable. I've worked with other breeds and they just don't train quite as easily when you throw a lot of tasks at them. You're right it is a lot for one animal, but usually it's the German Shepherds or the Belgians that law enforcement and the military use. The Collie is a very different breed. They're used to working independently and solving problems on their own, more so than the others."

Mike became slightly defensive at Dakota's comments about law enforcement dogs. "We've never used Collies before. They have light frames and are often small-boned, not as durable sometimes as Shepherds or Belgians."

Dakota was surprised how the agent kept maneuvering and framing the conversation to put him on the defensive. He didn't see the point, and he could not understand how he was allowing himself to be forced into justifying his points. He remained calm and in control of his facts. "I completely understand, but you may remember that during World War II, Collies were one of the top five breeds used by the military for many of these duties, *because* they are so smart and easy to train. Even today, they are one of the top three breeds still approved by the military. They just don't use them a lot unless they are the short-haired variety."

Mike continued his justification. "Yeah, because of all their long fur. They don't do so well in hot environments. The rough Collies are for colder climates," agreed Mike.

"Understood, but the short-haired or smooth Collies still have the smarts, just not all the thick fur."

"Yeah, but Collies are still sort of delicate."

"Sir, I don't mean to be argumentative, but a reasonably strong Collie can easily take a wolf or a German Shepherd or any of the Husky breeds in a fight. Because of their lighter frame, they are much more agile and still have the teeth and tremendous bite strength as well as the ability to slash like a wolf. Shepherds can't do that as well, they don't have the narrow turning and pivot radius and they are just not as fast learners."

"Sounds like you came over here to tell us we don't know what we're doing. Anything else you'd like to correct while you're at it?"

"Sir, I'm not here to tell the Bureau anything. Agent Boone simply asked me to come by and show you what I've been able to accomplish with Jack. No criticism intended. I thought we were having a technical discussion."

Jim jumped in to smooth things over. "Okay, Mike. Dakota is right. I just wanted you to see some new possibilities. I thought we might learn something and get some ideas about how we could use Jack or dogs like him."

"Got it, but what he's talking about is a whole change in the way we do things."

"I realize that," nodded Jim.

"That would potentially re-write the whole training program and all of our protocols. What he's proposing would be like starting from scratch. That's huge."

Jim countered cautiously in a soft reassuring drawl. "Mike, I'm not talking about changing what we already do. I just wanted to consider the possibility that we might add some new capabilities with a small group of dogs that could be more versatile for special types of engagements. We'd still have the regular training program for the dogs and missions that we have now. Instead of just the limited tactical roles, these dogs would be special operators, multi-faceted like

- 148 -

any SpecOps operator would be with the Bureau or the Corps or any other SpecOps organization."

Mike was not letting go of his criticism. "I'm not a fan of the idea. I think adding all those roles to one dog would be like building a house of cards. When the time really counts and you need to rely on the dog, it might all come crashing down. Right when you might need them to do something, they might freeze up, and then you have human operators at risk. That's my concern."

"Are you sure that's it?"

"Yeah Jim. … Dakota, Keith, thanks for your time. I really have to go. We're getting ready to start another exercise here shortly."

Agent Pearson headed back across the street. Jim's hands were in his pockets as he stared at the ground in front of his feet. Then he looked up. "Well. I'm sorry guys. That was not how I hoped it would go."

"Not at all Jim," assured Keith.

"I believe there is a lot of value in what Dakota has been doing. I think it is possible, just because it hasn't been done doesn't mean it can't be done. Jack, here, is one heck of an impressive dog."

"Thank you Jim. I'm sorry. I didn't mean to become argumentative with Agent Pearson."

"Quite alright. Mike, doesn't like to have his authority challenged. It's somewhat of an occupational hazard, but he's really proud of the work that he's done with the current program.

"Understood."

"When I suggested this idea to him he immediately got defensive with me too. It's my job to be on the lookout for new ideas, new paradigms and to make sure we have the best capabilities and the right mix of capabilities. It's Mike's job to train the canine teams and agents and sort of maintain the status quo. Sometimes our two different roles can cause some friction. But Mike's really a great guy. You just have to know how to stay off his hot buttons."

Dakota nodded. "Well. I still didn't mean for things to go that way."

"No harm done. Besides, he works for me, so if I decide that we're going to try some new things, he'll get behind the program and be the number one advocate of whatever the program is doing. It just takes him a while to warm up to change sometimes."

Dakota nodded. "I can certainly relate to that."

"So I have a question Dakota."

"Shoot."

"What Jack did was amazing. What I found more amazing is that the entire time he was out there, you didn't give him a single command; nothing verbal and I watched for hand signals. Only a few. How do you explain that?"

"Actually it is a little difficult to explain. I guess the best I can say is that after I have worked with a dog for a while, we just sort of connect. We understand each other."

"I see that, but still. How did he know what you wanted him to do next?"

"We have our own way of communicating. He seems to know what makes sense next."

"Well. That's the darndest thing. It was like you were reading each other's minds."

Dakota looked down sheepishly and grinned.

"I'd like to understand that a little better sometime."

Keith jumped in. "Jim, I really appreciate you inviting us out here and for this chance to show what Jack can do."

"Well. I'd like to go back to my office and tell you what I have in mind."

"Let's go," said Keith.

Saturday: January 12, 11:17 AM

Back at Jim's office, Jack lay comfortably on the floor as the three men spoke. Jim began to explain why he was so interested in Dakota and Jack. "Dakota. What is your clearance level if you don't mind my asking?"

"Uh. It's Top Secret."

"Great. That will be handy. I assume it's still active?

"Yes Sir."

"Good. So we could just transfer your clearance over to your new agency."

"My new agency?"

"You may or may not be aware, but the FBI works with a wide variety of state, local, federal and international law enforcement organizations and the intelligence community. Pretty much anyone who wears a badge I guess you could say."

Keith and Dakota listened intently.

"What I can say is that the Bureau is working with some organizations that could benefit from the types of capabilities that you and Jack have demonstrated. Now, Keith mentioned that you were undergoing some physical therapy?"

Dakota nodded. "Yes. I got a little banged up in Afghanistan."

"So what I saw out there with Jack, you look like you're pretty well recovered."

"Getting there. Keith's actually been helping a lot with that too. We've been doing a lot of martial arts training together for the past few months. That's been a huge help."

"Great. So you have a martial arts background?"

"Well, I mean, you probably know about MCMAP. I understand some of the agents work with the Marines on that. I'm a brown-belt, and since meeting Keith he's been cramming my brain full of new material and techniques as well. So Jack and I have both been learning a lot."

Keith jumped in. "He's definitely black-belt material, not quite yet, but in another year or two he will be."

"Outstanding. Well, the combination of you and Jack is really something to see, and again, that whole mind-reading or non-verbal communication thing you do still blows my mind. I'm surprised Mike didn't pick up on that."

Dakota had to intervene. "Sir, I don't mean to cut you off and this all sounds very intriguing, but Jack is not mine. He's Keith's."

"Oh, of course, I understand. But here's the deal. We would need you on board with these capabilities in less than a month. From where I'm sitting, you and Jack could play a major role and it would give your theory, which I would say is now a reality, a chance to be put into action. Keith could have Jack back, of course in a couple of months, but right now we're coming up on a critical deadline and I really need you and Jack on the team."

"Sir-"

"Jim," interrupted Jim trying to keep it less formal.

"Jim. Jack is not mine to offer or to loan out. I simply used him to try out my ideas and demonstrate that they could work. If you want me and the dog capabilities I could find another dog to work with."

"Dakota I'll be straight with you. There isn't time to train another dog. We need Jack."

Keith's eyebrows had been tightening the whole time as he listened. "Jim, how long *are* we talking about for whatever this is that you're wanting him for?"

"It would start in less than a month and would last nominally about three weeks – we hope. So, like I said, a couple of months give or take."

Keith inhaled slowly as he tried to process the situation. He remained silent as he and Jim stared at each other. Dakota broke the silence. "Gentlemen, Jack is *not* an option. He belongs to the Barnes family."

Jim looked down at his desk, then up again, first at Dakota, then at Keith. "Guys, I truly understand what you're saying, but this is a unique capability. The timing is good because by the time we get started, Dakota will be out of the Corps. He has the right skills and clearance for our purposes and this is a vital matter. Once we are finished, we'll return Jack to you and we'll work on finding other dogs to replace him. … Let me give you a little history lesson. Dakota, you mentioned using dogs during World War II. There's a little more to the story that you both may or may not know. During World War II, the military put out a call for war dogs. They needed a large number of dogs to perform a variety of tasks as you've mentioned. They were trained for specialized positions like, scout to find enemies waiting to ambush our troops, guard dog, ambulance dogs to find injured soldiers, and so on. But, like Dakota has been saying, each dog was really only assigned and trained for a single task. Families were asked to contribute to the war effort by volunteering their dogs. They could even choose which service the dog would go to. If the family wanted, they could also pay a small sum of money to purchase a rank for the dog and that money would help pay some of the expenses of the dog."

"So what are you getting at Jim?" asked Keith.

"There was actually the Collie mascot, Reveille, from Texas A&M. He was ranked General and thousands of other dogs ranged in rank from Private to Sergeant and various officer ranks."

Keith tightened his eyebrows as he listened.

"I'll be perfectly blunt. My point is that back then, people weren't happy about it, but they gave up their dogs in service to their country. It was the patriotic thing to do, and these dogs were a huge help and a valuable asset to our troops."

"So you want Keith the volunteer Jack," said Dakota.

"Jack could serve a similar purpose today and we really need his help. But today we need a very specialized type of dog, and as far as I know, Jack is the only one."

Keith and Dakota were silent as Jim's words weighed on both of them. Jim started back up. "I know I'm asking a lot."

Dakota started up. "Jim, my only reason for bringing Jack here today was to demonstrate what was possible, not to volunteer Jack."

"I understand."

Keith took a turn. "Jim. I don't like the idea. Not that I don't want to help, but Jack is just a family pet. That's why we bought him. He was a Christmas gift for the kids and unfortunately, he's had some problems that required surgery before he was even a year old. Not exactly the best gift depending upon how you look at it. ... I understand your sense of urgency. ... So the point of having Dakota is to be Jack's handler and you don't have time to set him up with a different dog."

"Exactly. We start in just a few weeks. We couldn't train a new dog to do half of what Jack can do. ... See my predicament."

"Understood."

"You came to me with this interesting idea and the timing is perfect. I'm saying it's an incredible capability and there's the quandary."

Keith questioned Jim. "How soon would you need an answer?"

"As soon as possible. We would need to start prepping Dakota and Jack and getting them used to other team members. The people who are interested are part of an organization called the OST – Office of Strategic Technology. They are part of the government responsible for the development and tracking of game-changing technologies. Dakota would become an agent in their organization. I'm merely responsible for building the team. I mean, like, Monday at the latest."

"Wow…." said Keith.

Dakota realized that Keith might be considering letting Jack go. Keith queried Jim again. "Three weeks huh?"

Jim nodded. "I can't just say yes. I have to discuss this with Linda and then we have to let the kids know."

"Just remember Keith, it's not forever. Tink of it as Jack taking a trip."

"And what if something happens to him?"

"There's always that possibility, but this is a highly trained and specialized team. Our whole approach is to minimize risk, not create it."

"I'll have to take the rest of the weekend Jim. I just don't know. This is crazy. I just never …. Jack is our first family dog. Now you want to turn him into Jack Bond or something."

"I understand, but like I told you, during the wars, that was a common thing that people did and they made the sacrifice."

Keith stood up. "Alright Jim, thanks for your time. We'll get back to you."

The men shook hands and Keith, Dakota, and Jack headed back out to the Jeep. The ride home what very quiet. Both men were deep in thought. After several minutes, Dakota broke the silence. "Keith, I don't have to be part of this organization. He knows what Jack can do. He knows that my training methods have been more or less proven. You don't have to do this. I get the mission. Every mission is critical in some way. That's my job, but that doesn't mean you, Linda, the kids and Jack have to go along with it. I can find another Collie and do the same thing, but that's later."

Keith looked out the passenger window, staring blankly at the passing trees, but listening.

He wanted to help Dakota, but how would the kids take it? What Dakota wasn't telling Keith was that during his vision quest he saw himself separating from the Marine Corps and finding a new dog companion. It wasn't totally clear, but he sensed that it was a new dog, not Jack, yet he also saw the Barnes saying goodbye to Jack. He envisioned a situation where Jack was in grave danger. Nothing was clear, but he sensed that he was on a mission with Jack, but at the same time, he also sensed a different dog was involved somehow. They were just fragments. He couldn't put them together so he just kept quiet about it. Dakota knew that somehow his future involved training and working with dogs, but the where and the how was unclear. It might not have even involved the FBI. He didn't know.

Keith broke through the clutter of thoughts flashing like fireflies sparking rapidly in his brain. "DX. I don't know what's going to happen. Definitely have to sleep on this one. I want to help *you* more than I care about helping the Bureau. Nothing against them, but that's not where I'm coming from. Linda and I are going to have to have our own mini-vision quest if we're going to figure out what to do with this situation."

"Keith. You guys have -"

"Just save it. We'll figure out what makes sense. We haven't come all this way to pull the plug."

They rode in silence the rest of the way.

Saturday: January 12, 12:43 PM

Linda was silent. She sat down in the wing chair in the corner of their bedroom and put her elbows on her knees and hid her face in her hands. Keith could hear her sniff as she began to cry. "Are you kidding me Keith? You're saying that Jim wants to take Jack from us and use him as part of some organization with Dakota and that there's a possibility he might be killed?"

"Jim isn't taking him from us. He's borrowing him … and no one said anything about Jack being killed."

"You didn't have to. I can read between the lines."

"I don't like the idea, but Dakota's chances of getting into this new unit or a new line of work are pretty much dependent upon being able to have Jack go with him."

"Keith …. Jack is our family pet. I can't believe you would offer him to the FBI."

"I understand. I told Jim, and so did DX, that we only brought Jack to show what Dakota could do with a dog. Neither of us had any idea he would drop that little grenade in our laps."

"But you're thinking of going along with it. Jack isn't some karate, FBI, whatever, war dog. He was a Christmas present for the kids. How's that going to work?"

"Babe I know. It's crazy. I'm kind of ticked at Jim for not giving me some heads up about what he was thinking."

"So you're okay with this? Loaning out Jack and hoping he comes back in one piece?"

"I didn't say that, but we both trust DX and if he doesn't have Jack with him then this opportunity could just evaporate into thin air. The need is now."

When she spoke, her voice was rough as she struggled through her tears. "How on earth are we going to explain this to the kids?"

Keith reached in his pocket and handed her a handkerchief.

"Well. Nothing has been as we thought it would be since we got Jack. Life just keeps throwing these weird curveballs. We also never thought we'd be taking him to the rehab center or spending time with troops, but we both agreed that's been a wonderful thing and now we have a new friend as a result."

Linda wiped her eyes and nose, then wadded the hankerchief in one hand and held her head up pressing her cheek into her fist with her elbow on one knee. Her thoughts and emotions collided somewhere inside as she tried to sort out the pros and cons. She struggled to see where any part of this picture made sense or gave her some handle to latch on to to figure out how to look at this new turn of events.

"I'm just trying to look at it from the angle that we're helping DX instead of that we're sending Jack off on some mission. That's the only way that lets me think it's ok to do this."

"So you think we should do this?"

Keith looked at Linda, both of their brains raced and reached for the rationale that would allow them to have some comfort in a decision that they both knew they did not want to make.

"I think it will work out okay. And I think the kids will understand."

Saturday: January 12, 2:37 PM

Wes blurted out. "So he's going to be like a secret agent?! …. Coooool!"

Keith looked at Linda. "Okay … Not what I expected…."

Allie and Sandra sat beside each other on the large footstool in front of the oversized easy chair in the family room. Allie, being the older of the two grasped the significance of what Keith had said. She teared up. Sandra was a little too young to really understand it enough to be much more than just curious. "So Jack's going away to stop bad guys?"

Keith tried to help her understand. "Sort of, but he'll be with a bunch of police and Dakota will be taking care of him. So we're just letting Dakota borrow him for a little while."

Allie was quiet as she processed what her dad had said.

Linda jumped in. "Guys. We all think DX is a really good friend don't we?"

The girls nodded. Wes listened half-heartedly. He was already cool with the vision in his mind of Jack running around basically playing paintball.

Linda continued. "DX has really done a lot to help Jack become better trained and he's helped him grow a lot stronger. … Now we have a chance to help DX. It's a good thing to be able to help our friend don't you think?"

"Mmmm Hmmm," replied Allie as Sandra nodded her head.

"So we're going to let DX borrow Jack for just a little while and then he'll bring him back home and he'll be all done. Do you understand?"

"Sure mom. DX will take good care of Jack and feed him every day and give him plenty of water right?" queried Allie.

"Of course, you know how much DX loves Jack."

"But Jack will still be ours right?"

"Yes, of course. We're not giving him away," assured Linda.

"Okay. ... I hope he helps DX catch lots of bad guys."

Linda smiled and turned her eyes toward Keith. They both realized they had more or less made the breakthrough that they needed. Sandra trusted her older sister to make sense of things at this point and determine if it was okay. Linda responded to Allie. "I'm sure he will sweetie. I know he will. You know when Jack smells trouble, he's always there to help."

Sandra tilted her head a little. "Mom ... What do bad guys smell like?"

Saturday: January 13, 1:07 PM

Keith and Dakota sat at the kitchen table drinking coffee.

"DX, we have already decided. It's not forever; a few weeks or so. Big deal. You're going to be fine and so is Jack."

Wes came walking in. "Hey DX, when you get out of the Marine Corps will you grow a Mohawk then?"

DX grinned, grabbed Wes and spun him around to tickle his ribs. "I might. Maybe for Halloween."

"Awesome! That would be cool. Maybe you could scalp the girls. They could use it. Nothing in their heads anyway," he giggled, as DX got him again for talking mean about his sisters.

DX pretended to get serious for a moment. "My people have a saying young brave."

"What?" laughed Wes, trying to recover from the tickling.

"When a man mocks his sisters to another, he is telling them him he admires them and will protect them."

"Yeah, like that's totally me. You're making that up."

"No, really. It's been a saying of my people."

"Since when?"

"Since about 10 seconds ago!"

"See. I knew. Just scalp 'em and get it over with," laughed Wes.

Keith intervened. "Wes, you're really pushing it buddy. Now, let DX and me finish please."

Dakota warned Wes. "Just watch your back dude. I may have to practice on you first!"

Dakota made two fingers pointing toward his eyes, then pointed them toward Wes indicating, 'I'm watching you.' Wes grinned and scampered off upstairs. Jack immediately scrambled to his feet at the sight of Wes on the loose and chased him down, growling and barking until he came to the bottom of the stairs and could go no further as Wes bolted up the steps.

Dakota shook his head as Jack took off as if chasing down a stray sheep. "Now that's instinct for you. Always herding. ... The force is strong within this one."

Keith laughed. "By the way I spoke with Jim this morning and he mentioned that there would be no problem with the physical fitness waiver. Since you're not going to be a regular Special Agent that requirement does not apply, you're more of a technical agent specialist. It's what they call a unique or highly qualified skills. You're the only one who has done this so that's why they're interested. The OST can hire you regardless. Jim said they would put together your job offer package and have it ready to pick up in a couple of days."

"Jeez Keith. This is really happening fast. It's hard to believe it's becoming a reality."

"Linda and I are incredibly thrilled for ya. I think it's going to work out okay."

Monday: January 28

Dakota was officially out of the Marine Corps. Since he was a young boy, he had listened to his grandfather tell the stories of serving during World War II. He wanted to serve in an honorable way as young men of every generation had done in the Lakota Nation. Now, because his injuries, he had been given a medical discharge. The course of his life was about to change. It started when he met the Barnes. Actually, it started that fateful day in Afghanistan. In that explosive blink of an eye; those miserable few seconds, lives ended, were impacted, and routed onto totally different trajectories.

It was time for a new beginning, new chapters. He felt that these next steps were part of the path to fulfill his vision quest. Jack was central to that as far as Dakota could determine. It seemed logical. Dakota had a thought, a sense, or a passing vision that he, Keith and Linda all had the same perspective. They all saw in their minds the same future or the same outcome to this course of events. Now, like some stage play, they all began to play the parts, embody the roles, and realize the course of the plot as though an invisible playwright had sketched out the basic flow of events already and the actors were realizing the playwright's vision.

The ironies made it that much more surreal. He had read Keith's book and fully embraced its concepts. The essence a true warrior; a noble soul who sought to serve his people; to protect the weak and defenseless and stand against aggressors. It was the code of the Samurai; it was the code of chivalry, of warriorhood, of the Marine Corps. Now he was continuing to follow that calling in a new form.

Wednesday: January 30
About three weeks to Go-Time

Dakota and Jack reported to Jim's office at the FBI Academy at 0700 Monday morning as directed. It was cold and damp and the wind was not particularly strong, but definitely a few notches above the "gentle breeze" label on the windy scale. Bleak light cast a cold hue across the campus. While he was excited to be there, the dismal wintry pallor that coated everything gave him an unwelcomed feeling, nothing against the FBI, this one was on Mother Nature.

Jim explained things as they walked. "We need to get you to the quartermaster for special operations. He will assign you a room in the training barracks. You and Jack will live here for several weeks while you're training."

Once Dakota dropped off a few personal belongings in his room, including dog food for Jack, he returned to Jim's office to report in. Jim took Dakota over to a classroom facility inside one of the buildings of Hogan's Alley; there Jim introduced Dakota and Jack. Agent Pearson was also there, sitting on the edge of a table on the small raised instructor platform in the front of the room. The other members of the team sat in the first few rows of theater-like seating. Dakota took a seat in the front row and made Jack sit on the floor beside him.

Agent Pearson stood up in front. "Gentlemen and lady, I would like to introduce the head of this new joint unit, from MI-6, by way of the British Royal Marines, Colonel Montgomery Wellington. .... Sir..."

Colonel Wellington stood up from his seat in the front row a few down from Dakota. He had the typical stiff, and proper British air about him as he stepped up onto the platform and rather quickly spun around. Dakota thought, the only thing missing was a riding crop tucked securely inside his arm. Dakota knew from working with the coalition forces overseas that while he might seem prim and proper in a briefing, the Royal Marines were some very crusty souls; among the best, just not quite up there with the U.S. Marines in Dakota's mind, but that was his professional bias. Wellington's salt and pepper hair indicated more than simply age. It conveyed experience and knowing the Brits, an ample supply of raw grit picked up along the way. As that thought expired in his brain, he could almost hear the voice of his DI at Officer Candidate School at Quantico reminding the platoon. "On the eight day, God created Marines."

Wellington's voice snapped Dakota back to reality. "Thank you Agent Pearson. Welcome to *Operation Light Saber*. Would someone cut the lights please?"

Colonel Wellington picked up a remote control from the podium and pointed it toward the projector in the back of the room. The first slide of a presentation appeared on the screen as he began to speak. When he did so, Agent Pearson flipped a switch on a control panel near the door which lit up several electronic signs around the room to indicate the level of the briefing. These signs were a reminder to the participants of the level of information to which they were being exposed. The signs read. "Top Secret."

"You are all cleared, so when I say that this organization, it's purposed and missions are Top Secret, you understand the international significance of maintaining that status.

I have been appointed chief of operations for a new international law enforcement unit for weapons tracking and recovery. It has been created as a partnership between Interpol through its European-based Fusion Task Force for counterterrorism, named Nexus and the United States Office of Strategic Technology (OST). This unit is not officially an Interpol unit and neither is it a unit of the United States or the United Kingdom. We do not officially exist. The Secretary General of Interpol, the U.S. Secretary of State and the Foreign Ministers of the other countries do not even know this unit exists. We have been given the code name *Striker-1*. Outside of our technical support team and those of you in this room, only six other people know this unit exists. We are strictly a black program. As you can see by looking around the room at your team members, it is composed of special operators from many of the top law enforcement and intelligence agencies on the planet, OST, FBI, British Royal Marines, Interpol, U.S. Joint Special Operations Command (JSOC), U.S. Marshal's Service, Bundespolizei (BPOL) - the German Federal Police, and of course Her Majesty's MI-6.

Normally an organization such as Her Majesty's SAS, Navy SEALS or Delta Force would be used in such situations. We have a different mission. I'm sure you chaps are all aware that international weapons smuggling is an old problem. Interpol has addressed it to some degree with their firearms tracking, individual countries have tracked the issue on a case-by-case basis, and various militaries such as the Yanks and the Ministry of Defence and NATO have put forth their own efforts when the need arose. Several top-level meetings have been held between Interpol and our various governments on the matter of weapons smuggling. The conclusion was that a capability to deal with these arms networks should be created. The participants in these meetings have no further knowledge than that. Our objective is to prevent or disrupt the transport and storage of these weapons *before* they even fall into the hands of terrorist operatives.

We are going to choke off the supplies of weapons going from dealers to organized crime and terrorist organizations at the source. However, in order to keep our targeted arms smugglers and cartels guessing and on the defensive, we must keep this organization utmost secret to maximize our advantage and the element of surprise. If they know that a new force exists, then they know to start attempting to infiltrate or counter our efforts in any way they can.

This unit is the first operational strike team. We will be backed with intelligence and communications support from Interpol and the U.S. Center for Counterterrorism using back channel networks and protocols so that even Interpol operators will be unaware that we are tapping into their databases and communications systems. Logistics and transportation will be provided by various sources depending upon the specifics of the mission.

This thirteen-person unit has been created for tracking international weapons smugglers, but not your typical smugglers. We are going after those blokes dealing in specialties, unique weapons, and those that provide strategic advantage. We are not concerned with run of the mill handguns or even automatic weapons; we're in the market for exotic goods. Are there any questions so far?"

When the Colonel stopped speaking, the only sound permeating the darkened room was the fan from the projector. Everyone had the same thought, 'He stopped just when it was about to get interesting.'

"If there are no questions then I will begin with the top level mission profile. We will be training for approximately three weeks, possibly longer until we receive confirmation of go-time.

The problem, gentlemen, is this … A band of international weapons merchants have stolen a prototype and several early production models for a new, man-portable laser Gatling gun, along with its operating instructions. These are intended to be next-generation battlefield weapons developed by NATO. NATO has asked Interpol for help in tracking the criminals and officially, Interpol has declined assistance other than to provide intelligence.

We are waiting to receive critical intelligence from Interpol elements that are already trying to locate these smugglers. They are doing this under the auspices of being a part of a normal Interpol weapons tracking operations. Interpol is working with the CIA and MI-6 to determine where the weapons have been taken. Once we have the data we need on the location and numbers of operatives we will move in. Our mission is to retrieve or destroy these weapons. Interpol knows the ID of the leader of the group that stole the weapons from a U.S. base in Germany. We are not even privy to that information.

The leader is a member of an international weapons cartel that is attempting to supply weapons to what we suspect are Russian-backed rebels living in Romania. These rebels are ethnic Hungarians. They live in Romania, but are politically in the minority and do not agree with the completely Romanian dominated political apparatus. A growing segment of the population in the northern regions of the country holds strong contempt for Romanian nationals. There has been friction and growing animosity between these regions of ethnic Hungarians and the native Romanian peoples for decades. The Hungarians resent being in the minority and have been building what we would consider to be underground resistance movements. We suspect that they want to overthrow the government of Romania at some point and install their own idea of the Romanian government. Somehow, they think that they will take on the Romanian military and stage some form of coup. There are also intelligence reports that suggest that elements of Romanian military might actually be involved or at least sympathetic to the movement. This would explain why they seem to have turned a blind eye to the movement of weapons in an out of the country. We're really not sure, it could be that that rebels are paying off local military figures to look the other way. It is even possible that the smugglers are simply planning to sell the weapons on the black market to the highest bidder.

What further complicates things is that we believe that the rebels are not just weaponizing for this cause, but also potentially supporting underground groups of Bosnian Serbs who may have an interest in rekindling hostilities in Bosnia and Herzegovina. In fact, we're concerned that like all good arms smugglers, they are supplying whomever is the highest bidder and they may have links to many fringe organizations around the globe.

So you see chaps, this mission is really about more than simply recovering the laser weapon. We are hoping to break this ring and find out exactly who is behind it so that we can disrupt a significant source of strategic weapons to undesirable organizations.

Now ... the rebels appear to be amassing weapons and supplies deep in the mountains northwest of the town of Rodna in northern Romania. They have chosen an ancient castle that is deep in the woods in Transylvania, but you needn't worry. Dracula won't get you. It's only a legend...."

Several agents chuckled, then U.S. Marshal Erika Roberts raised her hand. "Colonel..."

Dakota looked over at her as Wellington turned around to see where the question came from. She appeared to be about Dakots's age, attractive, self-assured, a cute blonde ponytail sticking out from the back of her black U.S. Marshal cap. Nope, he thought. Don't even think about it. Relationships just don't seem to work out. Besides, women are turned off by his occasional brashness and joking around and frequent lack of seriousness. He quickly dismissed the thought and looked back down at Jack. He stroked the fur along his back as Jack lay calmly at his feet.

"Yes," responded Wellington.

Roberts continued. "If this group is located in Romania, why doesn't the Romanian military or Romanian national police just go in and storm the castle or light it up?"

"This is technically a NATO matter since the weapons were stolen from NATO and because it falls under international arms trafficking, that logically brings Interpol into the picture, hence, this new team."

"But Sir, Romania *is* a NATO member nation."

"Yes Marshal and they are also an Interpol member. NATO leadership made the decision to involve Interpol. They would prefer to treat it as a law enforcement matter."

"Roger Sir."

A middle-eastern looking agent with two days' worth of dark growth on his cheeks sat in the second row. His body language and facial expression spoke before he did. With one tactical boot up on the top of the seat in front of him, he bluntly commented with more than a hint of chauvinism wrapped in a very French accent.

"We are going in so zat ze pretty American Marshal can sweet talk zee bad guys out of zayer boom boom laser toy – no?"

Sergeant Ranier Beringer, French Interpol, followed up his first insult as the other men chuckled at the first one.

"I sought ze U.S. Marshals were known for being a tough bunch of guys. ... Am I wrong?"

Roberts stared ahead at the Colonel, pretending she didn't hear anything. Then slowly, she turned toward Beringer.

"I hear French men are very sensitive and feminine, maybe you would prefer to give the sweet talking a try? – No?"

Wellington paused before speaking. "I can see that we are going to get along famously," then turned back to the screen. "Each of you has critical skills for this unit."

Beringer interrupted the Colonel. "I'm sure ze gurl has uzur special skills. No?" Wellington turned around toward the group to allow a moment for the friction to work itself out.

Roberts turned toward again Beringer. "Yes. Watching through the scope of my McMillan Tac-338 sniper rifle at fifteen-hundred yards as you drop your weapon and run. ...That is what you French boys do in a fight isn't it? Drop and run?"

Beringer grinned and raised his eyebrows. "Ah, you are good at long distances, but what if you and I whur up close?"

Roberts responded with a steely look. "I'm good with close. Close works. Would you prefer the cold point of my Stiletto blade in your throat, or should I snap both collateral ligaments in your knee when I sweep you down to snap your little French chicken neck? Or maybe you'd like me to strap you down for an afternoon session of waterboarding? I'm having a special this week on near-drownings. I could fit you in this afternoon if that works?"

Beringer laughed nervously, but Jean-Claude Chennault, his superior, also French Interpol, sitting beside his fellow compatriot, felt the need to intervene.

"Marshal, allow me to apologize for my friend here. He is lacking in certain, how do e-yew say, social graces."

Roberts panned her eyes toward Chennault without moving her head, then shifted her focus back to Beringer. "That would explain the smell. ... Just make sure your friend here showers once a month so he doesn't give away our position."

Grins appeared on faces across the room. DX shook his head almost imperceptibly as he looked down at Jack. He admired her no crap attitude. What the heck was Beringer thinking? Did he really think he could just sling sexist remarks around and go unchallenged …idiot.

Wellington stopped pacing back and forth on the stage as he had been during the verbal sparring match. It was always useful for a commander to gain a sense of the personalities with which he had to work, but it was time to continue the brief.

"Are we quite finished exchanging pleasantries? We need to get on with it. …You have been handpicked for your experience. Your contributions and roles are unique, however, for continuity; we will spend some of our time cross training. We must have some degree of overlap across the team as backup for each other. We begin this afternoon. … Do any of you lads have questions at this point?"

Beringer asked. "What is wiss zee Lassie dug?"

Wellington clasped his hands behind him, looked down, and took a step forward. "I'm told this dog has very special qualities and that they will be very useful for the types of operations in which we will be engaging. He will be assisting in a number of capacities and will be responsible for providing force protection. . … Are there any more questions?"

Erika mumbled under her breath. "Protection from a fluffy show-dog. …great."

Beringer piped in. "Is he being paid as much as us?"

Wellington wrapped up. "All right then. Gentlemen, your training begins at 1300. Make sure that you have checked in with the quartermaster if you have not already done so. Agent Pearson will be taking everyone over to the armory for equipping."

Jean-Claude Chennault became a French Interpol Agent after graduating from the French National Police College, Ecole Nationale Supérieure de la Police. It was located on the outskirts of Lyon barely three miles from Interpol Headquarters itself. A voice came from some compartment inside his brain that said, 'Interpol belongs to my country' and in the context of this international team, being the senior French agent, he felt that Interpol was his, and if it was his, then the mission should have been his to lead. Clearly, the Secretary General of Interpol had slighted him by making him executive officer of the mission.

It was hard to ignore the longstanding rub with the Brits. He detested their arrogance. The Brits were in charge; a major injustice. Normally Interpol would take the lead in such an operation and all tactical communications and data feeds would be provided through MIND/FIND, Interpol's technology for accessing their international law enforcement databases. All of their data races across their highly secured, i-24/7 web-based communication's system. Somehow, the powers that be determined that the stinking pigs, the Brits, the Ministry of Defense MI-6; those arrogant blue-bloods were to lead this effort. That would explain having an Aussie on the team, another British colony, a Mountie from the Royal Canadian Mounted Police, a New Zealander, and of course the Brits greatest allies, the Americans. They were all part of the British colony club; France wasn't.

This weird Indian and Collie thing was just bothering the crap out of him. These types of dogs were not used on missions and dogs played only a very limited role, usually sniffing for contraband or stowaways. It was a strange combination and he could not see how that could do anything but put the team at risk somewhere along the line. Certainly, he would never have made such a choice. This mission couldn't end soon enough.

Friday: February 1, 08:23

Dakota trained Jack on an agility and obstacle course he had constructed when the Colonel came walking up to their area. He stood arms folded, braving a moderate, and biting breeze. He watched with interest as Dakota finished coaching Jack through a large corrugated steel tube.

Next Dakota ignited a smoke bomb, which quickly created a large smoke screen that blew quickly in the wind. He stepped through the smoke screen on the same side as the Colonel and called to Jack to come through the wall of smoke. Jack came through once, then Dakota walked through the wall again and called Jack. Jack approached the wall, but then hesitated and snorted at the smoke and turned away, refusing to acknowledge Dakota's attempts to command him through the wall again. Dakota came through the wall of smoke to Jack's side. He hugged and praised him.

"It's ok Jack. We'll work through it. Good boy."

Then he turned around to see the Colonel grinning.

"How is he doing Lieutenant?"

"Very well Sir. One of the best I've ever had a chance to work with. He picks up everything just like that. I just keep drilling him constantly to keep it fresh."

"It appeared that he had difficulty with the smoke screen."

"Aye Sir, but that isn't a very important skill. Nothing we're likely to need. He still has a lot of other capabilities. We'll get him through it."

"Excellent. He is capable of a lot, but I need to know now whether you really believe that he will be able to become proficient on that entire list of tactical skills that I gave you this morning."

"Sir, I have every confidence that he will. Many of them I had already taught him before we joined your unit."

Wellington nodded. "Very good Agent Dixon. … And what about you?"

"Sir?"

"I read your bio. I am aware of your medical discharge from the Marine Corps. How is your physical condition and agility?"

"Sir, I have been training with and without Jack for months. I'm not quite up to Marine Corps standards, but then again we do set them very high. So even if I fall a little shy of that, I will be good to go."

"So you don't think much of the Interpol standards, or Her Majesty's Royal Marines?"

"No Sir. I didn't say that. Just that I feel confident in my abilities."

Wellington stared silently at Dixon for a moment. "I understand Devil-Dog. You know Her Majesty's Royal Marines and the U.S. Marines share a lot in common, so I hear what you are saying. …Very good. Carry on."

Dakota put Jack through an intense and highly compressed training schedule. Jack was already accomplished and versatile, but even more skills would be required for this mission. Dakota took him up several times in different types of Bureau helicopters and other aircraft to acclimate him to flying. He attached Jack to him with a canine rig designed to harness a dog to a parachutist. While they were in the plane Dakota strapped on a pair of canine tactical goggles to keep the wind out of his eyes. Over the course of several jumps, he accustomed Jack to parachuting with him into some of the open areas at the academy.

Dakota and Jack spent time in the water on the Potomac River in small speedboats and rafts. Jack spent time improving his doggie paddle, swimming. He had to learn to travel in cars and other vehicles at high speeds without restraints and even learn how to maneuver under fire, complete with smoke and random explosions. He had the chance to fast-rope with Dakota out of choppers and rappel down the sides of some of the mock buildings. Keith was right. Dakota was training Jack as though he was a canine James Bond. The only thing missing was the tuxedo and a vodka martini, shaken, not stirred. However, Jack *was* all black with a white chest – already dressed for the part.

Dakota worked with Jack to train him to protect a selected individual and to keep any aggressor from harming that person. On command, Jack became a canine bodyguard. He also gained a simple, but valuable skill as a scout dog. In one drill, Jack would go ahead of the team to locate any potential threats or intruders lying in wait. If he detected threats, he would return to the team and quietly signal Dakota.

They continued to work with Jack and training role-players who played armed assailants. On command, Jack knew how to attack and target a handgun, knife, or rifle. No armed assailant could follow through with their intentions with seventy pounds of aggressive Collie pulling their weapon down toward the ground and refusing to let go. Jack learned so much and he picked it up so rapidly that Dakota's only real concern was having time to drill it into him enough so that these new skills would stay solidly in his mind. Recall never seemed to be a problem with Jack. The issue was more one of mood, but Dakota had his old ways that enabled him to convey urgency to Jack if there was ever doubt about executing a command.

Dakota had no real problem with the wide variety of training protocols. This was the essence of his theory of the versatile canine special operator. He only wished, as any trainer does, that he had time to be more thorough.

The final training set for Jack was to learn the role of search and rescue, or as they were called in World War I, ambulance dogs. The Red Cross pioneered the idea of training dogs to go on the battlefield, locate injured troops, and carry medical and other supplies to them. Even having a dog with an injured soldier did wonders for his psychological state. These ambulance dogs were, in effect, the first therapy dogs.

Agent Pearson, the chief tactical canine training instructor outfitted Jack with a new tactical vest. It was black, bullet proof against 9mm and .45 caliber rounds, but also had attached to it several pouches including medical supplies, basic survival supplies, water, and a miniature built in day-night camera system and GPS. When Dakota had to send Jack in to an area alone, he could follow on a video monitor what Jack saw, even in total darkness. The GPS system provided his exact location. The vest weighed just under twelve pounds, including gear. Jack trained with this vest every day to become accustomed to it and to increase his stamina.

Dakota was proud of how Jack responded to all the training. A couple of times each week he called Keith for an update on Jack. He cared for Jack as if he was his own, but he knew well, that Jack was on loan. Inside the dorm, Jack slept at the side of Dakota's bed. At night, as Jack lay near Keith, he knew that his other people were missing. He longed for their familiar sounds and smells. While Jack was striving to meet Dakota's expectations and please his temporary master, but just beneath the surface, a short distance in Jack's brain from all the tactical excitement and his bond with Dakota was a sense of longing. Their absence created a large and unfamiliar void in the core of his spirit.

Friday: February 22
Five Days until Go-Time

Colonel Wellington and an intelligence analyst briefed Striker-1. The analyst provided photos and maps of the specific location in Rodna where surveillance satellites had been capturing imagery for the past few weeks. The images showed the layout of the surrounding countryside. Wellington pointed out the castle ruins where the weapons and supplies were suspected.

Rodna was accessible by the Romanian Railway, which wound its way throughout the mountainous countryside, but putting the members of Striker-1 on a public train was not even a possibility. How could a team wearing tactical gear, heavily laden with equipment and a Collie travel inconspicuously by public railway; too many major suspicions if any members of the rebel movement were to spot them.

Colonel Wellington briefed the group. "We will fly to Romania on a U.S. Air Force flight, landing at the Romanian Air Force Base of Otopeni, a few miles outside of the capital of Bucharest. From there we will board a Romanian Air Force C-130 Hercules from the 901st Strategic Transport Squadron. They will fly us over the region near Rodna. They only know that they are transporting a special tactical group, they do not know how we are affiliated or the nature of our mission.

We will parachute after dark. The landing zone is in a clearing in the mountains above the town, approximately five kilometers to the east of the castle. We have a small base camp set up. As you can see from the satellite photos, the castle is located on top of a rocky crag surrounded on all sides by forest and a raging mountain stream. The peak is surrounded mostly by jagged cliffs.

Weapons are smuggled in sometimes by horseback and sometimes by light trucks. We have tracked vehicle movement along an old stone road that leads to the castle gate. Weapons have been coming in over the borders from Hungary and other bordering countries. We are concerned that there may be some type of underground tunnels or caves that you may have to locate. Most likely, the weapons are being stored in the underground levels of the castle. The castle does not appear to be large enough to house all the munitions that we suspect are there, so underground storage or possibly nearby caves may be how they are doing it

Also, the trucks that we have seen approaching the castle do not actually enter it. The stone bridge that originally connected the stone road to the castle entrance collapsed centuries ago and there is no functional drawbridge. They appear to head off under cover of the forest a couple of hundred meters away. That's why we suspect that there may be either a tunnel through which they enter the underground layers of the castle or they are storing some of the weapons in caves hidden in the forest. That is what you will have to figure out. There are rushing streams and steep rocky cliffs all around and the entire region is known to be dotted with caves and caverns of various sizes."

Captain Herman Labatt, New Zealand National Police, spoke up with a frustrated tone. "Bloody hell. We have the same types of terrain in maw country. It's sounds like we're being dropped into a rats maze and we don't even know where the bloody cheese is. We could be wandering around in there for days."

"That's part of the reason for Jack. He will help track and locate where these chaps may be hiding out. I'd like it to be simpler for you, but that just isn't the way it is I'm afraid. You'll also be carrying thermal imaging scopes on your rifles so that maybe you can pick up local heat signatures that will give away their position. Between those and Jack, I have no doubt that you'll find our dealers."

Sergeant Rolf Pemberton, Australian Federal Police, piped in. "Colonel, do any of the locals know about this ployce? Do hikers or adventurers evuh go there?"

"Excellent question. As I said, there are vehicles at times that show up at the castle, but only at night and as far as any of the locals know, it's just a rundown castle keep from the 9th century. It is too remote for anyone to casually happen upon it. It is miles from anywhere. It wasn't until a few months ago that Interpol and the Romanian government even realized that this site was being used to cache weapons. We have also discovered that this same group deals in stolen art, diamonds, and other cash-generating operations."

"Sounds qwat lovely," interjected Labatt.

Wellington responded. "Yes. Quite. …Interpol has coordinated with the National Central Bureau office in Bucharest and requested that they keep the castle under surveillance, but not to engage or apprehend anyone. As far as we can tell, there is no electronic surveillance, cameras or sensors on site. The weapons cartel thinks that they are so remote that no one even comes near this place. Another factor is that many of the locals believe it is haunted. The Hungarians used it in the 9th century to defend against Bulgarians after they were forced to cross the Carpathian Mountains and settle in the region where Rodna is now located. They found their new homeland and have lived there for centuries, only now, they feel like an occupied people as their territory is within the current borders of Romania, not Hungary; displaced is really what they are. They have essentially been refugees for a thousand years.

One final battle occurred when the Bulgarians laid siege upon this castle outpost. It was highly successful … for the Bulgarians. They massacred everyone in the castle, and many atrocities were committed

- 179 -

in the process. The castle has never been used since. The locals don't even care to venture anywhere near it; seeing it as a bad omen of sorts."

Dakota interrupted. "Colonel."

"Yes Agent Dixon?"

"It sounds as if the only thing we know about this castle with any certainty is that the laser weapon may be inside somewhere, but it could be in some underground cave or tunnel. With so many unknowns, how are we supposed to engage these rebels?"

"You are authorized to use lethal force. It is very likely that once you are in, you will be detected and we will meet with armed resistance. How much, we do not know. That is why we have a backup support team standing by. This is a weapons trafficking task force. If you do capture any of the rebels, you will secure them and turn them over to the backup team who will process them. Once inside the castle, it probably won't be long before we're discovered. If the rebels turn and run, all the better, if they resist, we respond with lethal force. Once the threat is eliminated, then we can take our time and search the castle."

Dakota continued with a follow up question. "So how many hostiles do we expect?"

"Our best estimates suggest that at any one time, there are no more than twelve to fourteen and they are lightly armed and not trained as far as we know. They are criminals, not mercenary soldiers, or terrorists proper. They are the suppliers of terrorist organizations. Those chaps are just there to keep an eye on the castle and its contents. If, by chance, they surrender or any of them are captured, they will be charged with arms trafficking. ... Now then, once the weapon has been located, the backup team will come in to secure the castle and begin removing the weapons for inventory and disposal."

Roberts spoke up. "So we parachute in. How do we exfiltrate?"

We will be extracted by three Puma 330 support helicopters from the Romanian Air Force.

In summary gentleman, while there are several unknowns, we expect this to be a relatively straight forward mission. We really don't expect more than minimal initial resistance from the rebels at the castle. Once they are apprehended or eliminated, then we will simply search for the weapon and the other weapons will be confiscated as well. This operation will put a major hole in any plans for this rebel group to conduct or support any types of operations. I expect this first mission to be not much more than an evening stroll compared to what I know many of you are accustomed to dealing with."

Darren Goodreaux, Royal Canadian Mounted Police, turned to Marshal Roberts and spoke under his breath. "Famous last words, eh?"

She continued watching Wellington without saying anything.

Wellington continued. "If there are no further questions, Inspector Chennault will review our final rehearsals and prep activities with you. He has an itinerary of practice and training objectives for the last few days and helping you become more familiar with the terrain and natural features in the vicinity of the castle as well as the interior layout of the castle."

STRIKER-1 TEAM

Personnel | Organization | Specialties

➢ Colonel Montgomery "Monty" Wellington - British Royal Marines – mission operations and tactics

➢ Inspector Jean-Claude Chennault – French Interpol, planning and tactics – second in command

➢ Agent George 'Doc' Sung – Central Intelligence Agency (CIA), Special Activities Division: Special Operations Group - Intelligence and Covert Ops, Interrogations, Romanian Language Specialist, Special Operations Physician's Assistant

➢ Police Lieutenant - Helmut Faust - Germany – Bundespolizie, explosives, sniper

➢ Warrant Officer Ian Mackay - British Royal Marines – 4 Assault   Squadron – sniper, chief armorer

➢ Special Agent Mike Pearson –Federal Bureau of Investigation (FBI) – sniper, canine tactics

➢ Agent Dakota Dixon – Office of Strategic Technology (OST) – canine tactics, navigation, other undisclosed, special skills

➢ Sergeant Darren Goodreaux – Royal Canadian Mounted Police –   tracking and navigation

➢ Sergeant Rolf Pemberton – Australian Federal Police – medic, survival, communications

➢ Captain Herman Labatt - New Zealand National Police – man-tracking, survival, combat medicine, mountain climbing

➢ Sergeant Ranier Beringer – French Interpol – communications and intel systems

➢ Agent Manish Kumar – Military Intelligence-6, (MI-6) – Secret Intelligence Service – communications and cyber-warfare, mountain-climbing

➢ Marshal Erika Roberts – U.S. Marshals Service – pyscho-pathologist, negotiator, interrogator, sniper, martial arts specialist.

-10-

Go-Time

Thursday: February 28, 03:30 Hours, Mission Time
(United States East Coast)

Lieutenant Colonel Mike Ramsey worked methodically through his pre-flight checklist with his co-pilot. The two sat three stories above the tarmac in front of a hangar at Andrews Air Force Base in Camp Springs, Maryland. Their Boeing C-17 Globemaster III cargo transport aircraft would normally carry a payload like 158 troops or several Presidential Limos or even an M1 Abrams Tank, but today the payload was significantly smaller; a Collie and a thirteen-person Top Secret tactical team with a handful of support personnel and their computer and communications gear.

Ramsey glanced briefly out the portside cockpit window. The concrete reflected the bright area lights around the hangar area, but he could still clearly see the moon in the western sky. It was waning crescent and partly obscured by moderate, low-level cloud cover. Still a good night for flying he thought.

Wellington stepped into the cockpit. "Good evening Colonel."

"Welcome aboard Sir. Looking forward to being airborne and heading toward the sunrise in a couple of hours."

Mike did not know the group on his aircraft, nor their purpose. "Sir, this bird is fueled to capacity."

"Very good," replied Wellington.

"The flight plan calls for a direct route over the Atlantic Ocean for a nearly seven-hour flight across the pond. This leg of the journey will take us to Royal Air Force Station Mildenhall in Suffolk, northwest of London."

Mildenhall was home to the U.S. Air Force 352nd Special Operations Group, which Ramsey and his crew supported. That base had been used for decades as a departure point for the Top Secret Lockheed SR-71 Blackbird spy-planes flying over Western Europe and the Soviet Union.

Mike continued. "From Mildenhall we are scheduled to refuel, take on additional support personnel, and fly non-stop to the Romanian Air Force Base of Otopeni, outside of Bucharest. Once at Otopeni, that's where my boys leave you and you will switch aircraft to a smaller C-130 NATO transport."

"Roger."

That would complete the third leg of their journey to the ops post in the mountains outside Rodna. Inside the cavernous fuselage of the C-17, the team settled in, working with the loadmaster to secure their gear. Colonel Wellington reviewed the flight plan as he sat in one of the two observer seats in the cockpit, directly behind Ramsey.

Agent Manish Kumar from MI-6 and Sergeant Beringer from Interpol and other members of the support team focused and worked busily to set up and connect communications equipment.

Dakota watched them briefly and Manish explained to him. "This equipment is will keep us in contact with Interpol and the advance team. We are essentially staying connected to the cloud-computing infrastructure that will be critical for the mission."

"That's a long ways from hand-held walkie talkies." Joked Dakota.

Manish grinned. "The advance team is already near Rodna, monitoring the situation via satellite. All operations and comms aboard this bird will use Interpol's I-24/7 network. It gives us secure global police communications. And actually, we do have your 'walkie talkies'." Manish held up a small sat-phone to show Dakota. "These are Thuraya satellite-phones that connect to Inmarsat satellite for voice comms. You probably had something like this in Afghanistan."

"You're right. I'm familiar with those. Thanks for the tour Manish."

Dakota walked Jack over to their seats. Jack wasn't concerned about the team's communication capabilities however, or how their data would be securely accessed through the cloud. He sat calmly beside Dakota, panting, looking around trying to adjust to the strange feel of the cold steel decking against the pads on his feet. Dakota stroked Jack's head to comfort him. It comforted both of them. They were set and secured in their padded fold-down seats mounted to the bulkhead. All they could do was watch the support team plug in and adjust their equipment. They resembled a group of video gamers preparing for a convention. All they lacked were cans of Mountain Dew and Doritos.

A variety of monitors, equipment, and keyboards were mounted to steel cages and frames bolted to the deck in the center of the aircraft. The satin black equipment cages and racks combined with the black tactical cases mounted to them resembled one of the monitoring stations of a Wall Street trader, but these operators would not be concerned with any stock trading. A series of thick cables and connectors ran back and forth along the backsides of the racks and down to power outlets mounted in the deck. From these outlets, even thicker cables were duct-taped to the deck and ran a dozen feet or so forward, where they branched out to the left and right and connected to large power outlet boxes on either bulkhead. It was an airborne computer hacker's dream. What tech-nut wouldn't have fun at the controls of so much digital firepower?

Half of the tactical team sat along one bulkhead, half on the other. Piled up on an equipment pallet toward the rear of the cargo deck were their parachutes, their PROTECH Tactical Delta 4 helmets, the new ones with night vision mounts, ammunition, food, medical supplies and other gear. The agents had already checked and re-checked their weapons, ammunition and other gear. For now, it was time to settle in and try to find some way to doze inside the whale-sized tin can. Marshal Roberts had already put ear buds in and started a continuous loop of ocean surf on her MP-3 player. She hoped this would help calm her system and allow her to doze for a while.

Ten minutes into her tropical surf, she could hear the high-pitched whine of the four enormous Pratt & Whitney engines over the sound of the crashing surf as the engines. The engines began to wind up to idling speed in preparation for taxiing to the runway while the loadmaster ensured the hatches were sealed. Inside the cockpit, the pilots had completed the pre-flight checklist and the ground traffic controller stood at the ready with his orange-red traffic flashlights ahead of the port wing where Ramsey could see him.

The massive, flat-grey aircraft sat facing the tiny ground controller. A side-view of the scene mildly resembled an impossibly large shark facing the seemingly defenseless human on the tarmac in front of it. The ground controller guided the aircraft forward and on to the taxiway leading past the flight line, heading in the direction of runway 19-left. In another four minutes, the giant engines would generate upwards of forty-thousand foot-pounds of thrust each, to push the three-hundred and fifty-thousand pound aircraft down the runway and up into the night-sky. It shouldn't be possible, but it was. Something that heavy just shouldn't be able to lift off because of some air being pushed out the back of the four tube-shaped cylinders that housed the engines, but somehow it worked. Once aloft, it would make its way over the Chesapeake Bay, part of the Delmarva Peninsula and eventually out over the Atlantic Ocean to chase the sunrise.

Thursday: February 28, 03:50

Specialist Monica Petrov brushed a tassel of black hair back behind her right ear as she stood leaning over her computer monitor. The glow from the LED flat screen in front of her and a few small florescent desk lights were the only lighting in the room. She and a few other technicians busied themselves inside a doublewide pair of old and cramped Quonset huts in the far southwest corner of Mildenhall Royal Air Force Station. The base had been constructed in the middle of a region covered by local farm fields in the English countryside. The Quonset huts were remnants from WW II and had served as barracks for RAF pilots during the Battle of Britain. Today they served as a temporary staging area for Striker and their communications and intel support team.

They were linked into the intel satellites monitoring the area around Rodna while they awaited the arrival of the main Striker team. Petrov finished selecting some of the parameters that she would use for managing communications for the mission. She had been recommended to Colonel Wellington over a year ago, after her predecessor; Cathleen O'Neill had been killed. Miss O'Neill's car had swerved out of control and plunged into the Thames River. After days of searching, her body had never been found.

Petrov reached for her comm headset on the tabletop and placed it on her head, adjusting the microphone height to the side of her mouth.

She checked the volume and selected a secondary comm link over Inmarsat. Once the link was open, she activated an auxiliary voice channel normally only used either for test purposes or as a third-tier backup in the event that other channels were flooded or disabled.

"Werewolf this is Raven. Do you read me?"

A voice resonated inside her headset. "Affirmative Raven. What do you have?"

"I've confirmed the flight plan and mission itinerary. You should have a copy of it. I sent it through the anonymous file transfer utility as before."

"What is their ETA at Mildenhall?"

"Approximately seven hours."

"All right. And you've confirmed the final destination?" asked the voice.

"Affirmative."

"Copy. Out."

Monica deactivated the channel and shutdown the link.

Thursday: February 28, 04:22

Colonel Wellington sipped his Earl Grey from a steaming plastic cup as he walked casually along the port side of the equipment island inside the C-17. Manish looked up from his monitor as the fellow Brit approached.

"Sir, Her Majesty would be appalled … Earl Grey in a plastic cup?"

Wellington grinned and shook his head in mock disgust. "I know. I know. What we sacrifice for queen and country." Wellington gave him a pat on the back as he passed by on his way to a pair of flight seats bolted to the center of the deck. He settled in, sat his cup on a gritty anti-slip strip on the deck, buckled his seatbelt, and reached for his tablet computer.

Thursday: February 28, 18:40
United Kingdom Time

Ramsey captured the sunrise as planned and now evening approached as the massive grey C-17 descended from the overcast English skies to begin its final approach to runway 11. This vector put the aircraft landing in an easterly direction. Within moments, the craft descended to just a few feet above the pavement. Suddenly the fourteen, forty-one-inch main load-bearing tires directly under the center of the fuselage screeched in unison as they skidded against the pavement. Ramsey put the engines into reverse thrust to slow the metallic leviathan. Inside, the team lurched forward slightly against their seat belts. Dakota put his hand on Jack's back to reassure him. He had secured Jack's tactical vest to a harness attached to the deck so that he could land without being tossed about.

Within the hour, the team had offloaded their personal gear bags onto four Austrian Pinzgauer 716M transport vehicles for the drive to the staging area inside the Quonset huts. The same huts where Specialist Petrov and her team were located. The remaining gear stayed aboard the aircraft awaiting the flight to Romania.

Colonel Wellington rode in the front of the small caravan in an RAF Land Rover with a driver and Inspector Chennault. When they arrived a few minutes later at the Quonset huts, Wellington was first out of his vehicle. He waited for the others to come to a stop and watched as his team disembarked. The agents approached and formed a cluster around him.

"Welcome to RAF Mildenhall chaps. Well, we're finally here in God's country now," he said with a hint of sarcasm and a slight twinkle in his eye. "I trust you all enjoyed your inflight movie. Now we wait for further intel and instructions. A contingent of our technical team is already inside monitoring matters. We will be returning to the aircraft later for the flight to Romania. For now, catch up on intel and there are racks if anyone wants to catch some shut-eye. We will have a status briefing at twenty-hundred hours and we will be departing at approximately twenty-three hundred hours."

Jack walked with Dakota as the team approached the entrance of the first Quonset hut. He happily swished his tail back and forth as he trotted beside his partner. The original smooth concrete in this portion of the base had been tortured repeatedly over the decades by neglect and quick, sloppy repairs that had left a patchwork of different colored rectangles of newer concrete, asphalt, and tar, surrounded by crumbling pavement. The huts themselves were nothing more than half-cylinder-shaped layers of black and brown grime and moss with a little corrugated metal showing through to give the grime shape. A variety of weeds and vines grew along the foundation. Clearly, the weeds did not care that they were on the property of one of Her Majesty's airbases and that the proper British thing to do was to look ship-shape and spot on. No, these weeds were sloppy and obviously had no regard for keeping up proper appearances. They were probably American weeds.

The team made their way inside, where the interior revealed several technical specialists in black tactical dress hovering over different stations around another technology island. The island was populated much like the one inside the C-17, with monitors, communications gear, cables, and equipment racks. There was a colorful array of both steady state and blinking LEDs glowing from one side or another of nearly every piece of gear present. The scary thing was that Petrov could probably explain the meaning and purpose of each of the LEDs on each piece of gear; not that anyone would want her too, but she could. That geek streak was precisely the reason the Colonel had accepted her into this unit. He needed a geek. Wars, police work, and intelligence gathering had become more of a technology game in recent years than it had ever been when Wellington began his career. Cyberspace was the new battleground.

Wellington recognized his technical adjutant. "Petrov my dear. How good to see you slaving away over that hot silicon. How are things?"

Petrov responded professionally and in her Slavic accent. "Sir. Velcome. Vee are fooly operational and are tied into zee same satellite channels as the advance team in Rodna; the same feeds you should have been receiving during your flight Colonel." She looked in the direction of Dakota and questioned the Colonel. "Sir. Vutt is zat?"

"You mean who is that? Agent Dakota Dixon. He's a Yank, well sort of. He's a Native American."

"Sir, I meant zee animal."

"Oh, yes, quite. That's Captain Jack."

"Sir, a voolf?"

Wellington and Dakota chuckled, as did a couple of the others. Manish, sensed an opportunity for some good-natured ribbing. "Yes, we thought, in case the team runs into any werewolves when they get to Transylvania that Jack could do a handsome job of fending them off."

Wellington subdued his chuckle of surprise at Petrov's comment and explained. "He's a Collie. You know. A sheep dog."

"Vill he be herding sheep?"

Dakota spoke up. "No, hopefully, just bad guys."

Petrov continued to observe Jack. Jack was not a type of dog she had seen before.

"And you called him Captain? He has rank?"

Wellington answered. "No, Monica, that's just his name. Like a pirate."

Petrov gave Wellington a blank stare.

Wellington sighed. "You really must get out more Petrov."

She looked briefly at Dakota. "And he is, how is it? … An Indian? Are there cowboys too?"

Everyone laughed. Agent Sung piped in with an amazing John Wayne impersonation, which was weird to see coming out of a Korean. "Well Ma'am, I'm from a little place called Texas."

Monica looked very confused and slightly frustrated. Human socializing and especially humor was just not her thing. She looked strangely at Sung. "You are not Texas. You are Chinese."

Sung smiled, continuing his John Wayne drawl. "Korean actually darlin', but I can understand your confusion."

Dakota, Pearson, and Goodreaux doubled over with laughter and tried to turn toward each other to avoid laughing directly in Petrov's direction. Everyone was a little punchy after the long flight and lost it at the site of a terribly Korean-looking CIA Agent doing a very good John Wayne accent, causing total confusion in the mind of a very straight-laced, techno-oriented East-European who was having absolutely no luck sorting out the utterly confusing demographics of this supposedly highly skilled team of very professional special operators and their 'voolf!'

Sung had one last round as he turned toward Dakota who wiped tears of laughter from his eyes.

Sung pointed his finger at him and his John Wayne voice warned. "Um gonna be keepin' one eyeball on you at all times Tonto. Don't be givin' me cause to have to hunt me some Injun later."

Dakota wiped another tear away as he laughed. Sung grinned and fist-bumped Dakota.

Dakota laughed and cried at the same time. "Awesome bro! That deserves an Oscar. … You need to be on Saturday Night Live."

Marshal Roberts watched the scene, shook her head slightly, and muttered under her breath. "Looks like high-school is back in session." She walked off in the direction of the kitchen area in the other half of the dual Quonset hut structure.

Petrov shook her head as if to dismiss the whole episode, muttering under her breath as she returned her focus to the equipment. "I do not understand."

Wellington brought the scene somewhat back to reality. "It's okay Petrov. You're doing great. I much appreciate it. Once we reach Rodna and deploy the team to engage the smugglers, you'll be rid of this band of vagabonds."

Thursday: February 28, 19:16
United Kingdom Time

The group settled in. Some of the team stretched out on bunk beds and baseball caps covered their heads. A couple of the agents chatted in the chow area and drank coffee. Dakota set up Jack with bowls for food and water over in the chow area. He hung Jack's tactical vest over the edge of one of the lower bunks and gave Jack a light brushing to keep any knots from starting behind his ears and along his legs and belly.

Goodreaux walked by and gave Jack a pat on the head. It took a little while, but it seemed that most of the team had taken a liking to Jack. Dakota wasn't completely sure, but it also seemed that several of the team became impressed the more they saw of what Jack could do. Dakota set up a training protocol during their several weeks where he taught Jack to know the names of everyone on the team. As required by Dakota's own mischievous personality, he also used that new skill to set up a few pranks and gags against some of the team members at different times throughout the training, just a little something to help Jack reinforce their names.

Petrov finished briefing the Colonel on preparations and the latest intel from Interpol and the boys in Langley. The team completed their status meeting and just a few hours remained before it was time to head back to the odd-looking little Austrian vehicles that would take them to the flight line where the C-17 was being refueled and re-checked.

The kitchen area was empty except for Jack who crunched away, eating a good helping of his food. Someone had added a helping of leftover chopped chicken and rice to his bowl and mixed it in with his regular dry dog food. The smell of the additional helping drove Jack to eat most of the contents of his bowl. He had a habit of eating only until his hunger seemed satisfied and rarely consumed the entire contents of his bowl, but tonight he was leaving very little remaining in his chrome bowl. He continued savoring the scent of the food and then walked toward the bunks and laid down beside the one Dakota had used. His stomach was content.

Thursday: February 28, 22:00
United Kingdom Time

Wellington stood halfway between the tech island and the entrance to the Quonset hut. "May I have your attention? I suggest you gather yourselves and prepare to depart. We need to be on our way shortly. This equipment needs to be packed and pulled. Look alive chaps. Look alive."

The team members began moving around in all directions, quietly gathering clothing, equipment, and personal effects. Within just a few minutes, the computer monitors were unbolted from their mountings and snapped shut in tactical cases. Other gear was stowed in its cases for transport and the vineyard of cables strung everywhere, quickly disappeared into several large cases on wheels.

Dakota emptied Jack's bowls; rinsed and stowed them in Jack's tactical bag. He got Jack up and buckled on his vest, which he would need for takeoff. Once packed, the team members began filing outside to the awaiting transports and stowed their gear aboard before climbing inside. Wellington took one last walk around the place, flipped the lights off, and closed the door. Inside and out, it looked as if no one had been there in fifty years or more.

The small convoy headed toward the northeast quadrant of the base toward the awaiting aircraft. LtCol Ramsey completed his exterior visual inspection of the aircraft, while his co-pilot sat inside the cockpit beginning the pre-flight checklist.

The odd-looking Pinzgauers circled around the front of the aircraft and pulled alongside the hangar where they released their passengers and cargo. European trucks always have an odd look to them. Dakota wondered why they couldn't just look like a Chevy truck or something. He hopped out of the rear of his vehicle and picked up Jack, then placed him down on the tarmac before reaching back inside for their bags. The team members walked toward the rear loading ramp and headed inside for the next four-hour leg of their long journey.

Dakota walked ahead, assuming that Jack was behind or about to come alongside when he turned around and saw his K9 partner several yards behind, walking casually with no sense keeping up with him. "Jack. Come on boy! Let's go."

Jack picked up his pace a little, but still seemed in no real hurry to shadow his temporary master. Dakota walked up the ramp into the belly of the C-17 and stood in front of the pallet of gear. He turned around looking for Jack and saw him standing at the end of the ramp looking up at him.

"Jack. Come! Let's go!" Jack stood for a moment, staring at the ramp extending upward in front of him. "Jack. Come!" Jack put a paw forward and slowly walking up the ramp toward Dakota.

"Follow Jack." Dakota walked to his seat folded against the bulkhead and pulled it down and locked it in place. Jack walked to him and stood panting moderately. "Don't' tell me you're tired out from the little walk? … Okay. Sit."

Dakota knelt down and attached the security harness to the mounting fixture in the deck and the other ends to the mounts on either side of Jack's vest. Lastly, he secured both of their bags to the equipment pallet in the rear of the plane.

Twenty minutes later the loadmaster had once again secured the hatches and the ramp and reported to Ramsey that all stations were secured and ready for liftoff. Dakota looked down at Jack lying at his feet. Once again, he reached out and petted Jack to reassure him as the engines began their start up cycle. Within a few minutes, the aircraft was airborne and making the wide turn to the north briefly before taking an easterly heading in the direction of Europe.

They reached cruising altitude and Dakota unclipped Jack's harness so that he could move around if he wanted. He had been giving Jack a periodic visual check. Jack panted heavily and paced. He lay down completely on his side and continued his heavy panting, even drooling a little. Dakota noted, that the temperature inside the aircraft was comfortable, pretty much the same as on the first flight. He couldn't see any obvious reason why Jack would be panting so much and acting restless. Jack got up after a couple of minutes and paced around more, then lay down again.

"Jack. You okay buddy?"

He looked at his canine partner for a few seconds, then decided to go to Jack's bag to retrieve a water bowl. On the way back from the rear of the aircraft, Dakota picked up a bottle of water from a cooler that was lashed to the deck. He placed the bowl within reach of Jack and poured the contents of the bottle into it. Jack watched and paced around and then lay down again. Dakota frowned curiously and sat down in his jump seat, keeping his focus on Jack. After a few seconds, Jack rolled over on his side, panting. His eyes closed down to tiny slits. Dakota could see his distress. The question was why. Jack was used to flying in very small aircraft and helicopters, sky diving and fast roping. It couldn't be the motion of the C-17. It was as smooth as a commercial airliner. Dakota recalled that Jack was acting oddly before the flight, back on the tarmac.

He kept an eye on his partner for the next thirty minutes, leaning back on his seat. He looked up at the overhead of the aircraft for a moment and thought. When he looked back down at Jack, his eyes were completely shut. He continued panting and even whimpered occasionally. Dakota looked across the deck and saw Sung reading his tablet. Quietly, he got up, walked over, and sat down in the seat beside him. George looked at his Native American friend. "Hey DX, what's up?"

Dakota responded quietly. "It's Jack. …. I'm worried about him."

"What's the problem?"

"I know you're not a vet, but you have medical training right?"

"Yeah. I'm a spec ops physician's assistant. We actually do receive some veterinary training though. What do you need?"

"Well, could you come and take a look at him?"

"Sure."

The two went over to Jack. George began looking him over as Dakota described his recent behavior. "He started acting sluggish just as we approached the aircraft and very lethargic and was staggering around like he was drunk. A little after takeoff he started panting heavily and pacing around and then laying down on his side. He's even whimpered a few times. I know he doesn't feel well."

"What has he eaten?"

"His normal dog food. I think someone added in a little chicken and rice leftovers also. I don't know who, but I saw it in his bowl as he was eating."

George lifted Jack's eyes to check his pupils. "Is he allergic to anything in particular?"

"Nothing that I know of. He isn't on any medication except glucosamine and chondroitin for his joints and a daily vitamin."

"I'll be right back. I want to get my kit."

George headed toward the equipment pallet and came back a moment later with his tactical medical backpack. He laid it on the floor, and removed his stethoscope. He put it on and placed the chrome disc on Jack's lower rib cage to listen ….

"His heart rate is definitely elevated. ….I want to check his temperature."

George removed a rectal thermometer from a case inside the instruments compartment of his kit. He inserted it into Jack's rear and waited for it to beep.

"His temperature is 105.5 He definitely has a fever."

"What the heck is going on with him George?"

"He's had all his shots right?"

"Yes, a couple of months ago. It's a little far out for him to be having any kind of reaction and they're the same shots he's gotten every year without a problem."

George sat kneeling on his heels to think for a moment. "I can draw some blood and check for elevated white blood-cell count to see if he has an infection, but something tells me that isn't the cause of the fever. I think it's a reaction to something he ate and his body is trying make him sweat it out … or in his case, drool it out through his saliva possibly."

Dakota lowered the volume of his voice. "What are you saying George?"

"I'm saying, I think he was poisoned."

Dakota frowned. "Who?"

George shrugged his shoulders, then reached in his bag for a small flashlight and lifted Jack's eyelid again. He waved the light in front of his eyes. "His pupils are dilated and unresponsive; a sign of shock. Has he vomited at all?"

"No."

"We may need to get it out of his system. I'm going to give him a weakened solution of hydrogen peroxide to make him vomit. I'll need your help getting him up and getting this into him. Then we'll need to try and walk him around a little until he's ready to do it. Grab one of those nausea bags below the seat."

The two men got Jack awake and on his feet so that George could administer a syringe of peroxide in the corner of his mouth. Dakota held Jack's mouth shut while George squeezed the solution into Jack's mouth. Jack tried to wrench his head away and resist, but he was too weak. He just swallowed the solution.

George stood up. "Okay, we need to walk him around a bit, get him to vomit, then I'm going to shave away a little bit of fur on his left forepaw and give him an I-V with water."

Dakota looked surprised. "Water?"

"It's to activate his kidneys and literally help flush it out of his system. We need to make him pee, and the way to do that is just to pump some water into him."

Dakota put his head closer to the side of George's almost in a whisper tone.

"George, I don't want anyone, especially the 'Old Man', to know that we think Jack was poisoned. We have no idea who it might have been and that could be a problem."

George nodded. Dakota put Jack on a leash and led him around the aircraft. It was clear from the looks the other team members gave Jack as he staggered around, that they realized he wasn't feeling well.

Ranier was being his usual sweetheart self. "Is yur Lassie dug air sick Dakota?"

Dakota nodded. "Actually, yes, he is. Thanks for asking."

Ranier grinned a stupid grin. He was good at that. Yeah, it was hard to find much to like about him, but he was supposedly good at what he did. He just ticked off everyone around him in the process – jerk. Dakota continued walking Jack throughout the interior of the aircraft. Suddenly, Jack began to convulse. Immediately Dakota put the bag to his mouth and caught what Jack had to give him. Jack convulsed several times. Once it appeared that he had finished, Dakota continued walking him back to their spot where George waited.

"He did it. Now what?"

"I hate to say it buddy, but I think we need to give him another dose just to try and empty out his stomach as much as possible."

"Alright Doc. Whatever you think."

The two repeated the procedure and Dakota walked Jack again. This time when they returned to Agent 'Doc' Sung, Jack sat down and then lay down on his side.

George looked toward Dakota. "Let him rest for a minute while I get the I-V and fluids ready."

"Rog."

George reached in his bag and took out the necessary instruments. He walked back to another large black duffle bag and brought it forward, opened it and extracted from it an I-V bag of water. He hung the bag on a utility hook on the bulkhead between a pair of seats and strung the plastic I-V tube down toward Jack. Within a few minutes he had shaved a two-inch wide band of fur on the front of Jack's left paw and inserted the I-V and set the drip-rate.

"Now all we can do is wait about 30 minutes or so until his kidneys begin to process that fluid. Then he'll need to pee. You'll need to get one of those plastic tube-bags over there when he's ready. I'll make sure he has enough fluid in him that he won't want to hold his bladder. Meanwhile, I want you to give him this pill. It will help with any nausea he's likely to be feeling."

"Got it."

"After he pees, we do the I-V again. Meanwhile I want to get him some activated charcoal to help block the poison."

"George, this is all great. I really appreciate what you're doing. But do we have any idea what specific poison caused this? I mean, was it just bad food, or do you still think it was intentional."

George looked at Dakota. "I seriously doubt Jack ate any bad food. If the food *was* that bad, his sense of smell would have kept him front wanting to eat it. Besides, bad food probably wouldn't have caused him to react this quickly and if it was someone's leftovers, then they would be sick as well and I don't see anyone else looking like they're in as bad a shaped as Jack. I think someone put something into his food and might even have seemed appealing, possibly something sweet smelling. It wouldn't take much anti-freeze to kill a dog or at least make him sick for a couple of days. It smells sweet and animals are attracted to it. It could have easily been mixed in with his food and he would be attracted to eat most of it."

"So you think it was something like that?"

"Yes. In fact, when he pees, we'll take a sample and I can test it. We'll also take a little blood and check that as well. I'll probably be able to give you a reasonable answer soon. The only question then will be which SOB did it. … It had to be someone on this plane. No one else was in or out of the building at the air base."

"Like I said, not a word of this. I'll just have to keep my eyes out to see if anyone gives themselves away. I'd just like to know why. What's their problem ya know?"

"I don't know DX. It's weird to just poison a dog. That's pretty random, but my gut tells me there's nothing random about it. There has to be some motive behind it. Whatever was done to Jack was intentional man."

Dakota commented. "It's one thing to tease or not care for dogs or whatever, but to actually abuse or injure or poison one is just messed up."

"I know, sorry man. …. For what it's worth, I think he's going to be okay though. If we just flush it out and get that charcoal in him, it will clear it up, but it may take a day or two before he's back to normal. Guess that kind of cuts you two out of the mission profile."

"I don't know. We'll see. Just do what you can for him."

"Check."

Thursday: March 1, 01:09
Romania Time

The C-17 landed at Otopeni Air Base a few minutes past its scheduled arrival time. Some high altitude turbulence enroute forced LtCol Ramsey to change course slightly in search of smoother air. Jack finished the I-V of water and Agent Sung gave him some activated charcoal in tablet form. As the aircraft landed, Jack rested comfortably, but still panted heavily.

Once the aircraft began to taxi, the team started unbuckling and waiting for the aircraft to come to a stop at the hangar area. Otopeni was also home to the Romanian Presidential aircraft units, but the Striker-1 team would conduct their preparations at the opposite end of the airbase from them.

The team moved about as the loadmaster lowered the loading ramp in the rear of the aircraft. Team members looked at Jack who was still lying on the deck in obvious distress.

Colonel Wellington walked up to Dakota. "Agent Dixon, what has happened here?"

"Sir, I think Jack probably became airsick when he ate his food and then we took off. I guess I never worked with him during training where we did any airborne activity immediately after eating. He's probably just nauseous and has a pretty upset stomach. He'll be fine in a bit Sir."

"I hope so. We're counting on him. Keep me posted as to his disposition please."

"Yes Sir."

The team offloaded their equipment onto utility vehicles. The main team and support team headed over to the hangar. There were temporary hot bunks adjacent to the hanger where they would wait until near nightfall to depart for the northern region of Romania. Insertion of the team would occur by parachute at night.

Dakota slowly walked Jack to the barracks as the rest of the team went ahead.

George passed by. "DX, I'll see you two inside alright?"

"Sure. Thanks George."

Marshal Roberts was the last to exit the aircraft. She approached Jack and Dakota. "Dixon, is he going to be okay?"

"Absolutely, just a little air-sickness. He'll shake it soon enough."

She nodded and then continued on her way. Dakota wasn't quite sure how to read that. She was probably just trying to be polite. She never seemed too thrilled to have Jack on the mission in the first place … whatever.

The team assembled inside the barracks as they had done at Mildenhall. Everyone flaked out for a few hours of shut-eye.

Colonel Wellington stood near the center of the bunk area. "Alright chaps. Let's marshal up for a bit. … We could all do with some winks. I want everyone well rested. Before we do that, I just want to review the basics quickly.

The flight from here to Rodna will take just over one hour in the C-130. We will depart at 1800 hours, rendezvous with the advance team at their camp. The advance camp is located in the forest near the edge of a clearing. It is clearly marked on your maps and your GPS devices have the coordinates already uploaded into them. The camp is separated from the immediate area around the castle by a mountain ridge and a moderately wide mountain stream. The support team will leave their equipment here since the advance camp is operational.

The Striker Team will depart the advance camp by snowshoe at approximately 2130 hours, estimating the hike to the castle to take approximately forty-five minutes. We hope that arriving late will add to the element of surprise. With a little luck, most of the personnel will be asleep or drunk by the time we arrive. For now, we rest and once we arrive at the advance camp we will do a final intel brief and review of the approach to the castle, check equipment and head out. Thanks much chaps. Sweet dreams."

The group dispersed and made ready for some rest. 'Doc' Sung came over to Jack and Dakota. Dakota took a cot in a distant corner of the barracks. Jack lay on the floor beside him, still panting, but stable.

"DX, how's the big guy doing?"

Dakota gently stroked Jack's torso. "I think he's past the worst of it. … George, thank you. You saved his life."

George responded awkwardly. "Ain't no thang. I'm glad he is improving."

Dakota heard approaching footsteps and lifted his head to see the confident gate of the 'Old Man' silhouetted against the more brightly lit area of the barracks. Wellington queried Dakota in a friendly tone, but his British accent was still smart and dry with an ample hint of suspicion. "Dakota, how is our canine companion?"

"Sir, he's improving quickly."

Wellington stared down at Jack, then squatted down for a closer look. "He may be improving, but he certainly doesn't seem his usual chipper self. I'm quite sure of that."

"Sir. He'll be fine. He'll be ready."

"Dakota … That is certainly the question of the hour my good man. If I had to say presently … I'd have to put him on medical reserve. Can't chance it. You understand of course."

"Sir, he'll be ready," pleaded Dakota.

"Tell you what. We at least owe him a second look. … When it's closer to flight time I'll come and take another look. If he's up and at 'em, then he can go. If not, well …" Wellington looked down and stroked Jack's fur. "Sorry old boy. … another time."

George looked at Dakota, then down at Jack. Nothing needed to be said. George headed off to his equipment. Dakota lay on his cot and stroked Jack, hoping at least his friendly touch might bring him some comfort or assurance. It was eating at Dakota that he had taken Jack from his family. The struggle weighed down his normally jovial spirit.

Dakota was serious, focused and a consummate professional when it counted, but outside of mission parameters, he was a definitely undisciplined; free-spiritedness was not high on the list of qualities the military sought. It was his way of maintaining a healthy balance. He knew how to let loose and on more than one occasion his "letting loose" had landed him in front of his superiors. Right now, he was heavy, heavy with the weight of Jack's condition. As much as he wanted to prove his theories and demonstrate his particular blend of canine tactical skills in action, he really wanted Jack back to his carefree and crazy self. The two were kindred spirits, but right now sucked. Nothing more eloquent than that came to Dakota's mind ... the suckish factor at the moment was maxed out.

Sung came back a few minutes later. "Dakota, I analyzed Jack's samples, and it turns out that he had ethylene glycol in his system. Fortunately, the amounts were fairly low, which means I think either we got to him in time or maybe he didn't ingest a lethal dosage. He should be fine."

"Thanks again."

Thursday: March 1, 17:00
Romania Time

It was nearly time for the final leg of the Striker team's journey. Everyone was well rested and fed after the traveling and weird hours. It was time to pack their gear and prep for boarding the much smaller C-130 aircraft for the short flight to Rodna.

Jack moved around under his own steam, but not completely back to normal. Ten hours had made the difference. The 'Doc' saved him and for that, Dakota was grateful. Wellington spotted Dakota walking Jack. "Dakota, I'm glad to see the old boy up and at 'em." Dakota nodded as he kept walking Jack. "I'm afraid, Dakota, that he just doesn't look up to par however."

"Sir. Jack is plenty strong. He just needs a little walking and some fresh air for a few minutes. Once he's out in the snow and moving around in the cool air he'll be set. He always gets invigorated when he's in the snow. He- "

"Dakota. No. … No. I can't allow it. He is not ready. You don't have to be a vet to see it."

"Sir. He's a strong dog and resilient."

"I know he is, but he's not at the level we need him to be. We have to be able to count on him just as much as any other member of the team. …. I'm sorry. There will be other missions. He'll have his chance, but today isn't it."

"Sir, please. We can go along, make the jump, and stay at the advance camp. If he isn't ready after a few minutes of cold air, then we stay at the camp."

Wellington looked sternly at Dakota. "Agent Dixon …"

Dakota was silent as he looked down at Jack who stood still, panting casually, looking worn down from his ordeal.

"Aye Sir."

Wellington paused, looked at Jack, then back at Dakota who was still looking down at Jack, then he walked off.

-11-

Ghosts

Thursday: March 1, 18:00
Romania Time
Somewhere over North-Central Romania

The C-130 aircraft was a true workhorse; used for years by militaries around the world, but comparing the C-130 to the gigantic C-17 Globemaster the team had flown earlier was like comparing a little Ford Ranger pickup truck to the mighty Ford F-350; no comparison. The C-130 was noisy, bouncy and vibrated a hell of a lot.

Team members sat in their red nylon web-seats along both bulkheads. They faced each other silently while the engines droned just on the other side of the thin aluminum fuselage.

George sat near the rear of the aircraft slouched back in his web seat, staring mindlessly down at his black boots. He wondered how Jack was doing and what he and Dakota were up to. He was bummed that they couldn't be on the mission. He looked forward at the other team members; sizing them up briefly, then back at his boots. Who had poisoned Jack? He couldn't envision any of them really doing it. That was really over the top and what the hell could be the motive? He could make no sense of it. What it did do was make the CIA agent feel uneasy. It meant something, but what? Was there a traitor in their midst? The whole team was handpicked by Wellington. He knew everyone from past experience except for Dakota, and DX would certainly not poison Jack. That was nuts to even consider.

Wellington got up and walked down the center of the deck. "Alright chaps. We're approaching the jump site. We're going dark. We are now ghosts. Let's get those chutes on and secure your gear bags."

Each team member had a pack, which included the usual toys – or 'care package' as special operators often referred to it; extra ammunition, first aid supplies, in George's case, a large tactical field medicine bag. Other agents carried explosives, stun grenades, satcom gear, tactical cameras, night vision equipment, ruggedized tablets to serve as monitors for recon cameras, and backup weapons. Anything else they might need would be waiting for them at the advance camp. This much they had to take in themselves on the jump.

On the outside, the advance camp looked like a military combat operations center. It was a large olive drab tent structure with external generators for power and HVAC capabilities to provide a comfortable internal environment. Inside were several sturdy folding tables set up in a row. Each had multiple laptops with operators at several stations. The tables faced a fusion wall consisting of five large screen TVs mounted on a black steel framework. These screens provided the operators and the mission ops manager with high definition feeds of the satellite coverage of the area around the castle, local maps and real-time intel reports on activities and communications from the organization and players making up the smuggling ring. The center was equipped with Interpol comm links and database access for incoming intel via satcom. The base was also connected to a network of Interpol fusion centers manned by counterterrorism personnel and analysts.

Overhead were a series of florescent lights strung across the peak of the tent roof. The lights were low to prevent glare. While the lighting created a subdued appearance to the inside of this tactical control center, the activity level was anything but. The support team monitored the approach of the C-130 as it brought the Striker-1 team within jumping range.

Inside the bird, the loadmaster prepared to lower the loading ramp, exposing the cold winter air outside as the team readied to make their jump. Each team member donned a waist harness to which he attached his gear pack. The packs hung in front of their legs below the reserve chute in front of each agent. They each adjusted their goggles and lined up on the port side of the aircraft. There was a guy-wire about head-level running the length of the fuselage. Each agent attached the parachute static line snap hook to the line. The static lines were sturdy, bright yellow nylon straps that each jumper held in his right hand as he walked toward the aft of the fuselage and the waiting loadmaster. The fifteen-foot strap snaked its way down inside the parachute pack or 'D'-Bag (deployment bag) where the remainder of it was carefully folded. Once the jumper stepped off the loading ramp, the drop of the jumper caused the remainder of the static line to be pulled from the pack while the other end remained attached to the guy-wire with the snap hook. As the strap came out, it pulled the chute with it.

On the bulkhead near the loadmaster, the yellow jump light lit up. The loadmaster waited for the green light to switch on, signaling that they were in the jump zone. Eleven remaining members including Wellington, minus Dakota, plus four technical support members lined up along the guy-wire.

Eight-thousand two-hundred feet below the C-130 lay the advance camp base of operations. The jump light turned green. A split second later, the loadmaster waived on the first agent. He approached the end of the ramp and jumped, releasing his static line and opening his chute just a second later. The remaining team members followed suit. Within less than a minute, the entire team had exited the aircraft.

Their chutes enabled the operator to steer for a precisely controlled landing. As the chutes descended to a few hundred feet above the mountain ridge, they picked up some buffeting from turbulence passing over the mountaintops. The team coasted silently from the blackness of the night sky down to the edge of the forest that concealed the base camp. One by one they hit the snowy ground and began pulling in their chute lines and bunching up their chutes to shove into stuff sacks.

The chutes made a light scraping sound as they dragged across the partially frozen snow. Within a couple of minutes, the team had stuffed their chutes. They removed their packs from their waist harnesses with a single release clip. Each agent on the Striker team detached his or her padded weapons bag, removed the weapons, and prepped them. They strapped the empty weapons bags to the back of their packs and slung the packs onto their shoulders in preparation for the short hike to the advance camp. Above them, the C-130 had already circled around and headed back to base.

Thursday: March 1, 20:28
Romania Time
Otopeni Air Base

The C-130 touched down fifteen passengers lighter than when it had left a few hours ago. Dakota and Jack walked around outside the barracks. The cold night air gave Jack a spark that Dakota had not seen since before they left Mildenhall. Jack's eyes were full of life. His tail coiled tightly in its usual Husky-style; always a good sign. Dakota threw one of Jack's toys and made him retrieve several times. From what he could tell, Jack was operating close to normal. The two jogged around the large hanger-barracks so Dakota could see how Jack held up after some exertion. He didn't seem winded or weakened. That was all Dakota needed to know Jack was ready. He drank half a bowl of water in the past hour was alert, even playful.

A U.S. Airman walked in their direction as the two rounded the corner of the building. Dakota slowed and stopped. "Staff Sergeant. How would I find out about the C-130 that took off here a little while ago?"

"You can call the shift operations chief over at the central terminal."

"Great. How do I reach him?"

"Just hit 314# on any of the phones inside the barracks and it will connect you automatically."

"Copy that."

Dakota and Jack walked toward one of the doors to the barracks. He found a phone and inquired about the status of the C-130. It landed a short time ago and the flight crew had already gone to the flight crew facility next to the main terminal. Dakota scrambled outside to find the Airman who had helped him. The Staff Sergeant was outside speaking with another Airman when Dakota and Jack walked hurriedly to him.

"I need one of you to drive me over to the flight crew facility near the main terminal. It's urgent."

"Yes Sir. I can do that for you. We can take this vehicle here," as he motioned to one of the transport vehicles a few yards away.

"We need to hurry."

"Yes Sir."

"Pull it around over by that door. I have to retrieve some gear."

"You got it."

Dakota and Jack trotted quickly back inside the barracks. Dakota grabbed his tactical pack, helmet, weapons case, and Jack's canine vest. He ran back outside, with Jack in pursuit. The truck sat a few yards outside the door. The Sergeant waited at the wheel. Dakota opened one of the rear doors, threw his gear inside, and helped Jack up into the tall vehicle. He slammed the door shut and raced for the front passenger door to jump inside.

"Thanks Sergeant. Let's go."

The vehicle raced off. Eight minutes later, it pulled alongside an entrance to the flight crew facility.

"Here you go Sir, flight crew facility."

"Thanks Staff Sergeant. I really appreciate it."

"No sweat Sir. … Nice dog by the way."

"Thanks," said Dakota as he hurried to lower Jack to the ground. Dakota couldn't move quickly enough.

"Uh, Sir, your gear. …."

Dakota turned and looked back. "Wait here."

"Yes Sir."

Dakota nodded back, then turned to race to the entrance. Jack trotted alongside. The door swung open and Jack walked in first. Jack knew that when entering an unfamiliar area, he was to go first unless told otherwise. He walked in and sniffed the air as he looked around. He looked pretty good to Dakota, but he blitzed past Jack, leaving him to take the rear. Dakota walked quickly once inside the building, trying to orient himself rapidly. He spotted an attendant at a desk a few yards and rushed over to her. She looked slightly surprised to see someone in white, grey and black camo accompanied by a black Collie also in a tactical vest, rushing toward her.

"Miss, I need to find the crew of a C-130 that landed here in the past hour. It's urgent. Can you point me in the right direction?"

The attendant switched from being surprised to focusing on Dakota's question. "Uh …. I believe the crew you're looking for is right through that doorway over there."

"Thank you," Then he rushed off with Jack in pursuit. The duo blasted through the door and scanned the room. Three crewmembers sat at a table. Other chairs near them held their flight bags as the men filled out mandatory post flight paperwork. Dakota raced over to the senior officer.

"Major, did you just complete a flight over Rodna in the past hour?"

The Air Force Major looked up at Dakota, then down at Jack. "Who are you?"

"Major, is this the crew that just took a tactical team north of here for a jump over Rodna?"

"Look, I don't know who you are, but I can't discuss that with you."

Dakota explained the situation in an almost frantic manner. "Look, I'm not asking you to discuss it. I was supposed to be on that flight. My canine partner here became sick and we were delayed while the rest of the team took off. I need to get on a flight up there now! We have to get up there to help support their operation. It's absolutely imperative."

The Major had been calm, but became agitated. "I don't know who you are or what you think you know, but I'm not flying anyone anywhere. We've already secured the aircraft and are getting ready to get some chow."

The Air Force Captain who had been the co-pilot got up from his chair, walked around and stood beside the Major who turned in his seat toward Dakota.

"Major, you don't understand. It is absolutely critical that I get on a flight NOW!"

The Major became more forceful. "Listen pal. I don't take orders from you. Got it?"

In a flash, Dakota whipped out his Glock 19 pistol from its black tactical thigh-holster and trained it on the Major and the Captain.

"You do now. ... Jack – Protect."

Jack took a step forward ahead of Dakota and growled fiercely in a guttural wolf-like tone. Fangs barred at the pilots. The two stunned officers looked down at Jack, then at Dakota. The Major tried to push himself as far against the back of his seat as he could as if that would put any appreciable distance between him and Jack. It didn't.

"What do you want?!" shouted the Major.

"I'm a Federal Agent and I am commandeering your flight crew and your aircraft for national security reasons. You're going to fire up your aircraft and we're going to fly it back along the same route you took earlier with that team so that my partner and I can make that same jump. I told you I HAVE to get up there."

The Major looked at Dakota for a moment, still stunned. The Captain realized that any aggression toward Jack or Dakota was probably not a wise choice. The Major addressed Dakota in a more calm tone to try to diffuse the tension.

"Look Agent?"

"Dixon. That's all you need to know."

"Agent Dixon, if that's your real name, what agency are you with?"

"I told you, I was supposed to be part of that team you already delivered. That's all you need to know."

"I'd like to help you out, but I would have to get approval from my squadron commander and then file a new flight plan and get that approved. That takes time. If he's even willing to approve it. We aren't running a personal taxi service here."

Dakota was in high agitation mode. "I'll tell you what I'm going to do. I'm going to make it real simple for you. We're going to go get into a vehicle that is waiting for us outside, then we're going to the flight line and start up your aircraft so you can take me where I need to go. Got it?"

"You wouldn't use that," referring to his pistol.

Dakota stared down the barrel at the Major. "No?" He fired a shot directly at the chair between the Major's legs, blasting a 9mm hole a few inches from his groin. The Major looked down with his mouth open, shocked. Dakota continued. "… and you know what? (tilting his head down to motion toward Jack) He hasn't eaten all day and he's in a worse mood than I am. A few bites or lacerations won't keep you from flying. … That way I don't have to waste any bullets."

"You're out of your mind!"

Dakota was almost amused. "Then maybe you should do the smart thing and not test a crazy person. You don't know what I'm likely to do."

Jack growled again in the direction of the Major and the Captain.

"Now, let's get moving. … I have a flight to catch."

"Okay, easy pal. Take it easy. It's all good," replied the Major.

"Alright, that's more like it. Let's all move out that door now.

The flight crew got up and headed out the door without their bags, leaving their paperwork sitting on the table. Glock trained on them, Jack by his side, Dakota watched intently as the crew headed out the door to the waiting transport truck and climbed inside. Dakota helped Jack in and then climbed in the back, pistol still drawn. "Staff Sergeant, get us to the flight line."

A few minutes later, they arrived at the aircraft. Dakota was first out and continued training his pistol on the flight crew, but stayed far enough away so none of them could attempt to disarm him. They approached the aircraft and the loadmaster pulled open the forward hatch and crew climbed inside. Jack followed, then Dakota. Dakota followed the crew into the cockpit. "Get this thing started up. Contact the control tower and tell them you are making an emergency flight and there is no time to file a flight plan. Tell them you need priority clearance and that you are following the same flight plan you did earlier."

The crew did as they were told and settled into their seats; put on their flight safety harnesses and began flipping switches and turning on controls in a rapid, but rehearsed manner; avoiding the preflight checklist.

Dakota watched and kept his eye on the loadmaster seated in the jump seat. He posed the closest threat to a possible sudden disarming move if he was stupid enough to try it. Jack was in the main cargo compartment standing in the center of the deck waiting for Dakota.

Back in the cockpit, the crew continued an abbreviated startup sequence to get the craft airborne as soon as possible. Dakota instructed the pilot. "Now contact the tower and tell them what I told you."

The pilot switched the radio to the tower's frequency and explained the situation. The tower responded. "Attention flight Sierra, Oscar, Tango, six, niner, eight. That's a negative on your departure clearance. Repeat, negative, you are not authorized to depart."

Dakota turned to the Major. "Put me on speaker. ... Departure control, this is Federal Agent Dakota Dixon, credential id 7167 Bravo, Echo, Charlie. I am commandeering this flight by federal authority on a matter of national security. I need you to provide immediate departure clearance and instructions as the Major has requested. This flight must get airborne immediately."

The tower responded. "Sierra, Oscar, Tango, six, niner, eight, standby."

The flight crew continued with their abbreviated preflight check. Dakota stood behind the pilot seat. About two minutes later, the tower controller came back on the air. Over the loudspeaker, the crew could hear him say. "Flight Sierra, Oscar, Tango, six, niner, eight … You are cleared for departure on runway eight-right. Proceed to the taxiway. You may depart when ready. Traffic is holding for your departure."

The Major responded. "Roger departure control. Thank you for the assist."

Moments later, the rogue flight was airborne enroute to Rodna.

Thursday: March 1, 21:37
Romania Time
Somewhere over North-Central Romania - again

The loadmaster stood in the rear of the aircraft and lowered the loading ramp. A few moments later, the yellow jump light came on. For the second time that evening, they approached Rodna. Dakota mounted the skydiving goggles over Jack's face to protect his eyes from the wind. He attached his tactical bag, weapons case, and checked his chutes and gear. In a couple of minutes, he and Jack would walk the plank.

He stood at the forward edge of the ramp, watching for the light to turn green. He attached Jack with a short nylon tether strap to his own chest harness. When it was time, Dakota would pick Jack up, hold him against his chest, and attach two strap buckles to the top of his harness. This would effectively form a sling to hold Jack during the descent. He also outfitted Jack with a muzzle to keep him from opening his mouth in the face of the tremendous force of air they would encounter on the way down. He had already attached the snap hook end of his static line to the guy-wire. All that remained was a green light. . . .

It was nearly pitch black. The drone of the C-130's engines faded rapidly. Dakota felt the rush of frigid air against his clothing as he clutched Jack to keep him from moving within the harness. He could make out the outline of the trees and mountains in relation to the snow cover. The snow actually did provide some small amount of reflection of whatever moonlight might have been emanating from the clouds. His knees bent behind him, feet pointing up at the sky. The chute made an almost violent rustling sound as it deployed and straightened itself out. Once it deployed, he let Jack hang snuggly against him, secured by the canine jump harness. Dakota focused on guiding the tactical chute toward the southeastern side of the mountain ridge ahead of him. He recognized the arrangement of ridges and the tree lines from studying the satellite images of the area. The air bit his face like an icy hand slap. The only sound was the rustling of the parachute fabric. It was like someone rustling bed sheets violently and refusing to stop. He angled the wing-shaped chute toward the landing zone that his teammates had taken earlier. He hoped to come in like an aircraft, parallel to the ground at a shallow angle with the wing angled slightly upward until he made contact. Then he would be able to gradually tilt the wing and quickly come to a stop without him and Jack crashing on top of each other.

It worked. The chute slowly coasted forward under its own momentum and the violent rustling changed to a gentle ruffling like that of a large flag or a sail on a small boat. Suddenly the sound stopped. Silence took over. Dakota knelt down and detached Jack's harness and tether. He unclipped his chute pack and pulled in his chute, stuffed it in the pack and attached the pack to the back of his tactical pack. He removed his Mark 14 Enhanced Battle Rifle from its soft case, strapped the case to the back of his pack, and then slung the whole mess on his back as the others had done.

"Jack. Come!"

The two headed directly for the tree line about a hundred yards northwest of their position. Dakota checked his wrist-mounted GPS and they embarked on the short quarter-mile hike to the advance camp. At approximately 21:47 hours, they arrived in the small clearing a few hundred yards inside the woods. Before them stood the main operations tent. Attached to the tent were large corrugated plastic ventilation tubes that connected to HVAC units powered by silent-running tactical generators. A few feet away was the crew quarters tent and the mess tent. The tents were barely recognizable in the darkness; black hulking shapes outlined around the bottom by scattered patches of snow. The tops of the tents didn't really exist. They blended into the darkness of the forest. Dakota walked toward the operations tent.

Inside, florescent tubes provided subdued, but ample lighting. The interior walls were a light reflective grey to help create indirect, diffused light. In the center of the tent, tactical operators and support personnel sat busily monitoring laptop screens and alternating their sights on the large monitors on the fusion wall in front of them.

As the pair entered, a couple of the operators recognized him. He put his index finger to his lips quickly, shaking his head, signaling not to mention his name. The operators nodded understandingly.

Quietly Dakota conveyed his intentions to the ops lead. "Don't tell the Striker Team you know I'm here. I need to figure out how to insert myself into the flow at this point."

The ops lead nodded. Dakota put down his weapons, removed his tactical pack and helmet, and sat down at a small conference table with the ops lead. Within about ten minutes Dakota was fully briefed and up to speed with the latest intel and satellite surveillance. He discussed possible routes and terrain that might enable him to catch up with the team with minimal delay. The ops lead drew out the southerly course that the Striker team took. They entered the forest, headed southwest and came to a clearing downhill of the castle. From there, they planned to cross an old stone bridge that spanned a raging mountain stream. The plan was to follow the decaying stone road to the base of the rocky cliffs that protected the castle.

No hostiles had been spotted through surveillance for over two days. The hope was that the narrow pathway provided by the ancient road would afford a clear and rapid advance toward the castle gate, more importantly an undetected advance. Dakota could not afford to take that route or he would miss the siege of the castle entirely. He and the ops lead determined that the shortest possible distance was, in this case, going to be a straight line from the advance camp, over the top of the small mountain ridge hiding the camp, then down into a small cleave between that ridge and the next slightly taller ridge. Once over the second ridge, he and Jack would have to find a way to cross the mountain stream without the help of a bridge. One potential advantage to this approach was that it would take him and Jack directly toward the sniper position where Erika - Marshal Roberts, set up her sniper rifle to provide cover for the main team. Dakota was focused on the mission, but bumping into Erika wouldn't be an entirely unpleasant experience, even if she was covered in tactical gear and body armor. Not that he was interested or anything, but she did seem sort of okay to be around when she wasn't threatening to water board someone.

The Striker Team departed the advance camp at 21:30. It was 21:59; time for Dakota and Jack to pull chocks. He stopped over at Petrov's station for one last visual status check of the GPS tracks showing where the team had traveled. She looked up at Dakota, then down at Jack. "So you brought your voolf?"

"Yes," he said while studying the screen.

"He is better, yes?"

"Yes."

She continued making entries and adjustments on her keyboard. Dakota clicked on one of the function keys and switched the display input on the large screen in front of her station to her laptop. The large 55" monitor displayed the GPS tracks. They appeared as glowing neon green worm trails overlaid on top of a thermal satellite image of the area. The sat image showed any potential heat signatures of hostiles or large animals along with the bright blips and id-name tags of the Striker Team members generated by their wrist-mounted GPS units.

Dakota located the blip that was Erika's. Then he spotted the rock outcropping where she was heading to set up her sniper position. He made one final visual survey of the path he would take from the camp. It ran over the two ridges toward the outcropping that overlooked both the castle and the east fork of the rushing stream. The stream followed a cleave between the second ridge and a third ridge on the far west side of the castle. Just northeast of the castle, the torrent split on either side, effectively putting the castle on an island surrounded by a deep, wide, and violent mountain stream. No wonder the builders choose this spot.

"Petrov, Jack and I will go dark until I meet up with Marshal Roberts. Once I reach her position, I will reestablish comms with you."

She nodded. "I understand Agent Dixon. Good luck to you and … Jack? Is zat his nem?"

"Yes … that is his 'nem'. Thanks Petrov."

Dakota went over near the entrance to the tent where his gear lay in a heap. He outfitted himself once more to begin the trek with Jack. Jack watched Dakota, panting happily, looking for all intents and purposes, normal again.

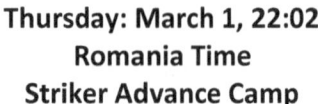

Thursday: March 1, 22:02
Romania Time
Striker Advance Camp

Dakota and Jack had ascended halfway up the first mountain ridge when an operator in the ops center opened up an instant message window on the console, selected a recipient for the message, and keyed in the following text.

"Additional Striker Agent and K9 enroute. Crossing over two ridges east of your position. Approaching from East. ETA 30 mins."

The operator quickly scanned the message to make sure it was accurate and sufficiently informative; hit send and closed the text window.

Thursday: March 1, 22:08
Romania Time
Rodna Castle, Rocky Overlook

Marshal Roberts had split off from the main team to hike toward a predetermined location. Her assignment was to establish a sniper position with good visibility of the castle and surrounding area. She would provide sighting and cover fire for the team. Jagged boulders and outcroppings were strewn across the path and a few spruce and fir trees scattered about in clearer areas. She wasn't in the forest, but a few yards beyond the thick of it. She climbed up on the sides of some boulders and down in a narrow space between others, weaving her way to an overlook she had spotted earlier.

After reaching the small summit of an outcropping, she nestled in, fishing inside her tactical pack and removing a night vision scope. Her perch provided a good vantage point looking down on the castle. She was approximately one hundred feet above the castle. From her position to the castle was about 350 yards, well within the range of her rifle. She pulled a thermal insulation pad from her pack and spread it over a boulder to her right. She would need this to keep the freezing boulder from draining all the heat from her body as she prepared to spend the next couple of hours leaning against the boulder to steady her sighting and monitor events.

Marshal Roberts spoke into her comm unit. "Overlook to Royal Eagle. I am in position."

Wellington's voice returned in the earpiece inside her left ear. "Jolly good Overlook."

Roberts grinned to herself and shook her head once. The Brits just had a humorous cadence in their dialog. It never ceased to amuse her.

Thursday: March 1, 22:10
Romania Time
Rodna Castle, Striker Team Bridge Approach

They continued through the crisp winter night. A nearly constant breeze created an invisible barrier that the team tried silently to push through as they trekked forward in the boulder-strewn field south of the castle. The main team took a route that led them southwest of Robert's position. They approached the stone bridge so they could follow the road to the castle entrance. Their route to the castle entrance was so direct, one might almost think they expected to walk up to the front gate and ring the doorbell. Their tactical snowshoes made the trek over the recent snowfall doable, but still required energy and concentration. Trudging through sixteen inches of snow in boots was not an option. They would be exhausted by the time they reached their destination and it would take three times longer. Snowshoes were the silver bullet.

Sergeant Rolf Pemberton, Australian Federal Police, was on point. His fist went up in the air. Everyone stopped. He flipped down his night vision goggles (NVGs) from their mount on the front of his helmet. He scanned the area and re-confirmed his course when he spotted the ancient stone bridge a few hundred yards ahead. Racing by underneath the bridge were the frigid waters of the turbulent mountain river. The NVGs flipped up and his hand motioned forward.

Thursday: March 1, 22:12
Romania Time
Rodna Castle, Dakota and Jack enroute to Marshal Roberts

Through the darkness, Dakota and Jack made good time as they humped their way over the top of the first ridge. Jack trudged alongside Dakota blasting out fresh clouds of breath as he panted moderately.

It was a short hike from the camp and he and Jack would only have to descend about two hundred yards into a small valley between the ridges and up the opposite face to the second ridge. That would put them in play with the rest of the team, something Dakota sought desperately. He quickened his pace, wearing the same Atlas tactical snowshoes as the main team. There wasn't as much snow in the thick of the forest as the main team had encountered in the open boulder field approaching the castle, but the snowshoes still minimized the sinkage. Even Jack had tactical canine boots that went up a little above the middle of his legs in the front and about the same with his rear legs. The boots had rough rubber-treaded soles for grip and were made of thick tactical nylon attached with Velcro wraps. At the top, they even had the elastic pull cord with a stopper clip. His boots prevented snow and ice from becoming lodged and building up between his pads and claws to minimize the chance of injury in rough terrain. They think of everything!

The two were down into the crease between the ridges. Jack continued alongside Dakota, trekking through the darkness, silhouetted against the snow. Suddenly a shot whistled past Dakota and ricocheted off a boulder past him. Jack barked. Immediately Dakota lunged forward into the snow.

"Jack, come!" He leaped toward Dakota. "Jack, duck."

Jack lay down and lowered his head to his front paws, making himself as low to the ground as he could. Dakota rolled to his side, unhooked his hiking poles, and reached behind for his rifle. He looked through a hand-held night vision scope to see if he could spot the shooter. The shooter crouched behind a tree about fifty yards up the face of the ridge. In front of the tree were a couple of boulders that provided the shooter good cover. Dakota got up, moved forward toward a boulder a few feet ahead of him, and curled up behind it.

"Jack, come."

Jack made his way toward Dakota. Immediately a second round exited the silencer of the shooter's rifle. It knocked Jack on his left side. He yelped out at the instant the round hit him. Dakota could only watch as Jack went down almost as quickly as he had gotten up. Jack lay on his side and pushed air out his nose, then quickly inhaled and exhaled twice. He raised his head, looking toward Dakota. The round struck his bulletproof vest and knocked the wind out of him as it buried into the fibers of the vest.

"Jack, crawl." Jack crawled on his belly toward Dakota until he was safely concealed behind the boulder. Dakota peeked above the top of the boulder through the night scope of his rifle. The shooter moved forward from the tree and took up position behind the nest of boulders, but Dakota could see his head and shoulders. He could not tell if the shooter had night vision capabilities. It was possible he didn't.

A small amount of moonlight struggled to pierce the thin cloud cover that blanketed most of the night sky. The snow reflected some of that light and made the entire area lighter. It was possible that with a simple day scope, the shooter could easily make out Jack and Dakota against the snow.

They couldn't stay pinned down here. Dakota knew if he wanted to live, he had to shoot and move. Stay put and he knew he would likely die. The best bet was to approach the shooter from two directions at once and put the squeeze on him. He wanted Jack to circle around silently and approach the shooter from the left, while he maneuvered around toward the shooter's right to attract his attention. This was Jack's chance, if only Wellington could see this. Dakota made an arcing movement with his hand in the direction he wanted Jack to go.

"Jack, sneak attack. …. Go."

Jack knew that meant to take a silent and indirect path to the target. Dakota popped up and fired a round toward the shooter, just to provide Jack cover. Jack began moving quietly in the direction Dakota had given him. He crept through the snow, rocks, and patches of bare ground, following a rough arc toward the shooter. Jack could hear the shooter whenever he moved. That was all he needed. He continued to close on his target.

Dakota moved quickly to a smaller boulder a few yards to his left. Another round came at him and missed. The shooter moved quickly, finding cover behind another boulder. Dakota also moved, beginning a high-intensity game of chess, only no rematch would be possible once one of the two combatants achieved checkmate. Dakota fast-crawled with his rifle, crossing a snowy patch of ground; not an easy thing with snowshoes, but he made it a little further. Another shot ricocheted nearby as he wondered how Jack was doing.

Jack quietly picked his way through snow, rock, branches, and frozen ground. He began to turn in toward the shooter's position, circling counter clockwise. Dakota moved more slowly, making a straight line northwest of the shooter, hoping for an opportunity to hang a right and approach directly. The shooter looked through his scope catching a glimpse of Dakota when he moved from position to position. The trick was to catch him in the open long enough for a clear shot.

He fired another round without even seeing Dakota, just hoping for a reaction – amateur. If he really knew what he was doing, he would know that firing at someone in a concealed position would not cause him or her to leave. He should have stuck with his first plan, wait until he spotted Dakota on the move, *then* shoot. Dakota stood halfway up, ran rapidly in a squatted position about six paces, and quickly crouched behind another boulder. These boulders had been here since at least the last ice age, dragged down the mountainside by massive glaciers. They were a Godsend to Dakota, providing him vital cover. They had been laying here for nearly ten-thousand years, just waiting to provide cover for Dakota and Jack.

Jack was behind the shooter to his left about fifty yards. He moved silently. He was close enough to hear *and* see the shooter. He crouched low, slowing as he closed in.

Dakota quickly pulled off his tactical pack and retrieved a small video monitor. He flipped it on and was able to see an image from the camera mounted on Jack's tactical vest. He switched his radio on to the frequency for Jack's receiver. Jack had a small speaker built into his vest near his shoulder.

Dakota spoke into his mic. "Good boy Jack. ... Sneak attack. Good boy."

Dakota continued to watch the view from the night vision camera on Jack's vest. He could make out movement from the sniper and an occasional reflection from his rifle. Jack was now only thirty feet away.

Dakota spoke quietly. "Jack. Lay down. .... Stay. Good boy Jack." Jack obeyed.

Dakota needed Jack to wait until he had a chance to close the gap on his end. In front of Dakota was a scattering of smaller boulders, just big enough to provide cover if he stayed on his belly. He removed his snowshoes, strapped them to his pack, and put it on his back. He crawled forward on his belly, dragging himself with his elbows and propelling himself with his knees and feet.

"Stay Jack. Stay."

Jack heard Dakota and continued to obey. He lay in the snow quietly, watching the shooter. Another round from the shooter's weapon whistled through the cold night air. He became impatient with no sign of Dakota. It was time; Dakota had maneuvered to within twenty-five feet of the shooter, but the shooter thought that Dakota was more like sixty or seventy. That was the last time the shooter caught a glimpse of the OST Agent. Dakota had his rifle slung over his back and pulled out the Glock 19 pistol from its thigh holster. He reached for a couple of baseball-sized rocks and dragged them beside him. He leaned up slightly and threw one about forty feet to his left. The shooter fired as Dakota had hoped. He reached for a second rock. Timing would be critical. "Jack ... ready."

Jack stood up and crouched slightly, head low, awaiting his next command.

"Jack, attack."

Dakota threw the rock. The shooter peered through his scope and saw the rock bounce. He fired randomly toward a group of boulders. He couldn't see Dakota. He panned quickly to the left twenty yards, looked and fired. He had nothing. Suddenly the shooter heard it, a deep growl that transformed into a fearsome medley of, growls and snarls as Jack ran and jumped on him from behind.

Wolf was the only thought that burst into the shooter's mind. The shooter pivoted around from his squatting position behind the boulders just in time to see a nightmare. Jack leapt from a boulder directly onto him. For all he knew, Jack was a wolf. The shooter screamed, dropping his rifle, doubly surprised by the fact that until this instant, he had not heard a sound from behind him.

While Jack grappled with the shooter, Dakota rushed, pistol drawn, the remaining few feet to the shooter's position. "Jack ... guard."

Immediately, Jack ceased the attack and backed off, continuing to growl.

"Good boy Jack."

Dakota pointed the barrel directly down at the shooter who lay on his back gasping for air. "Put your hands in the air."

The shooter complied.

"Up on your knees. Keep your hands in the air. Jack. Stay. Good boy Jack."

Dakota moved closer and removed handcuffs from the pouch on his belt with his left hand while keeping the weapon in his right hand pointed at his prisoner. He quickly stepped behind the shooter, putting a cuff on his right hand. He roughly pulled that hand behind his back, and then he pulled down the left hand and finished cuffing him. He unclipped the chest clip of his tactical pack and allowed it to drop to the ground. While the shooter kneeled, Dakota searched his pack and removed a roll of duct tape.

Jack knew that if the shooter moved, he was to attack him.

"If you move, the dog *will* attack you. Do you understand?"

The shooter nodded. Dakota put down his handgun and ripped out a piece of tape about six inches long. He slapped it across the shooter's mouth, then stuffed the roll back in his pack, slung it back on, clipped it and picked up his handgun and rifle. Then he put on his snowshoes.

"Stand up!"

Dakota pointed uphill where he could see the top of the ridge. That was his next destination.

"Start walking."

The trio began their ascent up the face of the mountain to the ridgeline.

Thursday: March 1, 22:25
Romania Time
Rodna Castle, Striker Team Castle Approach

The main Striker Team had just crossed the ancient stone bridge beginning the final approach to the castle. The sound of the rapids racing underneath the bridge faded into the background as the team carefully approached in two staggered columns. Pemberton was still on point, with Wellington a few paces behind him to the left.

In her nest of boulders, Marshal Roberts knew that if she spotted hostiles who posed any threat to the team, she was to begin taking them out. If hostiles were present, but did not appear to have detected the Striker team, she was not to engage. They hoped to remain undetected as long as possible.

The team continued their cautious approach, navigating a nine-hundred year old snow-packed stone road. Wellington didn't like it. Everyone wore the NATO black, white and grey camo, but he still felt exposed. They were still too outlined against the snow, with a glowing moonlit sky overhead. He reminded himself that the ops team was monitoring with satellite infra-red. Any hostiles that popped up would immediately trigger a notification message to their wrist-mounted GPS. Besides, Marshal Roberts was their overlook and he knew she was good. She would cover them.

The tactical march continued. Pemberton could see up ahead just a few dozen yards that the road began to curve to the right as it went up the hillside.

Thursday: March 1, 22:28
Romania Time
Rodna Castle, Dakota and Company

"Stop here a minute," said Dakota as he flipped his NVGs down from his helmet. He surveyed the scene below him on the opposite face of the mountain ridge. Jack stopped beside him waiting patiently. Dakota could see the general area where Erika was supposed to have established her overlook. He flipped the NVGs back up on top of his helmet and motioned for his captive to continue ahead of him. Jack followed.

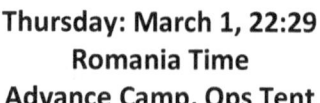

Thursday: March 1, 22:29
Romania Time
Advance Camp, Ops Tent

The ops team monitored intel reports from Interpol, CIA and other sources. They watched the Striker Team's GPS blips and id tags on the main situational display. It was their common operating picture for the mission that integrated all the essential mission information into a fusion display to provide a complete picture of the operation. Through the satellite infrared, the ops team could see the castle clearly in the CIA video feed.

One of the analysts reviewed the scene on a laptop and zoomed in on the area where Dakota and Jack were moving. It was apparent from the feed that a third person was moving with Jack and Dakota. There was no sign of any other humans near them. Erika was approximately two-hundred or more yards ahead of Dakota's position. The agent opened a text window and began sending messages and updates.

The recipient of these messages sat in a dimly lit space on the edge of a metal folding chair. He leaned forward, resting his forearms on his knees, as he reviewed the messages on his tablet computer. He shook his head as he read the incoming intel.

Thursday: March 1, 22:31
Romania Time
Rodna Castle Overlook, Marshal Robert's Position

Erika nestled in relatively comfortably behind a grouping of boulders near the edge of a drop-off. The thin luminous clouds provided a dim glow over the scene below her. The castle's hulking shape was visible even without the night vision equipment. Roberts scanned through her night-vision binoculars and found the main team advancing cautiously up the curving stone road. Although a foot or more of snow covered the road, they followed its path in their staggered formation. She could see that soon they would wrap around the northwest side of the castle as the radius of the road narrowed and completed its path leading up to the entrance. She panned right to find the castle and scanned the immediate area around it for hostiles. No one was in sight. Silently, she continued alone, monitoring the abandoned and possibly haunted castle, deep in the mountains of the northernmost part of Transylvania in the middle of the night in the dead of winter. She pondered these circumstances and thought sarcastically to herself, nothing creepy about this at all. She immediately refocused on scanning for hostiles.

She wore a thin black ski cap under her helmet, keeping the mask of it folded inside the cap. It was only about thirty-one degrees, and her face was the only skin exposed. It was tolerable for now. If the temp became noticeably colder during the night, she had already considered pulling the helmet and sliding the full face mask over her head. No point in being miserable, it could become a distraction. She wanted to be fully focused and on task. That was her nature. She was a professional and those who knew her knew that.

Dakota motioned for his prisoner to stop again. He checked through his night scope and spotted Erika about one-hundred and fifty yards down the hill. He motioned to move ahead again.

Erika continued her vigil, but within another minute, she noticed the sound of feet crunching in the snow. She turned around suddenly, drew her pistol, and trained it in the direction of the sound as she simultaneously adjusted her stance for better balance. The whole maneuver took barely a second and flowed together as one smooth natural movement. "Who's there?"

"It's Dakota and Jack! . . . and a prisoner!"

Thursday: March 1, 22:37
Romania Time
Rodna Castle, Main Striker Team

The main team approached the castle. As they circled around the north face entrance, Pemberton looked ahead and saw where the stone road approaching the main gate simply ended. There had been a bridge abutment where a wooden drawbridge used to connect when it was lowered into position, but most of the abutment had crumbled and deteriorated. There was no gate or drawbridge and probably hadn't been for nearly a thousand years; just a gaping open archway to the inner courtyard. Beneath the archway was nothing but a sheer jagged rock cliff with a drop off about forty feet.

Pemberton held up his fist, again, signaling a stop to the advance. Wellington walked up to his position while the rest of the team squatted. He scanned the terrain on both sides of the two columns of agents. Pemberton pointed up ahead where the road ended.

He spoke in a hushed voice with his thick Aussie accent to Colonel Wellington. "We're not going all the way up this road. There's nothing theya. Not loykly any smugglas are bringing weapons in the front door of this ployce. There must be another way in."

"Yes, but since we have no clue where there is another entrance, this is our way in."

Wellington noticed tracks in the snow and pointed toward them. "Look at those tracks leading off up the hill."

"Looks like vehicle tracks; possibly a snow buggy or two. The tracks dissapeya as they get closa to the forest."

Wellington thought for a moment. "They haven't shown up on any of the satellite surveillance that I can recall."

"I'm not surprised. They're barely visible here in person, much less from hundreds of miles up. We did see vehicle movement at different times though. Something about this bothers me. No sign of anyone patrolling the bloody castle. No obvious way in for anyone carrying cargo; tracks leading off into the mountains. Maybe there isn't even anyone heya."

"No. They're here."

"What if the whole castle situation is a decoy for the real location or the real base of operations, or it's a trap because they already know we're here."

"No. We've had this area under surveillance for quite some time. We've seen people walking around inside the courtyard and patrolling the castle walls. They're here."

"But did we ever see how they got in? How did they approach the castle?" asked Pemberton.

"We have not. As you said Sergeant, there may be some hidden entrance. It could be in the woods. Maybe they entered from a location outside of our surveillance boundaries. I don't know, but I do know that we're going in there to check it out. We can't just pass on by and not secure the location."

"Roguh that Sir. It just doesn't feel royt. That's all um sayin' Colonel."

"Noted. ...You know Rolf. The curious thing about this whole venture is that the last time this castle was under siege was nearly a thousand years ago. Rather strange when you think about it."

Wellington grinned curiously at Pemberton as he finished his historical observation. Pemberton looked at the Colonel. He felt even more on edge with the oddity of that statement. What did it have to do with anything? True it was, but why did it matter. Rolf felt like Wellington had just checked out for a moment or maybe the cold air was affecting Wellington's brain. The Aussie wrinkled his eyebrows and frowned in confusion down at the snow, then looked up and back at the two columns of agents scanning the area. He signaled to continue the trek.

They hiked a few yards further along the snow-covered road and then Rolf led them down the sloping right side of the road toward the rocky ravine some forty feet below the castle gate. From there they would begin a search of the entire base of the castle to see if they could possibly find some hidden entrance before committing to climb the cliff that would take them into the main gate.

Thursday: March 1, 22:41
Romania Time
Rodna Castle Overlook, Dakota, and Marshal Roberts

The prisoner told Erika and Dakota that his name was Dmitri Walachia. Beyond that, they had gathered no useful intel from him. Suddenly a voice crackled over Dmitri's radio, which Dakota had confiscated and stuffed into his pack. Quickly, he picked up his pack leaning against a nearby rock and reached inside and pulled out the radio. Holding it in front of him for a moment to read the text screen, he then looked at Erika and then at Dmitri. He reached forward and ripped the duct tape off Dmitri's mouth.

"You are going to tell them that the dog and I are dead. Do you understand me?" Dmitri nodded. "Anything else and I will just put a bullet in your head right here."

Dakota held the radio toward Dmitri's mouth and pushed-to-talk. Dmitri responded as he was directed. That was it. The call was over.

"Now, I'll ask you again. How did you know that the dog and I were here?"

Dmitri gave a steely-eyed look of defiance that flew all over Dakota. Dakota yelled at him again. "How did you know I was here!?" Silence. Dakota reached down along his left calf and pulled a knife from a sheath strapped to his leg. Dmitri's heart rate suddenly jumped. He looked with fear at the ominous black anodized blade. A prickly tingle ran through his body as adrenal squirted into his bloodstream.

Erika called out to Dakota. "Agent Dixon, sheath that knife!"

Dakota turned to his side to see Marshal Roberts training her pistol directly at him. He turned his gaze back toward Dmitri, then suddenly thrust the knife into the underside of Dmitri's thigh. Dmitri screamed out in agony and surprise.

Roberts lowered her weapon slowly, shaking her head in disgust. "Dammit Dixon!"

Dakota screamed in Dmitri's face like a drill instructor. "How did you know I was here!!!?"

Roberts cringed and looked as surprised as Dmitri and shocked at Dakota's tactics. Jack growled fiercely and emitted two barks toward Dmitri, adding insult to injury.

Roberts shouted out. "Dakota! ... Stand down! You can't do crap like that!"

She raised her weapon again. Dakota ignored her, knowing she would not shoot him. Dmitri screamed out and arched his head back in reaction to the pain, but he still did not answer. Dakota looked back for a second at Roberts.

"He tried to kill me and Jack! I'm going to find out how he knew about us."

Then he returned focus back to Dmitri. He slowly twisted the blade of his knife while it was still inside Dmitri's leg.

Roberts yelled out. "Dakota stand down!"

Dmitri responded. "There is a mole in your organization!!!"

Roberts looked worried and surprised as she heard the confession.

Dakota yelled in Dmitri's face. "Who is it!!!?"

Silence, then he repeated his question. "Tell me who it is!"

Dmitri and Roberts exchanged glances, more silence.

Dakota screamed in Dmitri's ear again. "Who is it!!!?"

Dmitri screamed out the answer. "Petrov! Her name is Petrov!"

Dakota looked back at Roberts who appeared relieved, but still trained her weapon at him. Dakota looked beyond the weapon at her face. He could see that she was surprised as well. Roberts holstered her weapon and Dakota pulled the knife out and stepped back away, satisfied and surprised with the answer. Roberts shook her head again in disgust. She stepped forward with a medical kit to help Dmitri.

"Dakota, you are *so* under arrest when we get back."

He came back sarcastically. "That's not going to be good for our relationship you know."

She looked at Dakota and shook her head. "You are in violation of international law Dixon! You have violated his rights and assaulted a prisoner while in restraints. … *And* you're delusional. Torture isn't part of our mission. Some of us actually operate within the law ya know!"

Dakota was revved up and not at all pleased with Roberts for pulling a weapon on him. "Listen sweetheart, he tried multiple times to kill Jack and me. He's the one guilty of attempted murder of an international law enforcement agent. So don't tell me about civil rights and international law. The fact that there is a mole inside this operation puts every one of our team members lives at risk, or doesn't that bother you just a little? Oh, and by the way, we are not subject to international law remember? Our organization does not even exist. Nothing we do exists either. Quit thinking like a Marshal. Out here it doesn't apply."

"I *will* write you up when we get back. Our orders are to apprehend suspects and retrieve the stolen weapons, not torture. Some of us know how to follow orders!"

She worked busily to find the right supplies in her medical kit to effect some quick treatment to Dmitri's damaged leg. She tore the side of his pant leg open for better access to the wound and hurried to bring the bleeding under control. Dimitri's blood stained the snow and the rock he leaned against.

Dakota continued. "And pulling information from this guy will allow us to apprehend those suspects and weapons," leaning in toward her face just to get his point in a little more.

She shook her head. Dakota paced back and forth thinking out loud. "Now I have to figure out how to notify Wellington without alerting Petrov and the ops team that we're on to her."

Thursday: March 1, 22:46
Romania Time
Rodna Castle, Main Striker Team

The main team completed their inspection of the rocky base surrounding the castle. Nothing suggested a tunnel, exit, or other way in. Clearly, the agents were not familiar with castle construction. Why build a massive, secure fortress with a single entrance secured by a drawbridge and then build in a lower entrance where the invaders would likely approach? That's an invitation for an assault force to walk right into the dungeon.

Pemberton walked over toward Wellington. "Sir, we need to get scaling that bloody wall. That's our only why in." Wellington nodded in agreement and then spoke into his mic. "Royal Eagle to Home Watch. Any sign of hostiles?"

Back in the ops center, Petrov responded. "Negative Sir. Zee satellite shows nussing."

"Copy Home Watch." Next, he checked with Roberts. "Royal Eagle to Overwatch. Do you have any hostiles in sight?"

Roberts looked at Dakota, then at his prisoner and then out over toward the castle, before responding. "That depends on how you define hostiles."

A confused look formed on Wellington's face. "Overlook, explain."

"Sir, we have a new addition to the team; two, actually."

Wellington lost his patience. "Overlook, quit dillydallying about. Explain your comment."

"Sir, our K9 team component is here and they have taken a hostage. A hostile engaged them on their way to my position. They captured the hostile."

Wellington was silent as he exchanged surprised looks with Pemberton.

Roberts continued. "Sir, there's something else you need to know."

Dakota reached forward quickly, covered her mic, and shook his head. Roberts realized she was about to mention the news about the mole over the mic. Petrov couldn't know.

Dakota chimed in on the mic finally. "Royal Eagle, Dog Whisperer here. I have a sketch I need to share with you. It's too hard to describe. I'll attach it to Jack's tactical vest and send him to you. Once you have it, a picture will be worth a thousand words. Then just send Jack back to our position after he delivers it."

Wellington was more confused, surprised, and angry. "Dog Whisperer! What the bloody hell are you doing here? Never mind."

Inside the ops tent, Petrov listened intently to the conversation. Dakota couldn't conceal from her the fact that he was still alive because she would have been able to see his heat signature on the infrared and his GPS signal. He could only hope that it might be a while before she considered notifying the same contact that Dimitri had that Dakota and Jack were still alive. The more important point was that no one let Petrov know they knew she was a mole. They had to try to act as normal as possible to keep from alerting her suspicions. Even so, she was more than curious, but she could not make out what Dakota meant about sending a sketch with Jack. She just didn't have enough information to know what was up. She decided to continue monitoring.

Dakota quickly scribbled a note about capturing his hostage who had likely been alerted by Petrov and the fact that he confessed that she was a mole in the organization. He folded and stuffed it into a pocket on the side of Jack's tactical vest.

"Jack. Seek whistle."

Jack took off and started working his way down the side of the mountain. Dakota spoke into his mic. "Royal Eagle, signal Jack with your whistle. He's on his way. You're going to want to see the picture I've drawn. I think it will help you determine the best approach to the target."

Dakota removed the camera monitor from his tactical pack so that he could use it to follow Jack's progress through the video camera mounted to Jack's vest. At the castle, Wellington knew that there was a message in what Dakota was telling him, but it was clear that he would not know what until Jack arrived. He decided to wait for Jack before laying siege to the castle.

Thursday: March 1, 23:11
Romania Time
Rodna Castle, Main Striker Team

Jack closed in on the main team. He lacked only a hundred yards to reach their location and deliver his message. Wellington blew the dog whistle one last time. As he peered into the darkness, he could see Jack approaching.

"Jack, come boy!"

He squatted down and waited for the Collie to come up to him. Jack arrived, wagging his tail and barked once, happily.

"Jack, no bark!"

Wellington immediately opened the pouch on the side of Jack's vest and removed the paper Dakota had inserted. The note read:

"Captured hostile confirmed mole in ops team. Petrov."

Wellington stared blankly out into the snow, stunned from the revelation. A moment later, he passed the note to Pemberton who frowned angrily as though he had been personally betrayed. Pemberton crumpled the note into a ball and clenched it in his hand.

Wellington got on his comm link. "Royal Eagle to Dog Whisperer, received your diagram. This will help much with the approach to the target. Before we proceed we're going to do one final comm check and recycle our radios."

Wellington signaled the team to shut off their radios. Once he saw they had all complied, he spoke. "Two updates for you. Obviously, Jack and Agent Dixon have arrived. How, I don't know. Regardless, apparently Dakota has captured a hostile and interrogated him, thus revealing that we have a bloody mole in our organization."

Looks of shock and anger formed on the faces of the team members as Wellington continued. "The mole is Petrov. There isn't much we can do about it right now. We'll need to rely solely on Marshal Roberts for visual oversight since we now know we can't trust any information from Petrov. We don't want to let on to Petrov that we suspect anything. The other members of the ops team at the advance camp could be in danger if she suspects that we know. Turn your radios back on. Let's complete the comm check with Petrov."

Wellington commanded Jack to return to Dakota. "Jack, seek Dakota. Royal Eagle to Dog Whisperer, Jack is returning to your position."

"Copy Royal Eagle," responded Dakota.

The Striker team prepared to climb the cliffs leading to the castle gate. Pemberton called in to Roberts on his comm. "Overwatch, this is Light Saber Leader do you copy"

"Go ahead Light Saber Leader."

"Have you spotted any hostiles at the target site?"

"Negative."

"Copy that. Keep us posted."

"Roger."

Pemberton and the others began the assault on the castle, while Roberts watched from her perch over 300 yards away. She scanned the area through the night scope on her rifle, no sign of hostiles. She tilted the rifle down and spotted a couple of the team members at the base of the cliffs. A moment later, they disappeared behind the boulders as they began their ascent. She tilted her scope back up to continue scanning the castle walls and tower. As she moved her scope to cover the tower, she detected two human figures. They appeared to be patrolling and carrying something long, too long to be a rifle. She turned the zoom on the scope. The figures were hazy, not giving off that much light. The long poles looked like lances. She decided to take a chance and see if Petrov could confirm her sighting through the infrared satellite imagery monitoring the scene from hundreds of miles overhead.

"Overlook to Home Watch. Do you have any sign of hostiles in the tower?"

"Ziss is Home Watch. ... Negative on zee hostiles. I have zero infrared on anything except zee team."

"Home Watch, are you sure? I'm seeing two hostiles patrolling the central tower."

"Zooming in Overlook. ... Zare is nussing, Overlook, no heat signature."

"Roger that."

Roberts looked through her scope again. She was sure she was seeing two vague human figures carrying something resembling lances. It didn't make sense, or maybe …. No, she thought. That's ridiculous. She panned right. She could see the northwest half of the courtyard beyond the east wall. The wall itself blocked her view of the southeast half of the courtyard, but the real-time satellite surveillance provided coverage of the courtyard, except it was being monitored by Petrov. Erika could see the team approaching the main structure inside the castle walls. She would deal with any hostiles that showed up within the range of her sights.

Dakota blew Jack's dog whistle. A few hundred yards away Jack heard it clearly and continued in that direction to return to his partner.

Thursday: March 1, 23:18
Romania Time
Rodna Castle, Inside the Courtyard

The castle walls were a silent testament to their ancient builders. Nearly a thousand years since the masons had laid the stones and the walls showed only minimal decay. Moss grew on the north facing walls as it did on most north facing things. The wooden drawbridge had probably been destroyed during the original siege. Aside from some minor siege-related damage, the ancient structure was in surprisingly good shape.

The team scaled the cliff directly below the main gate and quickly entered the courtyard inside the castle walls. A thousand years ago and such a move by enemy forces would have been met with flaming arrows and giant pots of boiling oil, but tonight, the only sounds were the occasional whistle of a midnight breeze and the dull thuds and scrapes of tactical boots against the jagged rock face.

Pemberton and Wellington took up positions alongside a stone building on the interior. They leaned back against the south side with a view of the main building and watchtower. The tower would be their entry point. Somewhere inside that structure or below it in a dungeon were the weapons, and in particular, the missing NATO laser Gatling gun. Wellington still breathed heavily from the strenuous climb; trying to catch his wind again.

Looking forward at Pemberton, Wellington commented. "I'm rather feeling my years quite noticeably. Not sure how many more castles I plan to conquer in the future," he chuckled.

The CIA Agent, George Sung, and the French Interpol Agent Beringer took up mirroring positions across from them.

Wellington spoke into his mic. "Next two up. Take the north wall."

Helmut Faust, German Police, and Warrant Officer Ian Mackay, British Royal Marines, quickly hoisted themselves up from a small rock ledge. They had been waiting just below the open archway of the main gate. The other agents were poised, ready to enter rapidly from other rocks below and to the sides of the gate.

Faust and Mackay ran quickly in a low, squat posture, staying inside the courtyard, moving past Wellington and Pemberton. They headed toward a set of partially crumbled stone stairs that led up to a ledge lining the interior of the castle wall. Centuries ago, guards watched from these positions as the invading army advanced on the castle.

Wellington signaled two more agents to take up a similar position along the south wall. The four agents on the walls were exposed from within the courtyard, but they had the advantage of a higher position. From there, they would be the last in after the rest of the team entered the main building. Agent Mike Pearson, FBI, and Sergeant Darren Goodreaux, Royal Canadian Mounted Police, rapidly moved inside and took up positions on either side of the main doorway of the central building; the watchtower.

A couple of hundred yards away in the darkness at the edge of the forest, uphill from the castle, a hostile looked through a pair of NVG binoculars, watching the agents with interest. Beside him was an accomplice.

He turned to his cohort. "Like mice to cheese."

Inside the courtyard, the agents could see the fifty-foot high tower in the moonlight. It rose some thirty feet above the tops of the walls and was probably seventy feet in diameter. Atop the round structure, the roof functioned as a watchtower, complete with parapets; exactly where Erika had noticed … whatever it was she noticed earlier.

The remaining agents entered the courtyard rapidly, with the carefully practiced, evenly spaced steps that ensured fast movement and sure footing. They took up positions on either side of the door along with Goodreaux and Pearson. It was time. Even though Inspector Chennault from Interpol was number two in charge of the overall mission, Pemberton was the assault leader. It was his job to get everyone in and out safely, while Roberts, Dakota, and Jack were responsible for force protection. Once inside, with the castle secured, Pemberton would turn over the control to Wellington and Chennault.

Pemberton entered the door quickly, weapon aimed into the darkness of the interior with eyes looking down the barrel and trigger finger poised. His NVGs provided enough illumination for him to maneuver around walls and avoid a few stones strewn across the interior. The other agents followed as the four agents on the walls covered their entry and monitored the perimeter for any signs of hostiles outside the castle walls.

Mackay spoke quietly into his comm link. "Home Watch, this is Light Saber 4. Do you copy?"

Petrov sat in front of her screen watching the GPS blips moving on the overlay of the satellite image of the castle. "Home Watch here. Go ahead."

"Any sign of hostiles anywhere in the vicinity?"

"Negative."

"Roger that."

Mackay and his three counterparts continued scanning as the rest of the team made their entrance into the castle. Then it was their turn to descend from the walls and enter last, providing rear cover.

Mackay spoke into his mic. "Light Saber 4 to Overwatch."

Roberts heard Mackay's voice come in clearly but quietly over her earpiece. The digital radio had a crispness to the sound that made it seem as though he were speaking directly into her ear.

"Overwatch here. Go head Light Saber 4."

"We're heading in. You have our six."

"Roger that. Proceed when ready."

Inside the main structure, Pemberton split the group into Alpha Team and Bravo Team. Bravo Team headed up to search the two upper levels. Alpha was assigned to search the ground level and lower levels. The teams had already memorized the layout of the building based on schematics they had obtained. Wellington even had the support organization construct a scale model for the team to study. Back at Quantico, they spent time nearly every day of the three weeks reviewing the layout of the structures inside the castle. Each agent knew this castle like it was his home. Pemberton led Alpha Team through a sweep of the current, ground level. Bravo Team was already at work upstairs.

Less than two minutes after they had split up, Bravo Team, led by Chennault, came back down a somewhat crumbled set of stairs that traced the edge of the north part of the room. Alpha Team had just finished searching the ground floor, which consisted mainly of a great room with fourteen foot arched ceilings and several smaller attached rooms and what appeared to be a kitchen or bakery.

"Nothing," stated Chennault to Pemberton. "All clear."

Wellington turned and responded. "Nothing here either." Wellington turned to Pemberton. "The only other location could be down. The other structures on the interior of the courtyard are not large enough to house any substantial supply of weapons as we have seen brought in here and laid out in the courtyard."

Pemberton commented to Wellington before beginning the descent of the lower stairs. "I'm just concerned that there are other entrances we don't know about. We saw the surveillance video from the satellite. There were suspects in the courtyard and patrolling the walls and watchtower, but we never saw *how* they got in. They just seemed to appear with crates full of weapons, like from inside the castle. It didn't make sense."

"Well then, we'll just have to go deeper and find those buggers now won't we old chap?"

Pemberton headed down the stairs, weapon drawn. Below the ground level was another floor. The ceilings were not as high as those in the great room, maybe six feet, if that. Folks were shorter back then. The agents had to crouch as they moved. The two teams spread out and quickly searched the perimeter rooms of the structure. In the center of the main room was a spiral staircase. A glow of light crept up from the stairwell. Pemberton and Goodreaux positioned themselves on either side of the first step leading down to the next level. Once the rest of the team secured the current level, Pemberton slowly and quietly descended the stairs training his rifle at any threat that might emerge. The light from the stair well cast a dim glow on the next level down.

Pemberton flipped up his NVGs to avoid being blinded by the source of this artificial light. He took two more steps. Suddenly two bats shrieked and raced out from under a ceiling perch that faced away from the light. He was completely caught off guard and with an uncontrollable reflex, he slipped backward, landing on his tactical pack on the stairs. Goodreaux trained his weapon past Pemberton toward the interior of the room to cover while Pemberton regained his balance. The surface of the steps where the bats had been hanging was slick with moisture and smelled of a general dankness and the aroma of bat guano.

The lead agents continued their descent of the stairs, staying close to the right wall. Once at the bottom, they squatted side by side and scanned to the left and right of the stairs. There was nothing in the room, but it was apparent that some light came from another room possibly on this level.

Pemberton commented in his mic. "This is where we were supposed to be able to use Jack and his video feed."

Wellington responded. "Drop it. Let's get on with it."

Pemberton removed a snake camera from his belt pouch and a small video screen. He connected the camera jack to the screen unit and flipped it on. He formed the semi-rigid fiber optic cable into a curve and slowly fed it around the corner of the wall on his right. He studied on the monitor. The camera showed nothing in the open room behind the stairs. There was an entrance to what appeared to be two smaller rooms along the exterior wall of the building. He handed the camera unit to Goodreaux who quickly curved the camera cable to the left so that he could feed it around on his side of the wall. After a few seconds, Goodreaux shook his head. Nothing.

The rest of the team positioned themselves along the stairs with several more agents waiting on the upper level. One agent stood guard just inside the door to the main structure. Goodreaux and Pemberton both stepped down off the last step and turned the left and right corners simultaneously. They quickly scanned the area, panning their rifles left and right maintaining their position as the rest of the team rapidly descended the stairs and fanned out in silence across the floor in a carefully choreographed movement. Once they were all down, Pemberton led the way toward the source of the light.

An exterior stairway along the west wall of the tower traced the curve of the outside wall. This stairwell had a much wider opening than the one they had just descended. From this opening emanated enough light to reveal a large area of the current level as the team approached. Pemberton was convinced that this next level contained the source of the light and quite possibly the arms dealers. Intel had reported that there were at least a dozen armed hostiles present at different times over the past few months. While surveillance could not detect when or where the hostiles entered the castle, the team had to assume that at least a dozen could be present, but Striker had the element of surprise – well, until they found out about Petrov. Wellington was not sure what to think. They simply had to press on and find the laser weapon and shut down this operation.

Pemberton and Goodreaux approached this new stairwell the same way as the previous one. As they neared the opening in the floor where the stairs began their descent, they heard voices. Pemberton signaled Goodreaux and the others. Wellington felt they might have found their perpetrators. Pemberton was extremely cautious, descending even more carefully than he had on the first flight of stairs. In a moment or two, several of the team made their way to the lower level while a few others stood watch on the current level.

They were at the lowest level of the castle tower structure and below ground level since the walls were below the rocky cliffs and the giant mound of rock on which the castle was built. This was the foundation level. There were no arrow slits on this level as on the upper levels. The arrow slits in the walls were a useful invention of Archimedes from the siege of Syracuse in 214–212 BC. They had become a standard feature of castles everywhere. This basement level was often used to store food and supplies and a section of it served as containment for prisoners. It was the level where they expected might be some type of escape tunnel – the only logical choice, since they had never seen anyone directly enter or exit the castle.

The blood pressures and heart rates of everyone were elevated from the moment they entered the castle courtyard. Adrenalin raced through the blood of each agent and senses were in a heightened state, as everyone knew the chance of an encounter with hostiles was imminent. They were each poking the edge of the fight or flight envelope. Pemberton noticed an electrical cable leading from the large room with the light. The voices appeared to be coming from that room. Two agents flanked either side of the entrance to the room as two more prepared to enter. Tension levels were peaking, but each agent remained focused and alert. Each practiced good breath control to maintain energy levels in the event some very sudden bursts of movement were necessary. Pemberton's hand signals indicated who would enter and cover to secure the room and who would follow. He scanned his team members to ensure they were ready.

In a sudden surge, the four agents burst inside the room, panning rapidly with their weapons, ready to engage any targets that might be present. Chennault and Beringer each went down on one knee while Goodreaux and Pemberton remained upright. Two hostiles standing near a crudely shaped entrance to a tunnel, drew their pistols, and began firing wildly. The agents focused on the hostiles and returned fire. The hostiles narrowly escaped, quickly disappearing into the darkness of the tunnel. Chennault and Beringer leapt to their feet and pursued them, firing into the tunnel. Goodreaux and Pemberton checked to ensure there were no other hostiles around the corners in parts of the room that were not visible from the doorway. Empty; no weapons, nothing but two sets of work lights on yellow, tubular tripod stands providing the only light in the room.

Goodreaux looked up along the ceiling and spotted a bundle of wires taped up to the joint between the ceiling and the wall, he anxiously turned his head and followed the wires with his eyes to discover they were feeding into plastic explosives mounted above the doorway. He whipped his head back around in the direction of the tunnel entrance and saw that the same wires leading inside and out of sight behind the archway, probably to another set of charges. The perfect placement. The arched doorways supported a tremendous amount of weight. Destroy the arches and part of the ceiling and nearby walls would simply collapse. He saw that the hostiles had also placed charges on the floor, flanking the entrance to the tunnel.

"Bomb!!! Everybody out!!!"

Goodreaux and Pembereton who had been standing just inside the door recoiled two steps back outside the door. Just as they exited, the charges above the outer door exploded. The blast threw them back on the floor a few feet from where the entrance had been. Rock and stone collapsed the entrance, trapping Beringer and Chennault inside. The charges mounted on the tunnel entrance exploded, blocking that entrance with rubble and stone. Smoke and dust filled the room instantly. Both French Interpol agents were on the floor, struck by various sized rocks.

Pemberton rose slowly from the rubble and dust.

"You okay mate?"

"Yeah. You?"

"I'm here, eh?"

Pemberton spoke angrily into his comm. "Overwatch come in!"

Roberts and Dakota heard the explosion through their headsets.

"Overwatch here. What is your status?"

"Beringer and Chennault are trapped in an interior room. The hostiles planted charges on opposite doorways. They were caught in the middle. Goodreaux and I escaped. Two hostiles took off down a tunnel way, but it is most likely blocked now."

"Copy that."

The rest were ok; spread out across the floor and a few on the upper levels. The inner room was dark. Beringer and Chennault lay on the floor, stunned and half buried.

Outside, Goodreaux and Pemberton switched on the tactical flashlights on their rifles to reveal the mound of rubble. A portion of the ceiling had collapsed and Agent Sung looked down through the opening, pointing his rifle, flashlight.

"You guys okay down there? Any injuries?"

Pemberton responded. "Goodreaux and I are good. I think Beringer and Chennault are trapped inside."

Pemberton tried his comms. "Goodreaux, Beringer come in. This is Pemberton. Do you copy?" Silence. He had dropped their code names in favor of their actuals since it was probably obvious that the hostiles knew of their presence.

The two Frenchmen were motionless. Inside the tunnel, two hostiles ran. The corridor led them up a short flight of stairs before curving around gradually to the right and then up another flight of about eight stairs.

Inside, Chennault struggled to sit up under the weight of debris. He wriggled and pushed rocks off himself. Berringer remained motionless. Chennault retrieved a small tactical flashlight from his equipment belt and shined it around the room. He spotted Berringer half buried. He cleared the remaining rocks and as Berringer came to, he discovered Berringer had broken his right ankle. He had no control over it and when he helped him try to stand he could put no weight on it. The pain was a searing heat. Chennault took a deep breath and felt a similar pain in one or two ribs on his left side. Blood dripped into his eye partially obstructing his view. He wiped it put the flashlight in his mouth as he helped his companion.

Jean-Claude! Pouvez-vous m'entendre?!!!" *(can you hear me?)*

He began to clear away some of the rubble around Chennault's head and upper body. Chennault's helmet had prevented any head injury from the falling rock. Beringer jostled Chennault on his shoulder. Chennault was face-down in the rubble. Slowly he stirred, pulling himself up and turning over on his side to face Beringer.

"Mon Dieu. Que la merde qui s'est passé," asked Chennault.

(My God. What the crap happened?)

"Nous étions pris entre deux ensembles d'explosifs," replied Beringer. *(We were caught between two sets of explosives.)*

The two agents gathered themselves and stood up. Beringer leaned on his good leg for support. Chennault searched and found their rifles. Both had been crushed. Their pistols were still in their holsters, strapped to their legs. They scanned the room to assess their situation. Chennault could hear Pemberton over the comm link. There was some crackle, indicating potential damage to the radio.

"Oui. I read you Light Saber Leader. We are trapped. Zee tunnul is blocked and zee entrance tue. … I can see your light moving around true some of zee boulders. I sink we may be able tue pull down some of zee rocks blocking de tunnul an climb over so we can find out where it goes."

Pemberton came back over the link. "Give it a troy mates. I can't see us moving any of these rocks. They're a couple of hundred pounds each. If we troy to blow them up it may bring the whole roof down."

"Roger zat."

The two Frenchmen began to pull back the somewhat smaller stones and blocks near the top of the heap blocking the entrance to the tunnel. Pemberton scanned around with his flashlight toward the tops of the arched doorways and stairs. More wires ran along the ceiling and more charges hung above the doorways. Suddenly it was all clear. They had been set up.

He yelled out to everyone on the current level and into his comm link. "Bomb! Bomb! Bomb! Out of the castle! Go! Go! Go!"

Chennault and Ranier made an opening in the rubble big enough to crawl through. Near the top of the heap, lying on their stomachs, they reached for rocks and stones and throwing them out of the way. They heard Pemberton on the comm link and immediately crawled through the opening and inside the tunnel. Chennault draped Beringer's arm over his shoulder taking weight off Beringer's damaged ankle. Hurrying down the tunnel, they hoped it would lead them out of the castle.

At the other end, the two hostiles climbed one last flight of stairs that led to an opening. Boulders surrounded the opening and concealed its presence. A wooden trap door covered the opening and natural materials camouflaged the top. To the naked eye, the escape hatch was indistinguishable from the surrounding area.

Inside the tunnel, the Interpol agents raced for their lives. The main body of the Striker Team raced up the stairs they had come down earlier, scrambling to get to the ground floor and out the exit.

Pemberton yelled into his comm link again. "Everybody out of the castle! Now!"

Every member of the Striker Team raced toward the castle gate. Running with their packs, gear, and rifles was awkward, but they had trained for moments like this. Sudden and rapid sprints were essential in combat, comfortable or not. When the agents reached the cliff at the opening of the castle gate, several sets of ropes that they had put in place lay waiting for the descent. Three agents hurriedly attached their harnesses to the ropes and fast-roped down the rock cliff in parallel. In the gateway, three more agents attached themselves to the ropes as the second set descended.

A shockwave from a large blast knocked several agents to the ground just inside the gate. A huge burst of dust and debris ejected out from the windows and gateway of the main tower, extending most of the way across the courtyard. A second explosion pounded their ears as another shockwave knocked them around again. A third, fourth and fifth explosion, probably several at once occurred in rapid succession as all of the charges detonated. In slow motion, the north half of the tower slid away from the castle gate, collapsing as the second explosion crumbled the center of the tower structure from the level below and the east face of the tower where the agents had just exited tumbled toward the front gate. Huge clouds of smoke and dust obstructed much of the mayhem from the agent's view. As the smoke slowly cleared, the moonlight revealed the total destruction of the tower and portions of the castle wall on both sides. The agents narrowly escaped becoming entombed in the ancient monument.

Three agents had attached their harnesses to the ropes when the shockwave threw them over the edge like dolls and smacked them into some of the outcroppings on the cliff face. The agents at the bottom of the ropes had just unhooked their rigs to make room for the next group. All remaining agents quickly made their way down the ropes and regrouped in the gulley at the base of the cliffs. Miraculously, no one was injured.

At the edge of the forest, the hostile with the NVGs slammed his fist angrily against the boulder in front of him. "We'll have to do this the dirty way. Monty will go out as he always wished; in a blaze of bloody glory … ignorant patriot."

Petrov's voice came over the comm. "Striker team, report. Vut is your status? Are you alright?"

At the base of the cliff, Pemberton and Wellington gathered the team for some quick re-planning. Pemberton looked at Wellington in disgust at the sound of Petrov's voice. "We're fine Home Watch. Preparing to regroup. Let us know if you notice any hostiles approaching."

He turned to Wellington and the others and spoke under his breath. "Like that will bloody happen."

Thursday: March 1, 23:27
Romania Time
Rodna Castle Overlook, Dakota, and Marshal Roberts

The prisoner's radio came to life as the text screen lit up with an incoming message. Roberts picked up the radio. The message read:

"Roberts. Free Dmitri. Kill the agent. Have Dmitri contact me."

Roberts put down the radio as Dakota looked over at her.

"What was on the screen?"

Roberts tossed the radio to Dakota. He caught it and turned it over to read the display panel. He looked up slowly to see Roberts training her pistol directly at him.

Roberts spoke with a deadly calm. "Remove your knife from its sheath, and toss it away."

Dakota complied, speaking as he did so. "What is going on Roberts?"

Jack emitted a low guttural growl as he saw Roberts pointing her weapon at Dakota.

She continued in the same tone. "Tell Jack to stay."

"Jack stay. ... Good boy."

"Now remove your sidearm and toss it on the ground in front of me." Dakota lifted his pistol from its holster, holding the stock with two fingers so the barrel pointed down. The pistol dangled in his grip.

He asked in a surprised tone. "You're part of this arms ring?"

"Yes and your Striker Team is an obstacle that must be dealt with. Now remove your backup weapon from its leg holster and then step away from your rifle." He complied again. Jack growled at Roberts, but stayed as he had been told.

"Since the explosions failed to kill the Striker Team, I will have to help my people pick them off," she explained. "Now, un-cuff Dmitri."

Dakota reached in a pocket, removed a set of keys for the handcuffs, and did as he was told. Meanwhile, he was formulating a plan, looking for options and making a mental map of the positions and distances of Jack, Roberts, and Dmitri.

Dakota's mind raced and his heart rate surged. He began to choreograph a play like a football coach determining how to deploy his offense. He freed Dmitri, then intentionally closed the gap between himself and Roberts by casually taking a couple of aimless steps toward her as though he was just coming within range for conversation.

Dmitri got up and walked past Dakota, back-fisting him hard on the side of his face. The blow temporarily stunned and blurred the vision in his right eye for a few seconds. Jack barked angrily at Dmitri as Dakota fell to the ground in front of Roberts. His legs were just at her feet. As he lay on his left side, he suddenly pushed his left shin against the front of her legs at the ankle and lifted his right leg and hooked it behind both her knees for leverage. Explosively, he executed a scissor takedown of Roberts, pressing his left shin in front of her ankle and slamming the back of his right calf against the backs of both her knees and scissoring them as he violently wrenched his torso to the right. Using all the strength of his core muscles, he torqued in opposite directions against her legs and ankles. She fell sideways to Dakota's right. Dmitri froze, not quite certain how to react.

Dakota yelled. "Jack gun!"

Jack stood up, took two leaps toward Dmitri as Dmitri fumbled around in the snow for Dakota's gun. Jack tackled Dmitri from behind, knocking him down, growling fiercely in his face and around his head. At the same time Dakota gave Jack his command, the former Marine leaped up and dived on Roberts, grabbing her gun while she still held it in both hands. He forced her to fire four times at Dmitri, just as Dmitri found the pistol and turned toward Dakota to fire. Dakota narrowly missed hitting Jack as he crawled all over Dmitri in a wolf-like rage. Dmitri rapidly sucked in his last breath with a sudden inward surge of air as the shock of the rounds rippled through his body. He fell limply to the ground as Jack continued growling and on top of him for a second.

"Jack. Down!"

Jack immediately stopped his attack and backed off. He continued to growl angrily at Dimitri's limp body. Dakota used a gun disarming technique on Erika, twisting the weapon counter-clockwise away from him using the barrel as a lever, while striking against the inside of her wrist with the other hand to twist the weapon out of her grip. In a split second, Dakota had it in his hands. He rolled backward off her to put distance between himself and his new prisoner. The weapon was securely clamped with both hands and trained on her. She lay in the snow on her left side, looking past the barrel at Dakota. Jack sat silently panting beside the body of Dmitri.

Roberts yelled out in desperation. "Dakota! Wait!"

She turned her radio off so the Striker team and the ops team would not hear what she was about to say. "I can explain!"

Dakota replied. "I'd be fascinated to hear what you have to say about this."

She spilled her story rapidly, racing to get it all out to convince him. "I was recruited into the smuggling ring six months ago as a mole working for them. I led them to believe I had been bought off and that I was working inside the Striker Team. They wanted intel so they could stay one step ahead of Striker. When the smugglers found out that the Striker Team was being formed, they used this castle as a trap to lure the team in so they could destroy us."

Dakota listened, but all he felt was a wave of skepticism wash over him like a cold shower. He heard words coming out of Robert's mouth, not believability. He kept listening, training his weapon on her.

"DX- "

"Don't! … call me that! … Only my friends call me that!"

"Wellington knows about me. I'm telling the truth. I had to play along so Petrov and the smugglers would believe I was with them. Petrov is the one who recruited me – or thought she did, months before Wellington had formed the team. I was their backup in case Petrov was compromised. Wellington's goal was to get enough intel to find the weapons cache and hopefully uncover some of the suppliers as well, but Wellington didn't know that Petrov was the mole. I couldn't tell him. The weapons were never here at the castle. That was all intentional just to bring the team here and take them out. It was my job to help take down the team if the initial plan to kill us failed, or if Petrov was exposed. I didn't know about the explosives in the castle though. I didn't know how they were going to do it. I'm telling you the truth! Confirm it with Wellington."

Dakota sensed that there might be an element of plausibility in her story, but it was so complicated that he wanted to hear it from the old man himself. He reached for his radio.

Erika stopped him. "Wait! … You can't do it over the radio or text. Petrov will know we're on to her. You'll have to send a message through Jack. I already turned my radio off before I told you any of this so Petrov wouldn't hear me. The problem is they're going to be expecting Dmitri to respond back after they think I've killed you. If they don't hear back, then they and Petrov will know something's up."

"Fine. We'll do that," still disgusted at the situation and not fully confident of her truthfulness.

"Wait. I can text Petrov that you're dead. That might buy us some time. We don't know if she is aware that Dmitri is supposed to contact the others once you're dead. I can tell her I'm about to move into position to start taking out the rest of the Striker Team."

Dakota stared at her for a few seconds. She looked at him awaiting his answer. "Do it."

Erika quickly texted a message to Petrov on the tiny keyboard of her digital radio. "Wait. Let me see the message before you send it."

Roberts keyed in the message, then handed the radio to Dakota. He reviewed the message, then handed it back to her.

"Add to it not to worry about the dog. He's worthless without Dakota."

Roberts updated the message and handed it back to Dakota one last time.

"That's good."

He pressed send.

Roberts shared her assessment with Dakota. "Wellington and the team have apparently destroyed their GPS units. I believe they know that Petrov is a mole and don't want her to be able to track their positions through GPS."

"How do you know this?"

"Petrov contacted me before you showed up. She said she had lost the GPS. … Crap! You have to put your GPS on Dimitri's wrist or she will see you moving around if you move more than a few feet or so."

Dakota took off his GPS wrist unit and draped it across Dimitri's left wrist. It would lay there with him and Petrov would think that heat signature and GPS was Dakota's dead body.

"But she can still see on infrared satellite."

"True, but now that she thinks you're dead, she won't be able to tell that it's you that's with me instead of Dimitri. The imagery on the satellite isn't clear enough to tell. I need to destroy my GPS. We can give her some excuse that I slipped and smacked it on a rock or something."

"That's fine, but she can still see the main team. She knows where they are. How does that help?"

Erika explained her plan. "I have to move into a closer position to be able to start taking out the Striker Team. The other hostiles will begin to engage from wherever they are. Once they do, we will have some idea where they are and I can begin to take them out instead. Petrov won't know the difference. If she suspects anything, she'll warn the others and we'll lose them. She'll think the Striker Team is taking out her people, not me. Once we get a location on some of the hostiles, hopefully we'll be able to track them back to the weapons cache and the leader or at least get a clue about where the weapons are stored."

Dakota processed what she had just proposed. "Okay. I still need to get a note to Wellington. Jack can get to him in about ten minutes or so. So you're saying the weapons are here somewhere?"

"Yes. I think, but not in the castle. There must be a cave, or bunker or some other structure. I don't know."

"But Jack will take twenty minutes or more round trip before he comes back with the response. We need to get moving soon."

"Wellington only needs to read the note. Then he can nod at Jack to let me know if your story is true. Jack will have his video camera on and I'll be able to see it on my monitor. Then Jack can head back here and meet us on the way to provide supporting fires. I'll know if your story is a load of BS as soon as Jack gets to Wellington."

"Okay. Can I have my weapon back?"

"Sure … Nice try Roberts. When I get the nod from Wellington. Meantime, cuff yourself."

Dakota reached over in the snow where Dmitri had dropped his cuffs and threw them at Erika. She looked defeated and frustrated as she caught them and began to put them on. Dakota reached in a pouch on his belt and pulled out a small notepad. He scribbled a note to Wellington to confirm Erika's story.

Erika looked at Dakota and shook her head. "I'm confused. For Jack to find Wellington, one of us will have to contact Wellington by radio to let him know to blow the dog whistle. If I do it, Petrov will know something is up. If you do it, she'll know I didn't kill you."

"Jack can find his way. He knows the route now."

"I hope so."

"Jack, come."

Jack got up and walked happily over to Dakota, wagging his tail on his way. Dakota placed the note in the same pocket on Jack's vest that he had used earlier.

"Jack. Find Wellington. … Go."

Jack took off in the direction Dakota pointed. He did know the way. He confidently began his descent down the hillside.

Roberts looked at Dakota. "The Striker Team will think I'm coming in to provide cover fire. Petrov will think I'm going to take them out. Wellington will wonder where you are though. I can't say you're with me if Petrov thinks I killed you."

Dakota paused. "Tell him what you told Petrov. She'll think you're just trying to maintain your cover. Tell her the prisoner escaped and killed me in the process."

"That would work. Sure."

With her hands cuffed, she put her radio back in its holder on her belt and plugged the wire for the comm headphone back in to the radio, turned it on, and set it to the proper channel to reach Wellington. "Royal Eagle, this is Overwatch do you copy."

"Go ahead Overwatch."

"Dog Whisperer is dead. The prisoner escaped and killed him in the process. I'm coming in to provide cover fire for you. Departing shortly."

Wellington sat backward against the rocks at the base of the cliff. He was silent for a moment as he processed the fact that Dakota was dead. He responded in a somber voice. "Copy that Overwatch. What about Jack?"

"He's here. He'll stay with me."

"Copy. Royal Eagle Out."

Dakota looked at Erika. "Now we wait for Jack to get to Wellington. I'll watch him on the monitor."

Dakota removed the control unit with the built in video monitor and flipped it on. In a moment, after the machine had booted up, the monitor showed an image of what Jack saw as he progressed down the hill. He was likely only about two hundred yards from the main Striker Team, but it required considerable concentration and effort to navigate through the hills, boulders and brush.

Dakota commanded Jack through the speaker mounted on Jack's vest. "Jack speak. … speak."

Jack barked twice. Wellington heard Jack's bark in the distance. Immediately he reached for his dog whistle, blowing it twice. With Jack's hearing, Wellington might as well have shined a spotlight on himself. Jack heard the whistle perfectly and zeroed in more quickly on Wellington's position. A few more minutes ticked as Jack zigzagged between boulders that led him on a final path to the team.

Wellington called out. "Jack! Come here boy!" Jack ran happily up to Colonel Wellington. "Hey boy!"

Wellington reached over and opened the message pouch on Jack's vest and removed Dakota's note.

"I'm not dead. Is Robert's under cover with the hostiles? If true, nod yes toward Jack's camera. I'm watching."

Wellington called Jack's name to make sure he was facing him and then nodded several times for Dakota to see. Dakota saw Wellington's response on the monitor, then he blew Jack's dog whistle. Jack stood immediately and headed off into the darkness.

Wellington sat and watched Jack as he disappeared behind a large group of boulders.

Dakota looked at Roberts. "Okay. I guess your story is legit. Let me undo those cuffs. ... This is turning out to be the weirdest first date I've ever been on."

He walked toward her and unlocked the cuffs. Roberts snapped at him. "Would you stop! This is NOT a date! So keep your fantasies to yourself."

"You're right. I'm sorry. It would have been better to start by going out for coffee, or a maybe you're the type who prefers smoothies. ... Handcuffs are a bit over the top."

He handed her pistol back to her and she put it back in her holster, shaking her head and refusing to give him the satisfaction of making eye contact just yet.

"Now, can we just get serious?"

Dakota grinned. "I don't know. This is all happening too fast for me."

"Dammit Dixon!"

"No-no. It's Dakota Dixon. ... See. I think we're hitting it off fabulously. Already we're bickering like an old married couple," he grinned.

"Ugghhhh!!!" screamed Roberts. His ceaseless innuendos began to rattle the psychologist just slightly. Somehow, his odd charm, humor or whatever it was had gotten inside her head. She was upset with herself for letting that happen. While proud of her ability to maintain her professionalism and emotional distance from subjects or patients, there was just something different about this one. His simple, but complex personality intrigued her, somewhat of an enigma.

-12-

Rules of Engagement

Thursday: March 1, 23:37
Romania Time
Hilltop Woods Overlooking Rodna Castle

The leader of the arms smuggling ring sat on a rock outside their main bunker. He peered through a pair of NVGs. Alfred Bainsworth was a mercenary, but he preferred to think of himself as an expert in business logistics, or as he preferred to call it, "Dark Logistics". The types of businesses he dealt with tended to be on the FBI's list of targeted organizations or at least in serious contention for inclusion. He had an axe to grind and the Striker Team was it, more specifically Wellington. He saw the team down below in the gulley at the base of the castle. They headed toward a boulder field strewn across the hillside moving in the direction of his bunker.

He turned to his second in command. "Spread your men out in both directions. Form a barrier between them and our location."

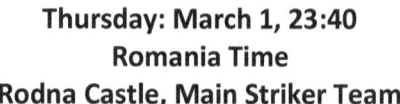

"Royal Eagle to Home Watch."

"Ziss is Home Watch. Over."

"Do you have any heat signatures that might be hostiles anywhere in the vicinity?"

"Affirmative Royal Eagle. To the Northeast, approximately 300 meters. Zere are eight or nine. Zey are dispersing to form an arc in front of you."

"Roger that Home Watch. Royal Eagle out."

Wellington turned to Pemberton. He had heard the same message over the comm. Pemberton spoke. "I think our target is in front of us. We need to engage them. If we can drive them back or take out most of them, then the survivors will likely lead us to the weapons cache as they retreat." Wellington nodded. Pemberton laid out the plan for the other agents. It involved a perilous crossing over the raging and frigid mountain stream to exit the island on which the castle stood. This would enable the agents to begin fighting their way up the mountainside toward the hostiles.

Thursday: March 1, 23:42
Romania Time
Castle Overlook, Dakota, Jack, and Roberts

The two hostiles who had set the charges emerged from the tunnel. Erika spotted their heat signatures in her sniper scope. She focused quietly and took careful aim, aligning the target in her sights. As the hostiles moved, she followed their movements through the scope, leading with the cross-hairs just ahead of the first target so that by the time the bullet reached the location in the cross-hairs, the target would also be there. She orchestrated the fatal intersection of bullet and target. She slowed her breathing as she tracked his movement, and then gently squeezed the trigger. A hot round rocketed out of the barrel. At seemingly the same instant, one of the hostiles was dead. She began calibrating for the second hit. She was a lethal guardian angel for her team.

Suddenly, Dakota realized something. "Wait! Hold your fire. That hostile could lead us to the others or to the weapons cache."

Roberts considered it for a second, then nodded. Dakota gathered his weapons and pack. "We need to head out as you told Petrov and get closer to the action."

He blew his dog whistle. Two hundred yards away, Jack heard it and continued in the direction of him and Roberts. Roberts gathered her gear. A few moments later, the two began working their way carefully down the hillside, navigating between boulders and a mixture of packed snow, covered with about a half a foot of fresh powder.

"Freeze!" Yelled a hostile who jumped out directly in their path from behind a nearby tree.

He stood in front of Roberts and Dakota, training an AK-47 rifle at them. "Drop your vepons."

The two agents slowly lowered their rifles to the ground.

"Now take out your pistols and toss zem toward me."

The gunman pushed the talk button on a radio mounted to his shoulder. "Diss is Tarik. The Marshal is working with an agent. Dimitri is not wis her."

They each slowly removed their pistols, holding the trigger guard between their thumb and index finger and tossed them on the ground in front of Tarik. Dakota spoke quietly into his mic, which was set to Jack's frequency. "Jack, gun."

Jack appeared out of the darkness from behind the hostile. He let out a fierce growl, startling Tarik causing him to turn suddenly to see the source of the growl. The instant Tarik had eyes on Jack, the angry Collie jumped him, knocking him to the ground, biting and slashing in a flurry of black and white fur and fangs. Tarik dropped his weapon in a vain attempt to fend off Jack with his arms. Dakota raced forward to retrieve his weapon. He saw Tarik hold up his left arm to shield himself as he reached for a knife strapped to his leg.

"Jack. Stand down!" yelled Dakota.

As the words left Dakota's mouth, Jack backed up a step and the hostile lunged upward toward Jack with his knife. Dakota fired and hit Tarik in the hand. Tarik rolled on his stomach and grabbed Erika's pistol on the ground beside him. Dakota fired two more shots, killing the gunman. Jack stood on the other side of Tarik's body, panting heavily from the encounter.

Dakota ran up to Jack to pet him. "Good Jack! Good boy!"

Erika muted her radio. She retrieved her weapons. "Well. I guess the smugglers now know that you are alive and I'm a mole in their organization. Which means if I'm not really part of their arms ring, then Petrov just heard what happened and now she has to figure that her cover is blown because I would be about to expose her at this point."

"Yeah, that makes sense."

"So, now we have to continue with providing cover fire, if needed, and see if there's any chance that any of the smugglers will lead us to the weapons cache. This whole castle siege was just a set up, so the weapons could be anywhere – even miles from here."

Thursday: March 1, 23:48
Romania Time
Main Striker Team, Base of the Castle

The main team heard the exchange between Roberts, Dakota, and the hostile on their comms. The hostiles knew Roberts was a mole, Dakota was still alive, and they knew that the Striker team was aware that Petrov was a mole. Nothing was left to conceal. All the cards were on the table, almost.

The team fanned out and headed in a northeast direction toward the hostiles. They worked steadily through the field of boulders. As they walked, they could hear the rush of the rapids from the mountain stream that separated them from the hostiles. Suddenly a storm of automatic weapons fire opened up a hundred yards or less, in front of them. The magnitude of the fire crackled and echoed off the rocks and rock cliffs drowning out the rush of the stream. Pemberton pointed for Wellington, noting that the firestorm appeared to originate up the hill on the opposite side of the river. In the moonlit scene the agents could clearly see the muzzle flashes coming from the automatic weapons of the hostiles. Immediately, everyone in the Striker team hit the deck, seeking cover behind the boulders and began to return fire.

Pemberton was pissed. "Pemberton to Home Watch."

Petrov answered. "Home Watch. Go ahead."

"Petrov, put Daniels on comm."

Robert Daniels responded a moment later. Everyone could hear the conversation in their earpieces as they maintained fire.

"Daniels. This is Pemberton. I'm ordering you to arrest Petrov and put her into custody. She is a mole who has been working for the smugglers. Do it now!"

"Yes Sir."

Inside the ops tent, Daniels turned around to see Petrov pointing her pistol toward him. Immediately another operator spotted Petrov and rushed to disarm her from behind. Petrov turned and fired at the operator, hitting him in the arm. Daniels grabbed Petrov's arm, pointing the pistol upward and grabbed the barrel from the side like a lever, pulling it down hard. That broke Petrov's grip. He thrust his right palm up into her chin, knocking her out. Petrov slumped to the floor in a heap.

Daniels yelled out. "Medic! I need a medic over here!"

He pulled a pair of handcuffs from his utility belt and cuffed Petrov while she was still unconscious.

Pemberton broke in. "Daniels! Are you there! We need support!"

"I'm here Sergeant."

"Now listen mate. We're pinned down. Call for the backup team and tell them to get a bloody chopper in here. Then I need you to help us pinpoint where the hostiles are located. You also need to be aware that Agent Dixon and Marshal Roberts should be visible on your monitor to the East of our position."

"Copy that Rolf," piped in Dakota. "Daniels. Everyone has destroyed their GPS because we knew about Petrov. We didn't want her tracking us. Jack's GPS is still functioning, so if you locate his signal you'll know where Marshal Roberts and I are."

"Copy that," replied Daniels.

Thursday: March 1, 23:53
Romania Time
Marshal Roberts and Dakota enroute

The trio of Jack, Roberts, and Dakota moved due north, parallel to the rushing stream. They hoped they could establish overlapping fields of fire to provide support to the Striker Team. They picked their way slowly through the boulders to find a route over the stream and up the hillside, more directly in front of the positions of the hostiles who had the main team pinned down. The Striker Team was attempting to drive the smugglers further up the mountain. They were trying to push them into the woods to see whether they would scatter or head for a central location that might lead them to the weapons.

Roberts was on point, Dakota in the middle, Jack took up the rear. Within a few moments, Erika located another suitable position from which to lay down sniper fire. She began to set up her targeting.

Dakota saw her prepping. "Alright, this is good. I'm going to move that way more, possibly providing a flanking position. Maybe I can effect some fire toward the rear of their positions. Come on Jack."

Roberts looked in the direction of Jack, then at Dakota. "Dakota, is Jack okay now? I mean, since his illness on the plane."

Dakota paused, almost surprised that for a second, Erika actually showed a little compassion instead of being pissed off at him for being a ham. "Yeah. ... Yeah, I think he's doin' just fine. ... Thanks for asking."

He left it at that, no sarcasm or joking. Erika looked at the two for a moment before Dakota turned and led Jack into the darkness.

Thursday: March 1, 24:00
Romania Time
Beringer and Chennault Escaping the Castle

Beringer and Chennault reached the tunnel escape. Beringer carefully let Chennault down so that he could open it. He pushed the heavy door out of the way, letting a wide ray of moonlight fill in the hole where the tunnel ended. He went back inside and helped Chennault up again and the two limped out of the tunnel together. Immediately a bullet struck Beringer. Chennault was crippled and on his own. He checked Beringer's neck and found no pulse. Kneeling, he exhaled slowly and felt himself sink with sadness at the death of his countryman. Pausing just a moment, snapped back to reality and reached for Beringer's pistol. He stuffed a couple of extra magazines from Beringer's belt into the large utility pockets of his tactical pants.

Chennault adjusted his mic and called in. "Pemberton, ziss is Chennalt. Ranier was just hit. He's down. I am injured. My ankul is broken or sumsing. I can barely move."

"Chennault. I copy. Find cover. We'll get help to you as soon as we can mate." Pemberton contacted Dakota next. "Dixon, can I interest you and Jack in a rescue mission?"

Dakota replied, trying to show Rolf a little respect in his moment of need. "Sir, how can I help?"

Pemberton gave Dakota the details. Meanwhile, Chennault was under heavy fire. There were two hostiles within fifty yards. He fired with both pistols, valiantly attempting to put up a wall of suppressing fire before running out of ammo. He quickly changed out both magazines, dropping the spent ones at his feet. The two hostiles moved a few yards closer. Chennault was acutely aware of the desperateness of his situation and began to fire more economically. Suddenly, the moderate clouds that had largely obliterated the moon, passed out of the way and a nearly full moon shone brightly on the entire scene. He took a quick look between some boulders and saw the two hostiles as though they were awash in a muted form of daylight. The brightness of the moon was ridiculous, good, and bad. Unfortunately, the light gave an even clearer view of Chennault to the hostiles.

Dakota contacted Chennault. "Jean-Claude. This is Dakota. I'm on my way with Jack. We're coming in from your three o'clock. The main Striker Team has already crossed the stream to your one o'clock. I'll be coming in behind the line of the main team."

"Copy zat Dakota. Just hurry. I haven't much ammo left."

"Roger."

Dakota picked up the pace and moved very rapidly through the snow with Jack at his heels. Dakota and Jack headed toward the river following its path north toward Chennault's position. In the bright moonlight, Dakota could see clearly, but he could also be clearly seen. Several rounds of automatic weapon fire blasted past Jack and Dakota, startling him so much that he lost balance and fell. He pointed his rifle in the direction of the fire as he pulled his legs up under him and crouched for cover against a rock.

"Jack! Come here."

Jack came quickly over to Dakota as several more rounds blasted around them. A thought flashed through Dakota's mind that this mission was not turning out to be the cakewalk that Wellington had described. Not that he was complaining. He was a Marine. They run toward the fight, not away from it, but it was Jack. He didn't want Jack going on this mission in the first place. Keith had outmaneuvered him into accepting Jack for the mission. Now he just wanted to make sure Jack made it home safely to his family. That was the goal. He owed the Barnes that.

Dakota popped out around the boulder for a second and fired a couple of rounds, striking very close to the hostile. In the moonlight he could see the hostile stand up partially as he prepared to return fire, then immediately, the hostile arched backward, dropping his weapon in a final convulsion as a round from Erika's rifle struck him.

Dakota spoke into his mic. "Erika?"

"Yeah ...," responding in a quiet voice.

"Thanks."

"Sure. ... Keep your head down next time. Don't they teach you Marines to shoot from a position of cover?"

Dakota took a deep breath, then stood up, speaking into his mic. "Yeah."

"Then do it! We can't afford to lose any more team members."

"Rog."

Dakota and Jack hurried to intercept the hostiles closing in on Chennault.

Friday: March 2, 00:12
Romania Time
Main Striker Team Pushing Up the Hillside

In the moonlight, Wellington and Pemberton could see their agents arrayed across the hillside in well-covered positions. Gunfire was inconsistent. The agents were well-trained and understood the importance of not wasting ammo, while the hostiles spent theirs indiscriminately, spraying in the general direction of a given agent as though they were trying to wet them down with a water hose.

George Sung, CIA, had his eye on a particular hostile who seemed to get a thrill out of jumping out from behind his boulder and firing in a wide rapid sweeping motion in the direction of George and Ian Mackay. George waited patiently and watched the idiot. For an instant it occurred to him, this guy only had a few breaths left and didn't even know it. His hostile was at his twelve o'clock at about forty yards. The hostile jumped out suddenly from behind the boulder, George was in sync with his somewhat erratic rhythm. It was the hostile's last appearance. George steadied his MK-14 against the boulder and squeezed off one round as the hostile finished spraying about fifteen wasted rounds. The hostile flew backwards from the force of Sung's round and crashed in an upright position against a tall boulder behind him. He inhaled sharply when the round hit him, but it was a shock reflex. Leaning back against the boulder he slowly slide down into a squatting position as the air leaked slowly out of his lungs. He slumped to the side before rolling and falling face down in the snow.

The rest of the team was also busy engaging hostiles. The odds seemed roughly even. There appeared to be about nine hostiles and maybe a leader or two whom Pemberton had spotted through his binoculars, but they were not engaged in the firefight.

Captain Herman Labatt, New Zealand National Police, and Special Agent Mike Pearson, FBI, paired up almost back to back in a fighting position. Their overlapping fields of fire prevented any forward movement from the hostiles. Meanwhile, they and the other agents were able to put down enough suppressing fire to allow them to move forward a few feet and close the gap.

Labatt spotted a new hostile he had not been able to locate previously. He knew that fire was coming from his direction, but this one was more coy than the one George had just taken out. Labatt fired a round to see if he could get the hostile to react. A split second after Herman's shot, the hostile stood in a crouching position and began to run a few paces toward another large boulder, possibly attempting to outflank the New Zealander. He didn't make it. A bullet from Erika's rifle took him down.

Higher up the hillside in a well-protected rock nest, Bainsworth and his compatriot Aleksandra Zuboff saw their comrade go down.

Aleksandra cried out into the radio. "Nicholas! Nicholas! Can you hear me." There was no response. Her husband lay motionless in the snow. His lifeless eyes stared up at the stars. Aleksandra turned to Bainsworth in anguish, crying out. "Ve vill crush zeez Interpol animals Alfred! Nicholas deserfs to know zat ve vill do zat for his nem!"

She stood up and began intently trying to locate one Striker agent's position after another and fire meaningless rounds in the direction of each.

"Die! All of you!"

Bainsworth yelled at her over the gunfire. "Aleksanra! Aleksandra! ..."

She stopped and looked at Bainsworth, sobbing. "Vhat?"

"Listen love. We'll make them pay, but right now we have to make sure they don't find the weapons cache."

As he spoke, Erika took out another of his henchmen. The odds were clearly in the favor of Striker.

Friday: March 2, 00:19
Romania Time
Dakota and Jack enroute to Chennault

Dakota and Jack raced through snow, gunfire, boulders, and trees, toward Chennault's location. Bits of rock exploded along the way, occasionally pelting them with rock shrapnel as each round of hostile fire attempted to find a target in Dakota.

Jean-Claude called into his comm link. "Dakota I hope you and Jacques are getting close. I only have one magazine left. I could use your help."

"Jean-Claude, I have you in sight. Look to your four o'clock."

Dakota was less than two hundred yards away and closing rapidly. He had to try to stay lower, moving from boulder to boulder with Jack. Dakota knelt on one knee and fired a few rounds from his Glock toward two hostiles who had Chennault pinned down. He maintained a low crouching position and continued to run with Jack, firing as he ran. Jack kept up with Dakota, running just at his heels. Jack winced from the gunshots exploding around him and arched his shoulders. He lowered his head with each gunshot, but in a strange way, he found this great fun, running at night, chasing Dakota. Something about this adventure touched a distant part of his ancient wolf DNA. The chase response required no training.

Dakota stopped and removed three magazines from his tactical pouch and put them into a pouch on Jack's vest.

"Jack seek the whistle. ... Jean-Claude, blow your dog whistle. I'm sending Jack with some fresh magazines. He'll get there faster."

"Roger zat. Dakota, sank you."

Chennault fumbled for his dog whistle. Jack heard the high pitch sound that no one else detected and bolted forward. Dakota slung his rifle off his back and provided several rounds of cover fire. Dakota continued moving in the same direction, ducking behind boulders, waiting until after each burst of fire, then moving on. Jack reached Chennault in less than two minutes while Dakota trailed behind.

Chennault called Jack to him. "Jacques! Here boy!"

Jack heard Chennault and increased his pace. The hostile fired several rounds in Jack's direction, narrowly missing him. Jack ran even faster, with his tactical boots helping him move rapidly over the rough surfaces and snow giving him more ease of movement than he would have without them. In another moment, Jack was with Chennault.

"Good boy Jacques! Good boy!"

Chennault's eyes became misty at the sight of Jack's happy face. Jack barked twice to greet Chennault. Chennault gave Jack a quick hug and then reached for the pouch and removed the magazines.

"Jacques, down. ... Dakota, I have Jacques and the ammo. Sanks much."

"Roger that." Dakota was less than one hundred yards away.

Chennault loaded a fresh magazine into his Glock and resumed returning fire. Finally, he hit one of the hostiles in the arm, forcing him to drop his weapon. As he reached away from his boulder, Chennault hit him in the other arm, then fired two rounds toward the second hostile, taking him out.

Dakota saw the second hostile go down. He took a chance, stood up, and ran as fast as he could through the moderately thick snow without his snowshoes, letting the adrenalin carry him the last few yards. Jack barked as Dakota dived behind a large boulder beside the one concealing Chennault.

"Dakota, I am glad to see you. My ankle is a mess eh?"

"Yeah. I've seen better my friend, but we can patch you up."

Dakota spoke into his comm. "Erika. This is Dakota. I'm with Chennault. We have a hostile at our twelve. I'd like to place an order for an extra-large serving of lead. Can you deliver?"

Roberts had just finished moving in closer to have better visual and choice of angles of fire for just such an occasion.

"Roger that Dog Whisperer. Your lead is heading downrange. Standby."

Within a few seconds, a 7.62mm round exited Roberts rifle, striking the hostile at Dakota's twelve o'clock. Suddenly, their little piece of the battle scene grew just a little quieter.

Dakota looked at Chennault's ankle. "Jean-Claude let's see about patching you up so you can travel."

"I can do zat now that the hostiles are out of the way, but I cannot travel. Besides, I do not want to slow you down. You must help the main team, how you say, … flush out zee bed guyz?"

Dakota looked down at Chennault's ankle and removed his pack, taking out the medical kit. He handed Chennault a couple of wraps and some gauze.

"Here, see what you can do with this, but we have to move you to a concealed position until we can come back for you."

"Agreed."

"And Jack is going to stay with you."

"Alright, sank you again."

"Don't mention it," grinning. "Come on. I think that group of boulders over there will give you nearly a full circle of cover and concealment. That will make a good position for you. Let me help you up."

Dakota draped Chennault's arm over his neck and held on with the opposite hand. The two limped the same way Chennault had helped Ranier. The location Dakota selected was only about thirty feet away. They made it there easily as Dakota gently helped Chennault down inside the surround of the boulders. Jack followed and came into the little den of boulders panting and watching.

Dakota ordered Jack. "Jack guard Chennault."

Jack barked once. Dakota felt good leaving Chennault with Jack and some fresh ammo. He would be okay for a while until the team could subdue the hostiles and take control of the situation.

"Pemberton this is Dakota. Chennault is immobile, but I moved him to a secure covered position and Jack is staying with him."

"Copy Dakota. Oy nade you and Roberts to provoid some supporting fire somehow. Way nade to advance up the hill and put the squeeze on the hostiles. Our backup team won't be heya for a while. They're caught in weatha."

"Roger that Sergeant. We're on it."

Erika left her perch to close in with more of a flanking position on the hostiles. Dakota raced back to meet up with her. His conditioning over the past many months was paying off. Running with boots was strenuous in snow on uneven terrain, but he paced himself and felt good, plus the cold winter air jam-packed with extra oxygen didn't hurt either. He just had to focus on breathing. Breathing was a good thing.

As Dakota came to within about a hundred yards of Erika, a hail of automatic weapons fire surrounded him. He dived for the ground. The hostiles seemed to open fire in unison and on cue, blazing with everything they had like the finale of a fireworks show.

Suddenly Daniels came in over the comm. "Pemberton, this is Daniels come in."

Rolf replied. "Go ahead. What have you got for us? Hopefully a backup chopper full of troops."

"Not exactly Sir. There are about five more hostiles showing on the infrared. Check your NVGs. You should be able to pick them up. They are a little further up the hillside, just above the ones you've been engaging. They're spread out in a line about forty yards across. Sort of a second line of fire behind the one in front of you."

Pemberton was silent for a moment. "Thanks Daniels. Is that it?"

"Yes Sir."

Pemberton turned to Wellington. "Okay. I don't know where the hell these new hostiles suddenly came from, but it's bloody well clear to me that they're protecting something. They don't want us getting up the mountainside, and that's exactly where we're headed." Pemberton spoke again into his comm mic. "Dixon! Roberts! Where are you two?"

"Roberts here Sir. I've moved in closer. I see the hostiles in my sights. Stand by Sir. Time to thin the herd."

She flipped open the bipod stand for her rifle and zeroed in on the first of the new hostiles. Working through her set up procedure, she targeted the one closest to her. Within a few more seconds, the first hostile was down. She adjusted her aim and tracking and took out the second hostile. Downhill from that hostile was one of the ones who had already been engaging the Striker Team. Because she was to the far left side of the hostiles' position, she had effectively outflanked them and could fire with impunity. She could kick their ass and they wouldn't even see it coming. She sighted, aimed, and removed a third hostile from play.

Just then, Dakota arrived, winded from sprinting. "Where's Jack?" asked Roberts.

"I'm fine. Thanks for asking."

She shook her head.

"He's with Chennault. He's immobilized. I secured him in a ready-made boulder fort and left Jack to guard him. He'll be okay until this is over." He continued to breath heavily, trying to recover from his sprint.

"I need you to set up a position on my eight. From up here we have clearer targeting than the main team. Once we get the hostiles on the defensive, the main team will be able to move up the hill to find out what's up there. Hopefully by then the backup team will be here."

"Roger that. Anything you say dear."

"Look Dakota, I'm sure you Marines joke around all the time like this is some way of relieving stress under combat or something, or you think everything is some big flippin' joke, but I need you on task and focused, got it?"

"Sorry, just havin' a little fun. Can't help myself. It's how I cope, like you said."

"Yeah, well we'll have our fun later...I mean. We need to get serious ... Shit! Just do your job Dixon!"

Dakota grinned to himself at her confusion as she tripped over her words. It was cute, but he kept it to himself, laughing on the inside. "Whatever you say. You seem to have the mind game thing all figured out. I'm on it. So where are you from anyway? I never got that."

Roberts turned slowly away from her rifle and looked at Dakota not believing what he was saying. "Really Dakota? You're hilarious. You just don't stop do you?"

"My people say there will be plenty of time to rest when you're dead. Besides, the small talk and the humor helps me cope, we already went over this."

"So you just want me to drop what I'm doing here in the middle of the mission and help you cope is that it?"

"Naw…. I mean…"

"Focus Dixon. Focus."

"Okay, now you're just creeping me out. You're starting to sound like Yoda or something."

"Dammit Dixon."

"Ah, you're still not getting it right. Remember? It's Dakota."

"Shut! – Up!" she yelled in a loud whisper.

"We're going to have to learn to get along better or our kids will get the wrong impression about us."

She shook her head in exasperation and looked incredulously at Dakota. "Did you hit your head on a boulder back there or something? You're completely delusional. You know that right?"

He faked a surprised look. "You say that like it's a bad thing?"

Roberts shook her head. Frustrated for allowing him to see her get flustered momentarily. He was really beginning to get under her skin. For a split second, the thought that Dakota was somewhat tolerable to be around when he wasn't being a complete spaz entered her mind, but not under these circumstances. She went back to the moment and being fairly pissed at his antics.

Friday: March 2, 00:27
Romania Time
Jack with Chennault at his Concealed Position

Inspector Jean-Claude Chennault, Interpol, was the executive officer for this mission; Wellington's number two, but he was down and out of the action. He had badly damaged his ankle in the blast inside the castle. He had to remain concealed in the mini-fortress of boulders Dakota had located for him.

Jack sat happily near the entrance of Chennault's enclave. In the background, both could hear the exchanges of gunfire. The acrid smell of gunpowder burned at Jack's sensitive nose as he continued Dakota's order to guard Chennault. Chennault could monitor the action through his earphones and keep up with the conflict.

Then he heard something that did not come through the earpiece in his left ear. A deep, throaty growl entered his right ear. The growl sounded evil and almost obstructed by a sloppy, spitting of saliva. Jack barked insanely. He growled back and barred his fangs viciously, but it did not compare to the menacing ferocity of the wolf. Chennault got up and crawled awkwardly toward the opening of the fortress. He pulled his pistol from its leg holster and flipped off the safety.

As he emerged at the entrance of the huge boulders, the scene in front of him looked like something from a movie. Jack's head was down low in a defensive posture, front paws spread in a wider than normal stance. A few yards in front of Jack was the grey wolf, the apex predator of this territory.

Immediately, the terrifying realization came to Chennault's mind that wolves typically hunt in packs. He pointed his pistol, but as he did, Jack pounced. The two canines became entangled in a death hug. Two sets of fangs slashed and tore at fur, ears, muzzles, and whatever they could reach.

Chennault could not fire. He didn't have a clear shot at the wolf. Jack was fully engaged, taking full charge of his duty to protect Chennault. Chennault lowered his weapon; helpless, only able to watch the death match and hope that the outcome was in Jack's favor. He fired two shots into the air, hoping to separate the two long enough for a clean shot at the attacker. The wolf paused for a second. As he did so, Jack lowered himself and prepared to leap forward to pounce on his foe. In that instant, Chennault had the shot he hoped for. With a two-hand grip, he double-tapped the trigger, dropping the wolf instantly. Jack stood up, looking at his nemesis, waiting, wondering if there was more, but the wolf was motionless. His fur was still.

"Jacques. Come. ….. Good boy!"

Chennault stroked Jack's head and patted his tactical vest as though he was patting Jack's side. It had to mean some type of appreciation to Jack. Chennault stood up, leaning against a boulder for support. He surveyed the scene and shown his flashlight off into the darkness. He saw no indication of any other members of a wolf pack. Then he returned to his fortress and called Jack to him.

"Well Jacques. It looks like zat was not a Transylvania type of werewolf. Good sing eh? Sank you Jacques."

He spoke into his mic. "Dakota, ziss is Chennault. Do you read me?"

"Go ahead Chennault."

"I sink zat Jacques should come back to you. I am fine here, but he could be of more use to zee team. Call your whistle and have him come to you."

"Are you sure Jean Claude?"

"Yes. I will be fine."

"Copy that. I'll call him." Dakota blew his dog whistle. Jack heard it from a few hundred yards away.

"Jacques. Seek zee whistle. Go Jacques!" Jack obeyed and disappeared into the darkness. As he ran off, he barked twice.

Friday: March 2, 00:36
Romania Time
Dakota and Erika Ascending the Mountainside

Dakota raced to climb a jagged rock face. He wanted to reach a downed tree that he planned to use as a bridge over the mountain stream. He attached Jack to his climbing harness and Jack dangled ten feet below him, suspended by Dakota's rig. An RPG exploded barely twenty feet from him and Erika. Clearly, someone had spotted them. He was halfway up the forty-foot cliff when it struck. The blast dislodged some boulders near the downed tree and jostled it enough that he feared the base of the tree might slide down and crush him and Jack. When the tree rotated, it caused Dakota's rope rig to twist and become jammed.

At that same instant, Jack's harness slipped and Jack skidded down several feet, but remained attached and dangling ten feet above some boulders at the base of the cliff. Dakota realized he had to lower Jack down on top of a boulder. With Jack's rigging jammed Dakota could not move up while Jack was still attached. The rope would also not allow him to climb down to join Jack. He lowered Jack on top of the boulder, then cut the line to free him.

Jack stood on the boulder, looking up at his partner and emitted two barks. Dakota continued his climb upward to the tree bridge. Jack leaped, jumped, and crawled across several boulders, using them as giant stepping-stones as some of the smugglers approached him.

Speaking into the microphone, Dakota ordered Jack to "escape" before the smugglers caught or shot him. As the smugglers approached, Dakota climbed upward toward the tree, but didn't have time to position himself better. He swung himself upside down, suspended by his rope rig and took careful aim from his awkward perch. He was able to take out both hostiles.

After Dakota and Erika made it across the stream, he summoned Jack with the dog whistle. When Jack arrived, he saw that Dakota and Erika were on the opposite side of the raging stream. Jack climbed and navigated boulders in the stream. Hesitating at the edge of a flat rock, he made a final daring jump to reach Dakota and Erika. As he pushed off, he lost his footing and fell short, sliding helplessly into the icy stream.

Jack struggled to make headway and find some place to escape the frigid waters as Dakota raced desperately downstream after him. Lying prone on a boulder, he reached out for Jack who flailed toward him. Dakota missed him as the current swept Jack away. He ran further down the stream and discovered that they were only a hundred yards or so from going over a twenty-foot waterfall. Dakota's heart raced and he felt the hot surge of adrenalin as he made a second attempt to reach Jack. He barely grasped a handle on the top of Jack's vest. With a tenuous grip, he pulled Jack close enough to get a second hand on his vest and pull him from the water. Once on dry land, the two collapsed together on solid ground. Jack was soaked and shivering. A moment or two later, Erika caught up with them.

"Erika, you need to get back to providing cover. I have to stay with Jack. If I don't get a fire built and warm him up, we're going to lose him to hypothermia."

"Roger that. Good luck." She headed off up the mountainside to find a new perch from which to snipe.

Dakota removed Jack's vest and Jack shook off the cold water. He hurried to gather wood for a small fire. Having been swept so far downstream, they were fortunately a safe distance from the battle scene as Dakota got the fire going. "Don't worry Jack buddy. We'll get you warmed up in no time."

Dakota removed a thin blanket from his pack, ran a line from a nearby tree out at a diagonal to the ground. He draped the blanket over the line so it provided a roof over the fire, then he carried Jack into the makeshift shelter. The half-Lakota Indian had built a traditional, small "Indian" fire that required very little wood and wrapping the blanket over the line as a roof help trap and concentrate the heat. He rubbed Jack's fur to expose his undercoat and skin to the warm air gathering inside the makeshift tent. With the entrance of the tent facing a medium sized tree, most of the heat from the fire remained inside and Jack began to warm up slowly. Jack looked in Dakota's eyes. Through his look, Dakota sensed that Jack understood what he was doing for him.

Friday: March 2, 00:48
Romania Time
Roberts' Sniper Position

Erika was in her sniper's perch focused on her task. She methodically took out several of the hostiles as she provided cover for the agents. Each downed hostile made the situation just that much safer for her team. Her efforts eased the job of the main team as they struggled up the rocky mountainside to investigate the cave fortress. As she scanned the terrain through her sniper scope, she noticed an entire new group of hostiles appearing from the same area along the mountainside. The new hostiles quickly halted any progress the agents had made. The thought flashed through her mind that the situation had the feel of a video game, where more adversaries appeared seemingly from nowhere, just after the current assortment of hostiles dwindled. They appeared to have grenade launchers and RPGs in addition to various styles of automatic weapons. The combined strength of the two groups of hostiles enabled them to quickly pin down and outnumber the Striker team. Erika was convinced that there must be some type of cave, bunker or otherwise unknown fortress buried in the mountainside. These scumbags weren't just spawned by some video game.

Friday: March 2, 00:57
Romania Time
Jack and DX's Tent Shelter

"Jack, you look much better buddy. Your fur is all warm and dry. We need to get you moving around so you'll generate some body heat. Common boy! Let's go."

Jack got up at DX's command. DX reached for his radio and re-mounted it on the side of his pack. He then donned his tactical microphone, adjusting it along the side of his left cheek.

"Dakota to Roberts."

"Go ahead."

"I think our furry friend is ready for action again. We're heading your way. Give us a few."

"Roger that."

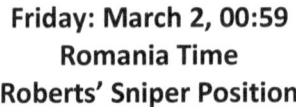

Friday: March 2, 00:59
Romania Time
Roberts' Sniper Position

Erika moved to a spot lower on the mountainside, hoping to flank the enemy. Her left foot snagged a tripwire, setting off a booby trap. The resulting explosion threw her clear and caused boulders on the hillside to dislodge. Before she could get up, some of the large rocks landed on top of each other, trapping her left leg. The hot searing pain in her ankle immediately suggested to her that it might be broken. Trying to ignore the feeling and work through the pain, she attempted to turn her hips and rotate her left leg, but her ankle was tightly lodged between the rocks. Several more attempts to do the same confirmed that she was trapped.

"Hey DX, you wouldn't happen to have a fork lift would you?"

"Explain."

"I'm stuck. Kind of got wedged in and ... oh shit."

"What?"

"Two hostiles approaching at my twelve. I could really use some help if you can fit me in your schedule."

"Hurrying. How far away are they?"

"About seventy-five yards. I'm not sure if they've spotted me yet. Hurry."

"Rog."

Dakota and Jack rushed to help her and within less than a minute, they arrived at her position. Dakota quickly assessed her predicament, then crouched behind a large boulder near her and positioned his rifle on it. He scanned through his scope, spotting the two hostiles, and quickly took out both of them. Dakota and Roberts exhaled heavily with relief that the immediate threat was gone.

"Ok, this rock ain't going anywhere without some kind of lever. Hang tight."

He spotted a nearby sapling and took out his knife and used a fist-sized rock to hammer the blade into the base of the sapling. In about a minute, he had cut enough of a wedge out of the trunk that he could push the sapling over and snap the trunk. He had his lever. He quickly thrust one end of the sapling under the rock that was on top of the trio of rocks that had her leg pinned. He toppled it out of the way and removed a second rock the same way. The last rock was twice the size. He could only lift it enough to lessen the pressure on Erika's leg, but not enough to allow her to pull herself out of the trap.

"Jack! Come!"

Jack, who had been watching Dakota remove the rocks, trotted to him.

"Jack, pull Roberts."

Dakota lifted the boulder as much as he could. As he did so, he commanded Jack again.

"Jack, pull!"

Jack clenched his teeth on the shoulder straps of her body armor and pulled backward with all his might. She wiggled backward with his help and pulled her leg free. Roberts breathed another sigh of relief. She attempted to stand when suddenly the ground beneath her shifted. The explosion had loosened some flat boulders on which she was standing. She slipped backward and landed on her stomach, laying on the edge of a drop off. Jack had pulled her back and stepped to one side, but she went toward the edge and lost her balance.

She reached out and grasped for anything to halt her slide over the edge. Dakota saw her struggle as she slid over the edge with only her head sticking up. Her hands reached unsuccessfully for something to grip. He dived forward on his belly like a baseball player sliding into home plate. She slipped further and balanced with only one tenuous foothold, which quickly began to give way.

"Give me your hands!"

Dakota reached out with both his hands for hers. He missed her left hand, but touched the fingertips of her right hand. It wasn't enough. He scooted forward a few more inches, careful not to put himself on an unstable surface that would cause him to go over the edge.

"When I tell you, push off of your foothold so I can grab you!"

"I can't! That's my injured ankle! It won't support me. I can't maintain it."

"You have to! Just do it! Now!"

Erika struggled to push off her single foothold and launch herself upward on her injured ankle. As she did, she reached as far as possible toward Dakota's hands and he grabbed her by both wrists. He torqued his waist as though he was rolling over on his back. The strength of his core muscles allowed him to drag her up over the edge where she could get her center of gravity on more stable ground. He pulled her the rest of the way over the edge as she crawled forward with her legs. For the third time in as many minutes, the two exhaled a sigh of relief.

Still breathing heavily. "Thank you," she said.

"Phew. Sure. Don't mention it. ...Let me have a look at that ankle."

She had badly sprained her ankle, and removing her tactical boot was not advisable as the swelling that would be occurring in the next few minutes could likely prevent her from putting the boot back on. The shaft of the boot would have to suffice as a wrap, but to immobilize it somewhat; Dakota tightly wrapped an elastic bandage around the outside of the boot in a crisscrossing pattern. The bandage allowed her to walk, but reduced the amount of flexibility of the boot to keep from aggravating her ankle.

"I think you're going to survive Roberts."

"Thanks again."

The hostiles continued to lay down heavy fire on the agents and the backup forces were still a considerable distance away.

Their radio earpieces came to life with the voice of Colonel Wellington. "Dakota, Roberts, I don't know if you have heard yet, but our satellite surveillance has just gone offline. I don't know if Petrov had anything to do with it, but it's a *damned site* inconvenient! Without our space birds, we can't track these crazy bastards or keep track of each other. We're going to have to fight this out old school."

"Sir, how bad is your situation," asked Dakota.

"Have a look through your NVG binoculars! We're bloody well trapped. They have us on three sides and we can't leave our cover. We're totally pinned down."

"Roger that Sir. I'm working on an idea. Standby."

"We need a might bit more than just an idea Dakota."

"Roger Sir."

Turning to Roberts. "We have to get them out of there or they're not going to make it."

"I suppose you have something in mind?"

"Yes and no. I don't want to take a risk like the one I did in Afghanistan. I lost some good friends that day, but this is pissing me off. That bit with the satellites going down is just like when we lost our drone surveillance. We were blind."

"Look. I'm sorry about what happened, but-"

"This time it's going to be different. This is *not* going to be a repeat of Takhar Province."

"So…"

"You know that miniature hand-launched drone in my pack?"

"Yeah."

"We can use that instead of the satellite surveillance."

"Ok…"

"I can use the night vision camera on the drone and see it on Jack's monitor. We'll be able to see what's going on and guide the agents out."

Dakota pulled his pack off and opened up the main section. Inside was a small plastic equipment box with the drone. The box was damaged and when he opened it, he saw that the blade housings and two of the blades of the miniature quad-copter drone were crushed. He lifted it out of the case.

"It's useless."

He slammed it down against the inside of its case and pushed it aside.

"This is crap!"

"What?"

"Now it's just *like* Afghanistan. No eyes in the sky. Blind and we're headed into an ambush."

"I guess history does repeat itself."

Jack whimpered slightly to get Dakota's attention. When Dakota turned to look at him, the two exchanged a brief look. Jack whimpered, then turned his head in the direction of the pinned down agents. Something in Dakota's psyche told him Jack was trying to tell him that he needed to go to them. Dakota sensed that Jack only lacked permission from him to do so. Erika watched the non-verbal exchange. It was clear to here that the two were communicating with what appeared to be only eye contact and head gestures. The effect seemed surreal to her, but Jack and Dakota seemed completely in sync with each other. Jack took a step in the direction where the agents were engaged in a firefight for their lives. He turned to Dakota and gave him a longing look as if awaiting the command. At that moment, Dakota realized that Jack fully grasped the severity of the situation. Jack understood his role. It was exactly as Dakota's grandfather had described. Jack's spirit told Dakota it was time. An image of Keith, Linda, Jack and the kids flashed in Dakota's mind and vanished as quickly as it had appeared. It was blasted away by the sounds of the intense battle raging in the background. Dakota realized this was the time for him to trust Jack. His vision quest and reality seemed to be aligning to each other and the reality of the situation was helping to make the vagueness of his vision quest clearer.

"Jack, wait."

Erika realized what was about to happen. "Wait. What just happened here?"

"What do you mean?"

"You and Jack, I mean, I don't understand. I just watched you two plan out an action and … you were communicating. … with Jack."

"Ok…"

"How can that be?"

"It's complicated. We just do. My people have old ways and I have them too."

"Oh sure. Got it. You just used the Force or something. Bullshit. What is going on here Dixon? How does he know what you're thinking?"

"I told you some things are just old and not easy to explain. My Grandfather called it a gift."

"Dixon, I saw it. He knew what you were planning and yet you didn't give him a single command."

"My people have always had a close connection to nature. Call it a sixth sense. When I pay attention to him, he pays attention to me. We are able to pick up on subtle things that others miss."

"So you were born with some special dog powers or something? Is that what you're saying?"

"Call it what you want. I need to equip Jack with this smoke bomb. It has a delay mode on it of sixty seconds. He's going to head down in front of the agents and run past them, creating a wall of smoke. Once he gets to the far side, I'll whistle for him to come back and that return trip will make a thicker wall of smoke to give the agents plenty of time to escape. Once Jack takes off toward the team, you and I will move up to find a new vantage point to provide cover while Jack is doing his thing."

Dakota removed a smoke canister from the side of his backpack and attached it to a utility clip on the top rear portion of Jack's vest. Down in the small, boulder-strewn valley, some of the hostiles moved closer to the agents, beginning to form a more complete choke point. The agent's time was running out.

Thinking as she listened to Dakota's plan, Erika struggled to remember something he had told her. "DX wait. You said your vision quest suggested that when you have become so close to your K9 brother that you are willing to risk him to save others that's when your spirit destiny will be achieved."

"Yes. What are you talking about Roberts," continuing to prepare Jack for his mission.

"DX, *Zoe* was your spirit destiny! You risked *her*. You were willing to sacrifice her to save your troops in Afghanistan. You said she understood that. Don't you see?"

"No! That's not how it's supposed to work!" Dakota felt the intensity of the moment as a fresh dose of hot adrenalin flowed rapidly into his bloodstream.

"You've *already* accomplished your spirit destiny! That's what I'm trying to tell you. You're vision or prophecy or whatever it is has been accomplished. You *are* a dog whisperer. You just haven't realized it. …Think about what I'm saying. You know I'm right."

"How can you be right! You don't understand. You're not one of my people! I have to be willing to sacrifice Jack not Zoe!"

"No you don't!"

"Oh, so now you're an expert on Lakota traditions? Do you think I *want* to do this? Besides, this isn't about what I want anymore. It's about saving those agents. Keith and Linda will understand."

"You don't have to do this! We can find another way....There has to be another course of action. Think about what I'm saying," grabbing his arm and pulling him back. "You have been so focused training Jack, trying to keep him from being hurt or killed that you've missed it.... Look, some people chase their destiny and some people never find their destiny, but I believe that sometimes, your destiny finds you."

"So what are you saying?"

"I'm saying, I think your destiny already found you in Afghanistan. You already got the dog whisperer thing down. With Jack, you've just had a chance to take it farther, but the whole gift and special powers that I've been seeing, that we've all been seeing between you two - it's pretty obvious something's going on even if the rest of us normal humans don't understand it. But you sure as heck better understand it."

Dakota was quietly angry and confused. An uncertain silence filled the space as his expression changed from anger to realization, the possibility that there might be something to what she was saying. Suddenly awed at the simplicity of her logic, he quietly composed himself as he looked at her. He shifted to his comfortable kidding around self as he began to accept her version of reality. "How do you do that!?"

"What?" she said innocently, realizing that she must have gotten through to him.

"Get inside my head like that."

She grinned. "It's what I *do*. I get inside people's heads; the criminally insane mostly."

"What are you saying Roberts?"

Continuing her grin. "Nothing."

The pair planned a new course of action to rescue the agents. DX and Jack would take one route toward the agents and Erika would go to the northeast, further up the mountainside. She was to find a new vantage point to continue picking off hostiles.

Dakota reviewed the new plan. "I think this will work. If Jack and I go down into that basin area and flank the hostiles from the opposite side, directly across the valley from you, that will put pressure on the hostiles while providing cover for the agents at the same time. Then they can make their retreat."

"Agreed."

"Alright, let's do this. Good luck."

"You too."

Erika gathered her pack and sniper rifle and limped slightly as she headed up between the boulders in search of a new vantage point. Jack and Dakota took off in the opposite direction, heading down into the valley. She turned back and spotted Dakota commanding Jack to head off in the direction of his original plan.

Confused and concerned, she yelled out to him. "DX! Where's Jack going?"

He didn't respond. "DX!"

He had gone back on their plan and was moving forward with the suicide mission for Jack.

Friday: March 2, 01:17
Romania Time
Jack and DX's Position down the Mountainside

Dakota commanded Jack to take off, but then he heard the words of his grandfather. A memory crept into his consciousness. A memory from back on the reservation at the campfire the night his grandfather told him of his special gift and the unique powers that went along with it. He sensed his grandfather's presence through his words. "Trust your canine companion."

Erika's voice burst through Dakota's near trance and bristled through his earpiece. "DX! Do you copy! I know you can hear me." He ignored her.

Wellington heard her calls. "Roberts what is it?"

"Not sure Sir. Trying to reach DX. He and Jack are heading your way to assist. It's nothing Sir."

"Copy."

Jack continued on his path as the battle intensified. The hostiles brought out more weapons, flamethrowers, high-powered machine guns, RPGs. They used seemingly everything in their arsenal to obliterate the agents. The "cakewalk" had quickly turned into a nightmare scenario for the Striker team.

Friday: March 2, 01:22
Romania Time
Roberts' New Sniper Outlook

Erika reached her new sniper perch and began scanning through her scope. She spotted Jack and Dakota running together now, but not in the direction she thought he had sent Jack a few moments ago. More confused, she radioed Dakota; still no response.

She spotted Jack as he climbed over several boulders and rocks in the stream. He ran in the general direction of the agents; not, where she and Dakota had agreed.

Friday: March 2, 01:29
Romania Time
Jack with the Trapped Agents

Jack arrived in the basin area where the agents struggled to fend off the smugglers. He carried many magazines of additional ammunition and a note from Dakota that read, "There is a way out that you can't see from your location. Jack will lead you."

Wellington greeted him with a smile. "Good boy Jack! Come here fella."

Pemberton stayed low, behind a large boulder and turned to Jack to unclip the saddlebag pouches of ammo.

Dakota arrived on the far side of valley area and moved uphill to find a suitable overlook. He set up his rifle and steadied it on a boulder, scanning for hostiles. He found and picked off several in just over a minute, as Erika did the same on the opposite ridge.

Jack barked at Wellington and Pemberton three times, then turned and took a step in a direction away from where they were firing. He was telling them to follow him.

"Ok Jack," acknowledged Wellington. "Boys, time to go. Jack will lead the way."

Erika continued to provide cover fire as the agents retreated. Two agents remained as the rest followed Jack. They put up a wall of fire, but one agent took a hit. Jack returned to him, grabbed the agent by the shoulder straps of his bulletproof vest, and dragged him behind a boulder. Jack barked several times for help. Two more agents rushed to aid the injured agent and join the retreat.

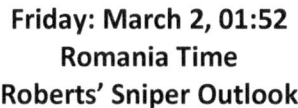

Friday: March 2, 01:52
Romania Time
Roberts' Sniper Outlook

Erika continued to scan and identify enemy targets. She worked like a precision machine, methodically adjusting the odds in favor of the Striker Team. The old adage about controlling the high ground to secure victory flashed briefly through her brain. While she felt the continuous effects of adrenalin coursing through her veins, she maintained focus and composure to steady her aim and calm her breathing to accomplish her deadly task.

She was completely unaware, as a hostile suddenly appeared behind her. The dark figure knocked her unconscious with the butt of his rifle, striking just under the rear rim of her helmet. A second hostile approached, and each took one of her arms and walked backward dragging her along to the north side of the mountain ridge. Less than fifty yards away, Dakota saw them through boulders and trees. He climbed and crawled up the hillside to return to her position. The agents had been rescued and were able to effect a retreat.

He arrived in time to observe the two hostiles drag Roberts into what appeared to be a cave opening. The cave was part of a defensive network of tunnels created when the castle was active. Dakota blew his whistle for Jack to seek him out. In the distance, with the team of agents, Jack stopped and turned his head toward the sound that only he could hear. He barked once at Wellington and Pemberton.

"Go Jack!" said Pemberton, realizing Dakota was probably calling him. Jack took off into the night.

Dakota waited for Jack behind a boulder, as he watched the two hostiles drag Erika further away. He blew his whistle one more time for Jack to zero in on his location. Moments later Jack arrived beside Dakota.

"Quiet Jack. No bark," as he held his index finger up to indicate silence.

Dakota moved forward. Jack followed. They quietly approached the entrance of the cave. A single guard stood watch. Dakota approached the location of the guard, taking advantage of every boulder for cover. He motioned for Jack to stop and stay. Dakota pressed his back against the boulder, squatting low. He peered around the corner cautiously and waited for the guard to turn his back. The guard didn't move. Dakota decided to direct the guard where he needed him to look. He picked up a small stone and threw it in the direction he wanted the guard to face. The guard turned quickly and drew his weapon, pointing where the stone had landed. At that instant, Dakota rushed out from behind the boulder, launching upward from his squatting position. He grabbed the guard from behind and applied one of his favorites chokes; one that Eddie used to hate, a bare-naked choke. A few seconds later, the guard slumped to the ground unconscious and Dakota and Jack snuck toward the entrance of the cave.

Thirty feet inside the mouth of the cave, they reached a large open area that essentially formed a room. Some type of lantern or other light source emitted a glow that provided just enough light for the two to navigate. The castle builders had dug out this space centuries earlier as evidenced by carvings and period symbols on the walls. They effectively turned several natural caves into an interconnected tunnel network, probably for storing supplies and weapons. The smugglers clearly had the same idea and had taken up residence as the latest tenants.

He moved cautiously, deeper into the wide tunnel, crouching behind a rock and part of the cave wall that jutted out near him. He spotted Erika lying on the floor in a semi-conscious state. Several hostiles stood nearby, paying no attention to her. He decided to use Jack as a diversion.

Pointing toward the hostiles, he whispered. "Jack go! Run!" Jack took off toward the hostiles and ran past them, around a corner and deeper into the tunnel. All of the hostiles gave chase, yelling in a Slavic dialect. Dakota moved in quickly, using the diversion to rescue Erika. He lifted her up, wrapped one of her arms over his back, and moved rapidly to the entrance. Barely conscious, her head hung down and her legs dragged as she struggled to lift them, making it difficult for the two to move very quickly.

A moment later, the two emerged from the cave and Dakota dragged Erika back behind the rock where he had hidden from the guard.

"Wait here a sec."

He rushed back toward the cave entrance and blew Jack's whistle with the signal for him to return. The hostiles heard nothing, but Jack did. Immediately, Jack turned around and raced toward the entrance, hostiles in pursuit.

At the entrance, Dakota ignited a smoke canister and rolled it into the cave. He ignited a second one and heaved it like a grenade, to the north and the group of hostiles with the heavier weapons.

He returned to Erika. She sat on the ground, more conscious, but still dazed and struggling to make sense everything.

"What did you do?" she asked.

"I lit a couple of smoke canisters. The red luminous smoke is actually a thermal marker for infrared weapons and they each have GPS transponders in them for attack aircraft to hone in on."

"Why?"

"Look, we have to get out of here fast. A little while ago I contacted the Romanian Air Force."

Coming out of her daze. "Ok ...And where are you expecting them to land?"

"They aren't. I called for an air strike on this position. That's what the markers are for. We have to go, now!"

"How did you pull that off?"

"I used a search and rescue frequency to contact a regional dispatch who connected me through to the ops manager at Otopeni."

She looked at him with dazed surprise as they began moving.

"In Afghanistan my unit coordinated supporting fires on enemy positions. ...It's what *I* do. ...Our care package should be arriving any moment."

Suddenly Erika seemed to clear the fog from her head and remembered that she was angry with him for earlier. "So hold on Dixon! You put me through all that! Making me think you were going to spare Jack." She staggered slightly and stumbled, but continued. "Then I saw you ordering him directly into that choke point in front of the agents and directly in the line of fire. Then you just backtrack and what? Pick up with the original plan? You owe me an explanation pal!"

"Wow. I guess that bump on the head stirred up a hornets' nest!"

"I thought I had gotten through to you."

"Yeah?"

"What was that all about? I thought your grandfather told you to trust your K9 companion. So what made you point him to the choke point and then suddenly reverse course?"

"You're right. I did trust Jack, and he told me that he trusted *me*."

"Trusted you?"

"Yeah."

"He just – *told* you that?"

"Yeah, you know, the dog whisperer thing. You get inside *people's* heads. I get inside *dog's* heads. ... They're much easier to communicate with."

"Communicate?"

"Yeah."

As he spoke, his radio came to life and the pilot of one of the two approaching fighters called in. "Dog Whisperer. This is Lightning Bolt. Delivering care package in approximately 45 seconds. Target sighted and weapons locked on. Standby."

"Roger that. Much appreciated Lightning Bolt."

Erika was furious. "So the whole time, you never intended to send Jack in front of the hostiles with the smoke screen, because you had already decided that wasn't part of your plan? Is that it?"

"Basically."

"Then you called in your own personal air strike, but you let me worry and think Jack was going to take one for the team." She shook her head in frustration.

Erika punched Dakota in the arm. "Wait! Where is Jack?"

"He's on his way. I blew his whistle."

"But the smoke screen near the cave, I thought you said Jack couldn't handle going through the smoke?"

"Crap!" Dakota raced back toward the cave entrance and blew Jack's whistle again. Inside the cave, Jack arrived near the entrance. He hesitated when he saw the smoke and backed away as he had done in training. He heard Dakota call him through the speaker on his vest. Dakota commanded him to come forward. Jack stepped toward the smoke, but backed away again. Dakota ran full speed toward the entrance.

Only seconds remained before the jet fighters unleashed their ordnance. Inside their dimly lit cockpits, the pilots had already locked on and armed their missiles. Dakota pushed through some pockets of smoke that had drifted away from the cave entrance. As he approached, he called out to Jack again. No response. He waited a moment and called again. A few seconds passed, and then he heard Jack bark twice.

Dakota closed his eyes. He could sense Jack's fear of the red cloud of smoke. He visualized Jack as he circled anxiously near the smoke. In Dakota's mind's eye, he coaxed Jack to focus and push through the cloud. He could sense Jack's mind clearing itself of fearful thoughts and trying to sense beyond the smoke. Suddenly, Jack burst through the wall of smoke, creating a swirling collie-sized vortex of red smoke behind him. Jack snorted a few times to clear his nostrils. Dakota knelt down and gave him a quick hug and a pat on the head.

"Good boy Jack! Let's go!" Jack barked.

Dakota checked his watch before the two raced back in Erika's direction. Jack and Dakota heard the jets thundering closer. Seconds later, the strike from the jets obliterated most of the newest wave of hostiles. The shock wave knocked both Dakota and Jack to the ground as they raced away from the vicinity, but both were unhurt. Only a few hostiles remained near the mountain bunker to the north and they had the laser, but the odds at least appeared more balanced.

Friday: March 2, 02:11
Romania Time
Dakota and Roberts' Location

The main Striker team re-engaged the hostiles guarding the bunker and headed up the hill, this time with much less resistance. Erika recovered from her assault and she and Dakota found a new perch from which to provide supporting cover fire for the team.

The smugglers had no idea where the two snipers were as the hostiles continued to lose strength in their numbers. The main Striker team continued to gain forward momentum in their quest to flush out the smugglers.

Daniels' voice came over the comm link, informing everyone that they had reestablished their downlink from the surveillance satellites. They had eyes in the sky again.

Dakota was frustrated at the irony. "Of course, now that we no longer really need the satellite coverage it comes back online. Gotta love technology."

Pemberton felt a wave of frustration when several new hostiles appeared and the odds against his team suddenly shifted very strongly in favor of the hostiles. The team was on the verge of achieving their objective after the air strike and the pendulum swung back in the other direction. Pemberton came to the brutal realization that the situation was still highly fluid.

In the distance, a welcome sound emerged as the agents recognized the low, choppy, pulsing of the main rotor of a Puma 330 support helicopter. The helo from the Romanian Air Force made itself known and quickly dominated the soundtrack of the situation. It carried reinforcements for the Striker team that would unquestionably shift the odds back in the favor of Operation Light Saber. Just as the helo began its final approach to the LZ, a strange voice came over the Striker Team's comm. At the same time, gunfire from the hostiles ceased and the only sound was that of the Puma.

"Hello Monty. I just wanted to say that I've enjoyed our little nighttime war game exercise. I hope you have as well mate. Do you copy?"

Wellington's face wrinkled into a new shape that was a combination of surprise and anger. Pemberton turned and looked at Wellington in anticipation of his response.

"Bainsworth? ... Alfred Bainsworth?"

Bainsworth continued taunting Wellington over the comm. "Well, thank you Monty. It's nice to know that old acquaintances are not forgotten or however that bloody song goes."

Bainsworth was a former British Royal Marine. He had served with Wellington, but had been court-martialed by him for aiding Croates who were involved in ethnic cleansing in Bosnia. The crimes happened while he was part of the NATO forces in Bosnia after the siege of the capital of Sarajevo. He was using the access to the encrypted channel that Petrov had set up for him before she was arrested.

"Bainsworth, what are you doing out here?" inquired Wellington, trying to remain calm and pump his former comrade for information.

"I've been working for Bosnian Serbs. It pays quite well old chap. I've kept tabs on you though Monty. I just wanted to know how my old commanding officer was doing. I mean, ever since you turned me in, I've felt compelled to check up on your wellbeing. I wanted to make sure that your conscience wasn't bothering you any about turning in a fellow Marine; a Bootneck."

Wellington was as confused as he was angry. "Cut to the chase Al. What are you doing here? You were broken out of prison and never found, as I understood it. What happened after that?"

"I have been freelancing. You know, sharing my skills with clients who value them. I've been training Serbs and others. They're most appreciative of what I have to offer."

"Bainsworth, I aim to take you down. You will be stopped."

"I believe that you believe that Monty. Please continue your fantasy, but I have a dose of reality that I must share with you."

"What Bainsworth? You traitorous-"

"Oh Monty. It's so heartwarming to know that your sentiments haven't changed."

The surprise was over. Wellington was just pissed as the entire Striker Team listened in on the awkward conversation between the two rivals.

"Monty. I knew you were forming some type of team or involved in an organization to shut down our operation. I'm afraid I can't let you do that. It would put a terrible sort of wrinkle in my plans."

"Bainsworth listen to me!"

"Monty. Monty. Don't get your knickers all in a twist. It's very unbecoming. I have a proposition I think you will find intriguing."

"How did you find out about this organization or operation?"

"Monty. You know the game. I spy. You spy. We all do a little spying. Sounds rather like a little song now doesn't it? ...I had Petrov on the inside working for me. You thought she was your trusty techie who had become compromised when you found out about her earlier this evening. She was never part of your organization. I planted her there intentionally. Surprised?"

Wellington paused. "Go on."

"Do you remember Cathleen O'Neill, Monty?"

"Why are you bringing her up? She was killed when her auto took a dive into the Thames. Her body was never recovered. I suppose you had something to do with her death, you -"

"Now, now, Monty, I did nothing of the sort. The accident was staged. It was a spoof, after which we took your lovely communications analyst hostage. Then we offered up Petrov to you to add to your glorious team. You really must learn to do a better job on the background checks and screening the people whom you accept into your organizations Monty."

"Bainsworth, where is Cathleen? Is she alright?"

"She's doing wonderfully. She's with me. She has provided a wealth of information during her internship with my organization."

Wellington seethed with anger at the thought that Bainsworth had potentially turned O'Neill and coerced her to join him. He gnashed his teeth, speaking almost gutturally. "Oh, Bainsworth, I'm going to -"

"Monty. Please .... Allow me to finish. I'm telling my story here. She has been loyal to your organization. She just doesn't have a very high tolerance for pain. She is quite eager to rejoin you I'm sure."

"What do you want!"

"I want what anyone in my position would want. A ride on that chopper that is arriving. I want to bring my prize possession, that laser weapon I acquired, and my people. Once we are safely on our way, I will tell you where to find your dear sweet Cathleen. She *was* dear to you once was she not Monty? I sense that possibly you two shared something?"

Bainsworth's sarcastic rant succeeded in getting under Wellington's skin. "Oh, I'm sorry; I forget that we are not the only ones on this comm channel. How clumsy of me. You probably would have rather kept that fact in confidence. I should have been more discrete."

Wellington was outraged as the situation and Bainsworth's taunting continued to drive deep into the Colonel's psyche. "I want to see her."

"Monty. Relax. You will dear friend. You will see her get on the chopper with us. We will fly to a safe zone somewhere outside Rodna where we will deposit her. Once we are safely gone, we will provide you the coordinates where you can retrieve her. Then we will be on our way. It's really that simple. I don't know what all the fuss is about. ...Oh, since you know that I am quite capable of piloting that aircraft, tell your pilots to disembark and turn the controls over to me. And one last thing old friend. I will disable the GPS tracker in the aircraft. I don't need you tagging along with me by satellite."

"I have no reason to trust you Alfred."

"My dear Monty, trust is not the issue here. You simply have no alternative. I'm sure you see it my way."

Friday: March 2, 02:32
Romania Time
Helicopter Landing Zone

The Puma helicopter approached the landing zone. Helmet Faust, German Police, removed flares from his pack and lit them. He placed them on the ground in a large triangle so the helo could land in the center of them. Bainsworth and his lowlifes watched from the security of their mountain fortress as the craft approached. As soon as it touched down, the members of the backup team jumped off and quickly joined the main Striker team, leaving the LZ vacant except for the helo. The pilot left the rotors turning at idle speed and both pilots exited the aircraft as instructed.

Bainsworth came over the radio again. "Monty. I believe we are ready. We have our cargo and your Cathleen. We will be coming down now from our position and approaching the aircraft. You and your men are not to move. If anyone approaches the aircraft or fires upon us Cathleen will die. Are we clear?"

"Yes. We are standing by. The pilots have left the aircraft."

"Monty, I love how this is working out old chap. It's wonderful to be working with you again."

"Bainsworth quit the game. You are not my friend. We are not working together. The sooner you get airborne, the sooner we can get Cathleen back."

"Monty. Please. Don't rush me. We're coming down now."

Several men dressed in a mix of winter jackets and tactical pants, boots and vests maneuvered between the various boulders and rocks toward the wide-open flat area where the running helo awaited. In addition to their automatic weapons, a couple of the men carried equipment cases the size of large suitcases; clearly the laser Gatling guns and their components. They loaded their loot on board and climbed in.

One of them took the controls of the chopper and prepared to take off. Toward the back of the line was, presumably, Bainsworth. He had a pistol to the back of a hostage with a black bag over her head. Another man led the hostage by the arm. They approached the helo and a couple of the men climbed aboard as the group clustered up around the large sliding door on the side of the craft.

Wellington watched the progression of events more than 150 yards away through his NVGs and focused intently on the hostiles. A trio of the hostiles took up protective positions as Bainsworth and Cathleen prepared to climb aboard the chopper. Pemberton put down his binoculars and looked at Wellington. Turning off his comm, Pemberton asked Wellington.

"What's wrong Sir?"

Wellington turned off his comm. He didn't look at Rolf, but picked up his NVGs binoculars again before he spoke. "Something isn't right ... That's not Cathleen. Cathleen is a wee lass of a girl, barely four foot five. That hostage is nearly six feet."

"Do you think-"

"It's a ruse. She isn't with them. They've played us. Damn him!"

Wellington turned his comm back on. "Striker Team, it's a trick. There is no hostage! Open fire! Open fire! Do not let them escape."

Immediately a deafening barrage of automatic weapons fire erupted as the Striker agents attempted to take out hostiles. The hostiles who had taken up protective positions returned fire.

Erika watched from her position and took out one of the gunmen, dropping him to the ground sideways from his kneeling position. A second gunman stood up in a ludicrous attempt to spray lead in the direction of the Striker Team. Through her scope, Erika noticed the "hostage" removed her black bag just before climbing into the chopper. She took aim and squeezed gently on the trigger. The fake Cathleen's forward movement was interrupted as she recoiled backward, falling to the ground.

The powerful Puma lurched upward off its landing gear and ascended rapidly. The front of the chopper angled toward the Northwest so that two men in the open doorway could fire broadside down toward the Striker agents. The chopper continued to ascend level, but sideways, putting distance as possible between it and the Striker agents as quickly as possible.

Several members of the Striker team rushed forward toward the LZ, firing as they ran. Three members of the hostiles continued to fire at the agents. Two of the hostiles raced up the hill toward their previous hideout while the third stayed in a vain attempt to hold off some eighteen well-armed agents who began rapidly advancing on his position. Several rounds converged on their target, finding their mark as the gunman went down in a hailstorm of lead.

The other two hostiles were essentially out of sight, ducking in and out of view behind boulders as they rapidly closed in on what must have been their hideaway. Wellington was concerned that they may be racing up there to whatever awaited them in their makeshift mountain fortress to destroy evidence or weapons or perhaps to pick up even more lethal weapons.

Wellington's voice came over the comm in Erika's earpiece. "Dixon, Roberts, you two are closer than we are. Can you get a clean shot or close in from where you are?"

Roberts replied. "Colonel, we are in pursuit. Sending Jack in as well."

"Copy that."

Pemberton ordered the rest of the agents to begin to converge in the direction of the fortified position that Bainsworth had occupied just moments ago. The Puma was already long out of rifle range and too far off in the darkness to see. Not even Erika with her sniper rifle had a shot.

Dakota commanded Jack. "Jack, sneak attack! Go."

Jack took off on a course to intercept the two hostiles, but not by direct route. He raced between boulders, leaping in and out of small drifts of snow scattered across the area. He closed the gap to the hostiles faster than any of his human compatriots. Jack's stride extended to his maximum reach. Like his wolf ancestors, he cruised low, streamlined in his stride, silent except for the crunching of his tactical boots against the snow.

Dakota and Erika took off on a more direct path to intercept the hostiles. They knew the hostiles would likely arrive at their fortification first, but the agents would not be far behind. The rest of the team approached, but at a slower pace as they challenged the steep rock face in front of them.

Friday: March 2, 03:12
Romania Time
Smuggler's Position

Dakota and Erika reached an area on the side of the mountain just south of the hostiles. Dakota checked his NVGs and saw what appeared to be a steel plate door or entrance spanning the mouth of what must have been one of the many caves in the area.

Jack completed his indirect route to come up behind the hostile's position. Dakota stopped, taking cover behind a boulder. There were two hostiles who had escaped from the LZ. None of the Striker team knew whether there were more lying in wait inside this makeshift vault. Dakota pulled out his canine video screen and booted it up. Within a moment, he could see what Jack saw through the mini-cam on his vest. Jack continued to arc around toward the rear of the hostiles. Gigantic outcroppings of Precambrian carbonate rocks framed the cave. Jack came around on the northeast side from behind the boulders. He was just a few feet to the side and above the position where the hostiles had stopped.

Dakota visualized Jack reaching his point of attack and crouching to await the order to move. Jack felt the intent of Dakota's spirit and crouched down as Dakota had requested.

Through Jack's camera, Dakota could see that there were only two hostiles near the cave entrance. It was a formidable natural position, further fortified by the large steel plate that Bainsworth and his people had put in place. Dakota and Erika moved a few yards closer.

Pemberton came in over the comm. "Dakota. How close are you?"

"About 100 yards or less. Trying to move in a little closer."

"Copy. We're still looking working this bloody steep cliff mate. Look mate, you're going to have to take those two yourself before they get entrenched in better defenses or bring out some kind of surprise from their arsenal insoyd that bunkah."

"Roger that. No worries."

Dakota pulled out his video monitor again to get a view of what Jack saw. Roberts took up a crouching position concealed behind a large boulder to the left of Dakota. A narrow passageway between the boulders where Jack had passed earlier separated the two. She flipped open the tripod of her sniper rifle and attempted to sight it to see what type of shot she had. Dakota adjusted the controls and looked at the monitor.

Roberts continued trying to sight some bad guys. "Get Jack in position. I need him to create a diversion with one of the hostiles so I can take a shot at the other one."

"Rog."

He adjusted his mic. "Rolf. This is Dakota. Jack is going to jump one of the two hostiles to create a diversion. Once he does that, Roberts will attempt to take out the other hostile. After that we'll wait for you so we can move in and secure the bunker."

"Acknowledged. We're almost there."

Dakota closed his eyes and visualized Jack getting up. When he opened them and looked at the monitor, he saw that Jack had stood up and was ready. He had a clear view from above and behind the two hostiles. "Erika, are you ready?"

"Yes."

"Jack, attack!"

Immediately Jacked leapt off the rock and jumped on the back of the hostile just below him. The second he did that, another 7.62mm round struck the second hostile, dropping him immediately. Jack continued to growl and gnash, and snarl toward the hostile.

Dakota signaled the team. "Pemberton, one hostile down. Jack has the second one engaged. Go now!"

"Roger that Dixon."

The Striker team augmented by the additional backup agents had only moments earlier created an arc-shaped perimeter around the hostiles. They immediately closed in and secured the area.

Pemberton commanded Jack. "Jack, stand down."

Jack stopped his fierce attack as quickly as he had started it. The hostile lay on the ground whimpering and still in shock from the sudden attack by this 'wolf'.

Pemberton ordered two agents to secure the entrance. "You and you, lead the entry."

Agents prepped themselves and lined the side of the steel plating covering the mouth of the tunnel. It resembled an irregular shaped warehouse door. One of the agents on the right side of the door pulled it open as three more immediately swarmed in, rifle flashlights lit and laser sights targeting the inside. The bunker was dimly lit from the rear. About forty feet back from the entrance, a couple of pairs of overhead florescent tubes provided just enough light. Stacks of crates and cases of weapons littered the area. In the middle of this space was a table with a few chairs and what appeared to be sectioned off bunk beds. The accommodations, if you could call them that, were crude. It was a cave, not a space that one could call livable. One of the agents heard a metal clinking sound. It appeared to be coming from behind a hanging tarp. Immediately, four of the agents snapped their rifles to the ready and surrounded that portion of the area as they trained their weapons toward the sound. One agent approached the tarp and ripped it back.

Cathleen O'Neill sat, bound, and gagged in a chair. Her eyes filled with terror. As soon as she saw the agents, she realized she wasn't in any danger and sank down relieved. She exhaled much of her stress. Immediately Rolf came forward to remove the gag.

"Ms. O'Neill?"

Gasping. "Yes."

Wellington walked briskly forward toward her. "Cathleen. … Ms. O'Neill. My God, are you alright?"

"Yes, yes, Colonel. It's so good to see you!"

Pemberton and Wellington both began untying the straps on her hands and feet. Wellington apologized. "Ms. O'Neill. I am so sorry that you were captured by these thugs. We honestly thought you were dead. The police never found your body – obviously."

"It's okay Sir. I'm just glad this is over."

"We can't imagine what you've been through."

Outside the bunker, several agents cuffed the sole surviving hostile. 'Doc' Sung looked over the hostile's wounds from Jack and began treating him for lacerations. Inside, Pemberton focused on the cleanup phase of the mission.

"The other chopper should be coming in shortly. I need a team led by Lieutenant Faust to go and retrieve Inspector Chennault and Sergeant Beringer's body and get them ready for medevac. Faust nodded and pulled several more agents out of the bunker to join him.

Wellington turned to Pemberton. "Rolf. I need you and a few of the men to stay here and process this evidence and get it ready to be airlifted out of here in the morning. We'll have the evidence team come in and take over from you once they arrive.

"Roguh that Sir."

Wellington looked around the room for Dakota and George Sung, but they were outside with Jack, Erika and a couple of the others. Wellington left Cathleen with a couple of agents as he navigated his way through a near maze of weapons and cases as he approached the entrance.

"Agent Sung, what are you doing with this man?"

"Sir, I'm treating his injuries."

"Miss O'Neill is inside. I need you to have a look at her and ensure that she is okay. He can wait. Let me know as soon as you have an assessment of her physical and emotional condition."

"Yes Sir."

George gathered his medical bag and headed into the bunker to locate Cathleen. Wellington turned to Dakota and Erika. He leaned over to pet Jack who sat patiently at Dakota's heel.

"Agent Dixon, I – The whole Striker team owes you and Jack a rather large Bravo Zulu for your contributions today. You too Marshal Roberts."

A mildly pleased look formed on her face. "Thank you Sir." Then she looked down modestly.

"You three made quite a team today and we owe you our lives."

"I was just pointing that out to the Marshal here. I mean, that we made quite a team, Sir."

Wellington grinned. "Jack was truly amazing. Every bit as reliable and effective as our agents. You've convinced me beyond any doubt of your approach to canine training. We will need to continue this."

"Yes Sir," responded Dakota, beaming with pride. At that moment, he felt as though he had just hit the winning home run in the World Series and he began to sense something that he had never really felt before – that somehow, with the odd international assortment of agents, he belonged.

He turned and grinned with satisfaction at Erika. She looked up somewhat reluctantly at Dakota and managed the slightest hint of a grin back. It didn't exactly qualify as a smile, but it was enough. Dakota saw it, a visible chink in her armor.

"Agent Dixon, I think it's fair to say that you and Jack have earned a spot on this team."

"Thank you Sir, however, Jack's special agent days are over. I will have to find a new partner, as I will be returning him to his family."

"Understood Agent, just get that partner soon and get him trained."

"Aye Sir."

Wellington turned to and walked away. The team focused on mopping up the mess as they awaited the choppers.

Friday: March 2, 05:51
Romania Time
Advance Camp

Erika, DX, and Jack stood outside the cave bunker watching the sunrise over the mountains. It was the beginning of another cold wintry morning, but the scene in front of them exuded a kind of quiet serenity, something that had been missing for the past many hours.

She turned to DX. "I understand achieving your spirit-destiny is huge and all that, but you shouldn't be concerned about acceptance. Those members of your tribe you told me about, the ones who rejected you when you were a boy … If they are so intolerant they couldn't accept you and your gift, why would you care? Their acceptance or admiration is worthless. Who are *they*?"

"It's just that I've never really felt accepted by my people since I'm not a full Lakota. I was always the outcast. That eats at you."

"But not everyone at the reservation is full-blood Lakota. There are many like you."

"True, but I always seemed to be the one they choose to cast out. Probably because of the whole dog whisperer thing."

"Maybe they were just jealous or even a little afraid. Anyway, who cares? They're jerks. … Dakota, you don't have to be accepted. If it happens, great, but you can't spend your life hoping you'll satisfy someone else's criteria. I don't think we're put here to chase after the favor of others. Ya wanna know what I think?"

"It appears that I'm about to find out," he said grinning.

"I think, being the outcast means you get to find your own better path, not the path others would have you take. You get to chase your destiny, not have it handed to you by others."

"Yeah, but I didn't choose this gift or these funky powers."

"Ok, so maybe it's a little of both, you find your destiny and it finds you. I don't know."

Dakota looked down, grinned and shook his head.

Roberts looked a little surprised. "What?"

"It sounds like little boy stuff now, but when I was a teen, I told my grandfather I would become a great warrior and make him and my people proud and achieve my spirit-destiny. I thought that would be my way of fitting in somewhere."

"I think it's noble, and besides, look at what happened here tonight. … I think you're there dude. Maybe I'm wrong. Maybe you need to go back to the reservation and see if they accept you now. If they did suddenly welcome you with open arms, would that really make you feel fulfilled? Is that what you really want? …Didn't think so."

"You really have this all figured out don't you?"

"It's my thing."

"Maybe you need your own TV show, weekdays at four."

DX was silent as he looked out at the sunrise.

"Gaining their acceptance or respect is a battle not worth fighting."

He grinned. Erika asked. "What?"

"My grandfather said something very much like that."

"I think your grandfather was a wise man."

"Am I being charged for this counseling session? 'Cause I don't know if I can afford your rates."

Erika grinned. "Yes. I'll bill you later."

"I'm certainly glad I have you here to straighten out my life and tell me how it should all unfold. Is there anything else you'd like to add Dr. Roberts?"

She took a sudden step toward him, took his face in her hands, and kissed him. Completely surprised and silent, he stood motionless, eyebrows raised, as she turned and walked away.

She turned her head back and grinned. "That one's on the house."

Friday: March 2, 07:32
Romania Time
Advance Camp

During the next couple of hours, the choppers came and went, extracting all the team members and beginning the process of removing the cache of weapons. The chopper with Bainsworth, his thugs and the laser Gatling guns was tracked by a secondary transponder in the Puma. Bainsworth was unaware of an inconvenient feature – a backup transponder. The Romanian Air Force was already set to intercept him as soon as he landed. They would retrieve the laser and take Bainsworth and company into custody; mission accomplished.

The team of agents returned to the advance camp. Inside, Petrov was cuffed to a chair. Since the operation was nearly at its end, the attention could shift back to her. Dakota walked from the mess tent where most of the agents downed hot coffee and food. He headed over to the ops tent with Jack beside him. When he entered the tent, he spotted Petrov in a chair in a corner and walked over to her. He came to within a couple of feet of her with Jack beside him.

"Jack. Guard me." Immediately Jack growled menacingly at Petrov.

"What's wrong Petrov? Does my 'Voolf' scare you?"

A worried look formed on her face at the sight of Jack coming so close. "He's mean."

"Yeah, he's real mean. Is that why you poisoned him? Did he scare you? … No. You tried to cripple us in any way you could while you worked for Bainsworth."

"I don't like your dug."

"You know what Petrov. I don't think my 'dug' likes you either. You're going to an international court and they're going to fry your butt. I'm going to make sure of it. Jack and I will be there. … You and Bainsworth are both a couple of sorry sacks of …. You make me sick. … Come Jack."

Dakota and Jack left and returned to the mess tent.

Friday: March 2, 08:04
Romania Time
Inside a Romanian Puma Helo

Jack sat beside Dakota. Dakota had secured his tactical vest clips to restraints inside of the helo for the ride back to Otopeni Air Base. Roberts sat across from them, looking at Jack. She hunched forward resting her forearms on her thighs and held her rifle upright as its stock rested on the deck. She tilted her head down and stared blankly at the floor for a moment as Dakota looked out the porthole beside her. A moment or two passed before she looked up at Dakota.

"Texas," she said, over the pulsing whir of the engine.

"What?"

"Texas. …You asked where I was from. What country are you from?"

-13-

Homecoming

Saturday: March 6, 13:17
United States East Coast Time
The Barnes Home

Linda finished making a huge fruit salad for the cookout. Allie and Wes helped take various fixings out to the deck and Keith ran a wire brush over the grate on the grill before firing it up.

Little Sandra sat on the front porch swinging restlessly - watching. A moment later, Linda heard a scream of excitement come from the front of the house. "Daddy! Mommy! They're here! They're here! DX and Jack are here! Come' on! Come' on!"

A Jeep drove down the slight hill from the stop sign at the end of the street. As it neared the house, Dakota stuck his arm out and gave a wide wave to Sandra. By now, she was in the front yard jumping up and down, screaming with glee. He turned the Jeep around in the middle of the street and parked along the curb in front of the house. He stepped out and walked around back to open the swing gate door and reached inside to pick up Jack. He placed him down on the pavement.

Sandra yelled out. "Jack! Jack!"

Jack galloped toward her, up the grassy incline of the front yard. He barked repeatedly and with intensity as he wagged his fluffy tail in wide swipes and barked more. Sandra raced to meet him and dropped to her knees to hug Jack.

Dakota reached into the open back of the Jeep and helped another Collie, putting her down on the pavement. The new Collie trotted up the hill toward Jack and Sandra. In a moment, Sandra was drowning in a sea of tri-color and blue merle Collie fur as the two surrounded and circled her, sniffing and licking and nudging her until she fell over giggling.

A woman opened the passenger door and stepped out. She walked around toward the back of the Jeep and took Dakota's hand as the two walked toward the house. Linda appeared at the front door; waiting a brief moment, taking in the scene with Sandra and the Collies, and then the surprise of Dakota and whomever it was that was with him.

Sandra looked up from the Collies, pointing toward the new dog and asked Dakota. "Who is this?"

"Her name is Sierra. I adopted her."

"You mean she's yours now to keep?"

"Yep. She was a rescue Collie and now she's found her forever home, with me."

"Where did you get her?"

"I adopted her from some friends of mine with a Collie Rescue down in Texas. She needed a home and I needed a Collie. Did you know that there is a place called Stafford, Texas where the Collie rescue is? There's actually another Collie there named Captain Jack. How weird is that? Stafford, Virginia and Stafford, Texas; both have a Collie named Captain Jack."

"Huh," said Sandra non-plussed.

She was quiet for a moment as she continued hugging the two Collies. Then she looked up at the woman with Dakota. "Who is she?"

"Her name is Miss Erika."

"Hi Sandra," as she knelt down to play with Sierra. Linda walked down from the front porch.

Sandra had another question. "Is she your girlfriend DX?"

Dakota and Erika looked at each other. "She is a girl, and she is a friend. So … yeah, she's my girlfriend."

"Are you two getting married?"

Erika, Dakota, and Linda laughed at the sweet, but blatant interrogation to which Sandra was subjecting Dakota.

"Sweet little Sandra, you're always thinking inside that pretty head aren't you? We're just kind of working on the friend part right now. Is that okay with you?"

"Sure. Dad's making salmon burgers and hot dogs. I hate salmon. Do you want some? You can have mine. It's hideous. I'm going to eat a hot dog instead."

"That sounds awesome. Sure, I love hideous salmon."

Dakota grinned and muttered to himself. "Workin' on phase one."

"What?" asked Erika.

"Oh, just a little something I got from Eddie."

Erika raised her eyebrows with a mildly confused look, but decided to let it go.

Linda redirected Sandra. "Sandra would you go let Dad know that Dakota is here?"

"Okay Mom."

She stood up and bolted toward the house, tilting her head from side to side happily, as she ran.

"Hi, I'm Linda," offering her a friendly hug.

"Erika. …Nice to meet you. DX has told me a lot about you guys."

"Welcome to our zoo of a home. We take the animals in at night."

Linda turned to DX and hugged him. Her eyes welled up. "Welcome back stranger."

"Thank you. Good to be back."

Linda knelt down, hugged Jack, and ruffed up his fur. Jack barked several times and licked her face as she continued ruffing up his fur. She hugged him again as Sierra licked her face.

Linda stood up and guided everyone toward the house. "I'm glad you're here. Come on inside, I'll introduce you to the rest of the clan."

As they headed into the house, both Collies followed and barked.

Dinner was over, but dessert had to wait a bit. The kids played in the backyard with Jack and Sierra, as the adults looked on from their seats at the table on the deck. The waterfall washed over the rocks on the hillside and splashed into the small pond with a relaxing and refreshing sound.

Keith turned toward Erika. "So you are part of the group Dakota is with I take it?"

"Yes. We were sort of paired up during most of the operation."

Linda was interested to learn more about Erika. "So are you a Marine, or FBI or what do you do?"

"I'm with the Marshal's Service."

"So you're a Marshal?" asked Keith.

"Yes."

Keith commented. "So I can see you two would obviously have a lot in common then."

Dakota joked. "Well, she does have a rather *arresting* personality."

The four adults chuckled. Erika turned to Dakota with a grin. "DX just seems to have a way of making up his own rules sometimes. Don't you? For some reason the word *rogue* comes to mind," grinning.

"I don't know what you're talking about Marshal. I do like *all* Marines, adapt, and overcome."

Keith wanted to know more. "So what is your area of specialty?"

"I'm a pyscho-pathologist, or profiler. I do interrogations. I'm also a sniper and martial arts specialist. If I can't talk a fugitive into surrendering I'll either shoot him or kick his butt I guess," she laughed.

"So pretty much the same skill set as my wife," laughed Keith.

Dakota paused for a moment before commenting. "So, Linda - Erika is also from Texas."

"Oh *really*," smiled Linda. "I *knew* there was something I liked about her."

Keith piped in, turning to Dakota. "Okay, so DX check this out. They're both Texans. I'm a Redskins fan and you're an Indian, so that's two on two, and something tells me we're still outnumbered."

Linda laughed. "So you two are a real-life pair of Cowboy and Indian?"

Dakota laughed. "I hadn't quite thought of it that way Linda, but now that you mention it."

Erika changed the subject. "You know guys; I wanted to tell you that Jack was really amazing during the operation. I would never have thought that dogs could be used that way. He saved a large group of agents and several others on multiple occasions. He was able to do things that were just as critical to the operation as what the agents did. He made an awesome operator. He even fought off a grey wolf out in the mountains, while protecting an injured agent. DX has really done an incredible job of training him. You should be very proud."

Linda raised her eyebrows in surprise. "That's really great to know. Wow, a grey wolf. That sounds a bit scary. I'm glad he could help you all out so much and help DX prove his new ideas about K9 training."

Dakota chimed in. "Yes, but Jack's secret agent days are over. He is officially retired and home to stay. It's time for him to enjoy the good life and just be a family guy. Keith, you and Linda helped me achieve my dream. I saw this happening in my vision quest, but I could not say anything about it until now. Now it's time for you guys to take Jack and live out your dream of having that crazy, funny Collie as the king of this clan."

Linda commented. "We're really glad that everything worked out. That's so amazing that Jack could be a part of all that. So DX, since you accomplished the mission, has that satisfied your vision quest? I mean, are you a dog whisperer now?"

He nodded, then looked toward Erika. "Apparently, a vision quest can be about more than just achieving your spirit destiny. Sometimes it can help you look back and see what you've already achieved."

Erika grinned. Dakota continued, looking at Keith and then at Linda. "And I have you and Jack to thank for that. I also appreciate *your* help Keith. That whole line of conviction thing came in handy. It helps if you know that going in, kind of gives you an extra set of mission parameters that come in handy when you come to a fork in the road."

Keith nodded.

Dakota continued. "He's okay now, but we had a bit of a scary bout with some food poisoning just as we got started, but one of our guys who's a doctor took great care of him and got him through it."

Linda commented. "And now you two have met up. Looks like you accomplished more than one mission."

Dakota grinned and looked toward Erika. She reached out a hand to his. Then she jibed. "Well, I've just taken DX on as a new patient. Maybe I can show him the errors of his ways."

Keith turned to Linda. "You know, maybe we need a rescue Collie to add to the mix. Whadda ya think?"

Linda quickly responded. "Oh. I think we're good. How about if we just have DX bring Sierra over from time to time. … and Erika of course. Let's see how Jack and Sierra get along. … Who knows, maybe this thing will work out between you two– I mean between Jack and Sierra. Did I *say* that or was I just thinking it? … Jess sayin'."

Erika looked down and shook her head, grinning at Linda's not so subtle suggestion.

Keith turned to Dakota. "So what's next?"

"Well. Erika is going to come with me for a few days on some unfinished business."

Keith and Linda waited for the other part of his comment. "When I was in the hospital and the rehab center I couldn't follow through with it, and then this new opportunity came up with the Bureau. Everything happened so fast, but now that we have some down time and I'm operating on all cylinders, I have to go to see the families of the two Marines I lost in Afghanistan. I have to close that loop. Those families need to know what their fathers and husbands meant to me and their fellow Marines."

The group was silent, and then Linda spoke. "God bless you DX; and your men, and thank you – both of you."

The End

Saturday: March 6, 16:04

KEVIN BRETT

About the Author

Kevin Brett has been owned by and loved Collies all his life. As a young child, his family had a humongous mahogany Collie named Macintosh. Later, in his teen years, his family had a sable and white Collie, named Piney Branch Lindsay Lad. His current Collie is a tri-color, named Captain Jack Sparrow. Kevin works with numerous Collie, Sheltie, and dog rescues around the country helping them raise funds to further their rescue efforts with autographed copies of his books. Many copies of Jack's story have been sold by these rescues to help raise money to save these animals in need.

Kevin is a certified enterprise architect who has led numerous DoD enterprise architecture projects, and is a former software engineer and operations analyst for the Space Shuttle/Spacelab Team. Kevin is also a certified martial arts instructor with nearly three decades of martial arts training and teaching experience. He has authored several martial arts books and is also an experienced outdoorsman, survival practitioner and a life-long Jazz Saxophonist!

He and his wife Lana were two of the five co-founders of the United Karate Institute of Self-Defense, Inc., in Alexandria, Virginia. He has taught martial arts, self-defense classes to local and federal law enforcement, and military.

KEVIN BRETT

He lives with his wife, three children and their mischievous Collie, Captain Jack Sparrow, who is just "trouble with a tail."

Send me an email.
KevinBrettStudios@yahoo.com
I'd love to know what you thought of this book,
or post a review of it on Amazon.com or Goodreads.com

Keep up with Jack and his other Collie friends on Facebook

Jack's Facebook page is:

Jack: The Christmas Collie

Other books by Kevin Brett

$11.95

Paperback: 223 pages

ISBN-10: 0981935044

ISBN-13: 978-0981935041

Product Dimensions: 9 x 6 x 0.4 inches

Author: Kevin Brett

$11.95

Paperback: 240 pages

ISBN-10: 0981935001

ISBN-13: 978-0981935003

Library of Congress PCN: 2008909902

Product Dimensions: 9 x 6 x 0.4 inches

Author: Kevin Brett

$7.95

Paperback: 101 pages

ISBN-10: 0-9819350-5-2

ISBN-13: 9780981935058

Product Dimensions: 5.06 x 7.81 x 0.23 inches

Author: Kevin Brett

www.ingramcontent.com/pod-product-compliance
Lightning Source LLC
Chambersburg PA
CBHW060353260626
47160CB00006B/2300